Fitzwilliam Darcy

such I was

Fitzwilliam Darcy

such I was

CAROL CROMLIN

Published by Worth Saying, LLC
P.O. Box 541, Old Greenwich, CT 06870
www.worthsayingllc.com

This book is a work of historical fiction, which draws its central characters from the literature of Jane Austen. In order to give a sense of the times, names of real people and places, as well as events have been included in the book. The story is imaginary, and the non-historical characters and events introduced herein are the product of the author's imagination. Any resemblance of such non-historical characters or events to actual ones is purely coincidental.

Cromlin, Carol
Fitzwilliam Darcy, such I was / Carol Cromlin
ISBN 978-0-9890811-0-8
1. Historical Fiction 2. Georgian England - Fiction 3. Austen, Jane, 1775-1817. Pride & Prejudice. 4. Darcy, Fitzwilliam (Fictitious character).

Cover Design by Charles Brock

Cover Art John Smart, artist unknown, oil on canvas, National Portrait Gallery, London

Typesetting services by BOOKOW.COM

First Trade Paperback Edition June 2013

For Mom and Dad

*I offer my sincere thanks
to all who helped along the way.
In particular, I thank my husband;
my window into the male mind.*

PREFACE

Pride & Prejudice was first published in 1813, but Jane Austen actually wrote her story, under its original title, *First Impressions* between October 1796 and August 1797. She specifically matched day with date in Chapter 13, where Mr. Collins' letter to Mr. Bennet states that he will arrive at Longbourne on Monday November 18th.

Taking 1796 as my point of reference, the first previous year in which November 18th fell on a Monday was 1793. There I began, then worked backward to determine the dates of my story.

PROLOGUE

Fitzwilliam Darcy was born into a family whose lineage spanned many centuries of refined and noble blood lines. At the age of eight and twenty, he stood as patriarch of the much esteemed, Darcy family. This monumental responsibility would have been, to some, a burden too great to bear; but Darcy, throughout his entire life, had been most carefully prepared for his duty. To him, it was simply what Providence meant him to do. That he did it creditably, at so young an age, lent him tremendous distinction.

Having since a child, been given to keen observation and deep reflection, Darcy was universally recognized as a man of extreme gravity and taciturnity. Knowing the circumstances of his life, one would most certainly understand from whence came these traits. Alas, there were amongst his acquaintance some in want of such knowledge.

CONTENTS

Chapter I

NETHERFIELD PARK

1793

EASILY clearing the paling on their return to the manor house, two riders and their eager mounts still felt an heightened sense of exhilaration. It had been an invigorating tour. Landing solidly, Charles Bingley quickened his pace. Drawing alongside his friend he queried with much exuberance, "Darcy, is not this an excellent property?"

After a moment's reflection, came a response, " 'Tis pleasingly situated, I grant you Bingley."

" 'Tis pleasingly situated?!' Darcy, we have been touring all morning. Is that the most you can afford me in reply?"

Looking askance at his good friend, Darcy laughed, "Bingley, I do not consider a mere two hours, the whole of a morning, but to your point, I believe the grounds to be of a reasonable size and condition for you to manage. Yea, there are some places where it has been allowed to become rather wild, but the house itself has been well maintained. If you believe yourself ready to live as a landed gentleman, I have seen nothing here that should prove too much for you."

Hesitantly, Bingley queried, "You approve then? I mean, now that you have seen the whole of the estate, do you think I have done well to let it?"

Considering a moment, Darcy replied, "Yes Bingley, I can

safely say I do."

Relief evident in his voice, Bingley laughed, "Good then for I have told Mr. Morris I should take it for a twelvemonth at least."

Darcy did not question why he had been asked for his opinion after the deal had already been made for he was well acquainted with his friend's impetuous nature. He simply returned, "The best of it is, Bingley, you may learn what you are about, *here*, where you are not known to anyone. With no local attachments, at the end of your lease, you may leave what mistakes you have made behind and your connections need know nothing of them."

By now, the gentlemen were making their way into the court yard. As they dismounted Bingley said, "I am truly grateful you have been able to come and see Netherfield for yourself. I feel much at ease knowing you think well of it." Darcy acknowledged the compliment with a quick nod and Bingley continued, "Have you indeed managed to arrange your affairs so you can stay for the whole of the autumn?"

"Yes, actually I have. From time to time I shall have to return to town for a few days, but aside from that I expect to remain these two months complete. It will be of great benefit to find myself in such very quiet country at this particular time, so I thank you again for your kind invitation."

"You are most welcome, but truly it is I who stand to benefit most from your stay for I plan to ply you with questions about running an estate." With a sheepish grin, Bingley added, "As a matter of fact, if you are willing, perhaps we might make a start right now. What say we meet in the library in… perhaps… an hour's time?"

"Very good; an hour it shall be, and Bingley, try not to be late."

With a feigned look of injury, Bingley replied, "Very well Darcy, I shall try. In the mean while I shall have some refreshment brought up to your room." Noting Darcy's nod of acknowledgement, Bingley handed his mount over to his groom and hurried away saying, "I am off post haste so as not to keep you waiting."

"Very good." came an over-the-shoulder rejoinder as Darcy who had been scratching his horse's forelock, offered up the apple he had carried in his pocket throughout the tour. Darcy chose to ride his own horse whenever he was in the country, thus he had directed that Albion be brought from Pemberley in anticipation of his stay. Bred of impeccable blood lines, Albion stood a full sixteen hands high, his sinews barely tethered beneath a glistening chestnut coat. He was also an alert and most spirited animal, thus he elicited no little concern amongst Bingley's stable hands.

As Darcy handed over the reins, he assured the anxious groom, "My mount is quite tired and shall give you no trouble." As he watched Albion walk docilely along with the groom Darcy thought back over the ride and began to hope Bingley was indeed up to the challenge of becoming a landed gentleman, for he knew only too well, how great a challenge that was.

Upon entering his room, Darcy saw fresh clothes lain out on his bed and heard the welcome sounds of Wilkins orchestrating the preparation of his bath. On the writing table lay a silver salver which held the morning's correspondence. Immediately he saw the neat flowing hand on the piece atop the pile, Darcy seized Georgiana's letter. Missives from his young sister had always been pleasurable and diverting. Now he read them with disquiet, wondering if they brought good tidings or bad. It had been under three months since a most disturbing incident had dealt a devastating blow to Georgiana's sensibilities. Darcy had, thankfully, managed to preserve his sister's honour, but the shame and disillusionment she suffered was deep, and likely to remain a torment to her for a very long time.

The anguish Darcy felt at having so nearly failed his sister in his duty as her guardian, gnawed incessantly at his conscience. After all, he reasoned, *"Providence has placed me where it has, so that I might protect my family, and all who are, and all that is Pemberley. Yet in this, my first crucial trial, I have so nearly failed completely. My vigilance must be increased tenfold..."*

A rap at the door broke in upon his reverie. At his call, a servitor entered and laid out a tray of cold sliced ham, bread hot from the oven, served with newly churned butter and a steaming pot of coffee. Once the young lad had done and gone, Darcy broke the seal and unfolded his letter. *"Please God, let her fare well."* he prayed. As the fragrant Arabian heightened his senses, Darcy settled into a high backed chair, cup in hand and began to read.

Pemberley House
Thursday, October 3, 1793

Dearest Brother,

Received your letter of September 30th and have sent this direct to Netherfield Park as you requested. I hope it finds you well and that all is to your liking. Please do not be overly concerned for me dear brother. I have caused you so much grief already that I am heartily ashamed of it.

Mrs. Annesley and I are getting on quite nicely, for she is kind and very patient with me. We have begun taking long walks in the park and discussing all manner of things. You have chosen an excellent companion for me brother and I thank you.

These past months, you have been so devoted to my restoration that I am glad you have at last taken some time for your own enjoyment. I hope your visit with Mr. Bingley and his family will be in every way pleasurable.

I look forward to seeing you at Christmas. In the mean while, please offer my warmest regards to all the Bingley family and know I remain your respectful and ever affectionate sister.

Georgiana Darcy

Relaxing back in his chair, Darcy slowly released the breath he had been holding. Closing his eyes, he thought, *"Dear Georgiana. Pray God, all is truly as well as you say. You sound cheerful enough, but the brevity of this letter is not at all like you."* He would write to her that very evening, once he had carefully crafted his response. As for now, he could more calmly enjoy the hot bath Wilkins had informed him was ready and which his muscles so earnestly yearned for. Then of course Bingley would be expecting him in the library.

Ready in no more than three quarters of an hour, Darcy headed downstairs; lest he should have to await Bingley's appearance (which he thought quite likely) Darcy carried with him one of the books he had brought from home. As he had anticipated, there was no one in the room so he chose a comfortable chair and opened his book. Not far past the appointed time, the door opened and Bingley appeared, shewing no surprise at having been preceded by his good friend.

"Well Darcy, have I been prompt enough to suit you?"

Laying aside his book, Darcy replied, "Yes, Bingley, quite so. In fact I am most impressed."

"If truth be told, I am rather impressed myself. Now where would you suggest I begin?"

Darcy laughed and said, "As you say the owner has left behind the household accounts, I believe we should begin there. By perusing the ledger we can determine what sort of outlay has been required in the past *and* you might also see where there is room for improvement. There is hardly an estate in the realm that could not be run more efficiently."

"Excepting Pemberley, you mean."

"I do *not* mean that particularly, no. Still, it is true Pemberley is exceptionally well run. The management of it has been perfected through many generations of skillful direction and exceptional servitors."

Bingley groused, "I cannot think how I should ever be able to run an estate such as Pemberley."

"You might make a start by learning how Netherfield has been run. True it is much smaller and it is not a working estate, but I dare say there are valuable lessons to be learnt here. What ledgers have the housekeeper and overseer given you?"

At least an hour had been spent in diligent review of the household accounts when conversation moved from the management of Netherfield to the enjoyment of Netherfield and its surrounds. "Darcy, I think it is just as important to learn how one conducts himself as a landowner, as it is to know how actually to manage his land."

"Yes Bingley, I quite agree. One cannot be too careful. Everything you do will be under scrutiny and every word you utter will be seen to have great import. Once you establish yourself, you will be looked up to as a leader of the community, so naturally you must act, always, with the utmost comportment and respectability."

Clearing his throat, Bingley offered, "Yes... well... I was thinking more along the lines of protocol when considering invitations to entertainments. You know, shooting, hunts, dinners; things of those sorts."

"Certainly that is important as well. In town, you will want someone to handle correspondence for those and many other business and personal affairs, but in the country it will not be so daunting a task that you cannot attend to it yourself."

"I am glad to hear you say so, for I have attempted to make a start already. You see, when first I came down, one of the near neighbors who paid a call was a Sir William Lucas. He seems a very agreeable sort of fellow; we chatted at some length." Collecting a tri-fold sheet of vellum from his desk, he handed it to Darcy, saying, "Next day, he sent along this invitation and I am happy to say I have accepted it."

As he read the missive Darcy stiffened in his chair. When he had done, he looked up in dismay. "Bingley, you cannot be serious. Am I to understand you have already sent off your acceptance of this invitation?"

With no little consternation, Bingley said, "Why yes."

"On behalf of us *all*?"

"Yes. Yes, of course."

"Are your sisters aware?"

"Well... no. Not yet, but I cannot see why they should have any objection? It is a good opportunity to go out into society and meet our new neighbors."

"Really, Bingley; sometimes you astonish me. A simple country dance in environs such as these; what society can it possibly afford, to which you should aspire to be known?"

"I should think it an admirable opportunity to pass a pleasant evening amongst friendly people." Bingley stated flatly.

Incredulously, Darcy riposted, "It is insupportable. What can you have been thinking?

"It never occurred to me that any of you might object."

"Though I believe I know your sisters' minds on this score, I cannot speak for them. As for me, I should find it the greatest trial to attend an assembly such as this."

Bingley exclaimed, "Really Darcy, it cannot be so very bad as that."

"Bingley, if you wish to become a true gentleman, you will have to associate yourself with other gentleman and gentlewomen. At this dance, it is hardly likely you shall have opportunity to associate yourself with anyone of consequence."

"Come now Darcy. Surely you exaggerate!"

"Whether I exaggerate or not, I am sure this will be a complete waste of an evening." As Bingley did not immediately reply Darcy realized perhaps he had sounded a bit harsh and so he explained, "Bingley, were I in a better humour, I might be more willing to contend with the prospect of a night spent in such a fashion; I could not ever like it, but for your sake, I could accept it with grace. I will not burden you with any specifics; suffice it to say that at present my mind is engaged with far too many weighty concerns to allow me to suffer such a prospect with patience."

His thoughts immediately flew to his sister and her private anguish, for he was certain she was still far from recovered. Furthermore, the man responsible for her plight had been in the protection of the Darcy family his entire life. Having impressed himself upon Darcy's notice in so untoward a fashion, Darcy had been left feeling utterly betrayed; he also felt he must now be ever more mindful, knowing not, what new offense he could expect of this man.

In rapid succession, a multitude of other concerns ran through Darcy's mind. He was just considering one of his tenant farmers who had lately become very ill and wondered if the man's family could manage the farm on their own when his ruminations were interrupted.

"Darcy, I had not realized how strongly you felt. Of course we can send our regrets. I can say we have been unexpectedly called back to town."

Darcy considered and responded, "No. I realize *you* are eager to attend and since you have already accepted for me, I shall attend as well, but I am afraid I will be very poor company."

"Darcy, I thank you kindly; you are a true gentleman and you are right. I cannot tell you how very eager I am to attend! I rather wish it were tonight for I long to become acquainted with my neighbors."

"To-morrow is soon enough, Bingley. Becoming acquainted with your neighbors is all well and good, but an assembly is hardly more than a marriage mart. When you are ready to look in earnest for a wife, it is in town you are likely to find a suitable companion; not here."

Darcy thought, *"If Bingley would just learn to rein himself in a little; to behave more as one of his station ought..."* But it would seem Bingley was not so easily to be reined in; somehow he was always willing and able to find pleasure where Darcy could not imagine pleasure was ever to be found. To

Darcy, it seemed almost as if his good friend *created* happy situations by his presence alone. This was a quality so absolutely foreign to Darcy that he could not at all make it out and it was, at times, most trying. It was, however, a quality Darcy found he greatly *admired* and he had come to believe, one of the primary reasons for the depth of feeling he and Charles shared. Perhaps Bingley's love of life taught Darcy to hope that he would not always feel so keenly, the sorrows of his own life, Perhaps it was that as Bingley sought Darcy's guidance, it put Darcy in mind of the close relationship he had shared with his own, much esteemed, father. Whatever the reasons, the concern and regard were most genuine.

Still perplexed and growing more dismayed with each passing moment, Darcy wondered, *"What can possibly have possessed him to think he should accept such an invitation? Surely he must know there are rules of decorum that must be followed in polite society... Difficult as it may be, I must prevail in setting Bingley to rights, for he must not continue in this manner. If he persists in associating with anybody and everybody, he will be hard pressed to maintain his reputation. As gentlemen, we have responsibilities above and beyond our desires, and propriety demands that we see to those responsibilities."*

It was, Darcy felt, his duty to guide those he cared for in the proper direction and in his opinion Bingley needed a great deal of guidance; a very great deal.

Chapter II

AN HEIR IS BORN

1766

WINTER in Derbyshire can be bracing. Betimes the weather may turn a bit dank and dreary, but hardly ever more unpleasant than that. Now and again though, when Mother Nature sees fit to remind us of her supreme power, the placid winter air will turn quite raw and biting. Chill breezes in the Derbyshire peaks whip themselves into fierce, frigid winds that drive disquiet into the hearts of man. This mid February night was such a one as neither man nor beast ventured forth without compelling cause; yet this night saw one of the Darcy carriages making its solitary way as swiftly along the Lambton road as the many deep and jagged ruts would allow.

Within, huddled Dr. Braxton, who thought he just might freeze right there in that carriage, for despite the warming blocks and blankets that had been supplied against the hardships of his journey, the cold seeped right into his bones. He could only thank God for the relatively short distance he must travel and that the coachmen had the light of a full moon to guide their passage. He prayed he might soon arrive; but even more fervently, he prayed the night would end well, for on this night, the benefactors of farmers and townspeople for miles round awaited a blessed event. Pemberley was in want of an heir and if prayers from far corners of the shire were answered, this night would bring it one; so whilst much of Derbyshire slept, news of its fortune was near at hand.

Childbirth was always a hazardous undertaking, but even more so when, as now, it was one's first thus it was not a surprise the family entrusted this responsibility to no less than a Scottish trained physician. 'Twas nearly half after three in the morning when the carriage slowed and turned in at the lodge gate. Progressing through the park the doctor prayed, *"Dear Lord, let there be no complications this night and guide me that I may see her safely through. It is not oft' I must ask so great a favor of you Lord, so please hear me this night."* He blessed himself with the sign of the cross and said aloud, "Amen."

Once the carriage broke through the trees, affording a view across the valley and the lake to the great house, one could see the blaze of candle light that illuminated it from tip to toe and end to end. The light of the moon from above, the candle light glowing from within and the reflection of both on the lake created an imposing specter that gave the impression of divine intervention. Dr. Braxton hoped this was indeed a portent of an imminent blessing. When the carriage entered the courtyard, a footman threw open the door almost before it had come to a stop and Mrs. Marshall, the old housekeeper hurried out to fetch the doctor just as fast as her legs would allow.

"Praise be, you are come doctor. This way please."

Hurrying after her, the doctor inquired, "How does Lady Anne fair?"

"The mistress is in great pain. She had some small pains come since near on eleven, but she has been very bad for the past hour or more."

"Then it progresses quickly. She may not have so long a confinement after all. That would be the greatest luck."

Mr Darcy had been dividing his time between the hall outside the birthing room, from whence he would be gently shooed away whenever someone entered or left; the library where his brother-in-law, Lord Fitzwilliam was keeping vigil with him, and lately, the great front hall where anticipating the doctor's arrival he could step outside and listen for the sound of his returning coach. On hearing the distant sound of hard driven, hoof beats and the rattle of wheels, he heaved a great sigh of relief.

The doctor was very much surprised to find Mr. Darcy in the hall to meet him when he entered. To be greeted by the master himself, was unprecedented. He stammered, "Why, Mr. Darcy, sir. Good morning sir. I started out as quickly as could be."

"I thank you for that. I do not doubt you did, and I am best pleased you are now here. This is early, is it not? We believed my wife would not be delivered for another three weeks."

" 'Tis a bit early," advised the doctor, "but not too early. Once I have been to see her, I can better advise you of her current state."

"Why, yes, of course. Mrs. Marshall, please shew Dr. Braxton upstairs."

"Yes Mr. Darcy, sir. Come this way doctor."

On the way up, the doctor instructed, "I shall need lots of linen, a warm blanket or two… and oh yes, some water for I should like to clean the dust from my face and hands. Make it hot for my fingers feel quite numb from the cold."

Mrs. Marshall announced the doctor at the confinement room door then went off in search of the required supplies.

After saying a quick prayer, Dr. Braxton entered to find Lady Anne abed, eyes closed, her sister-in-law, Lady Margaret on the one side, holding her hand and whispering soothingly to her; on the other side, Constance the mistress's lady's maid stood mopping Lady Anne's brow.

Lady Margaret now whispered, "Anne, dear, the doctor is come." Slowly, Lady Anne opened her eyes and even more slowly did a weak smile touch her lips.

"I am glad you are come." said she. "I have heard the wind howl so; I did not like to know I had occasioned anyone to be out of doors this night."

"Lady Anne, you are too kind. Think not of me. Your thoughts now must be with yourself and your baby alone."

"Yea, so very dearly do I want to give my husband a healthy baby."

Lady Margaret offered, "We have been trying to make her rest whenever the pains allow."

"Good," said the doctor, "Very good. She will need all her strength at the end." The doctor then cleared his throat and addressed his patient rather awkwardly, "Lady Anne, if you would be so kind as to permit of an examination, we shall know better what we are about."

"Of course doctor."

Doffing his jacket and rolling back his sleeves, Dr. Braxton availed himself of the ewer and basin that had lately been supplied for him. The good doctor proceeded quickly with the examination; this, as much in defense of his own sensibilities as of his patient's. He was soon able to pronounce that all was well and he assured Lady Anne the baby, though quite large, was in the correct position and it appeared the birth was not far off. He then begged to take leave momentarily to carry the news to Mr. Darcy.

In the library, Mr. Darcy was pacing about in a determined effort to keep his wits about him. He could sit no longer than thirty seconds before beginning again to pace. All the while, one hand plowed furrows in his hair and the other grasped a much abused brandy glass. "Edward," he began, "you have been through this twice. What can be happening up there? I am sure I shall go mad if I do not hear some news soon."

"George, it is not easy, especially the first time. It seems that hours go by with no word of what is happening. When someone does come, it is only to say there is nothing to report. Though you are glad they have come, you wonder why they even bothered to come at all, for they have given you no peace. Then, just when you are sure you shall spend eternity thus, someone comes to tell you it is over and you are a father."

"Not a very comforting representation, that."

"No, not very, but not far off the mark either. Here, let me refill your glass."

"Thank you, no. This will do for now." With a small chuckle, Mr. Darcy said, "If you continue to ply me with spirits I shall not be coherent enough to grasp the news when at last it does arrive." Returning to his seat, once again, Mr. Darcy said, "Until today, all I could think was how very much I want and need an heir. Now, all I can think of is Anne and what she must suffer to give me a child. One hears stories. Still, I was not prepared for the tortured screams I have heard coming through the chamber door."

"George, that is precisely why we men are sent to wait in the farthest reaches of the house. We can watch with complete equanimity, as a traitor is drawn and quartered at the tower; we can go into battle and strive on with composure through the sights, sounds and smells of agony and death; yet we have not the mettle to stand idly by while those we love suffer pain."

Just then there was a rap upon the door and Mr. Darcy sprang from his seat as he called, "Enter." The doctor was shewn in and Mr. Darcy gained some little comfort from the relatively composed look of his countenance. "Mr.Darcy, sir," he began, "all appears to be well. The baby is rather large, but it faces as it should and Lady Anne is a strong lady, so I do not foresee any difficulty beyond what is to be expected in a first confinement."

"You have greatly eased my mind." said Mr. Darcy, "I would like to see her."

Dr Braxton started visibly and stammered, "Oh... but... Mr. Darcy, sir. That would be highly irregular. Highly irregular, sir."

"But it is what I want." To the earl, he said, "Edward, I shan't be long." and offhandedly he added, "Whilst I am gone please avail yourself of whatever you wish."

"George, do you think this is wise?" Lord Fitzwilliam cautioned.

"I cannot say if it be wise, but it is what I require."

"Then do as you must." the earl replied.

With a quick nod, Mr. Darcy was through the door, leaving the stunned doctor to follow as he might.

When he reached the confinement room, Mr. Darcy took a deep, steadying breath, then rapped and entered before anyone could respond. On seeing who was come, there were gasps of disbelief all round, save for Lady Anne who smiled wanly and said, "I knew you would escape your guard and come to me if you could."

With a shift of his eyes, he sent the servitors quickly from the room. Then he asked, "Lady Margaret, would you allow us a few moments alone."

"Of course, George." she said somewhat uncertainly. "I shall be right outside the door. Call if you need me."

"Thank you Margaret." he replied. "I shall be brief." He quickly strode the distance to the bed and as he lowered his tall frame to sit beside his wife, he saw with apprehension that she and the bed clothes were drenched in sweat. She smiled at him as he took her hand; its trembling telling him she was making a valiant effort to hide her pain. He said quietly, "I suddenly felt a great need to see for myself how you fare."

"All is well my dear. All is well."

He kissed her hand and said, "All must be well. I *need* to have you beside me. I very much want this child, but I need you."

"I know Dearest and you shall have us both. I am truly blessed that I am yours and I have no mind to leave you." Just then, a great pain seized her and she cried out in spite of herself. Mr. Darcy, certain she was then to die, jumped up and called loudly for the doctor.

Within seconds, Doctor Braxton was attending his patient and Lady Margret was at Mr. Darcy's side. Gently placing her hand on his arm she said, "You must leave now for I believe it may be time. I will come to tell you how it progresses." Not trusting himself to speak, Mr. Darcy merely nodded and quitted the room.

Once the other side of the soundly shut door, he leaned against it for much needed support. Very soon, he knew he must leave, for the fierce struggle that ensued behind the door would not give him peace. Verily, he thought he should go mad if he continued there much longer.

Mr Darcy's face, on his return to the library, gave Lord Fitzwilliam pause, so pronounced was its pallor. Shaken to his core, the expectant father knew not how he had arrived there for he could remember nothing of traversing the Pemberley halls or descending its stairs. All he knew was that he was gripped by a terror so great it threatened to consume him. Seldom in his life had there been cause for him to feel any serious apprehension. He was observant, intelligent and quick witted. From an early age, he had been carefully taught how to assess and conquer whatever challenge he faced, but at this moment he knew what it was to be completely lost to fear. Lord Fitzwilliam did what he could to calm him, reason with him, but so fully in the grip of his sensibilities was he that there was really little of consolation in anything that could be said.

Thankfully, his torment did not last over long, for it was not two hours later when Lady Margaret entered the library with the news that most of Derbyshire awaited. "George," said she through myriad smiles and tears, "you are a father and Anne fairs well." Joy threatened to swallow her voice as she continued. "She is safely delivered of a healthy, baby boy. Oh George, he has the soundest lungs, the biggest eyes and such a head of dark curls. He is a handsome baby." Mr. Darcy seemed rooted to the spot where he stood, so Lady Margaret prompted, "Would you like to see your wife and son?"

"Yes, yes, of course." He saluted her cheek and clapped Lord Fitzwilliam roughly on his back in acceptance of their congratulations, then he was off, taking the stairs two at a time.

As he reached to open the door to the future of Pemberley, Mr. Darcy found it necessary to pause a moment to regain his composure. When he did open the door, he was not fully recovered, but he was well enough. The scene before him was completely different from what he had left there just two hours gone. A gentle calm now suffused the room and although Lady Anne looked quite wan, she now lay dozing serenely in a fresh, dry gown and clean bed clothes; Constance sat attentively by her side.

Mr. Darcy's keen senses registered the wholesome scent of a newborn babe and though he was only aware of it on some distant level of his thinking he found it most reassuring. Perhaps it was that he associated it with the foaling of the Pemberley mares, or the lambing of its sheep or the whelping of its hounds; whatever it was, it was a very good thing for it bespoke stability, continuity; it meant there would be a future.

On seeing him, the doctor lifted his tired body from his seat by the fire and crossed the room, offering congratulations as he came. "All went very well." said he. "For a first confinement, Lady Anne had a surprisingly easy time of it. Once the baby was ready he came quickly and gave little trouble.

Lady Anne will not be herself for at least a month and for the first few days she will have to be watched closely against the onset of fever, but there is every reason to expect her to regain her strength afore long. As you see, she is taking a much needed rest at present, but she is quite calm so I have administered no sleeping draught. She will wake if you call her."

"Thank you, no. I will let her rest but I *will* see my son."

"He sleeps, as well."

"Then let him stay where he is and I shall see him there."

"Very well sir."

"Thank you doctor, for everything. I have no doubt you would welcome a good rest yourself, having been roused from your bed. We had not expected we should need to call upon you before first light."

"No matter sir. I was glad to come."

Mr Darcy nodded in acknowledgement and said, "If you go below, Mrs. Marshall will order you some refreshment and the carriage for your return home."

"I am most grateful, Mr. Darcy, sir; most grateful." The doctor collected his things and betook himself from the room.

Mr Darcy made his way across to the claw footed, mahogany cradle that bore the ornately carved Darcy crest. As he approached, he was struck by the realization that *his* son now lay in this, the same cradle he had lain in. Looking down upon the form that reposed within, his sensibilities jostled within his breast; now pride, now joy, now duty foremost in his thoughts. He took in every detail; thick, dark, curly hair even now, with tiny ringlets plastered on a high forehead; long voluminous lashes hooding somnolent eyes; full ruby lips that seemed to smile now and again; a shallow cleft to his chin, that promised to become more pronounced with age; fingers, long and thin, that peeped from beneath the bunting, where he had managed to wriggle a small hand free. *This* was his son; this was *their* son. Continuing to watch, he thought, *"Welcome my boy... How long have I dreamt of this day... How much will one day be entrusted into your keeping... You are a Darcy of Pemberley... One day you will understand how very much that means..."*

He was not sure how long he had been standing thus when he heard a long, deep, contented sigh from the direction of the bed. Turning, he saw that his wife was now awake and intently watching him. Her smile, when their eyes met, stopt his voice in his throat. With the slightest shift of his eyes toward the door, Constance scurried from the room, then he was quickly across to the bed. "Anne," he murmured, as he sat carefully on the edge of the bed. He reached out, wanting very much to hold her, but he hesitated.

"I will not break, you know. It is not my arms that have been so abused this day."

Very much relieved that she felt well enough to jest, he again reached out and cradled her in his arms; so gentle was he that had she not seen, she might not have believed herself held. He smiled and said, "You have given Pemberley an heir and Providence has spared you. I can want for nothing more." Words did not offer an adequate answer, so she simply smiled and clung tighter; savoring the emotion that flowed between them as he gently caressed her hair and tenderly kissed her forehead.

Pemberley had an heir. By the next day, expresses had carried the joyous news to London and to Kent where Lady Anne's elder sister, Lady Catherine de Bourgh lived. Lady Catherine had not traveled to Derbyshire to attend her sister, for she was herself with child and the rigors of traveling so many tedious miles and in such thoroughly hazardous weather would have been most unwise. Besides, being as yet childless herself, clearly no one would expect of her, so great an act of impropriety as to attend someone else in the confinement room.

In two days the news had made its way throughout the entirety of Derbyshire. Town folk drank rounds to the young master and multitudes of people flocked to morning matins to pray for his health and long life, for all knew well that Pemberley's good fortune was their good fortune. Such was the environment of heartfelt gratitude, complete approbation and unqualified respect into which young Master Darcy was born.

Not four months later, Lady Catherine's confinement commenced and Lady Anne Darcy, fully recovered of her health and vigor, dutifully journeyed to Kent to attend her elder sister's lying in. More than ten years her senior, Lady Catherine's months spent with child had been far different from those Lady Anne had spent. From their onset, they had been fraught with difficulty and things were only to grow worse, for the child lay breach. Lady Anne called to her sister, as she sat beside the bed, mopping Lady Catherine's brow, but there was no response. The torturous process of labour had begun yesterday noon and it was now gone seven in the evening. For the better part of the afternoon, Lady Catherine had been drifting in and out of a sleep from which she could not always be roused and the midwife was growing ever more concerned both for Lady Catherine and for the baby.

There were still signs of life from within, but only just. That there was life at all, was in and of itself cause for thanks. This could not go on; measures needed to be taken to end the struggle and now that Lady Catherine was no longer able to direct what was to be done, the midwife could do as she saw fit. Thus two hours later, and owing to much rough kneading and prodding by the midwife, Lady Catherine was delivered of a slight wisp of a baby girl, though it was not even certain she still lived, for the cord was tight round her neck, she was ashen and her lips were blue. Once the cord was severed and a closer inspection done, it was found that she did indeed breathe, though t'were but ever such shallow breaths. Nearly three hours more would pass before Lady Catherine found the strength to speak and it would be nearly a fortnight before anyone would venture to predict whether mother or child would survive, but survive they did.

Not for a month, did Lady Catherine feel sufficiently recovered, that she would condescend to hold her child for the first time. When she did, so awkward was she that the child wriggled and cried till Lady Anne took her up and comforted her. "Anne dear, I am quite sure she would have stopt mewling on her own. I will not have her spoilt as you already spoil your son."

"There is a difference, sister, between spoiling and loving you know."

"Nonsense. What can one so young know of love?" countered Lady Catherine.

"A great deal, I should think." replied Lady Anne earnestly. "Our little boy responds quite nicely when we speak kindly to him or sing to him. He laughs and coos and wriggles about."

Lady Catherine was utterly exasperated with her younger sister and her ridiculous notions. "I seriously doubt the veracity of that claim. Children need nothing but strict instruction, and to think you have actually traveled with yours. You had better have left him with his wet nurse."

"I have no wet nurse, sister."

"What? No wet nurse? But... That is impossible! You *cannot* mean to say you attend him yourself."

"Sister, that is precisely what I do mean to say. You know

I have never been one to follow convention, simply for convention's sake. I do not believe it wise to send a babe off to live in someone else's home or even to bring a stranger into our home, just so my child can nurse. I want to tend my own child."

"Foolish, headstrong, girl; you have ever expressed your opinions most decidedly, be they sensible or no but this is ridiculous." chastised Lady Catherine and she continued, "I know there is no changing your mind once you have made it up, but consider what you are about. Had you a girl, it would be bad enough, but we are talking of the rearing of your husband's heir. You will make the child soft and weak minded; then what use will he be?"

"Oh, Sister," laughed Lady Anne, "do you not think you exaggerate perhaps just a little?"

"No Anne, I do not."

Looking now to the babe in her arms Lady Anne offered, "I do believe your daughter would disagree with your general assessment. Do you not see how peacefully she sleeps?"

It was true; throughout the whole of this conversation, Lady Anne held her niece and gently rocked her. As a result, the child had soon gone off to sleep and continued so with a most contented look upon her face. "She is a pretty, little girl, your daughter." As if in response to the compliment, the child opened her eyes and smiled up at her aunt. "La. See how she smiles, sister?" Eyeing Lady Catherine playfully, she continued, "To be sure, she knows what we say."

"Anne, I love you dearly, you know that, but you really must give over speaking such nonsense. It sets my teeth on edge and it does not at all become a daughter of the house of Fitzwilliam."

Lady Anne could no longer contain her mirth and she began to laugh. This of course, her sister very ill brooked. So it had been since they were children. Lady Catherine, eldest of the Fitzwilliam children, saw it as her duty, always, to help guide her younger brother and sister in the proper direction. Her younger brother and sister; however, saw no such need, for they felt quite able to manage on their own. Thus it became a bit of a game for them to occasionally rile up their elder sister, provided there was no chance of detection by their parents. It was not that they were bad children; on the contrary, they were really quite good, caring, well mannered children. 'Twas simply their juvenile way of keeping their controlling sister at bay; besides, the temptation was often times far greater than their resolve could bear.

Nevertheless, that was then and this was now, and as Lady Catherine, was still really quite weak (despite her assertions to the contrary), Lady Anne did not wish to upset her unduly. She stopt laughing and gently said, "Sister, I meant no harm. 'Tis just that I am so very taken with your precious little girl. She is so dainty and her bright eyes are the most beautiful shade of green that ever I saw."

"They are quite nice, yes. You know, Anne, I had been thinking to name her after you, and as she seems already to have won your approbation, that might be just the thing."

"I would be honoured if you should give her my name. That way, she and I shall always be connected in a very special way."

"I am glad to hear you say so, for you know Anne, I have been thinking of something else; there is yet another way you could be forever joined with my daughter."

"Whatever do you mean?" laughed Lady Anne. "Despite your harsh talk, I know you could never mean to give her over."

"I mean, dear sister that you have a son and I now have a daughter. What a wonderful thing it would be if they were to unite in marriage and join the houses of Darcy and de Bourgh."

"I cannot say I had thought so far ahead, but yes, it would be lovely if that were to happen."

"*I,* dear sister, do think ahead and for me suddenly to find myself with a daughter at this particular time, and after all these years, tells me they were meant for each other. What is more, the de Bourgh estate is not entailed in any way, so Lady Anne stands to inherit all. If our children should unite, just think how vast would be their joint holdings."

"Yes, they would have much indeed, but I should sooner wish for their happiness than the increase of their wealth. They are each already very wealthy so I think they would benefit far more from happy marriages."

"Oh Anne, you can be so tiresome. Their happiness is all well enough, but the good of the family is what matters. These four months, have I thought that if I should have a girl, it would be my favorite wish that she should marry your son."

"If they should chuse it, it would make me truly happy indeed."

"Then we are of the same mind."

Just then Lady Catherine's wet nurse came to fetch the baby and brought with her the news that Sir Lewis' coach had been spotted coming up the long drive. Being himself even older than Lady Catherine, he was of a different generation altogether. His was a time in which a father's place was as far away from the birth of his children as possible, thus he and a party had hied themselves off to his Scotland estate, for six weeks of hunting, shooting and fishing.

At the end of another month, Lady Anne and her son returned home and most happy was she to be back. Lady Catherine was daily regaining her strength and whilst the little, Lady Anne was still very small and tended to be colicky, she lived. Considering her very difficult beginning, that was a blessing, indeed. Thus it was that when the young master entered the world he had two cousins already there to meet him and almost as soon as he arrived, did he gain a third.

Chapter III

THE YOUNG MASTER

1769

HEARING the happy sounds of a child at play, Mr. Darcy looked up from his *London Chronicle*. Across the nursery, Lady Anne and the young Master Darcy sat upon the floor, engaged in quiet chatter and play. Whilst they were thus employed, shafts of late morning sunlight streamed through the many windows, illuminating Lady Anne's golden tresses and her son's raven curls. Taking in the sight, Mr. Darcy was filled with pride and happiness. Just on three years old, the young master was growing tall and strong; he was become quite agile and he already displayed a propensity to be engaged in whatever went forward about him. Clearly he was not someone destined to be idle, whilst others achieved; he would play an active part in shaping his world.

"*Yes,*" Mr. Darcy thought, "*I have much to be thankful for.*" It was a warm day in early April, and he thought aloud, "I do believe it is high time this strapping young buck takes his first ride out and I think today would be just the day." Having gained their attention, he added to his wife, "I am sure we should *both* be much pleased if you would join us."

"I should like that very much, and, as your son already exhibits your sense of purpose, I am quite sure he would enjoy it greatly." She then asked her son, "Shall we go and ride horses with Father?"

"Ride horses? Yes Mother." He stood quickly and solidly as he spoke, then he went to his father.

Mr Darcy rang the bell for Mrs. Nichols, the nursery maid. When she arrived he commanded, "Mrs. Nichols, see to Master Darcy and have him ready to ride in an half hour."

"Yes Mr. Darcy, sir." With a curtsey, she gathered the young master into her arms and whisked him off, humming to him as they went.

Taking his wife's arm in his, Mr. Darcy said, "Anne, I shall hold him very carefully. You need not worry."

"I am not worried for I do not doubt that you will. Besides, if he is to have a confident seat, he must never know a time when he did not ride."

Earnestly, did he reply, "Daily, do you give me cause to thank Providence for leading me to a wife whose thinking is so like my own."

Smiling up at him, she teased, "Was it Providence, or our parents who led you to me?"

"Both," he replied. "Our parents put us in each other's way, but Providence shewed me the wisdom of their choice."

"Do you mean, Sir, that it was not my many charms that won your approbation?"

He flashed that impish twitch of his lip that she so dearly loved. He then drew her to him, kissing her deeply and the look that followed left naught in want of words. Clearing his throat he said, "We had better prepare for our ride or we shall have our son cooling his heels in wait." Reaching for the door he regained his formal demeanor, and asked, "How quickly can you ready yourself?"

With one brow cocked, she said, "I shall be to the stables before you, my dear."

"Really?" said he, "We shall see."

Mrs. Nichols and young Master Darcy could be seen in the courtyard before the stables as Lady Anne stepped through the kitchen door. She had come down the service stairs and through the back hall, knowing that to be the most direct route to the stables. Seeing no sign of her husband, she hurried out and quickly made her way along the path. As she passed through the hedge that separated the kitchen garden from the courtyard, she came up short, for leaning against a majestic elm stood none other than Mr. Darcy, fully attired for a ride.

"After you," he offered and his lip twitched ever so briefly.

"So," she countered, "I see you are not to be outdone today."

"I think not." he said mirthfully, "but I must admit I have not been here long." Taking her arm, they moved on in easy conversation to join their son.

Fletcher, Mr. Darcy's gentleman's gentleman, had sent word ahead to the stable hands so a pair of groomsmen now had the couple's horses saddled and waiting in the court yard. "Fitz, you are going to ride with me today."

With fulgent eyes, the young master affirmed, "Yes Father!" Lady Anne's ascent into her saddle was then performed with the usual ritual. The groom who held her horse offered his assistance (because such was his duty) and Mr. Darcy gently rebuffed his offer, legging his wife up himself. Then, after swinging himself up into his own saddle, Mrs. Nichols handed up the young master. Settling his son securely before him, Mr. Darcy asked, "Are you ready Fitz?"

"Yes Father."

"Then we shall be off."

"Mrs. Nichols, you shall not be required for upwards of two hours." advised Mr. Darcy.

"Thank you, sir." she replied as she gave a curtsy. As the horses turned, the young master called out his adieu to his nursery maid with a grin that employed his entire face. She replied in kind and watched as the trio moved slowly through the cobbled courtyard and out beneath the crested arch.

As Mrs. Nichols ambled back to the house, she past through the herb garden, where she came upon Mrs. Macey, the cook. She had one arm laden with lavender sprigs, her other hand bore a basket of thyme, sage, rosemary and comfrey. Falling in step with her, Mrs. Nichols relieved her of the basket and said, "The family is off on the young master's first ride out. How fast they do grow."

The cook replied, "Yea 'tis true. I remember well how quickly my own wee ones grew up."

Mrs Nichols went on, "It seems just yesterday I came to this house, yet it is quite three years since, and I could not want for a better situation than I have here. Young Master Darcy has the most even disposition; never does he fret or cry or give trouble as young ones are want to do."

"I do not doubt it," the cook confirmed, adding, "He is blessed with the most, good natured and loving parents a babe could ever want. Of course, nothing is ever denied him but he is taught to be grateful too. The baps my mother taught me to make are one of his favorite breads and whenever I send them up, the mistress herself actually brings him down to the kitchen to thank me. You can but imagine my surprise the first time ever I espied the mistress and young master standing right there in my kitchen. Master Darcy came straight up to me with his, "Thank you," he did. We are very lucky to be in service to a family such as the Darcy's. There are but few houses where our lives would be what they are here." Mrs. Nichols agreed wholeheartedly.

By this time, the Darcy's were passing through a grove of fruit trees and as proud parents are want to do, both father and mother marveled at their son's identification of apples and pears. They were also quite pleased with his determined, though not entirely successful, attempt to say quince. The rest of the forenoon was spent traversing a fair part of the Pemberley lands. They started by circling round the lake and riding up the hill beyond; from there they struck out on a path that meandered through dale and copse; over stone bridges that spanned streams and one over a shallow ravine. They continued beside the river that eventually made its way through Lambton. Along the way they saw (to the young master's delight) two separate herds of deer grazing peacefully. Some falcons kettled high overhead, whilst countless rabbits, hares and squirrels foraged and a family of foxes stole from some tall grass into a copse. These last, caused Mr. Darcy to proclaim that a hunt was in order.

The excursion took them past low hills and pasture lands where they saw large flocks of sheep tended by the occasional young shepherd, leisurely carrying out his duties. Once when they came within speaking distance of one such lad who happened to be sitting beneath a lofty oak, Mr. Darcy called out, "Master Stephen, good morning."

Somewhat surprised to hear who addressed him, he quickly removed his dog's head from his lap and was to his feet in an instant. Coming quickly toward the Darcys, he said, "Good morning, Sir; Ma'am; Master Darcy."

Lady Anne nodded and smiled; Mr. Darcy asked, "How are your parents, and your brothers and sisters?"

"They are all very well, thank you, sir."

"And how goes it with the sheep?"

"Real good, mostly, sir. Whenever Marshall, there spots any vermin, 'e barks like a banshee and runs hard at 'em so we've not lost many wee ones this year."

"I am glad to hear it. Good morning to you Stephen. I had best let you get back to your flock. Give your parents my regards."

"I will sir. Good morning to you, Sir; Ma'am; Master Darcy."

Moving on, Mr. Darcy made a mental note to find out how many lambs had been lost from other flocks. During this conversation, Marshall had stood as well, somewhat ruffled at having had his pillow so unceremoniously plucked from beneath his head. He was hardly impressed by the stature of the intruders. He had given a quiet snort, stretched first his fore legs, then his hind, shook himself indignantly and trotted off to find a more peaceful spot in which to curl up and resume his nap.

As the Darcys continued on, the path skirted past open fields where tenant farmers were industriously preparing to plant the year's crop; here they saw fields being plowed and others already harrowed. "Good morning Mr. Martin." called Mr. Darcy, "I see you are making fine progress."

"Good morning Mr. Darcy, sir; Lady Anne, ma'am. Oh, the young master grows fine, he does." God bless him, and you and Lady Anne as well."

"Thank you, Mr. Martin."

"As you say, we are making fine progress *indeed*. What with all the rain last fall and the mild winter, the soil is cut right through in two shakes of a stick. We shall be ready to sow in no time."

"That is excellent news. Young Fitz is out for his first tour of the estate and busy as you are I am sure you do not wish to be detained any longer so we will be quickly on our way. Good day to you."

"Good day to you Sir; Ma'am; Master Darcy."

The Darcy's acknowledged everyone they met, with Mr. Darcy able to address nearly all by name. As he often rode out over his lands with his steward, Mr. Wickham, he was well known to his people and they to him. The interest he took in the affairs of his estate and the wellbeing of his people was keen and it earned him the genuine respect not only of his own people but of those on neighboring estates who heard of it, or saw the results.

Though the young master could not have understood what he saw that day, this was to be but the first of many such outings, during which he observed the workings of the estate and experienced his father's interaction with those who contributed to the prosperity of Pemberley. Having been thus exposed, frequently, and from so young an age, he grew naturally to understand activities on the estate, to appreciate their interdependence and to regard them as the substance of life.

Chapter IV

REMEMBER WHO YOU ARE

1774

THE young master was eight years old when his uncle, Sir Lewis De Bourge breathed his last. Relations, friends and acquaintances from every corner of the realm, travelled to Kent to attend a funeral, the likes of which, the shire had never known. When the time came for the mourners to take their leave, Lady Anne remained behind to console her bereaved sister.

Lady Catherine genuinely appreciated having her sister to stay with her. So reassured was she, that in less than a fortnight, she was enough recovered of her spirits that she found the strength to resume offering Lady Anne an elder sister's advice in all sorts of matters. One afternoon, whilst they sat taking tea in Lady Catherine's favorite of her garden houses, their conversation, not surprisingly, found its way round to mortality. "Anne," said she, "I am very much concerned for you."

Much surprised, Lady Anne replied "Whatever for, sister?"

"You must have more children. You need, at the very least, one more son, for there are any number of ailments that carry young children off. You know that! and unlike Rosings Park, Pemberley is entailed. What will happen to it if your husband should die with no living issue?"

"Catherine!" Lady Anne exclaimed almost as if she feared giving voice to such a horrible thought might bring it to bear.

Making no acknowledgement of her sister's discomfiture, Lady Catherine forged ahead, "Are we to see Pemberley in the hands of some obscure Frenchman who has never heard of the place or even set foot in England until he finds he owns a bit of it? Oh think how the shades of Pemberley will be polluted if it should fall to a master who does not have English blood coursing through his veins."

"Catherine, do you not think you are being a bit over zealous in your estimation? My son is strong and healthy and we are ever so mindful of him. I see no reason why he should not grow to manhood. Besides, all these years we have hoped for more children but Providence has not seen fit to grace us with any but one."

"Perhaps you are not so attentive to your husband as you ought."

"Sister!" Lady Anne really believed her ears must have deceived her. Recovering of her surprise she said, "Whilst it amuses me greatly to hear you speak so, for never would I have thought it possible, I would ask you not to pursue that avenue of conversation ever again. Not only is it exceedingly insulting, it is incredibly far off the mark."

Making no apology for her inappropriate comment, Lady Catherine simply returned, "Then let us hope you shall soon meet with success, for you see how suddenly the flame can be extinguished. My Lewis did have his gout and his stiff joints, but there was never anything to make me think he should be so unexpectedly carried off as he was."

Lady Anne replied, "It was a complete shock to *us*, so I can only imagine what it must have been for you, who lived with Sir Lewis day in and day out, yet saw nothing to alert you beforehand."

Lady Catherine readily picked up this thread and Lady Anne, thankful she had been able to redirect the conversation, at length had her sister speaking of pleasanter, less intrusive topics.

At the end of a month's time, Mr. Darcy very much wished to have his wife return to him and she, just as heartily, wished to be at home again. Chusing to travel to Kent to escort his wife home to Derbyshire, Mr. Darcy determined that the young master would remain at home in the care of his governess. Wanting to spend a few days in town before heading north, it would be a se'nnight before the young master's parents arrived at Pemberley.

During that time, Master Darcy's lessons continued as always, but without his father there to make useful employ of his empty hours, he found himself in the company of George Wickham far more often than usual. George, the son of Mr. Darcy's steward, lived on the estate so he was always about and as he was but one year older than Master Darcy, it was natural they had come to be friends. They enjoyed much innocent fun. They swam and fished; they rode and jumped; they had various sorts of races. They even fancied they could, through some trickery, outrun the young master's dog, Excalibur, whom he called "Cali," but that belief was soon disaffirmed. They played at marbles and blind man's bluff; they trundled a wheel and they rolled each other in a barrel.

Alas, not all their adventures ended as they had expected. Neither chose to be barrel rolled a second time, and when they tied wads of cotton to the front paws of two cats, in the hope that the cats would fancy themselves great pugilists, the cats would have none of it. They simply yowled and struggled, each on its own, 'til they had freed themselves. The boys did not get quite the pugilistic exhibition they had sought, but none the less, they found it great fun to watch the antics as the cats rid themselves of their mitts.

Finally, arrived the last lazy afternoon before the young master's parents were to return. The boys, having wandered all the way to the eastern reaches of Pemberley, rested at the edge of a meadow, wondering what next to do. Whilst Cali trotted about, happily picking up interesting scents, the boys stretched out in the grass, hands behind their heads, the sun warming their faces. They began to admire a bee hive affixed to a low hanging branch of a nearby tree. They figured a hive of that size must contain a fairly large supply of honey and one or other of them remembered having heard somewhere that smoke made bees fall sleep. If that were so, they determined it should not be difficult to appropriate a bit of honey for themselves.

Neither had ever actually seen anyone attempt the process but it seemed straight forward enough; they would set the end of a dried branch alight, smoke out the bees and draw down the branch that held the hive. Their plan was really quite ingenious for they constructed a rope from plaited vines, slung it over the branch then secured the ends round an exposed root, employing a large rock for ballast.

This all likely would have worked, had they not taken so very long to consume their prize, but as they leisurely dined on dripping bits of honey comb, the smoke began to die out and the bees that had remained quiet within the depths of the hive began to turn their attention to their new formed *door*; first one bee emerging through it, then another, and another. By the time the boys realized the danger, it was too late and they found themselves rushing about, desperately seeking cover. In their haste, they tripped over their vine noose, causing the branch to spring free and the hive to careen through the air.

Pursued by some exceedingly irritated bees, the boys quickly took up the smoldering branch and sprinted headlong through the meadow and down a small hill. The pond at the foot of the hill proved their salvation for they jumped in and remained submerged with naught but their noses surfacing periodically to take breath. Continuing in this attitude for what truly was far less than ten minutes, indeed it felt, an hour complete. Once fear subsided, pain replaced it and for nearly a week, itching, swollen welts would prove effective reminders of how not to gather honey.

When finally they thought it safe to emerge from the pond, it was time to assess the damage to their persons. Wishing to confirm the wellbeing of his dog, the young master scanned the area. Realizing Cali was nowhere to be seen, he called and called; he whistled; he clapped; he called louder still, yet he received no reply. The horror of the bee attack all but forgot in the face of this new calamity, the young master dared to venture back in the direction of the bee tree, leaving George to follow as he might. When not even there could he see any sign of his dog, the young master was thoroughly alarmed. "What can have happened to Cali? Where can he have got to?"

George replied, "He has probably just run off after a hare or something."

"No. He never goes so far that he does not hear me call him back."

"It would seem this time he has."

"Perhaps when the bees... I must keep looking."

After nearly an hour spent tromping up and down; back and forth; round in circles, they had no better idea where Cali was, or in what condition he might be. George was not at all pleased to have spent so significant a portion of his afternoon searching for Master Darcy's dog. He rather doubted he should have been inclined to go to such great lengths in search of any dog, even were it his own. Besides, he had just been through a truly harrowing experience, his bee stings were a great bother *and* he was really very hungry.

"Fitz, we have looked enough and I am half starved. Let us go back home or better yet, into Lambton for we are nearly there."

The young master would not hear of it. He was by this time beside himself, but he would not give up.

"The sun has already begun its descent and there is hardly any moon this week. If we do not start back soon, *we* will be lost. Do not be daft."

Even this unassailable logic did not alter the young master's resolve. He would go home, but he must follow a circuitous route back to the manor house, covering as much ground as ever he could. George reluctantly agreed.

They moved north into a thick copse; this part of the estate was rarely traversed, thus it was not so familiar to the boys. Moving on, they had ventured deep into a cedar forest when something odd registered with George, "I think I smell smoke."

A moment later, the young master said, "I smell it too, but no one lives about these parts and there is no wind. Why should we smell smoke?"

"That, I should like to know as well."

"Let us go nearer and try to find out."

George immediately took charge and directed, "I believe it is coming from this direction. Let us move through here." Now that there was an adventure afoot, George did not think tromping through the wood half bad.

Wide eyed, the young master nodded and followed after George. Soon they heard the cracking of twigs underfoot and a boy came into view; a pair of hares slung over his shoulder. The boy looked like no one they had ever seen before. He had long, straight, black hair, piercing, deep set, black eyes and olive skin. His height and form proclaimed him to be about the young master's age yet he had the face of a man; its bone structure and expression incongruous with his person.

Despite his youth, the young master had already imbibed a solid understanding of what was considered acceptable and what was not. He knew his father turned a blind eye on poaching, so long as the privilege was not abused, but to endanger Pemberley lands was abuse beyond the pale. If this boy had started a fire to cook what he stole, that was not to be borne.

George jumped out and said, "Hey. What do you mean killing our hares?"

Shewing not the least surprise or concern at being thus confronted, the boy replied, "Who says they be yours?"

"You are on our land so they must be ours!"

" 'Hapse I dint caught 'em in your land?"

Taken aback, George knew not how to respond. Finally he blurted out, "Well I know they aren't yours so give them to me!"

"If you be smart, you'll go 'bout your business and forget y'ever saw me."

George, sized up this slight wisp of a boy and said, "You're just a thieving gypsy!" He made a quick grab for the hares, but he was too slow by half. The angered gypsy boy hooked his foot round George's ankle and instantly felled him, locking his foot across George's neck. The young master now ran over and jumped on the gypsy boy's back, but no sooner had he done so than the gypsy boy flung him off, sending him sprawling into a briar patch.

Master Darcy yelped in pain as he scrambled out of the prickle bushes and George squirmed in a vain effort to free himself. The gypsy boy said, "I'll not hurt you if you go 'way and let me 'lone. Just go 'bout your business and forget y'ever saw me."

He took his foot from George's neck allowing him finally to stand and catch breath. His pride severely wounded, he quickly backed away, panting, "You're lucky I have to get home or you'd end up like one of those hares. Com'on Fitz."

The young master certainly did not wish to stay behind without George, particularly if he had, for the very first time, come face to face with an actual gypsy, but neither was he ready to abandon the search for his dog, so he pleaded, "But what about Cali?"

"Forget Cali. We need to go home."

The young Master looked stunned and the gypsy boy asked, "What is Cali?"

"He is my dog."

The gypsy boy's ears perked up for he sensed an opportunity. Assuming a friendly tone he asked, "You have lost your dog?"

"Yes. That is why we are here."

"My grandmother can help you find him."

"Truly? Can she?"

"Yes. She has a magic eye and she helps people find what they have lost. Can you go get some money to pay her?"

"I *have* some money."

As Master Darcy began to fish through his pockets, George said, "Fitz, we should go."

The young master's fingers closed round a shilling and a ha'penny. Drawing them from his pocket he asked, "Is this enough?"

George gasped.

The gypsy boy, shewed nothing of the excitement he felt at the prospect of so rich and easy a gain. He said evenly, "It will do. Come. I will take you to her."

George said, "I would not even give him the ha'penny. They cannot find your dog and they will probably kill you!" Seeing the young master still wavering, George concluded, "You can stay if you wish, but I am going home."

The gypsy boy was incensed by George's insults but sure as he was that he had a fish almost on his hook, he tempered his response. " 'Tis nothing to me if you find your dog or not, but my grandmother's magic eye can help you."

The young master knew not who to believe, but if this lady could help him find his dog… "George, please do not go."

George replied, "I am and if you are smart, you will come too." and he began to walk away.

The gypsy boy said, "Let him go." and he gifted George with such a menacing glare that he would not have stayed, had he wanted to. Once George had gone, the gypsy boy continued, "If he would leave you when you ask him not, he be no friend. Do not trust him. Come. We'll find your dog and I'll see you come to no harm."

Master Darcy could only hope he had made a right decision, but he had to go on. After the longest two minutes of his life, he began to discern voices hard by. Soon they arrived at a spot where a huge cedar had snapped halfway up its trunk, creating a natural arch. Beyond this was the gypsy camp, which consisted of six or eight oilcloth tents of varying size and condition. Smoke rose through holes cut in the centre of their roofs. The men were away at present but there were women and children busy everywhere; some cooked; some carried wood for the fires; some retrieved clothes from lines tied between trees; some weaved baskets; an old woman sat against a tree singing as she mended socks; here and there, small children played.

When the gypsy boy and Master Darcy walked through the arch, nearly everyone stopped what they were about. At first a silence descended over the camp; next there arose a great confusion in a tongue unlike anything the young master had ever heard before. A particularly sturdy woman wearing bright colours and many gold bangles on her wrists came quickly to the gypsy boy and began a stern tirade during which she looked often to Master Darcy. Once the gypsy boy could get his say, it would seem he reassured her, for she grew calmer. At last he gave her the hares he had caught and she stood back letting him lead the young master into the camp, but still her eyes followed them.

"Who was that and why was she so upset?" The young master queried.

"That is my mother and she thought I was too long away."

"Why then did she look so often to me?"

"She thought you to blame, but I told her not."

This may have assuaged the young masters concerns, but it was far from an accurate account of the conversation. Characteristically leery of outsiders, the boy's mother had chastised her son for having been so foolish as to endanger the gypsy family's peace by giving away the location of their encampment. She had begun to quieten down only when he told of the riches that could be had from his new acquaintance. She had been further pacified by the boy's assurance that he would take a most indirect route in seeing the young master away to his own home.

Coming up before one of the tents, the gypsy boy called within to his Grandmother, "Mirri Purri Dai."

His call was met by some rustling and the swift appearance of a woman who, though of middle years, looked to be much more, for life had deeply etched her dark, weathered features like fissures in the dry, hard ground of winter. She too wore brightly coloured clothes and even more bangles than her daughter. As the boy and his grandmother spoke, the young master listened intently, but could discern nothing of their conversation; so completely unfamiliar was their language. Naught of its syntax, inflections or cadence bore any resemblance to English; or for that matter, to any other language the young master was learning.

If Master Darcy's ears would not vouchsafe him knowledge, he must seek recompense through his eyes and he studied the woman intently. She was tall and looked very strong; her hands he thought to be the size of his father's. Her face, when first she appeared, had looked foreboding and unyielding, but when her eyes fell upon her grandson, her features had softened. As they spoke, she seemed at times contemplative; at times amused. The young master was mesmerized by the Purri Dai's eyes yet he was not quite sure why. When at last she turned her gaze on him, he realized what it was. Her eyes were different. Studying the one, he saw that it was a very light brown, almost gold while the other was dark. Never had he seen anything such before, and it unnerved him.

"I hear you have lost your dog." said she.

"Yes. Ma'am. I have."

Now the Purri Dai began to ply her trade. "I can help you find him but you will have to pay me for my trouble."

Producing once again the shilling and ha'penny, the young master said, "I have these. I hope they are enough."

"That will do for now. When my grandson sees you safe home, you might send back some food for me."

The young master had not expected a request such as this, but he was more than happy to comply.

"I will need something of your dog if I am to find him. Perhaps you have some of his hair on your clothes." the Purri Dai said.

"Why yes. Most like I do." Quickly he searched the legs of his breeches and soon came away with some hairs.

The Purri Dai took the hairs and clasping them in her hands, she closed her eyes and began incanting some words over them; she threw some hairs to the East and some to the West. When she had finished, she told the young master his dog would return home before the sun had set twice more.

Completely enthralled by this strange ritual and no doubt *wanting* to believe its veracity, the young master said, "Thank you *very* much."

"She gave a quick nod and a little smile and said, "Give me your hand and I will tell your future."

The young master did as he was bid and the Purri Dai ran her fingers over his palm saying, "I see here that you will have great responsibility in your life… and I see too that you will have great sadness."

The young master gasped and tried to pull his hand away but the Purri Dai held tight.

"Ah, I cannot stop now. Once I begin, I must tell all."

That golden eye now seemed to bore straight through him as if it had a mind of its own. It was such an unusual colour that it forced him to stare at it and that made him immensely uneasy.

Quickly she continued, "I see another boy who is often with you. He has been with you today; your brother perhaps?"

"I have no brother."

"That is good, because the boy I see, you must not trust; he is no true friend to you. One day he will try to bring harm to you or your family and it will be for you to stop him."

For a second time, the gypsy woman had foretold of injury to the young master's family and he could not like it. "That is enough." he said. "I do not want to hear any more. I want to go home now." This time he pulled away with such resolve that the Purri Dai let him go saying, "If you are determined, then you shall leave, but you must forget you ever saw us."

The gypsy boy accompanied the young master home and hid a safe distance from the house while Master Darcy went quickly into the kitchens. There was no one there so he went round on his own and found an empty grain sack which he filled with some bread and cheese, a loaf of sugar, a ham bone with a fair amount of meat to it and a pickled tongue.

As soon as the gypsy boy had the bundle securely in his hands, he disappeared and the young master made his way round to the front of the house. He was nearly to the stairs when he heard a great scramble above and looked up to see Cali bounding down to meet him. It was difficult to tell who was happier or more relieved, for the young master ran to meet his dog and knelt on the stone stairs to pet him. Cali's tail wagged his entire body whilst he furiously licked his master's face.

When the bees attacked, Cali had been off on a small adventure of his own. Having followed a fresh scent, he was quite some distance away. On his return, he had tried devilishly hard to follow the many crisscrossed tracks the young master and George had made in the meadow. He had lost their scents completely at the pond, so he did the next best thing; he awaited his master's return to a place he was sure to eventually go.

Finally ascending the stairs, the two made such a great noise entering the house that they were instantly discovered.

"Master Darcy," said Mrs. Reynolds. "Where have you been? Your parents are home a day early. They have been here these three hours, but as you were not about, they have gone for a rest. You are to join them at supper."

A cozy, quiet meal had been planned in the small breakfast parlour, but at no time during the whole of that supper did anything resembling quiet fall over the room. Everyone had interesting events to relate but naturally the topic that arrested all other conversation was that of the gypsy camp.

During the young master's recounting of the day's adventures, a cloud had come to rest over his father's features. By supper's end, Mr. Darcy had grown quite sober indeed and after sending a messenger to fetch Mr. Wickham, he had his son accompany him into his library. Cali went with them and promptly curled up at the young master's feet.

"Son you say the gypsy woman helped Cali find his way back home. Why should Cali have required help in returning home?"

"Because he was lost." explained the young master. "We got separated and he got lost." The dog had looked up on hearing his name, but as no one seemed to take any further notice of him, he once again settled his head on the young master's foot.

Mr Darcy took a deep breath and began slowly, "Son, various people chuse to make their way in the world by various means. Gypsies travel about selling items they have made; sharpening tools; mending chairs and such. Many of them go throughout the season, moving from farm to farm helping with the harvest, but there are some gypsies who make money through deceit. They lead people to believe they can do things they really cannot do, like seeing what is to be in the future or even more deceitful, they pretend they can somehow direct the course of events. Son you must remember that only Providence determines what is to be, therefore only Providence can truly say what is to happen in the future. Do you understand?"

"I suppose so... but did not the gypsy lady guide Cali home?"

"No son, she did not. Dogs are very able creatures. They have a keen sense of direction and an even keener sense of smell. They are also incredibly loyal; just notice where your dog is at this very moment." He paused as his son looked down. "So long as they have command of their senses and are not physically hindered, they will prevail. I assure you Cali found his own way home; he needed assistance from no one." The young master was clearly taken aback.

Mr. Darcy said kindly, "In future, when someone tells you they can do something, think on this experience, consider what they claim and decide for yourself if what they say is reasonable."

"Yes father."

"It is a hard lesson to learn that people are not always to

be trusted, but the sooner you learn how to judge, the better." Mr. Darcy gave his son a moment to digest his words then he forged ahead. "There is something else that concerns me greatly about these gypsies you came upon. They were living, without permission, on someone else's land and still they saw fit to make fires there. If somehow their fire had got out of control, what would they have done to stop it? What could they do? A hungry fire will devour everything in its path.

Putting our land; our home; our lives and the homes and lives of our people in danger is an unforgivable transgression."

It was not long before there was a rap upon the door and visitors were shewn in. Having heard of the gypsies himself, Mr. Wickham, with George in tow, had set out to pay a call right after they took supper and had met the messenger midway along the path. Both Mr. Darcy and Mr. Wickham knew full well that having been discovered, the gypsies were likely already gone. Mr. Darcy explained to his son, "Their home was discovered so I would expect they have moved it, just as a cat will move her kittens once something finds where she has hid them."

Nevertheless, it was arranged that Mr. Wickham and a few able farm hands would accompany Mr. Darcy early next morning to assess any damage and if perchance the gypsies were still there, they would see to their immediate decampment. The young master would come to shew the men where to look. George was anxious for the chance to be of the party as well; there would, this time, be no threat.

Coming upon the broken cedar, the young master knew, beyond doubt, they were in the right place, yet there was nothing at all to say any living thing had ever walked there before. Master Darcy was shocked. The whole party got down from their horses and walked about, looking for some slight sign that the gypsies had been there, but they could find nothing. Even the ash from their fires was gone; buried or scattered in the wood, the young master knew not which, but the gypsies were nowhere to be seen.

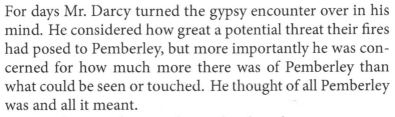

For days Mr. Darcy turned the gypsy encounter over in his mind. He considered how great a potential threat their fires had posed to Pemberley, but more importantly he was concerned for how much more there was of Pemberley than what could be seen or touched. He thought of all Pemberley was and all it meant.

One afternoon later in the week, when the young master had finished his lessons for the day, Mr. Darcy collected him for a ride out and headed north toward the highest ground on the estate. They had been riding about an hour, engaged in pleasant conversation the whole of the journey, when Mr. Darcy said, "Fitzwilliam let us take this hill. There is something I wish to share with you." Turning off the path, they began their ascent. It was not o'er steep; still the crest of the hill was far distant. The two made their way up with ease and as they rode, they fell into a companionable silence, each in his own way absorbed by his surroundings.

At the crest of the hill Mr. Darcy reined in his mount. Reaching his side, the young master saw that their vantage point afforded an expansive view and from a goodly distance overlooked the great house and its lake. Dismounting, Mr. Darcy proceeded to tie up the horses and together father and son walked to a point where the prospect was completely unobstructed. "This is Pemberley's highest point."

Mr. Darcy explained. He then commanded, "Fitzwilliam take a good, long look round you. Search as far as your eyes can see and commit all to memory, for *this* is our home. This is *us*, for we *are* Pemberley."

Fitzwilliam's eyes were drawn initially not, as his father commanded, to the vista before him, but to *his father*, for there was something in his voice the young master had never heard before. The mix of immense pride and humility his father felt, completely changed the timbre of his voice.

As Mr. Darcy looked out over the great expanse of Pemberley, he went on to recall, "The first time ever I saw this sight I was about your age. Your grandfather had brought me here, just as I have now brought you. I remember feeling truly humbled by all I saw before me; but I felt great pride as well."

Now searching the landscape, the young master said, "I cannot imagine feeling anything less than proud. I do not think I ever realized quite how much there is of Pemberley."

"The park alone is ten miles round, but it is not the magnitude of Pemberley that matters most. Of paramount importance is that Pemberley is what connects a Darcy to all the Darcys who came before him, and to all who shall follow. *We* stand where Darcys have stood since Norman times. It is for us to do what is required to preserve our home so that Darcys shall continue here through eternity. It is Pemberley that makes a Darcy who he is. It is Pemberley whence a Darcy draws his strength. That is a great gift, but it is also a great responsibility.

Fitzwilliam, you have been breeched these three years gone. You are a young man now and must begin to learn the responsibilities attendant on your position. As a Darcy of Pemberley, one day this will all be yours; yours to enjoy, but yours also to cherish, to nurture and to protect.

You have lately seen a situation arise that could have posed a serious threat to Pemberley and you have seen me ready to act in her defense, if need be. One day it will be for you to protect Pemberley. Whenever that day comes, you must be ready for the challenge, and a very great challenge it is, but you will *be* Pemberley so you must be ready.

All that your mother and I have ever taught you; will continue to teach you, is intended to make you someone worthy of the name Darcy and worthy of the great gift that Pemberley is. A Darcy's life must be ruled by duty, honour and decorum. You are a Darcy. Remember who you are."

"How shall I know what I am to do, father?"

"Remember who you are and let that understanding guide your actions. You are rational and intelligent. Follow your conscience and you shall not err."

Mr Darcy chose always to give the young master just a bit more information than he thought him currently equal to, for he knew his son would remember all and would not rest until he had mastered the understanding of it. To Mr. Darcy, learning to think was as important as, if not more important than, any knowledge he could impart.

Chapter V

LIFE LESSONS

1776

O F the utmost importance to the Darcy family, was the education of their son. When at the age of six, it had been time to begin the young master's formal education a tutor had been procured. By the age of eight that single tutor had been replaced by an assemblage of no fewer than half a dozen, all carefully chosen from amongst the most accomplished in their several fields. Now that the young master was ten years old he had long since proven himself an eager and able student, possessed of boundless curiosity and great natural intelligence.

Throughout the years, he took lessons in spelling, grammar, writing and literature. This last required him to learn the languages in which various works had been written, thus he learnt French, Latin and Greek. He studied arithmetic, astronomy and the natural sciences; he learnt of various peoples and cultures round the world and of the conflicts that had sometimes arisen amongst them.

As he lived in an age of unparalleled British nautical might, there was much to be learnt of valiant seafarers and triumphant naval battles. As a result of these maritime successes, there was much to learn of the distant lands that could now be counted as part of the Empire. Alas, he had also to learn the currently unfolding lesson of how an empire might lose control of a colony, if not managed wisely.

There were, as well, lessons in riding, fencing, swimming, shooting, fishing, dance and song. His lessons increased in intensity as he progressed and would continue until he went up to university, but important as it was, his formal education would have been nearly worthless had it not gone hand in hand with the many life's lessons learnt throughout the years.

"So Master Darcy, you have been riding out with us for nearly two months now. What have your rides taught you about Pemberley?" asked Mr. Wickham.

"They have taught me I shall spend much of my life atop a horse." This candor was characteristic of the young master; nevertheless, both Mr. Wickham and Mr. Darcy laughed at the unexpected nature of his reply.

"And would that be such a bad thing, Fitzwilliam?" his father asked.

"Not at all father; I love to ride. You know I do."

"Indeed, I know it well. I believe you are like to become as avid a rider as your mother and I."

Of late, the young master's riding ability had become so skilled that Mr. Darcy had begun to bring him along quite frequently when accompanying Mr. Wickham on rides out over the estate. As a result, Master Darcy was becoming quite familiar with the various Pemberley fields, forests; and waterways. He knew where the best hunt grounds were; the best trout streams; the best swimming spots and the best climbing trees. He was learning which cart roads connected with which and what paths served as shortcuts to various favorite spots. He could identify the different crops and was coming to recognize the characteristics of the land that determined which crop should best be planted where.

Gesturing out over the field of barley, beside which they now rode, Mr. Wickham asked of Mr. Darcy, "What say you to this?"

Most pleased with the goodly height and general health of the vast field of waving grain, Mr. Darcy replied, "I have been noticing it of late. It is a far better crop than last year?"

"It is indeed, sir." replied Mr. Wickham. "If the weather continues as it has done, we shall have an excess of barley this year. So much so, that I believe we shall have to seek another miller."

"Really?"

"You know sir, that Stubbs' mill is not very large; he could barely manage all we sent him last year."

"Yes, I remember." concurred Mr. Darcy. "How much more do you anticipate we shall have this year?"

"At least half again as much as last; perhaps more."

"That much?" queried Mr. Darcy.

"Truly sir. We have had just the right amount of rain and the temperature has been perfect. I have walked among the rows myself and they are all fine and healthy."

"Wickham, I think we have not only to thank the weather for that, but your irrigation ditches as well."

"Ah sir, I cannot take credit for that idea. Last year on my way north to negotiate with Morrison for the price of our wool, I saw such in some fields in Hawick. It seemed quite ingenious, the way they blocked or opened the channels as need be, so I thought it worth a try."

Mr Darcy said sincerely, "That was a keen observation and good judgment on your part." Then he addressed himself to the issue at hand, "Whilst I understand what you say about the bigger harvest, I am concerned that Stubbs depends on our grain, as do we depend on his buying from us each year. I do not wish to damage a valuable business relationship."

"I too thought of that, sir. I have been looking only to place the excess. There is a man, Barker, in Sheffield who can take more than he currently has promised him. He can use an extra two hundred bushels at least."

"Very good Wickham and Sheffield is not far. What price have you discussed?"

About to answer, Mr. Wickham slipped slightly in his saddle. He thought it a bit odd but clearly his horse had just taken a slight misstep so he righted himself and continued with his conversation. "He will match Stubbs' price, sir," he said.

"Excellent," replied Mr. Darcy.

"If you are in agreement sir, I can arrange with Barker straight away. He is so anxious to have the grain, that he is willing even to send his own carts to haul it away."

Mr. Darcy chuckled, "What a shrewd bargain you exact Wickham. Thank heavens I do not ever have to deal against you." Surveying the field once again, he mused, "You are a master negotiator, Wickham." Lost in thought for a moment, Mr. Darcy was recalled by the alarm in his son's voice.

"Mr. Wickham, sir! Father!"

Mr. Darcy looked upon his steward and called, "Wickham! Are you alright?" for Mr. Wickham's face had grown pallid and it was skewed aside. As Mr. Darcy spoke, Mr. Wickham teetered and slid quite far down the side of his horse. In trying to right himself, he found that his left arm and leg were practically useless. Mr. Darcy swiftly drew his own horse to Mr. Wickham's side and firmly clamped his hand round the flailing man's forearm. He righted him and held him steady. Still maintaining a tight grip, he asked urgently, "Wickham, can you ride? You need the doctor."

Mr. Wickham's reply was somewhat garbled but he managed to say, "Only just."

They were many miles from the manor house and all there who could help, and clearly Mr. Wickham could not manage the long ride back on horseback. As Mr. Darcy deliberated, his son offered, "Father, I should like to ride ahead and raise a call for help?"

Mr Darcy considered going on himself for he did not wish to send his young son alone over the desolate miles that lay between them and help; besides, he could ride much harder and faster than his son. Still, tending the stricken steward was surely not a burden he wished to place on one but ten years old, so in the end he acquiesced. "Very well. Mr. Wickham cannot ride the full distance to the house. He and I shall wait here while you ride ahead to seek help." Alighting, he eased Mr. Wickham to the ground, where he propped him up as best he could.

"Take this path to the cart road and follow it until it meets the West Walk. That will take you through the park, thence back to the house?"

"Aye, sir. We have ridden thus enough times that I believe I know the way."

"Good. Once you reach the road, the West Walk is little more than five miles off. Go straight to the stable; find Mr. Abbott and tell him what has happened. Ask him to send someone into Lambton to fetch the doctor and to ready a small gig for Mr. Wickham. Tell Abbott I should like him to come with Cooper to collect Wickham." Mr. Cooper, the overseer knew every inch of Pemberley, so there was no one better suited to accompany the young Master back.

"Yes father."

"Take this just in case…" Mr. Darcy secured the holster bearing his own pistol over the edge of his son's saddle. "Fitzwilliam, be careful."

"I will father."

Mr. Darcy nodded and gave the young master's horse a slap on its rump, sending the pair off at a trot. Looking after them, Mr. Darcy felt a strange mix of pride and concern for this was the first time he had ever entrusted his son with a serious responsibility. There were dangers present as well; there was a chance the horse might stumble and go lame or be startled and throw his rider, and not every animal living in the wood was docile; neither was it unheard of for beggars or poachers to travel deserted cart roads and these were often not the most honorable of men. Mr. Darcy felt certain Fitzwilliam was able to meet the challenge, but as he watched the figure of his young son, and heir, fade from view, it was disquieting none the less.

As the young master rode on, he too felt some disquiet. He thought first of Mr. Wickham, then of George and he was determined to succeed. He retraced their steps along the path, quickly coming out onto the cart road. Riding for what seemed a long time he began to wonder if he might have overshot the West Walk. Strange how a crisis slows time to a crawl.

"I will find my way… I must find my way. I remember seeing a very tall, broad linden tree just before the place where I must turn off. I am sure I should have known it, if I had seen it, for

it is so very large and it stands well apart from any other..." He stopt and looked about; he even considered doubling back, but in the end he decided to forge ahead. Riding at least another ten minutes, he still had past not a solitary soul along the way. With no one to assist, there was nothing for it but to push on.

At this point panic began to set in. *"Mr. Wickham's very life may depend on me, yet here am I lost! ... What am I to do? ... I cannot fail him. I cannot."* Again he considered turning about, till he convinced himself, *"I cannot have past that tree. It is so very large a tree I would have to be completely daft, not to have seen it. Even had I not seen it, I should have smelt it."* He had let his sensibilities take hold of him, but now logic once again assumed the reins, and with it, so too did his confidence. He realized now that he could not indeed be so far off the mark as he had allowed himself to believe. *"No, that just is not possible."* he reasoned. *"I have ridden this way before. I cannot have past it yet. I shall find it; I shall."*

He knew he would. After all, he was a Darcy and his father always said a Darcy did not accept failure. He began to grow annoyed that he had allowed himself to be frightened. It would not take many more such lessons for him to learn to forbid his sensibilities to obstruct his judgment. Immediately he came to this decision, his crop told his horse it was time they quicken their pace and so they pressed on. Finally, on rounding a curve in the road, he saw in the distance, a welcome sight. At last he had come upon the marker tree.

Turning into the West Walk, he felt he had lost much precious time so he decided to abandon caution and ride as hard as possibly he could. He leaned in, issued a stern kick and rising up on the balls of his feet, gave his horse its head. He had never ridden quite so fast before but he had seen others do it and felt it well within the scope of his ability. He knew how one should position oneself and how one held the reins and crop; he just prayed to God that no obstacle would present itself in his horse's path. Having ridden about a quarter mile without losing his seat, he became more at ease. In time he came within sight of the lake. He was almost there.

It was upwards of an hour before Mr. Darcy heard hoof beats and wheels approaching on the hard dirt road. When he could make out that it was indeed his son and his men coming into view, he exhaled a great sigh of relief for it heralded Fitzwilliam's safe passage and because Wickham would soon receive the care he so badly needed. The transfer was made quickly and carefully; at last they could be on their way.

By the time they finally made their way back into the familiar courtyard, it had been nearly three hours since Mr. Wickham took ill. Never had Mr. Darcy been quite so grateful to pass under his arch. Mr. Wickham was taken to a store room next the kitchens that had been fitted up with a bed brought down from the servant's quarters. The doctor, having arrived before them, now escorted his patient within.

Father and son watched as Mr. Wickham was borne inside. After directing a stable boy to fetch George, Mr. Darcy turned to his son and said, "Fitzwilliam, I am *that* proud of you. It is largely due to your efforts that Mr. Wickham is now to receive the care he needs."

"Father, what has happened to him? How is it he suddenly could not ride?"

"I am not absolutely certain myself, but we shall know better once the doctor has seen to him." Guiding his son to the solitude of the orchard, Mr. Darcy advised, "Fitzwilliam, I fear that what has happened to Mr. Wickham is very serious indeed. Only time will tell what the good Lord has planned for him, but we must accept whatever comes to pass."

"I do not understand, father"

"No… No… I am sure you do not. You see… even before each of us is born, God has a plan for the purpose we shall serve in His glorious world. Whilst we are here, He cares for us and guides us. If we fulfill our duty in this world, by living as good, caring, honourable people, God believes we deserve a reward and He calls us up to live with Him in heaven."

"Is that where Uncle Lewis went?"

"Yes son. It is."

"And Mrs. Wickham too?"

Thoughtfully, Mr. Darcy replied, "Yes son. I believe it is."

Mrs. Wickham had been a good sort of person, but she had also been very weak minded. Sadly for all concerned she had learned to find pleasure in drink and because her husband was so well paid for his exemplary efforts as steward, she was always able to fund her vice. The presence of ready money put her also in the path of those eager to encourage her to seek pleasure in games of chance. After years of hard living, Mrs. Wickham had succumbed not quite a twelvemonth since, and now this.

"Father, how old is Mr. Wickham?"

"He is five and fifty years old so he is not young."

"Is he much older than you?"

Mr Darcy could easily see where his son's thoughts were

heading and he answered reassuringly, "He is more than ten years my senior."

"Oh." said Master Darcy.

Just "Oh" but the release of tension in his young shoulders spoke volumes and his father said, "You need not worry Fitzwilliam. Your mother and I are both whole and hale so I do not believe we shall be going away for many, many years to come."

The young master's eyes glistened as he replied, "I hope not."

Mr Darcy thought sadly, *"You have been through far, far too much today, my boy; enough of this cheerless talk."* Earnestly he said, "Whatever happens is what Providence deems best; we must not question it. Now, let us go and find your mother. I believe she does not realize we are back and she would want to know what a brave and responsible son she has." Their conversation may have been at an end, but whilst it had answered many questions for the young master, it had raised as least as many more; some of which he would struggle with for years to come.

It was not long before Dr. Braxton came out and gave his pronouncement. "Apoplexy," he said. "No doubt about it. He may not last the night. If he does, he may linger for a while, but I have seen this before; it is not to be expected that he should recover."

Mr Darcy answered with a sigh, "I only wish we could have gotten him to you sooner. He suffered much on the journey back."

Dr Braxton replied, "Unfortunate though that is, it made no difference in his condition. When this happens, there is nothing anyone can do for the person beyond trying to make them as comfortable as possible."

When Mr. Darcy made George aware of what had happened he went to great lengths to ease his pain, preparing him for what he would see, but it could not be enough. When the door to the sick room opened, George was struck by the incomprehensible sight of his father, still wearing the shirt he had been wearing when they had broken their fast that morn. Only now, he was slumped abed, pale and weak... and in the middle of the afternoon! George could not remember ever having seen his father abed in the day; and to be laying so lifelessly, this man of boundless strength and fortitude. George's mind was totally at a loss to comprehend what was happening.

Breaking in on these tortured thoughts, Mr. Darcy asked, "George, shall we go in?" George, knowing there was nothing for it, steeled himself and gave a slight nod. As they crossed to the bed, Mr. Darcy called quietly, "Wickham, George is come to see you."

Mr Wickham opened his eyes and turned to face them. As comprehension slowly dawned he said with difficulty, "George, my boy." and he managed to produce a half smile.

Reaching the bed, George was devastated by the appearance of his father's twisted face. "Father, what has happened to you?"

"Not sure." answered Mr. Wickham slowly.

"Will you be better soon?"

"Hope so."

Mr Darcy was confident George would manage to handle the situation, so he thought it proper to give father and son their privacy and he excused himself telling George he would wait for him in his library.

With Mr. Darcy gone, Mr. Wickham studied his son for a long while and George stared openly up and down his father's entire left side. Finally Mr. Wickham said, "Be not afeared. Trust Providence."

George really could not like the sound of that. Instinctively he now knew there truly was very real cause to fear. "Father," he said, "how bad are you?"

"Quite bad, I believe."

"Why are you not at home? We have Clara; cannot she help you?"

"No George."

George's voice cracked slightly as he replied, "I just wish we could both go home now; that is all."

With a sigh, Mr. Wickham said, " 'haps soon." His strength was waning but he forced himself on, "... grateful to be here. Few would take such ... interest in ... steward and his son."

This conversation was raising more concerns for George than it was resolving and he did not reply. It would be quite some years before George could put words to the emotions he felt regarding the Darcys but the fact was, he was just becoming aware of the distinction between master and servant, and he realized he was on the wrong side of the division. He wanted not to be dependent on the kindness of others; he wanted to control his own destiny, for that he believed, was the only way he could be sure he would not be desolate. No matter who else left him, he would always have himself.

The effort required to hold so lengthy a conversation had quickly drained the energy from the weakened Mr. Wickham; his eye lids had long since begun to droop. George, realizing his visit was drawing to a close, excused himself saying, "Father, it would appear you need your rest. I shall go now and return later."

The sad expression on Mr. Wickham's face was painful to see; he nodded his head and asked George to pray for him; to which George replied, "I will father. Indeed I will." and he briefly grasped the hand his father held out to him.

When George left the room, he desperately needed to think so he sought the freedom of the outdoors and slipped through the service door next the kitchen. Once outside, he headed for the path on the far side of the lake. The farther he went, the quicker he moved, till he had run so far and so fast that he literally dropt to his knees from exhaustion. Panting for breath, he looked up through the trees to the blue sky above and let out a primal scream. "Why?" he shouted. "Why is this happening to me? It is not fair!" He took a much needed deep breath and thought, *"Father, why has this happened to you? I have no mother, and if you die I shall have no father... no family. I shall have no one and nothing at all. What is to become of me?"* His energy all but spent, he began to cry.

Mr Wickham survived that night and in time he even began to improve. During the time he was ill, his son was afforded the use of a room in the servants quarters so he could be nearer his father. Mr. Wickham appreciated this dearly; George did not. The young master saw very little of George during those days. When he did, he was struck by George's seeming insouciance. *"How,"* the young master wondered, *"can he be so unconcerned? I should think I would be beside*

myself if I had to watch my father face what Mr. Wickham is facing."

What the young master did not know was that George was *indeed* beside himself, with a concern that knew no bounds. Alas, it came to pass that George was concerned far more for himself than for his father.

Though the young master did not see much of George, the steward's son was very much about, and he was acutely aware of every move Master Darcy made; every privilege granted him; every favor bestowed upon him. Unbeknownst to Master Darcy, George had long since harboured some little resentment of him for "*it was,*" George reasoned, "*not through anything more than luck that the young master held the exalted position he held,*" whilst George had, as he saw it, "*been left to gather crumbs beneath the young master's table.*"

As George groused about this, he did not consider that whilst all Pemberley staff were well treated, the Wickhams inhabited a substantial and very comfortable home, situated in a most attractive prospect on the grounds; or that their table was never without such extreme luxuries as sugar, butter or fresh, lean meats; or that the logs in their hearths usually shared their place with very large chunks of coal. Such benefits as these were of consequence even in the greatest of houses; they were unheard of in the homes of the middling sort.

Something else George did not consider was that far from merely being fortunate beggars, he and his father lived as they did as the reward for his father's exemplary efforts as steward. Mr. Wickham had much to be proud of for he had earned what he had. Still George groused, and as the length of Mr. Wickham's convalescence increased, so did George's resentment. It seethed and would eventually develop into an all consuming jealousy, for yet again had he been cheated by life, only this time, the ill-treatment was complete. He was not convinced his father would ever again be as before, and he was scared; monstrous scared.

Mr Wickham, by sheer will, did at last recover. He was determined to be well again and after some months of praying and forcing himself forward, he was again able to do the things he had once done. This miracle did not; however, come before the young master had gained a completely new understanding of what George was about. That young man, was well aware of the benefits to be had by staying in the good graces of Mr. Darcy, who had always thought very highly of him, thus he most scrupulously kept from his benefactor anything that might betray his burgeoning want of principle. In Mr. Darcy's eyes, his godson remained a fine example of what a good natured, well mannered young man ought to be.

Wickham felt no need to hide his true self from the young master for *his* good opinion was of no consequence. In the young master's eyes, George was beginning to change into something very different indeed and though his limited experience did not yet allow him to put names to everything he saw, what he saw, were the beginnings of the deceitful, scheming, lascivious, gaming propensities that would eventually come to characterize George Wickham.

The young master did not understand how someone could be so changed in so short a space of time, but there was very little resemblance between the George of just a few months gone and the George whose father had lately taken ill. The young master turned this change over in his mind for a long while but he never could quite decide why such would happen; could happen; should happen.

Chapter VI

GEORGIANA

1778

A dozen years had past since the birth of the young master, yet no siblings had come to join him. There had been no miscarriages, no apparent ill health; no want of affection; still the Darcy's had not been blessed with one single child more. To be sure this was the cause of some concern, particularly during the young master's early years when healthy though he was, it was not at all unlikely he, like so many others, could have been carried off by disease. With each successive year that he grew and enjoyed good health, the vital importance of producing an heir presumptive diminished but the *desire* for further issue had remained strong, so when finally the news came that Lady Anne was once again with child, it was met with well nigh the same degree of jubilation as had met the first announcement.

That joyous news had come summer last and the months since had past with ease as the Darcy family anxiously awaited the blessing of their second child. It was now Sunday the 12th of April and Lady Anne's time had come, but not all was well. Her lying in had begun nearly twenty four hours past and now as day began to break she lay wan and much weakened by the violence of an arduous but as yet fruitless labour. Long hours ago the doctor had informed Mr. Darcy that the baby was not only long but was turned about as well. Upon hearing this news, Mr. Darcy had blanched for he knew only too well that when a baby presented breach it meant almost certain death for the child and often for the mother as well; he could only pray such did not come to pass this day.

For hours he had waited helplessly, trying determinedly not to listen as the tortured cries of his dear Anne found their way down the hall to his unwilling ears. His mind tried desperately to wrap itself round what was happening; to come to some sort of understanding; to find some assurance that all would be well. *"Things went as they ought for her first lying in"* he reasoned, *"and is not the first expected to be the more difficult? Why should it not now be as before? Anne, you are such a completely good person. Why should you be made to suffer so? Can this truly be how Providence has planned it?"* He searched for answers that did not come; his mental anguish nearly matching the physical anguish of his wife.

Finally, it came to pass that a healthy daughter was born, but she came at great cost to her mother. The protracted difficulty of Lady Anne's labour had left her so weak that she would surely have lost her baby, had it not been for the determined efforts of the doctor. So severe had her contractions been that her strength was compromised to the point where she was unable at the end to help herself as she would need to, were she to survive.

Only thrice more did she see the sun rise. On the Thursday, Mr. Darcy and the young master attended the Lady Anne as she lay in the Pemberley picture gallery, amidst paintings and statuary now draped in black crepe. Wearing an expression of complete peace and tranquility, she lay in an oaken coffin so highly polished that the candles surrounding it seemed multiplied into a myriad of dancing golden flames. The image put the young master in mind of the story he had read so many times of King Arthur, for this was exactly as he imagined the final voyage of the dead King floating down river to Avalon.

A week later, a procession led by three matched pair of plumed, midnight steeds made its solemn way along the carriage road into town and to the door of the Church; the large glazings of the hearse glimmering in the sun. The Lady Anne was attended on her final journey by her husband and son; the Fitzwilliams and DeBourges; friends; acquaintances and connections from every corner of England; as well as all the Pemberley staff and cottagers. Towns' people standing along the side of the road bowed their heads and made the sign of the cross as the procession past; some fell into spontaneous prayer; some shed tears.

The service, dignified and somber, had been planned completely by Mr. Darcy. Throughout, the young master Darcy sat betwixt his father and Lady Margaret, quietly taking in all that went forward. When it was over, Lady Anne was borne back to the waiting hearse and as the horses took their first steps the Church bells awoke to bid her farewell. Master Darcy was particularly struck by the effect of the bells. Passing beneath the steeple, the slow steady tolling made such powerful vibrations in his ears and chest that his eyes were drawn almost forcibly, to the belfry. The sound and image of that knell would stay with him forever.

Lady Anne was to be buried in the family cemetery, on the grounds of Pemberley. She would rest in the protection of generations of her husband's ancestors, in a spot he had chosen for her, beneath a then fully flowered cherry tree. Coming upon the freshly dug grave, the young master's heart gave a lurch. That huge gaping mouth waiting to swallow his mother was far too real, too final and he looked away. Lady Margaret, seeing and knowing, placed her arm gently but securely round him. When at last the coffin made its descent, a sizable portion of the young master's heart went with it.

The Lady Anne had died during the week preceding Easter and the fresh mound of earth in the Darcy family grave yard was bedecked with white lilies, this as much for Lady Anne's pureness of heart as for the timing of her demise.

Finally it was over and Mr. Darcy looked for some time at his son, who still stood beside Lady Margret. He looked, but seemed not to see him. He said nothing; not to his son nor to anyone else. Lord Fitzwilliam made some quiet remark that Mr. Darcy seemed incapable of comprehending. For the whole of the ride back to the manor house he sat and stared silently through the glazing.

The Darcy's knew full well, the dangers of child birth. It was never a surprise to anyone when a mother was carried off in this manner; yet Mr. Darcy had never once allowed himself to consider the possibility that such might befall his lovely wife. Now he tortured himself incessantly with thoughts of the degree to which she had suffered. The fact that she had had to suffer at all was a horrible burden for him to bear; would that he could have borne the suffering for her. So completely had they understood and admired each other; so secure, in every way, had their bond remained throughout all the years of their marriage that it was incomprehensible to him that he should ever be without her. If pressed to account for their eventual ends, he would have imagined that he should be first to draw his last breath, but providence had not seen fit to grant him that more acceptable reality and now he was faced with the unthinkable. He knew not how to go on without her.

If there was one thing the privileged life of a Darcy did not offer in abundance, it was instruction in how to suffer hardship. So undone was Mr. Darcy by his grief that for a time he withdrew into himself, leaving his children bereft of his attention. This was not truly a difficulty for his infant daughter, for Pemberley was a veritable well spring of capable, trusted servitors, but for the young master, with whom he had always shared an uncommonly close bond, it was insufferable. First, to have lost his mother to an interloper and now for all intents and purposes to have lost his father as well, was a trial too great to bear. Yea, everywhere he turned he found someone whose purpose in life it was to see to his all and sundry needs, but such alone would not do. He needed a confidant; he needed a mentor; he needed his father.

Faced with so monumental a personal tragedy, the young master's sensibilities clouded his judgment and with no one to guide his understanding or to ease him through his pain, his youthful mind managed to come to some most inaccurate conclusions regarding the wherefore of his grief.

Life at Pemberley House had gone on thus out of kilter for nearly three months when one day, after what now past for lessons were through, young Master Darcy sat in one of the bright windows of the nursery trying desperately to lose himself in a particularly fantastical Greek myth. Upon his peace encroached Millie, the nursery maid who came in cooing at Georgiana who she held lovingly in her arms.

"Good afternoon Master Darcy," said she.

Without looking up, he answered perfunctorily, "Good afternoon to you."

Holding Georgiana up before her brother, Millie went on, "Ah just look at how your sister smiles at her bonnie brother."

Concentrating even harder on his reading, Master Darcy did not look up; he was neither convinced of this particular reasoning nor was he amused by it. *"Everyone is always trying to make me think she is so perfect. She will never be nearly so perfect as Mother was."* he thought.

"Now will you look at that;" Millie went on, "if she doesn't hold out her hand to you..."

"I hardly think she has the faintest idea who I am or who anyone else is."

"Oh but she does Master Darcy. Many are the times you walk by and the poor little dear starts to cooing with her big blue eyes on you till you pass out of sight."

Seized by a fit of the most bitter sarcasm, he thought, *"Oh yes... Poor little dear... What deprivation she suffers; this mewling brat for whom everyone falls over themselves... She did not know mother so what has she lost?"* He rose, soundly closed his book and thumped it down on the seat in his stead. It rankled his nerves to think of the excessive amounts of attention paid this little trespasser, who had taken the place of his dearly loved and sorely missed mother. *"This is not to be borne."* Completely lost in painful reflection and having not the faintest idea where he was going, he marched down the stairs, across the breadth of the reception hall and out through the massive front door.

⌘

"Enter." called Mr. Darcy, at the rap upon his library door. He was deep in thought, staring blankly at some papers on his desk. When he heard the door open he did not look up but waved toward the barely picked at dinner tray and said, "Take it. I am not hungry."

Clearing his throat, Fletcher began, "Yes sir." and he picked up the tray but remained where he stood.

Realizing the man tarried, Mr. Darcy asked, "Is there something else?"

"Yes sir… there is… but… I am not sure how to…"

Impatiently, Mr. Darcy cut him off, "What is it? Speak and have done with it."

"Yes sir. Very good, sir… It is that… I am sorry sir, but we cannot find the young master." The poor man was so pale by the time he had finished that he looked as if he would faint dead away.

"Have you taken leave of your senses? What are you saying?"

"I am afraid it is true sir. The staff has searched every inch of the house; above stairs and below. We have all looked until we are sick. He is not here sir."

When Mr. Darcy's only reply was a disbelieving stare, Fletcher felt it necessary to go on, "The staff only realized something was amiss sir, when the young master did not come down to supper. The last he was seen was before 2 o'clock in the afternoon. He had been reading in the nursery; it is not known where he went after he left there and he has not been seen since."

"He must have told *someone* where he was going."

"No sir. I am afraid not. No one knows a thing."

"You must be mistaken. Why would he go off on his own without a word to anyone?"

"I wish I were mistaken sir, truly I do, but he is not to be found."

Getting up and beginning to pace as he tried to make sense of what he was hearing, Mr. Darcy questioned, "Supper was served at 8 o'clock. Why has it taken till nearly 10 for you to alert me?!"

"It was never thought sir that he would not be found. At first it was believed he was somewhere about and just not wishing to eat."

As the reality of the situation began to sink in Mr. Darcy began to feel sick.

"Sir, a search party is being formed even now. They plan to comb the park with torches then to move on to the cottages and out buildings."

Mr Darcy's mind raced and his heart pounded. In mere seconds so many questions tumbled over each other in his thoughts. *"How could Fitz suddenly vanish? Surely he would not just wander off aimlessly. Where can he be? Something must have happened to him, but in Heaven's name, what? Oh dear Lord, please do not let him have come to harm..."*

"Did he take his horse?"

"No sir."

"And the carriages; any missing?"

"No sir. Not a one."

"Then how far can he have got to? Has anyone been here today who did not belong here?"

"No sir."

"What about the village; has anyone gone there?"

"Yes sir. Mr. Wickham himself has gone into Lambton and taken four men with him but they have yet to return."

"If Wickham is leading the party in Lambton, I shall lead the search of the grounds. Fletcher call for my horse."

"Right away sir." And he was off.

Mr Darcy would not await Fletcher's return. He rushed to his dressing room and with some difficulty found for himself his breeches and boots and got them on. By the time he reached the court yard, an assembly of no fewer than fifty men was there to meet him and more were steadily making their appearance; there were stable hands and gardeners; the keeper of the hounds was there with some of the dogs; many of the tenant farmers and their sons were there as well. Some rode, some were on foot but all were anxious to begin. There was a palpable sense of true concern; these men were not driven simply by duty or self interest.

Mr Darcy was taken aback by the sight and he was humbled that so many had so quickly and eagerly answered the call. A groomsman handed Mr. Darcy his reins and in one swift motion he was in the saddle and turning toward the crested arch. As he did so, he rattled off a silent prayer then he spoke, "I sincerely thank all of you for your help. Glancing skyward he said, "The moon is waning but it is bright enough still to be of assistance. If we break into separate groups we shall cover the grounds much faster. Search every cottage, every barn and every hay loft; anywhere he might be." Mr. Darcy knew every face before him and he addressed the men by name as he assigned them to cover specific areas of the estate. "If you find *anything*, set off a shot every few minutes till I reach you." To his own group he said, "Let us begin with the old mill and..." his voice cracked, "the weir next it."

The party moved along calling out the young master's name but their only replies were the occasional rustle of leaves, the hoot of an owl or the call of a juvenile fox who had strayed too far from its den. The mill and its environs shewed no sign of having been visited any time in the recent past; nevertheless it was thoroughly searched. Then it was time to turn their attention to the weir and Mr. Darcy felt for only the second or third time in his life, an all consuming fear. He knew his son to be an excellent swimmer, but this was a weir. He was visited by the awful memory of his helpless hours whilst his dear Anne's life hung in the balance and he began to sweat profusely. He had lost her and he did not know how he should manage if his son were lost as well. The deceptively still waters beneath the crest were perfectly clear and though the darkness did not allow of complete certainty, after a time it seemed reasonably sure they had claimed no victim. Relief coursing through him, Mr. Darcy thought, *"Providence has spared me this grief at least. Dear Lord, please let my son be found alive and safe."*

As the search party moved from cottage to cottage, it grew in number. When at last it had been to every edifice, used or unused, standing or felled and nothing had been seen or heard of the young master, Mr. Darcy reluctantly directed, "We have done all that can be done here tonight. Those of you who ride shall accompany me north to the high ground; those on foot I shall thank heartily and send back to your families. Thank God for them and when you arrive, give them to know you love them." No one wanted to be known as the man who went home to sleep when Pemberley was in need and someone called out, "Sir, we shall keep searching till the young master is found."

Mr Darcy had to clear his throat to reply, "May God bless

you all." Then to those on horseback he said, "The young master and I often go to the look-out point on the high ground to the North; I must search there next." In a more distant voice he continued, "If he is not there, at least it is a good spot from whence to watch and listen." Grieved as he was, he did not know whether he more wanted to hold his son tightly to his breast or to strike him for what he had done. As he rode, still calling out the young master's name, Mr. Darcy had much time to think and he began at last to realize how far he had removed himself from his dear son; Anne's son; his heir; the future of Pemberley. Regret and shame settled heavily on his mind. It now finally dawned on him that Fitzwilliam must be feeling a grief similar to his own for they (all three) had shared an uncommonly close bond. Theirs was not like most families. Having chosen not to send their son off to pass his early years living with a wet nurse, the Darcys' chose not to send him off to school either, though so many of their acquaintance did. They had wanted him to be with *them* and for Pemberley to be an integral part of his every memory. *"Dear God, please let him fare well. Please let us find him safe and unharmed."*

They rode deeper into the wood, the path getting steeper as they went. More than once they heard the not far distant cry of a wolf. No one commented, but all duly noted, raising the level of tension even higher. When they reached their destination there was no trace of Master Darcy. They were disappointed still to have found nothing; disappointed yet relieved not to have found that the young master was seriously hurt or worse. Looking out over the prospect before them everything was absolutely still. Mr. Darcy now stayed his horse near the edge of the precipice and prayed, *"Dear God please do not make my son pay for my sins. I have thought*

*of myself and my grief alone. I realize now that I have been
completely remiss in my duty as a father, but that shall change
from this instant if only he still lives."*

Continuing the search as they made their way back to the
manor house, hope began to fade. They had gone miles
beyond the park, yet they had found nothing. If Master
Darcy were still out there somewhere on his own, the likelihood was great that he was badly injured, yet Mr. Darcy
was forced to acknowledge that little more could be accomplished till day break. He and his men returned to the courtyard. There it was learnt that Mr. Wickham was lately back,
having found nothing; the same was true for many of the
parties that had been combing the grounds.

Unwilling to await the break of day, Mr. Darcy and Mr.
Wickham together would head back out. To one of the
grooms who waited in the court yard Mr. Darcy said, "Have
fresh horses brought round and see to these."

"Right away sir."

Whilst he and Wickham waited, the distant sound of hard
driven hoof beats became apparent. Soon one of the tenant
farmers rode into the courtyard with the news that early in
the afternoon, Master Darcy had been seen by some harrow-
ers working a field near the edge of the estate that bordered
the Bakewell Road.

This area had already been searched, but possibly not well
enough so Mr. Darcy and Mr. Wickham lead whichever
men were about, on another search of that part of the estate. Whilst they combed the area, hours past and the sun
rose, but even in the light of day they could find nothing.
By now the shoppes and businesses in Bakewell would be
starting to open and possibly someone there would have
seen or heard something of the young master so Mr. Darcy

and Mr. Wickham, riding abreast and accompanied by four searchers struck out for town.

"Do not lose hope." offered Mr. Wickham, "Fitzwilliam is intelligent and resourceful; I expect this will yet end well."

"I pray God you are right but I cannot help feeling this is my penance for how poorly I have behaved toward him lately. I am ashamed to call myself Darcy, for where has duty been in my thoughts of late?"

"You are a Darcy true, but you are entitled to feel the pain of loss just as keenly as the next man. I know how hard it was for young George and me when we lost our Aggy and you cannot be feeling any less grieved for Lady Anne; God rest them both."

Mr Darcy immediately recognized and appreciated the deep and genuine concern from whence stemmed Mr. Wickham's words. He chose simply to offer a polite nod of acknowledgment and say nothing, but he was sent into most solemn reflection. *I might be entitled to feel the pain of loss but not to shirk my responsibilities. Duty is the driving force of a Darcy; has to be. Is not that what my father taught me and what I have always taught Fitzwilliam? Yet here am I having failed so miserably. Oh that I should let pernicious sensibilities cloud my judgment.*

To Mr. Wickham, he said, "If someone had told me even yesterday that I should find myself searching through the night for my son because I had failed him, I believe it would have taken every ounce of will for me not to demand satisfaction, yet here am I and truly do I deserve every bit of the agony and shame… Where can he possibly be? We are running out of places to look. Wickham, I know not what I shall do if he is not found."

When the great, heavy front door had closed behind Master Darcy that afternoon he had had no plan. He had simply felt an overpowering need to distance himself from what had become an increasingly unbearable situation. His mother was gone; his father had largely absented himself from his life and there was an intruder in their midst who upset whatever vestiges of normalcy remained. Cali would comfort him, he thought but standing there at the head of the stairs he realized he had not gone to fetch Cali after his lessons. To fetch him now would mean a return to the house and that just would not do, so he alone had marched down the long flight of stairs, thence striking out across the lawn and into the park. Some long time later he had cut through part of the wood and found himself on a public road, though which road, he was not quite sure. Funny how different a road can look when on foot than from the elevation of a horse or carriage; besides, there was no mile stone and no sign post in sight. He walked on, only stopping to consider what he had done whence he became too tired and hungry to go on. Resting under a large oak to take stock of his current situation he realized he had with him no food, no drink and no money. Worse yet, he had not an idea where he was or how far it might be into town for there were still no sign posts within view. Alas, self recrimination would have to wait, for as he pondered, his eyes began to close and his mind refused to take on any more.

"Is summat up wi' 'im?"

"Ah cannah say."

"E's got nice clothes."

"Yeh … Could be someone giv em to im fer the fancy would n' be lyin i'the road."

"Yer right."

Young Master Darcy, suddenly aware of voices, awoke with a start to see two simply dressed boys of near his own age standing over him.

"E stirs," said one to the other, then to Master Darcy he asked, "Are you awreet?" but the young master looked puzzled and did not respond.

The second boy explained, "He asked if you are alright."

"Oh… Yes… Quite well, thank you."

"E talks fancy." said the first boy to the second. Then to the young master he said, "Ah nivver seen you before. Were dy you live?"

As Master Darcy's faculties awakened, so too did his ability to recognize and understand a dialect he was marginally familiar with, having now and again heard it used among some of the farmers. Thinking it best not to be too forthcoming, he replied, "I live about a mile from Lambton, more or less. Where am I now?"

"You're come close ter the edge o'Bakewell."

Pleasantries were exchanged as the two boys joined Master Darcy. One sprawled out on the grass in the sun, the other sat on the trunk of a fallen tree. The first boy, who happened to be two years younger than Master Darcy was called John. The other boy was called Martin and was the same age as Master Darcy. The young master thought it best to give his name as William only. Upon hearing young Master Darcy's reason for flight, John said, "You never ought to have done it. They'll be bang frit to death fer you back home."

Young Master Darcy considered that prospect and replied gravely, "No, I really do not think anyone will be very frightened for me. I dare say I shall hardly be missed."

"Then come wi' us. We're headed ter town fer summat ter eat." said John, who for his young years was quite full of confidence. Young Master Darcy quite happily rose to join his new friends as they continued on their way into Bakewell. He had never known boys such as these before. On his trips into town with his mother or father he would often see local children talking or playing and he would sometimes wonder what they were like, but he had never had reason or opportunity to converse with any of them. This promised to be something of an adventure and he felt easy and happy for the first time in a very long while. The day was turning out just fine.

Their first order of business was to find something to eat but as none of the three had any money and the boys lived on the far road out of Bakewell, this would require some skill.

Coming into the town Martin said, "Ah'll see what ah can get a the bakers."

John replied, "Good idea," and he directed Master Darcy to walk on with him till they were just beyond the drapers shop. As the two boys sat at the side of the road and waited, Master Darcy thought his friend seemed perhaps a little distracted but as friendly chatter continued he thought no more of it. Abruptly John said, "Let's go." and ran full on down the road, leaving Master Darcy to follow as he could. The two weaved in and out among people in the road, not stopping till they had rounded a corner and run halfway down a narrow alley. They were still trying to catch their breath when they were joined by Martin. With a toothy grin he said, "C'mon" and led them round to a hidden spot behind the shoppes.

"So?" questioned John. "What have you got fer us?"

From under his shirt he produced a large loaf of hard crusted bread and proudly asked, "What d' you think o' this?

"That be a good un." John said as he reached out and tore off a big piece. With wide eyes, Master Darcy waited appreciatively for a piece to be handed him.

"Ain't ye havin' any?" asked Martin and he held out the loaf for Darcy to take some off.

This protocol was a bit surprising to Master Darcy but it was easily understood and the three ate as if they had not eaten in weeks. Looking round, John said, "Sure wish we had summat ter drink."

"Me too," agreed Martin.

"So do I," added Master Darcy.

Martin said, "What about the inn. Tis not far along."

"Aye," John concurred

Master Darcy said, "We have no money. They will not serve us at the inn."

Rising, Martin said, "Who's lookin fer ta be served? All I want's a few swigs o'ale. Com'on." and he led the others to the inn. Standing at the door and looking about the tap room they saw that it was not full but there were a good number of people about. Not too far from where they stood was a man who seemed to have had more ale than he ought, for his head rested heavily on the table. Staying low and moving with stealth, Martin found his way up behind the drunkerd. Slowly removing the man's glass from the table, Martin took a long draught and quietly replaced the glass, then made his way quickly back to the door. "Tha's how 'tis done." He exclaimed proudly.

Master Darcy simply looked stunned but John said, "Th' was a good un. Now me." and he went off for a share of the man's ale. Back in no time, licking his lips he said, "How was that?"

Master Darcy again looked stunned so Martin said, "T'ain't nothin' to it. Ye try it."

Something told the young master this was not an advisable course of action but he was very thirsty. "Perhaps I could just ask the man for a sip."

John and Martin were overcome by laughter that threatened to expose them.

Master Darcy did not see why they should find this so funny. "It is but a small sip I would want. Why should not I just ask the man kindly?"

Still laughing, John said, "Go on then; try it."

As Master Darcy walked away he could hear the boys giggling. Coming up beside the man, he stood tall and tapped him gently on the shoulder. The man only grunted and shrugged his shoulder as if shooing off a bug. Master Darcy tapped again. This time the man lifted his head and made an effort to see who disturbed him.

"Sir, I am very thirsty and wonder if you might be so kind as to allow me a small sip of your ale."

The man looked to his nearly empty glass, then yelled some garbled oath and rising unsteadily to his feet, tried to strike the young master. He dodged the blow but while the man promptly toppled back down, Master Darcy knew to be gone and he ran. He ran right into the Inn keeper, who having been alerted by the commotion grabbed him by the collar. "Run, will you? Not so fast!"

Immediately this happened, John and Martin turned on their heels and made a hasty departure, leaving the disbelieving young master to fend for himself as the Inn keeper led him gruffly out the door. "Get on with you, you dirty, thievin' rascal. Can you no' see this be a respectable place? Take yourself away before I give ye a good thrashing."

Master Darcy's mind raced as he worked at trying to comprehend what was happening, but he could not get on. Never in his life had he met with such incivility. The vulgarity of the patron and the inn keeper's insolence struck him of a heap. When a member of the Darcy family entered an establishment the publicans rushed to his service; they did not throw him out. *"But then,* he thought, *"he does not know who I am."* and things began to make sense. It of a sudden struck him how very different some people's lives must be from his own. He had wondered earlier why it was necessary to run into an alley to eat bread and now he began to think he might understand. "Sir, I am not a thief. I asked the man politely for some ale and had he said no, I would have withdrawn, but I was not given that chance."

"That be some fancy talk for a thief."

"Sir! I am not a thief." cried Master Darcy.

"If you be not a thief, what then d'you want to bother my customer for?"

"It was not my intent to bother anyone. I merely wished to ask a favor, for I am very thirsty and I have no money with me."

The Inn keeper found he could not truly be so angry for he was rather amused and there was something amiable about the boy. "Come to town with no money did you? Not very wise, that. Are ye willing to work? I could use some help for one of my men did not come to work today. You look like a strong boy; if you will mop up the tap-room and drag in the barrels of ale for to-night's guests I will see to your thirst and you will get a good meal besides."

Young Master Darcy was a little slow to respond as he processed the idea of having to work for a meal. Imagine this man suggesting that he clean a filthy tap-room or haul barrels in to serve the middling class. Great heaven's, what would his father say? Then again, did his father care what he did? Why not try something ridiculous? Finally he said, "That would be very kind of you sir; very kind indeed."

"Right then. Your first pint shall be on credit as ye be so thirsty." Taking Master Darcy to the taps he poured him a pint and said, "What's your name then?"

Even less forthcoming than earlier in the day the young master said, "I am Will, sir."

"Well then Will, in return, I expect good work of you." And to one of the regular workers, he said, "Jamie, Will here is to 'elp you t'day. Shew 'im what's to be done."

"Aye, sir. C'mon Will."

Soon Master Darcy began rolling barrels of ale and dragging crates of gin from the alley. They were heavy and the distance from the alley to the store room long and obstructed so the young master very much welcomed the watered wine he was offered to quench his thirst whilst he worked. Unaccustomed to this sort of labour, Master Darcy grew weary, his muscles felt sore and he began to sport rather large blisters on his hands, thus he was relieved indeed when he had finished and grateful was he when at last most of the guests had finished their supper and it was time for the servants to eat.

The young master sat to table in the kitchen with whichever of the staff were not currently needed. Up and down the long trestle table people reached over and under each other's arms for the various dishes. When Master Darcy asked for a napkin he was asked what was wrong with his sleeve. When he asked someone to serve him some potatoes, he was told he was close enough to take them for himself.

General chatter rang out all round but little of it involved Master Darcy till Cook who had just taken her place at table beside him said, "You be new here. You the one what's called Will?"

"Yes ma'am."

"Where you from, Will?"

"I live not far from Lambton." he replied.

Cook too had noticed the young master's fine clothes and she asked, "How d'ye come to be workin' here?"

Jamie replied, for he had maintained constant chatter whilst he and Master Darcy worked. "Seems as he 'as a mind to run away from 'ome... but he's not much used to the way o'things."

Cook addressed Master Darcy, "Beat you, do they?"

"Why no!" he replied in surprise.

"Starve you then?" asked a chamber maid.

"Certainly not!" Master Darcy said in shocked disbelief.

"No," determined the cook, "He has good meat on 'is bones. You can see as e's not starved." Observing him closely as she now did she added, "...except perhaps for today."

Many had noticed the refined manners with which Master Darcy ate, but they had also noticed how much he was eating and the cook's words seemed to give them license to laugh. Mortified that the whole of the table was having such fine sport at his expense, he coloured and became sullen.

Noticing how very ill Master Darcy brooked this offense, the inn keeper's wife took pity on him saying, "To be sure this is hardly a way to treat a guest and Will is our guest tonight as sure as if he were a paying customer."

"Aye, so he is." said one of the maids. "To your health Will." and she lead them in a toast as they started a new round of the small beer that had been served at table.

Conversation strayed to other topics but so out of place did this unlikely visitor seem that Cook would not give over trying to understand what had brought him to the inn, and she soon asked, "Do your parents know you are here?"

Master Darcy winced almost imperceptibly, but Cook saw it. "I have no mother and my father will not notice I am gone."

The chamber maid asked, "There be a lot o'you then?"

"No. There are but two of us. I have a sister."

"So way would y' be runnin' away?" she asked.

Master Darcy said, "I am *not* running away. I just need some time on my own to sort things out."

The inn keeper whose regard for Master Darcy had improved through his hard work, was sitting at the bottom of the table and he asked with a bit of a smirk, "What kind of things could one so young as you need to sort out? You are not beaten, you are not starved, you have fine clothes on your back, even if they are dirty, and you speak as you've had schooling. What more could you possibly want for?"

Master Darcy knew not how to respond for he was quite alarmed at being so easily seen through. He was not at all pleased with the direction this conversation had taken. He tried very hard to steer it into more mundane territory, but try as he might, talk kept coming round to him and to how he came to grace their table that night.

Jamie now observed, "If your sister be anything like mine you best hope *she* 'as no' missed you or she'll 'ave raised a holy racket by now jus' to see as you get a good thrashin.'"

"I need not worry there. My sister is but a babe."

"Aye. There it was." Cook's suspicions had been correct. She was a mature and perceptive woman who had borne eleven children of her own; of those, nine had grown to adulthood and now had children of their own so she was keenly aware of the workings of a child's mind. That small wince had told her Master Darcy had probably not been long without his mother and she wondered if perhaps father and son were suffering from the loss, for certainly this did not seem like a neglected child.

Everyone else at table had his or her own hard luck story to tell and Cook scanned the table trying to determine which it would do their visitor most good to hear. Her eyes alighted on one of the chamber maids. "Mary," said she, "it would seem you and our guest 'ave somethin' in common for 'tis but you and one elder brother."

"Aye, tis true; only there's just us two. We have no mama, nor no papa."

"Really?" Master Darcy heard himself ask.

"Really."

"Do you not miss them?"

"Ah nivver knowed neither one of 'em so tisn't much to miss. Me brother says our papa went into the regulars 'fore Ah was born but the neighbors said he was kilt for robbin' coaches. Me mama died when she 'ad me so Ah nivver could ask her... Sometimes Ah wonder what they were like... Anyway me brother looked after me just fine by himself so Ah nivver really thought much 'bout it."

"How did you live, just you and your brother?" Master Darcy asked. Part of him didn't want to know, but part of him needed to know for here he was shunning his sister when this girl's brother had looked after her even as a father would.

"Well first we stayed a' home by ourselves but when we couldnah pay the rent, the rector and 'is wife took us in and me brother worked to 'elp pay our keep. When me brother got married he took me to live with him and 'is wife but when she started 'aving babies of her own she said she couldnah see to me as well and me brother brought me to work here."

"How long have you been here?"

"Since Ah was six."

Master Darcy gave a start in spite of himself. "So you *never* had a mama or a papa?"

Mary shook her head emphatically. Others round the table told their stories and for the first time Master Darcy realized there could be others whose grievances were even greater than his own. He had terrible sadness yes and always would, but there were those whose daily existences were fraught with sadness; people who at times did not know where or when they would find their next meal or where they would rest their heads at night.

The conversation continued but it began to make Master Darcy's head pound. There was so much to absorb, so much to reflect on; he had also to contend with the combined effects of extreme fatigue and too long a time without sustenance followed by a large meal eaten far too quickly. As if this were not bad enough, he was also feeling the effects of too much drink. He was only vaguely aware of being in motion when he was guided to a bed in a guest room situated just above the tap-room.

Some long time later the Inn keeper's wife came into the kitchen with a report. "E still sleeps but at least this time 'e made some noises when I spoke to 'im." The Inn keeper said, "It has been hours. No matter what the boy says, his father will be frightened to death for him. I am sure of it."

Cook asked, "But how can we know where we are to take him if he does not tell us who he is?"

The inn keeper said, "I do not like this one bit. That is some gentleman's son, I am sure of it, and he will have my hide for getting his boy so addled and keeping him hidden for so long. He is right above the tap-room. How is it he has not been roused by all the noise? Something is surely amiss."

His wife replied, "He is not being hidden, he is being cared for and I am sure his father will be glad of it once he knows.

The inn keeper said, "I am not so sure as you my dear. These men of the fancy can be funny sometimes."

The inn keeper's wife had an idea. "He said he lives near Lambton."

The inn keeper replied, "If he is to be believed. If he lives *this side* o' Lambton we are done for! That is all Pemberley Wood along there. If he be the Darcy boy, his family owns half of Derbyshire and if his father takes it in his head to give us trouble for this, we will rue the day we were born… We must rouse him and send him away. He cannot be found here." The more the poor man considered the situation, the more alarmed he became.

His wife said, "We cannot just throw the boy out. First of all we do not actually know he is a Darcy, and if he is I should think we would do much better to get the boy safely home. I have heard of the Darcys' goodness and I should think his father would look kindly on someone who helped his son when help was wanted."

The inn keeper said, "I suppose you are right my dear. Calling for Jamie he charged him to, "Go upstairs and do not leave till you rouse that boy and get 'im to speak. Do what you must. Throw water on 'im. Shake the stuffing from 'im. Anything. Jus' make 'im wake and speak. Find out who he really is!" Growing steadily more alarmed, the inn keeper thought better of his plan and said, "Wait. I shall go… No. I must see to our guests; the tap-room is still full."

"*I* shall go." said his wife. With a side long glance at her husband she added, "All the better for the boy I should think."

"Never you mind." said he. "Just see you find out where that boy belongs."

"I shall see what can be done but if he is still in a bad way, I think it better for us if we let him sleep and get 'im home in the morrow when he is himself."

The Inn keeper thought a bit then he grunted, "I don't like it but 'tis probably best that way. E wouldn' reflect so well on us now, would 'e?"

Making their way into Bakewell at nearly half after five in the morning, Mr. Darcy and Mr. Wickham met few stirring. Whenever they did come upon someone, they would ask after a young boy appearing in town the prior day but they could find out nothing of the young master.

They were headed for the Inn, which surely would be open at that hour, for among their guests would be some who needed to be early on the road to take advantage of every possible hour of day light. Reaching the inn Mr. Darcy approached a man who was just done seeing some travelers off to their carriage and asked whether he was the proprietor. When the man acknowledged that he was, Mr. Darcy said, "Sir, I require your assistance." Shewing the inn keeper the miniature he had brought with him he said, "This is my son; he is called Fitzwilliam. Can you tell me if he was here yesterday?"

The inn keeper, believing he recognized the face that stared back at him swallowed hard and replied, "There were three boys in here yesterday taking ale from one of my customers. I caught the one but the other two got away. The one had no money so he worked in exchange for supper and ale. He looked very like, but I cannot say as he is one and the same sir."

"A boy taking ale from a patron then working here, you say?" Mr. Darcy's heart sank, *"Another blind alley have we entered."*

"Yes sir. Good worker he was too. Cleaned this very taproom top to bottom and stocked it right well for the night's guests."

Mr Darcy did not like to waste this time for surely this would not have been his son. He needed to get on with his search. "Thank you but I fear I have wasted your time. My son was alone so he would not have been amongst those you speak of." He did not add that his son would not have stolen ale or come looking for work.

"I am Darcy of Pemberley. If you should see or hear anything of one boy alone, looking such as this, please send word immediately." He handed the man two gold sovereigns to ensure his assistance and turned to leave. His long strides had taken him nearly to the door by the time the nervous inn keeper mustered the courage to call out, "Sir. The boy I spoke of is still here and he is called Will. He was feeling poorly and we could not get from him where he belonged. Would you not like to see him?"

Mr Darcy saw little point in such a meeting. It was hardly likely a wandering, sickly boy would be his Fitzwilliam; more like, he was some beggar newly drifted in from some other parish, but again there was logic in speaking with him. Could be he had seen or heard something of Fitzwilliam in the town. "If he is still here, then yes it would not hurt to speak with him."

"He is above. This way, if you please."

Mr Darcy and Mr. Wickham followed the inn keeper up the stairs, Mr. Darcy holding out little hope this meeting would yield any useful information but it was the most he had had to go on at any point throughout the whole of that long painful night so up he went. Morning sun was beginning to brighten the upstairs, where the remains of a lone candle burned forlornly in a sconce halfway down the hall. Passing along, all was still save for the rustle of travelers preparing to take their leave or the occasional vocalizations of deep slumber. Arriving at the front most room, the inn keeper rapped lightly, then opened the door. Immediately he did so, their olfactory senses were accosted by the foul odor of stale sweat tainted with strong drink and the stench of someone having violently heaved their stomach. Thoroughly sickened, Mr. Darcy thought, *It was foolishness to waste time coming up here. Surely this scalawag can be of no assistance in my search.* He was about to say as much and turn round to leave when the inn keeper entered the room and asked of its inhabitant, "How do you do now?"

"Not so well, I fear."

In a kindly voice the inn keeper replied, "By now you must have lost all you took in so I think you will soon be on the mend."

Mr Darcy was struck of a heap for well did he know that voice. Fear, joy, horror, relief, shame, remorse all warred in his mind as he recovered himself and burst into the room.

"Fitzwilliam." he called gently. The figure that knelt beside a bucket in the corner of the room turned its drawn, dirty face towards the door and Mr. Darcy could barely recognize his own son.

Weakly, Master Darcy said, "Father, you have come for me." The faint note of surprise in his voice smote his father as no lance ever could.

"Yes Fitzwilliam, I have come."

So softly as almost not to be heard came the response, "I had not expected it but I am glad of it."

Piteously his father asked, "Do you truly think so ill of me that you thought I would not search until I had found you?"

Whether for want of strength or from knowing not what to say, Master Darcy did not respond and his father hung his head in shame.

The inn keeper withdrew, quietly closing the door behind him before heading back downstairs. Mr. Wickham, having quickly assessed Master Darcy's condition, had long since come down and instructed the searchers to return to Pemberley with news that Master Darcy had been found safe and to have a carriage brought round to the inn.

The young master was by now a bit more comfortable, though his head pounded and he felt awfully dizzy. His father helped him to the bed where he collapsed in a heap. There was so very much Mr. Darcy needed to say, so much he wanted to know, yet there was nothing for it but to wait until an intelligent conversation could be had. Standing next the bed, Mr. Darcy observed the dishevelment of his son and studied his drawn features intently. Tracing with his eyes, the paths of some curls that sweat had plastered to his son's forehead, Mr. Darcy remembered having studied curls plastered to that self same forehead, the first time ever he saw it. Thanking Providence for Fitzwilliam's safe return to him he wondered, *"How can we have come to this?"*

By eight 'clock the inn keeper and his wife had been most heartily thanked for their kindness and a promise had been made that the inn keeper would be duly recompensed for his troubles. Mr. Darcy himself, helped his son to the waiting carriage. Pity the young master could not be more aware of the care and concern with which his father attended him. Mr. Wickham, respecting their need for solitude rode home, guiding Mr. Darcy's horse along with him.

In the coach, there was very little conversation. The young master slept and Mr. Darcy fell into sober reflection as he sat next his son, supporting him against the jostling of the ride. The sun was full up when the carriage turned in at the lodge gate and even beneath the trees it was easy to see. A few minutes later, when the road broke through the wood, offering the first view of the house, every inch of Pemberley was awash in bright day light. Mr. Darcy gazed at his still somnolent son and thought, *"How differently this night could have ended. I have truly been blessed that my folly has not cost me most dearly."*

When the carriage entered the court yard the servants knew to make themselves scarce, but most instinctively made the sign of the cross. As the young master was helped down from the carriage Mrs. Reynolds, who yet had tears in her thoroughly bloodshot eyes whispered, "Praise God for your mercy."

Again it was Mr. Darcy who helped his son up to his bed

chamber and with the aid of Mrs. Reynolds situated him comfortably in his bed. That dear lady had known the young master since he was but three years old and as she smoothed back his hair and quickly sponged his face clean she had to wipe away tears in order to see. When she had done she kissed him gently on his brow and quietly took her leave. Mr. Darcy moved a chair next the bed and there he sat dozing and telling the quarters till nearly noon when at last his son stirred.

Opening his eyes and quickly sitting up in confusion, Master Darcy held onto his head as the room swirled round him. From somewhere in the fog he heard his father's voice saying, "Lie down and be still son. You want time before you feel yourself again."

Swiftly turning toward the voice he managed a feeble smile but he had made himself so dizzy he felt he might keck.

"What has happened?" he asked.

For the first time in a very long time Mr. Darcy wanted to smile, but he durst not acknowledge amusement at his son's expense just then, so he quietly and evenly said, "That is precisely what I have been wanting to ask of you Fitzwilliam but it can wait till you are feeling better. Right now more rest and perhaps a little to eat would do you far more good than conversation." As he spoke he rang the bell.

Within minutes two maids entered carrying for Mr. Darcy, a tray of cold ham, biscuits and tea and for the young master, one of dry toast and warm milk with an egg and a small bit of brandy to it. Both ate, Mr. Darcy noting with surprise that he himself actually felt to eat. When they had done Mr. Darcy said, "It would seem you had a very trying day yesterday so I think it best if you make an effort to get some more sleep. We can speak when you are better able." Master Darcy had strength for not much more than to nod his head and he soon again was fast asleep. Calling for Fletcher to attend him, Mr. Darcy betook himself to his own bed chamber for a very much needed respite. When Fletcher was leaving he was given instruction to wake Mr. Darcy immediately the young master was alert.

Having awakened long before his son, Mr. Darcy had time whilst he waited, for a long talk with Mr. Wickham who came round to see how the young master fared. He recounted the whole story of the prior day's events as told him by the inn keeper whilst they awaited the arrival of the carriage. Mr. Darcy was beside himself. He told Wickham he was amazed at what had taken place and he wholeheartedly agreed with Mr. Wickham that Master Darcy was very lucky he had fallen in with such kind people.

They spoke a while longer then Mr. Darcy asked Mr. Wickham to go himself and make generous reparation to the inn keeper. Mr. Wickham carried out this request with dispatch and the inn keeper was more than happy with his compensation.

Father and son conversed long into the night, resolving many painful issues and each gaining a new understanding of the other and of himself. They only gave over the discussion when neither had the strength to continue. The events of that fateful day could not erase the pain or render father or son instantly able to deal with his grief, but it was a powerful first step in bringing about the healing they both so desperately needed. Perhaps *more* importantly, it made each an integral part of the other's restoration. It re-established and even strengthened the incredibly close bond they had always shared; a bond which from that day forward never wavered.

There were countless positive outcomes of that experience but one of paramount importance was that the young master no longer saw his sister as a combatant but as someone who had been injured just as he had. His father shewed him a miniature taken of his mother's likeness when she was but five years old and already they could make out so striking a resemblance to Georgiana that she became their link to Lady Anne. The young master began to see himself as Georgiana's self-appointed protector and later, once he was able to consider the events of the past three months rationally he vowed he would never again allow his sensibilities to cloud his judgment.

Chapter VII
LADY EVELYN

1781 & 1784

IN 1781, for the summer of Master Darcy's fifteenth year, Pemberley was alive with house guests. For the first time in the three years since Lady Anne Darcy had died, the sound of laughter could be heard echoing through the halls of Pemberley. Mr. Darcy's long time friend, Lord Casterley had taken a post with the East India Company and had been living abroad, with his family, for many years. Unlike most of the directors, who had their offices in London, in Leadenhall Street, Lord Casterley preferred to be in the midst of things. He believed he could get a much better understanding of things that way.

The situation in the East had, of late, been growing steadily less secure and it had now become necessary for Lord Casterly to return to England to attend a series of special meetings of Parliament, where proposed solutions were to be discussed.

On the evening after the Casterley's arrived, the two old friends sat in Mr. Darcy's library, chatting as companionably as if it had been a week rather than a decade since last they had seen each other. "Darcy, I cannot tell you how happy I was to receive your kind invitation, for I did not feel at all comfortable leaving my family behind."

" 'Kind,' you say? It was nothing of the sort? I knew a

visit from you would be immensely... well... shall we say diverting."

"Oh ho! Is that it?" Lord Casterley laughed. "Well I have a month complete to entertain you, before I must leave for London. I should be able to do myself proud in that space of time."

"Quite so. It will be just like University days. You know Casterley, I never did understand how you could spend so much time making everyone else laugh and still be the best of us all."

Swirling his cognac contentedly, Lord Casterley smiled and said, "Just lucky, I think."

Cocking a brow, Mr. Darcy replied, "I believe luck played very little part in it."

"Ah well... Those were good days my friend; very good days."

"Indeed they were." Mr. Darcy agreed. Laughing, he asked, "Do you recall how we all used to flock to the Red Lion to await Oliver's waggons and see which of us had got parcels from home."

"Well, do I recall. Every Friday. It was a high point in the week. We were sometimes upwards of a dozen of us there to receive the waggon when it arrived."

"Yes and you could never quite tell which were there expecting parcels of their own and which were simply hoping to prevail upon others to share their good fortune." The gentlemen shared a hearty laugh then Mr. Darcy said, "The best was racing to be at the Rose by seven to catch the Fly for a jaunt in London at the week end."

Laughing even harder, Lord Casterley said, "I more remember the many times we almost missed it for the return trip next morning. I am convinced the driver's watches must have run fast, for we cannot have been so tardy all that often."

"No?"

Lost in thought, Lord Casterley did not immediately reply. At last he mused, "You know, looking back, everything was so much simpler then. Sometimes I wonder if I have made the right choices in my life. I have such fond memories of my life in England, but my girls know nothing of what should be their home. Emily is now sixteen years old and Evelyn fifteen but they have lived all these years in the East." Lord Casterley stopt here, very deep in thought. Finally he looked up and said, "Darcy, all joking aside, I am truly grateful to you for giving me this opportunity to shew my girls the land of their ancestors."

"I have sometimes wondered if it was a good thing to take your girls away so young, before they could know England, but Casterley I have known you long and known you well. Almost from the start I have held you as my closest friend and never have I known you to second guess yourself. You think and rethink every decision you make, so I can only suppose these comments arise from the current turmoil in the East; but let me tell you, you have given your girls an experience most females could never even dream of. You have done what you thought best and no one can do more, or better than that."

"I can but pray you are right." Lord Casterley answered. We never know what Providence has planned for us so all we can do is make the best decisions we know how and hope they are the right ones."

"Quite true... I have often rethought the time I had with Anne and prayed I made always the best choices where she was concerned."

The Darcys and Casterleys had been great friend's before the Casterleys left for the East thus Lord Casterley felt completely confident saying, "There is not a doubt in my mind that you did so, for I never knew anyone always so completely happy as your Anne."

"It is good to hear you say so. I have always *believed* I made her happy but it is sometimes difficult to see one's own actions plainly." Now it was Mr. Darcy's turn to drift into deep reflection.

Observing the melancholy and longing in his friends face, Lord Casterley ventured, "It has been three years and you are still young. Have you given any thought to marrying again?"

Mr Darcy's voice seemed to come from somewhere far off in the distant realm where his thoughts had lately wandered. Very quietly, he said, "Marry again? No Casterley. I think not, for where should I find another such as I have known? I should daily look to the one and wish to see the other; that would not do... No. I believe I am better off as I am."

"Truly it does not much surprise me to hear you say so. I had rather thought those might be your feelings."

Their conversation lasted long into the night and covered many topics, some serious, some not, but throughout, there was complete understanding, one of the other. During the course of the next weeks the gentlemen spent hours visiting old friends and old haunts; whilst the Casterly ladies generally occupied themselves with Georgiana or in entertaining Lady Casterly's old friends and their daughters with teas in the Pemberley gardens or dinners in the drawing room. The girls had seen the visit to England simply as a wonderful opportunity for adventure. So far, they had been disappointed for they had seen nothing of adventure save for the journey itself.

It had been about a month since the Casterlys' arrival and now it was time Lord Casterly strike out for London. Mr. Darcy and he had left at first light for the Darcy's London townhouse. Lady Casterly was just now setting out for a day of visiting in Lambton, and the girls, accompanied by Master Darcy and George Wickham had come out to see her off. Taking in all that was going forward, Master Darcy thought, *"George has completely captivated the Casterley ladies for they spend whole days together in his company. They talk and laugh as if they have always known him."* Given George's easy manners, this was nothing extraordinary at all, so Master Darcy was not quite sure why it seemed to bother him; such had never bothered him before. In fact, he was not quite sure why it even garnered his attention, but bother him, it did; immensely.

Master Darcy was noticing *particularly,* everything Lady Evelyn did. When she was anywhere about, it seemed he could feel her presence before he saw her. It was becoming quite bothersome for him. He could not think when she was near. For that matter, he could barely think when alone. Every subject he tried to concentrate on seemed to find its way round to Lady Evelyn, yet she remained totally unaware of his presence – or so he thought. This did not surprise him either, for he knew he lacked George's gift of easy conversation. It was not within his power to engage in idle chatter; he simply would not speak if he had nothing of value to say.

As he watched Lady Evelyn say goodbye to her Mama, he admired the grace of her figure. Her long auburn hair flowed down her back in ringlets gathered up in satin ribbons and as it glistened in the summer sun, his breath caught-up in his throat. *"How very beautiful."* he breathed. *"She is grace itself.*"

The carriage made its way down the drive and as it passed out of sight Emily turned to say something to her sister and walked off with George. Lady Evelyn then turned, and to Master Darcy's utter astonishment, walked the twenty feet or so directly to where he stood. As she drew nearer he became aware that he had been watching her far more intently than was proper so he quickly diverted his gaze to the house and asked awkwardly, "Is there anything I can get you to occupy your time in your mother's absence?"

"I rather hoped you might have some time to ride out with me and shew me the Pemberley lands."

"Well, yes," he said, though more than a little flustered by the request. "I suppose I can, but when my father returns, I think he would be a much better person to do justice to a tour of Pemberley." As he spoke, words poured over words. "Perhaps our families can go all together and make a day of it."

"That sounds lovely," she replied, "but I think I should much prefer to see it today... with you alone... if that is agreeable."

Though taken aback, Master Darcy replied, "Of course. That can be arranged. I shall call for the horses to be brought round to the courtyard. When should you like to strike out?"

She replied confidently, "I can be ready in an half hour." Master Darcy had expected more time to prepare his mind for the prospect of a ride out alone with a lady, especially *this* lady, but it appeared he would not have that luxury. "An half hour it is then. I shall meet you in the courtyard beside the stable block."

"I shall be there." she said with a smile and taking her

leave, she seemed to float up the stairs and into the house. Some time past before Master Darcy could recall his senses, but when he did he moved up the stairs with dispatch for he had lost precious minutes of his sparse half hour.

When Master Darcy entered the courtyard he found, to his great relief, that he was the first to arrive. On seeing him, a pair of groomsmen led out his spirited horse and the gentle, bay mare he had ordered for Lady Evelyn. "Master Darcy, sir." the two said in unison.

"Thank you Giles; Matthews." he replied, nodding to each. One of the many lessons he had learnt from his father was that true respect must be *earned* and if one wanted to earn respect, he must first give it. Knowing the proper names of each of Pemberley's servants and addressing them by such was one way of shewing that respect, but it was something Master Darcy was naturally inclined to do regardless.

Rubbing his horse's nose affectionately Master Darcy tried to collect his thoughts but he had little time to do so before he espied Lady Evelyn striding down the path to the courtyard, dressed in full riding attire. She did not approach from the house, but rather from the direction of the lake. This surprised Master Darcy, but only a little for in the short time the Casterlys' had been at Pemberley he had come to realize that Lady Evelyn could always be expected to do the unexpected. "There you are." she called when she saw him.

Walking toward her, he thought, *"How in the world can she have readied herself fast enough to even have time for a stroll by the lake?"* Once again she had befuddled him and that very much intrigued him. In an effort to relieve his restless mind, he joked, "I see you are anxious for your excursion to begin."

"I am." she answered with conviction, "I hope you have given me an agile horse for I dearly love to ride and I am always ready for an *adventure*." Giles and Matthews had followed behind with the horses and as Matthews now moved forward to offer the lady a leg up into her saddle, Master Darcy was left to wonder, *'Exactly what sort of adventure is she expecting to find during a ride upon Pemberley's lands?'*

It was about a quarter past ten when they walked their horses out of the courtyard. They rode round the lake and up the hill on its far side. From there they past through a copse of flowering shrubs and struck out for the northern reaches of the estate.

"Master Darcy," Lady Evelyn said as they made their way along a tree lined walk, "What is your earliest memory of your home?"

Surprised by the topic, but pleased that Lady Evelyn would chuse to ask about his favorite subject, Master Darcy thought a moment and replied, "I would have to say it was the first time my father and mother ever took me for a ride out. I am told I was but three years old and I do not think anyone has ever truly believed that I remember, but I do. Certainly, I have forgot much about it, but I remember the ride and I distinctly remember father stopping often along the way to acknowledge people." He laughed, "I especially remember one shepherd and his dog. The dog shook himself and ruffled his hair till he looked twice his size."

"What a vivid memory." Lady Evelyn breathed.

Master Darcy then returned, "What is your earliest memory of home?"

"Oh," she laughed, "it is nothing quite so serious as your memory, nor was I nearly so young. There is a wall that surrounds our home. Just beyond, is a gentle waterfall that creates a shallow pond. The native children swim there and run about under the falling water; you can hear them playing and laughing from the edge of our garden. We were not allowed to go there but behind our shrubbery, Em and I found a small breach in the wall. Sometimes, we would crawl through and join the fun.

That is where I first learnt to swim; we felt so free and so alive when the cool water hit our bare bodies." After a dreamy pause she continued, "It is only for small children but I often wish I had a place like that still. Master Darcy was at a loss for how to respond, so he said nothing. Some minutes later, the path brought them to a clear mountain stream and they stopt to water their horses. Whilst they waited, Lady Evelyn asked, "Does this stream lead to a pond?"

"I think not." Master Darcy replied, a bit more firmly than he intended.

"Pity." Lady Evelyn murmured, but Master Darcy chose not to acknowledge her reply. Soon the path lead into a forest situated on rising ground. Here the path narrowed, requiring the pair to ride singly and Master Darcy took the lead. Conversation became difficult, but he suddenly felt very much more alive to Lady Evelyn's presence, now that she rode, unseen, behind him; and did he imagine? or could he actually distinguish among the various fragrances of damp earth, dewy mosses and forest greens, the subtle sweetness of the lavender water he knew her to be wearing?

When at last the ground began to level off, the tree cover grew a bit thinner. Master Darcy and Lady Evelyn made their way to the edge of the forest. There the path widened and the fulgent sun shewn through a sparse awning of branches. Before them was a large clearing that sloped gently down to reveal a distant vista of immense proportion and beauty. Lady Evelyn brought her horse to a stop and lifting her face to the sun's warmth, she breathed in deeply. She then sighed gently and gave Master Darcy a sidelong glance that disconcerted him as much as it thrilled him. "It just takes your breath away." she said. Master Darcy thought surely she referred to the view, but something told him caution was required.

"Master Darcy, may we rest here a bit? We have ridden quite far."

"Why yes. Yes… of course…" he stammered. "I… I am sorry. I did not realize you were tiring."

"Not to worry. I just thought it might be nice to enjoy the prospect from here for a while."

"You have chosen to stop in a spot that has always been a favorite of mine." Not quite sure why he had shared this intimate knowledge, Master Darcy plunged on nervously. "Since I was first able to ride out on my own, this has been a place to which I come when I need to sort things out. It is both calming and invigorating at the same time…" and he thought *"much as are you,"*.

Smiling demurely Lady Evelyn asked, "Would you help me down?" Not at all prepared for a request to dismount, Master Darcy was a bit flustered. *"What for, I wonder? You do not appear to be tired."* Still, he could hardly deny the lady the chance to rest, if rest she needed. In the one fluid motion that had already become characteristic of him, Master Darcy swung his long leg over his horse and was to the ground. Quickly tying up his horse, he walked with manly grace over to Lady Evelyn's horse as she looked out upon the vista that lay before them. He knew that to help her down he would have to hold her about the waist and he felt a mingled sense of being mightily unsettled yet quite pleased at the prospect.

Upon reaching her side, he looked through her, rather than at her.

"Lady Evelyn." he said gallantly with a slight nod, but he was not sure whether he should await some signal from her or just lift her down and be done with it. Thankfully, she relieved his distress by leaning forward and placing her hands on his shoulders. She seemed to weigh nothing as he easily lifted her from the saddle. As she alighted, her skirts brushed ever so gently against him. It was hardly more than the brush of a feather, but it was enough to send his senses reeling. She smiled and leaving him to tend to her horse she walked to the edge of the clearing where she chose to seat herself beneath a tall, wide elm.

Tapping the spot beside her she called, "Come join me."

Again he was torn between disquiet and desire, but his feet seemed to decide the issue for him, for they were in motion even as his mind deliberated. As he walked, questions flooded his brain, *"What shall I say?... What ought I to do?... She does not appear to be tired... I thought she did not like me... How can it be that she seeks my company?"* He even wondered if he might be the subject of one of Wickham's cruel jokes, for he could not fathom what might possibly draw her to him. It could not be his personality for though he knew himself to have impeccable manners, he knew too that he very much lacked finesse. Neither did it mean anything to him that he had already gained much of his eventual height of over six feet, or that his constant riding, swimming and fencing had gifted him with a sinewy frame. Modest as he was, he had never taken the slightest interest in considering his own aspect, so he truly was unaware of how very fine of person he was.

He placed himself about three feet from her, but this

would not do. Beckoning him closer, she assured him mischievously, "I am not likely to grow long teeth and bite, you know." Master Darcy felt himself colour, but said nothing and did as he was bid.

Once again taking in the beauty of their surroundings Lady Evelyn breathed, "I can easily see why you are drawn to this spot. Never have I seen any place so beautiful."

"Oh, a hit to the heart, direct." Master Darcy thought, *"She could not have found any more perfect compliment than praise of Pemberley – especially this most extraordinary part of Pemberley."*

He hadn't much time to revel in accolades of his beloved home for it seemed the joust was on in earnest and it now took a decidedly different turn. "Why," Lady Evelyn asked pointedly, "have you never brought me here before?"

"Pardon?" he countered in great surprise.

"I asked why you have never brought me here before?"

"Forgive me but I do not take your meaning."

"Well," she began in a soft but steady voice, "it is that we have lost so much time."

"Lost so much time?" Master Darcy queried. He had no idea where this conversation was leading and he was become most uneasy.

"Why yes. I am in England not a full month longer and it would have been lovely to come here sooner and often."

"It never occurred to me that you might like to come."

"Pity, that." She sighed and leaned gently against his shoulder. His mind raced in an effort to comprehend just what was happening; it would seem his arm too was capable of independent movement for without consulting his reason it wrapped itself gently round her. *"Take care what you are about."* his conscience warned him for he was not quite sure how much longer he could maintain his composure. Just then Lady Evelyn drew his attention to a pair of hawks circling overhead. "They are dancing in the sky," she said "and they seem quite happy together."

He agreed that indeed they did and she giggled. When he looked to see why she giggled, her eyes drew him in and he was struck anew by her great beauty. So intent was he on studying this vision before him that he did not immediately realize that he was beginning to lower his face to hers. By the time he did realize, he was so close there was nothing for it but to kiss her. It lasted but a second and she did not resist. In fact, it would seem she invited it. He realized it did not seem nearly so awkward as he had imagined his first kiss would be. Rather it seemed natural and pleasing; most pleasing and so he kissed her again. These were beautiful, chaste kisses, but they transported him to raptures. Alas, his euphoria was soon dashed to bits by the rude intrusion of reason. *"What must she think of me? She will be roundly insulted. What would her father say?"* But oh, how little he knew her mind at that moment.

During the remainder of the Casterleys visit, Master Darcy and Lady Evelyn each seemed often to find their way to where ever the other happened to be. They read together in the library; they wandered and talked together among the flora of the conservatory; they took long walks in the park; and of course they often rode out to distant parts of the estate. Not surprisingly, that summer Master Darcy very much perfected the skill he had first practiced that glorious midsummer afternoon.

In the autumn of 1784 the young master would reach a significant milestone, when for the first time, he would go up to university. For the summer preceding this monumental event, Mr. Darcy invited his friends the Casterleys for another visit. This time there was no awkwardness between the young master and Lady Evelyn. Their shared experiences of the past gave them topics of conversation to which he could easily contribute. Happily, this put him at considerable ease and rendered him really very good company. They got on well from the start, often riding out together, laughing; sharing stories; exploring areas of Pemberley which Darcy wished to share with Lady Evelyn. His feelings for her had remained strong and he began to feel alive in a way he had not in her absence.

This particular morning, as they were setting their course for a day's ride, Lady Evelyn said, "You know, you have shewn me many beautiful parts of Pemberley since my return, but there is one place we have not been; a place I would very much like to return to."

With blissful anticipation he asked, "And where might that be?" He was sure he knew; at least he hoped he knew, but he thought it best to make sure.

"I want," she said simply, "to return to our spot."

It pleased him that she still remembered and thought of it as *their spot*, for that is how he had come to think of it, and he was not fully able to hide the pleasure from his voice when he said, "Then that is where we shall go."

"Do you know," said she, "I have been charting your lands in my mind these past weeks and I believe now that I might find my own way there."

"Shall you lead then?"

With a small laugh she said, "I believe I shall." and she urged her mare to quicken her pace. With only a small amount of assistance from Master Darcy she brought them to the crest of that fondly remembered hill and stayed her mare before a most breathtaking view. "It is even more beautiful than I remember." she breathed. "I have thought of this place quite often lately for it brings back memories of a happy time."

Master Darcy responded, "If it is possible, I come here even more now than ever I did before."

She smiled in acknowledgement and asked, "Will you help me down?" This time, he felt no awkwardness at the request. In fact, he was happy she had made it. As he lifted her from the saddle, she drew herself toward him and slid fluidly down the entire length of his tall frame. Taken completely by surprise, the moment her feet touched ground he quickly released his grip and would have stepped back, had she not just as quickly locked her arms round his waist. As she did so, she lifted her head, looked him full in the face and maintained an intense gaze which demanded he return it.

Aside from their few chaste kisses when first Lady Evelyn had visited Pemberley, Master Darcy was wholly inexperienced in matters of amour; however he was not altogether unschooled, for George Wickham had on a number of occasions, secured copies of *Ranger*, the gentlemen's magazine. Ever seeking ways to prove his importance, Wickham was always quick to triumphantly offer his prizes for examination by Master Darcy and Darcy's cousin Reynold Fitzwilliam. What *Ranger* lacked in tastefulness, it boasted in thoroughness, for what it did not shew in graphic sketches, it described with precision; hence it proved most illuminating for a young man.

Somewhere deep in the recesses of his mind, Master

Darcy knew he should not, could not, *must* not, let whatever was happening continue. Lady Evelyn was someone
who had wholly earned his approbation and she was also
the daughter of one of his father's oldest friends, but those
thoughts were being seriously compromised by her skillful
and persistent ministrations and by his newly discovered
passion. When she slid her hands up the cleft in the center
of his impressively muscular back and pressed even closer
against him, he felt other, new sensations as well. After
what seemed ages, Master Darcy finally managed to return
Lady Evelyn's gaze and he knew his face colored for he felt
it do so.

Propriety is a driving force of a true gentleman and Master Darcy was nothing, if not a gentleman. This situation
clearly was not proper, thus every thought in his mind told
him it must stop... now. Yet every nerve in his body told
him to proceed, so when Lady Evelyn closed her eyes and
stood on her toes, inviting him to kiss her, he acted instinctively and lowered his head till their lips met; but this was
not the same as the chaste kisses they had shared three years
gone. No. How could it be? He had now admired her,
longed for her, these three years and his desire found its way
into his kiss.

No one had garnered his interest since Lady Evelyn. For
that matter, no one had ever done so before her. This just
seemed as it ought to be... and yet... Drawing back abruptly
he choked, "Lady Evelyn." Then clearing his throat, he continued, "This is not right. We must not... We cannot... We
must return to the house at once."

She said nothing but maintained her grip and stared intently up into his eyes and he found he could say no more.
That ardent kiss was followed by another and another; their

intensity and technique increasing dramatically. Her experienced hands were coaxing him out of his unease. His hands were beginning to find useful employ as well. Soon the pair found a comfortable spot in a bed of wild grasses and nature being a dynamic and powerful force, it was inevitable where things would lead. The gentle soughs that escaped her throat at first disconcerted him, but once she gave him to understand they arose from pleasure rather than pain, they encouraged him, till the pair reached a crescendo, the magnitude of which shocked his unlearned senses.

It took some time for conscious thought to return, but when it did, he began at once to have serious misgivings. *"I have forgot myself, completely!"* he thought in horror. Accustomed *always* to being guided by his conscience, he found his present circumstance utterly intolerable and he began quickly to apologize, "Lady Evelyn, I am sorry. I should not have allowed myself..."

But there are some things one cannot fight and this appeared to be one of them, for she quickly silenced his apology with a kiss so deep it barred the escape of sound. When finally they stopt to seek air she looked into his languid face and whispered, "At first I had thought this might be your first time, but now I believe I must have been wrong."

Thoroughly undone by the nature and boldness of this observation, but none the less proud of its implication, he did not correct her impression in any way other than that his cheeks once again colored. He realized he would need to school his sensibilities, but that was a thought for another time.

It was very late in the afternoon by the time the pair made their way into the Pemberley courtyard. Darcy knew they had missed dinner and hoped their absence had not aroused too much attention or concern. He was most thankful when Giles appeared to hand Lady Evelyn down from her horse, for, the whole of the ride home, he could think of nothing save what had happened when *he* had helped her from her horse. So disordered were his thoughts that for the whole of the ride back, he had scarce been able to put two words together. They entered the house through the conservatory and parted quickly, but not before Lady Evelyn bestowed a quick salute on his cheek and said, "I believe now we know each other well enough that you might dispense with calling me Lady." He knew not how he could look anyone in the eye at that moment and prayed he would meet with no one on his way to his chambers.

Thankfully he past unseen through the halls; entering his bed chamber, he threw himself facedown across the bed in misery. *"How, how, how..."* he thought, *"can I have allowed this to happen? Oh dear God, what have I done? I love her, yet I have allowed myself to ruin her. I must marry her. But how can I? I have yet to go up to university. As I am now, what sort of husband would I make for a lady of quality? Oh, but what is to become of her if I do not marry her? She can no longer have any hope of a good marriage elsewhere and I am to blame."*

He knew it to be a gentleman's bounden duty to protect a lady's honour; to conduct himself in a gentleman-like manner. For hours, his conscience tormented him mercilessly. When supper was announced he had no interest in food and remained in his chambers. After a time, the house grew still; some long time later, Darcy heard the clock at the head of the stairs chime yet again. This time it struck but once. By now too emotionally exhausted to think, he just lay there in a fog and told the quarters till three, when at last fatigue brought on a fitful and abbreviated sleep.

The following morning Darcy arose even earlier than usual, and went down to break his fast, hoping he would be alone. His mind was mightily unsettled for he still had not come to terms with his actions of the previous day; nor had he determined what he must now do. If ever he needed to ride out and think, this was the time. So early was he that breakfast was just beginning to be laid out when he entered the dining room, but that was hardly of concern to him. He would not have eaten at all had he not felt weak from want of nourishment. He gently dismissed the servants' apologies, grabbing two coddled eggs, some dry toast and a cup of coffee, all of which he scoffed down without tasting any of it. Then he was off to the stables to fetch his horse.

As he rode out of the courtyard, he thought, "Where to go?" Now that his favored destination had a new significance, he certainly could not go there. He decided to strike out for the outlying hay fields. There would be no one about at this time of year, and he could sit in a deserted hay loft, undisturbed for hours, whilst he determined how to resolve this terrible predicament. As he rode, the scent of damp earth registered in his senses. The sun was breaking over the horizon and the initial swirls of morning mist forsook the cold earth as they began to rise from the ground. As he rode up to the first hay loft he came upon he thought, *"This shall do just fine."* He tethered his horse and entered the ancient edifice; whose door he knew would though closed, never be locked. He began pacing about, but soon decided he could much better think if he climbed to the loft, from whence he could look out over the lands of Pemberley.

He had been there in solemn contemplation upwards of

an hour, when a second horse came up beside his own. Its rider dismounted and tethered the reins then scratched both horses on their forelocks, earning appreciative whinnies, before quietly entering the building. As it was now bright outside it took a moment to grow accustomed to the dim light. Once oriented, it became clear the original occupant must be above for there was nothing and no one to be found below. The ladder that led to the loft was mounted with a tread as soft as a cat's. Darcy had been so intent on self recrimination that he had not been aware anyone approached; he gave a start when he heard, quite near him, the whisper of a familiar voice, "You need not hide and brood for you have done nothing wrong."

Darcy swung round to espy Lady Evelyn, examining him intently; still perched a'top the ladder, he could see only her face. "I am not hiding and I most certainly am not brooding! I am merely trying to sort things out in my mind." He was astonished that he could have the insolence to be angry with her after what he had done, but for her to insinuate that he would have the cowardice to run and hide was more than his manly pride could brook. "Have you sought me out simply to compound the great burden which my conscience has already to bare?"

"No, I have come to ease your struggle."

"Then," he thought, *"your skill is quite limited."* He could not believe he was again thinking such mean thoughts. *"How is it she can so completely disorder my mind, even when I feel such contrition on her behalf?"*

"I have come to tell you of things you do not know; things that change everything. May I join you?" she asked.

Darcy nodded his consent, though he felt it not at all a wise decision, and with his help, she completed her ascent into the loft. She seated herself on the floor squarely in front of him, but a reasonable distance away. "First of all," she began, "it is I who should have apologized yesterday, not you. Perhaps I was a bit too bold, but I have learnt to go after what I want."

"I cannot believe what I am hearing?" Darcy thought. *"Was I a prize to be won?"* Again his feathers had been ruffled; nevertheless, clearly the fault had been his and he was about to say so when Lady Evelyn held up her hand to silence him. "Please let me finish. If you fear that you have ruined me, be not alarmed, for you have not. You see, I have been married."

"Oh dear God!" Darcy blanched, *"I have lain with another man's wife. My sin multiplies daily."*

"I am a widow." she continued and he sighed a great, deep sigh.

"But Lady Evelyn, how is it we have never heard of this? Our fathers are the closest of friends."

"Well might you ask, but the fact is, Papa has only lately heard of it."

"Beg pardon?"

"You see, we eloped."

"You what?"

"It is true. Edward, my husband, was an officer in a regiment tasked with protecting the interests of the Honourable East India Company. Papa did not think an army officer worthy of his daughter but we thought otherwise and we married secretly. We had hoped that Papa would change his mind once Edward had earned distinction, as he was determined he would. In the mean while, I continued to live at home. Almost immediately we married, there were reports of problems on one of the tea plantations and Edward's regiment was sent to quell the disturbance. He and some of his men died there of Cholera; we had been married but three months."

Darcy was struck of a heap; so far was this from anything he could ever have imagined.

"We were perfect together, Edward and I, but as soon as we began, it was over, so you see, sometimes life teaches you to go after what you want for you may not have a to-morrow."

"I am truly sorry for you," Darcy said with genuine concern. "for well do I know what it is to lose someone you dearly love. When did this happen?"

"We married not a twelvemonth past; I was still seventeen and my Edward was five and twenty. He died right after my eighteenth birthday."

Darcy said, "I wish I could tell you it gets better, but not a day goes by that I do not see something to remind me of my mother or cause me to hear her voice. Sometimes I wonder if it shall always be that way."

"You will never forget. There is no reason why you should, but in time your pain will grow less... At least, so I am told."

"Yes. I have heard the same and can only hope 'tis true, but it is difficult to believe."

"Poor Papa. He was mortified when he learnt of it. *I* am the reason he applied to your father for another invitation. All he could think was to remove me from there. I believe he was far too ashamed to tell anyone of 'my indiscretion,' as he called it; particularly not so close and respected a friend as your father."

"Yes, I can see how he might feel that way."

"Besides, he thought it would materially hurt my chances

of marrying again if suitors knew of my head strong nature. That is Papa's thinking, not mine. I haven't the heart to tell him, but it truly does not signify what other suitors would think for I cannot brook the thought of marrying again. I would not marry where I did not love and I cannot allow myself to love again for I am too afraid of suffering such awful pain a second time. Thankfully, Edward's father had left him well enough settled that I am now spared the necessity of having to marry."

Darcy's warring emotions felt a great sense of loss and he said, "I can certainly understand your feelings, but I hope one day they will change."

She looked at him intently and said, "I have told you my story not to gain your sympathy, but rather to ease your conscience. I sincerely hope I have done so."

"Indeed you have," he whispered. It was true. She *had* eased his conscience; very much indeed, but she had misread his thoughts for it was not sympathy he felt. His thoughts were rather more self-serving just then, for he truly did feel deeply for her. Though it would have been disastrous to take her to wife at that particular time in his life, the thought would have been most palatable once his gentleman's education was complete. True, Darcy did feel tremendous relief to know himself innocent of so fowl a deed as he had believed, but his relief was tempered by great sadness and he said so.

Had he been an experienced lover, he would have realized from the start that he had good cause to doubt himself culpable of so heinous a transgression as he had feared. Alas he was not experienced. Had he that small but valuable bit of understanding, many hours of painful self-recrimination could he have been spared; but then, a tremendous life's lesson would he have lost.

Finally at ease and really looking at Lady Evelyn for the first time since her surprise appearance he cocked a brow and thought aloud, "How is it you knew where to find me?"

She smiled that unnerving smile and said, "A servant girl said she had seen you leave, very early, in your riding clothes. I figured you would not have returned to our spot so I did what the men do at home when they are hunting wild tigers."

"So you liken me to a wild tiger now, do you?" he thought, but he was not quite sure whether he was offended or pleased.

"I looked for fresh tracks on the ground; the earth is soft after last night's rain so it was rather an easy task." She moved closer as she spoke and her eyes mesmerized him.

He wondered, *"Will you ever stop amazing me?"* They shared a very intimate look and as penance had been duly served, perhaps even for undue cause, there was nothing for it but to prove there were no hurt feelings. Their experience the day before had included touch, sound and scent. Today sight was introduced as well; introduced and mutually gratified. After a time, the two lay in spent exhaustion, in a languid heap, atop a soft pile of linens, silks and doe skins.

"Do you really like living in England?" Lady Evelyn queried as she gently traced the lines of Darcy's face with her finger.

He replied instantly, "I could not imagine living anywhere else. I know I will visit the continent, but I know too that I shall return. America seems to me yet a wild, lawless place, so I do not believe I could be happy there either. No, I shall always live in England; and always, I should expect at Pemberley for I am not even much for London."

"Sad." Lady Evelyn murmured softly.

"Pardon?" Darcy said as he strained to catch her words.

"Oh, no matter." After a short pause, she said, "Things here are very different from life in the East. Life moves much slower there and people are much freer. One does not have to be so proper and reserved all the time."

Darcy was not sure what was so bad about having to conduct oneself in a proper manner but he did not challenge her statement.

"How," she continued, "can you be so sure you would not like living somewhere else, if you have never been there?"

"I suppose I cannot be absolutely sure, but I do not believe I would be happy if I were to leave my home."

Lady Evelyn replied, "My papa lives half way round the world from his home. He has people to let his estate and others to work the fields whilst he is away."

Darcy knew there were some who chose to live away from their ancestral homes but he had never been able to understand how anyone could do such and so he explained, "These have been Darcy lands since time immemorial; a Darcy built Pemberley; Darcys' have lived at Pemberley, cared for Pemberley, loved and respected Pemberley for centuries; in fact since Norman times. This is our home. It is the place from which a Darcy draws his strength; it is the place from which *I* draw *my* strength. Pemberley is a part of who I am, as much as are my features or the hue of my eyes. Besides, I *am* Pemberley. One day I will be master of Pemberley, and that is a responsibility I could not possibly take more seriously than I do." Darcy thought he heard Lady Evelyn whisper, "Pity that." but he was not sure and he did not ask.

They rode back together in much better spirits than they

had come and this time Darcy was able to enter through the main door and without regret, still, over the next few months, he past many hours of painful self recrimination. No matter the provocation, no matter how genuine and heartfelt were his feelings for Lady Evelyn, knowing he had been capable of so far forgetting himself, left him with a profound sense of guilt and fear that he could so transgress again. For someone to whom propriety was the central cog, this condition was unacceptable. It was only through the kindness of Providence that he had not been guilty of bringing about a lady's ruin; a very special lady at that. He realized with humble gratitude that Providence had granted him a monumental reprieve and he was determined, in future, to be worthy of that great favour. He was resolute that from that day forward, there would be no situation in which propriety would not be master of his decisions; no situation in which he would not maintain absolute control of his actions; no situation whatsoever.

The Casterleys stayed on through the summer. Darcy and Lady Evelyn were often in each other's company but so totally discrete were they, in the company of others, that no one ever suspected the depth of feeling they shared or the nature of their association. Alas summer came to an end and Lady Evelyn returned to the East, to the life she knew; the life she felt comfortable with. Darcy was about to begin a new phase of his life for in October he would be going up to university. For this he felt great excitement but he felt a very great sense of loss at Lady Evelyn's departure. He would have to be content with his many exceedingly fond, private memories.

Chapter VIII

GENTLEMEN AND SCHOLARS

1784-1788

D ARCY watched from the head of the Pemberley front stairs as one of the family coaches made its way up the drive. Excitement and a small measure of apprehension attended him as he thought, *"I am about to begin the first real adventure of my life."* It was early in the month of October, 1784 and within minutes he and George Wickham would be traveling to Cambridge for the Michaelmas term. This was not new to George as he would be starting his second year, but for Darcy, it would be his first time going up to university.

Mr Darcy said with a broad grin, "Well son, by the time you lay down your head tonight you will be a Cambridge man and you will have begun one of the most important and exhilarating experiences of your life." Then he addressed them both, "Look after each other."

Neither young man wished to be saddled with the responsibility of looking after the other but as the trio descended the stairs Darcy and George both allowed that indeed they would comply. There was a little more conversation, and then it was time to leave. Their trunks and furnishings had preceded them by a day so they had naught to carry but themselves. Mr. Darcy told them he expected nothing but the finest reports of them both and wished them good luck and God's speed.

A few hours later their coach had entered the town of Cambridge and come to a stop in Trumpington Street. Before them, the Great Gate of Trinity College stood beckoning them into a different world. The term would not officially begin until the 10th so the young gentlemen from Derbyshire could look forward to a few days leisure before facing the rigors of the year.

Early next morning, when the bells of St. Mary's rang loud enough to raise the dead, Darcy awoke with a start. Wickham had not warned him of this Cambridge tradition; for that matter, neither had Rennie. In the latter case, at least, he suspected good natured mischief. Much would he have liked to cuff his cousin just then but that would have to wait, for Rennie was not due to arrive for another fortnight. He, who like Wickham, would be starting his junior soph year, saw no need to rush back after the long vacation.

What with the shock of the bell, the severe chill in the room and being too excited to sleep any longer, Darcy arose quickly. By eight he had readied himself for the day, read a few chapters, broken his fast and was then out for a tour of the town. He found Deighton's Book Store, the White Bear Inn, a coffee house, the market, the various schools, the Senate House, and across from this last he found the source of the morning bells. At Trinity, Darcy had been entered on Lynam's side, so this learned Fellow was to be Darcy's tutor. At half after nine Darcy went round to present himself at Lynam's rooms. The weather being unusually cold for that time of year, he was grateful for the hot cup of coffee offered him whilst they discussed a plan for his studies and decided which books he was to begin reading.

Over the course of the next few days Darcy and some of

the other young men began to make friends. This would have been most difficult for Darcy, had there not been amongst the group some far more outgoing than he. After a couple weeks, Rennie arrived to find, very much to his surprise, his younger cousin already well installed as a university man.

One Saturday evening in November, Rennie and Darcy were heading over to the White Bear and as they passed down the hall they saw light under the door of one of Darcy's new friends.

"'Tis funny, that." Darcy observed. "When I asked if he should like to join us this evening he declined owing to his having somewhere else to go."

"Really? Then let us see what you can already have done to cause him to throw you over."

With Rennie heading for the door Darcy grabbed at the sleeve of his gown and said, "Rennie do not. Leave him alone."

Shaking Darcy off, Rennie said, "I will not!" and rapping soundly upon the door he added mirthfully, "Darcy, you have been here but a month. If you are already guilty of an offense that has caused someone to throw you over as a friend, I want to know what that offense can have been."

On opening his door the young man stammered, "Darcy! I thought you would have gone before now."

Darcy, feeling most uncomfortable said quietly, "No, I am only just now leaving."

Rennie said in a stern voice, "I must know what my cousin has done to offend you."

"Pardon?" came the reply. "I do not take your meaning."

The young man was completely perplexed and Darcy equally mortified. "This is my cousin, Reynold Fitzwilliam."

At this, Rennie bowed comically and said, "Pleased to make your acquaintance, sir."

Darcy, lifting up his eyes, continued, "Rennie, this is my friend Edmund Bingley."

Edmund nodded and said, "Pleased to know you as well."

In a most impish voice, Rennie addressed his cousin, "Your friend? As he has chosen not to venture abroad with you this evening, it would appear you have been set aside as friend… most probably for want of manners or something such."

Edmund was beginning to come out of the fog, though he was still not quite sure whether he or Darcy was the intended victim of Rennie's mischief. Inviting them in, he addressed Rennie thusly, "I am afraid you have quite mistook the situation. I would very much have enjoyed an evening abroad. It is just that… Well… Now that I am caught out, I might as well own up to it. You see I have stayed behind simply to…"

Rennie, who had caught sight of the desk spread every inch with books, papers, quills and ink, completed the sentence for him, "… to study."

"Well yes… that is it, precisely."

"At this hour on a fine Saturday night?" Rennie asked in horror.

"At nearly any hour on any given night, I am afraid."

"Good heavens, Darcy. I would not have thought it possible that there should be anyone who loves books more than you."

Bingley laughed, "Believe me, I am not so great a lover of books. I have no choice. My father's hopes and dreams all depend upon my success here and this is what I must do to keep up."

Darcy asked if they might help him. This offer was politely refused but Bingley's voice did not seem to agree with his words so Rennie, who was by now standing over the desk said thoughtfully, "Newton might be just the thing for a Saturday night; something quite new. Have you a good bottle of wine? If so, I think we can make a pleasant evening of it right here. That is, if you do not object."

Surprised but most grateful once he knew the offer to be genuine, Bingley acquiesced and by the end of the night the cousins had fully illuminated the theories that had so vexed him. He proved to be amiable, willing and quite able to learn. His difficulty lay in the fact that, growing up, he had not the benefits of a first class education, thus he had come up to university ill prepared for the challenge that lay ahead.

During the course of their discussions it was learned that Bingley had come from an old and respectable family in the north of England; that he had three siblings, an elder sister Louisa, another just after him called Caroline and the youngest, a brother Charles. Their mother had died many years since and when she had, their father had felt *that* much more, the responsibility for the welfare of his children. He had responded by pouring himself even deeper into his business than before and had eventually become quite wealthy. The sisters were currently attending an excellent school for girls in London and his brother was at home where he had a tutor. The family's wealth having come during their lifetime, the style of living they now knew was much different from what it had been.

"My father," said he, "constantly reminds us of where we started and how far we have come, lest we become complacent and cease to appreciate what we now have, but I *do* appreciate, very much indeed, and I want nothing more than to earn my father's approbation by continuing and even bettering his legacy."

By the end of the night Darcy had gained great respect for his new friend and during the whole of their time at Cambridge they were often to be found going over whatever they were currently assigned to read. People might tend to look down upon those whose money had come from trade, but Darcy saw nothing in this young man to make him seem any less worthy than had he been born a gentleman.

Darcy, still as eager to learn as when a boy, had fallen easily into the rhythm of university life, attending Chapel each morning at seven thence taking a constitutional walk at seven-thirty; attending lectures from eight till ten at which hour he would return to his rooms to study. Two was the accustomed hour for relaxation and making calls on friends, of whom it is no great wonder Darcy made few, though the ones he did make were to remain his friends for life. At three he would dine, often with friends; supper too was usually taken with friends then after evening Chapel at five he would generally read till it was time to go to sleep. In this measured way did Darcy pass his freshman year – or might he have, had there not been cousin Rennie about to remind him there was life beyond study. There were indeed many diversions to be found if one only looked for them and Rennie knew how and where to look. There was shooting on the fens, fishing in the rivers, smoking one's pipe on the banks of the river after an exhilarating boat ride. The list of divertissements was virtually inexhaustible.

Collecting Darcy, early one evening toward the middle of term, Rennie set off in a direction different from that in which they usually seemed to head. He was taking Darcy to meet an acquaintance of his. Turning up a very tidy looking row of houses that spoke of refinement, Rennie indicated as their destination, a house toward the far end of the block.

Darcy said, "I did not know you were acquainted with any of the town's people."

"Yes well... There are people it is good to know."

Having rapped at the door, a manservant admitted them and led them to a drawing room saying, "Please wait in here. Miss Watson will attend you shortly."

Rennie replied, "Thank you Munroe."

With a bow and a quick, "Sir," Munroe had gone.

Looking about, Darcy noted that the house was furnished in a tasteful and comfortable splendour. There were generously upholstered chairs; mahogany tables and book cases that were intricately inlayed with fruitwood and rosewood; the carpets and draperies were of silk; and placed about the room were some most impressive pieces of art and statuary. In a few minutes the lady appeared. She was very pretty, exquisitely dressed and looked like sophistication itself.

Extending her hand she exclaimed in a very familiar tone, "Reynold, it is good to see you again."

"And you, my dear." Rennie replied bussing her outstretched hand.

"I do not believe we have met since before your long vacation."

"I believe you are right."

Assuming a coquettish attitude she said, "I did so fear you had forgot me."

"Never, my dear Jemima. Never. This evening I have

even brought you a new acquaintance. This is my cousin, Fitzwilliam Darcy."

"It is my pleasure to know you Mr. Darcy."

Rennie interjected, "You need not be so formal. You will make him even more full of himself than he already is. Just call him Fitz, as I do."

The lady laughed and Darcy said, "Please forgive my cousin. He seems to have forgot how to behave as a gentleman."

Coming over and linking her arm round Darcy's, she said, "Oh your cousin is *quite* the gentleman, and I suspect I shall find you to be the same."

Rennie saw that Darcy was a bit taken aback by the lady's familiarity and added to his discomfiture by saying with a devilish grin, "Mind your manners Fitz. As I am the one who has brought you here, you should be more polite to me. I trust I can depend upon you to reflect well on my judgment in having made the introduction."

Darcy was speechless but Ms. Watson laughed, "Rennie, behave yourself."

Munroe returned just then to serve glasses of port and the gentlemen remained a few minutes more, engaged in pleasant conversation.

When they were leaving, Miss Watson said, "Reynold, I hope I shall see you soon again." to which he made a polite nod. Then she said, "Mr. Darcy, now that we have met, I shall be happy to receive you if ever you care to send round your card." Now Darcy returned a polite nod. Once a distance from the house, Darcy verified his understanding of the lady's meaning. Yes there were divertissements of all kinds to be found if one just knew where to look.

That first term seemed to pass very quickly by. Far sooner than Darcy would have expected, he, cousin Fitzwilliam and Wickham would be travelling north to Pemberley, for it was December and Christmas tide was upon them. Save for the first five years following the death of Lady Anne Darcy, it had been customary for the family to gather for Christmas at Pemberley, which was always a most festive place. Understandably, that first year, neither of the Darcy men had any feeling for celebration so the Fitzwilliams' had taken on the family Christmas with the proviso that as soon as Mr. Darcy felt it proper, he would consent to bring this special gathering back *home* as it were. Mr. Darcy gratefully acquiesced, but to no one's surprise the Darcys' chose not to attend that first year, passing their Christmas very quietly at home. Four more Christmas's had past, Georgiana had grown and the young Master had gone up to university, so for many reasons Mr. Darcy felt the time was right to resume the old tradition.

On Saturday the 11th of December, Rennie's parents and brother had arrived, to find Pemberley most tastefully and beautifully decorated. There were garlands of ivy, myrtle and laurel draped over all the doors and windows and along the entire length of the banisters and down the newel posts. Vases filled with holly, rosemary and red and white flowers adorned tables, side boards and chimney-pieces. Evergreen sprigs hung at the glazings and wreathed the bases of the tall Christmas candles that stood proudly either end of the side board in the dining room. There were even orange and apple pomanders hung about to add a spicy element to the scent in the air. Everything had come from the Pemberley grounds or greenhouses and orangery. To complete the picture of a house in want of Christmas celebrations, there stood in the centre of the table in the large dining room, an expertly rendered sugar sculpture of Pemberley. So accurate was it in its intricate detail that it truly gave one pause. Even the lake was depicted in melted sugar that, now cooled, glistened like the smooth glassy surface of the frozen lake outside. Everywhere one looked there was decoration of one sort or other; still there was a decided air of understatement to it all.

Lady Catherine and Lady Anne De Bourge travelled into Derbyshire early the following week, arriving on the Tuesday. With the house full of guests there was a great deal of activity but as the young men were still away at university there was not so much of noise. This deficiency was soon to be remedied for in two days time masters Darcy, Fitzwilliam and Wickham would arrive for their Christmas vacation.

From early afternoon Thursday, Georgiana awaited the return of her brother, going countless times to the windows. Finally near on four 'clock it was *she* who gleefully heralded the news of his arrival. Pointing down the drive she called, "Look there; brother is come home!" The others came to look and indeed she was right. Within minutes the dearth of noise was no more. Immediately Darcy walked through the door, Georgiana ran to him and jumped up leaving him no choice but to catch her up in his arms. He laughed, "Can it be that you have missed me so much?"

"Oh yes brother. Yes."

Rennie asked, "And have you missed me as well?"

After a slight pause she said, "Yes but not so much as brother."

This of course brought about a round of banter between the cousins and great laughter from all. Even Lady Catherine laughed, choosing to overlook her little niece's breach of etiquette.

St. Nicholas' Day had come and gone whilst the young men were still at school but the celebration of it had awaited the assemblage of the entire family. Dinner the next day was served in the small dining parlour, and included a large leg of mutton made with onion sauce, roasted hare, stewed capons, larded oysters, beef olives, savoys, potatoes roasted with leeks, transparent soup and salad. Amongst the many offerings in the dessert course were, a Dish of Snow, stewed pears, Flummery, Black Caps and various sweet meats. After dinner, any who Rennie and Darcy could convince to join them, played at a rather lively and messy game of taking an apple from a pail of water. In the evening, supper was a light meal followed by the traditional exchange of St. Nicholas' Day gifts; then the family played charades.

On Friday Mr. Darcy organized a winter picnic beside the lake, in the same spot where there had been winter picnics on so many occasions in the past. The weather that winter being some of the coldest anyone could remember, the lake was completely frozen and skating was the order of the day. As before, everyone crowded round the fire seeking its warmth and the camaraderie of fireside chatter and laughter. From within, they were warmed by a constant supply of hot chocolate and spiced wine particular to the Christmas season; both of these were heated beside the fire.

As is often the case, next morning the excess of time spent out of doors, in the fresh air, rendered everyone quite tired. It was near ten by the time most in the party had stirred abroad and so began a rather lazy day. Mr. Darcy and Lord Fitzwilliam spent a fair amount of the forenoon conversing in the library. Lady Catherine was quite content to sit and chat amiably with Lady Margaret, even owning that she thought it a good idea when Lady Margaret suggested they go for a walk-about in the conservatory. Lady Anne found pleasant employ entertaining and being entertained by Georgiana for the better part of the day. The only ones of the party who shewed any interest in active pursuits were Darcy and Rennie who went for a long ride through the snow that lasted till it was time to come back and dress for dinner.

The next se'nnight past pleasantly by and on Christmas Eve the Wickhams and a few friends from neighboring estates were invited to attend the festivities, which began just after supper. To allow for the keeping of tradition, the Fitzwilliams had carried with them from Greystone, the brand saved from last year's Yule fire. Earlier in the day, this had been placed as kindling in the great hearth of the saloon and two footmen had labored to haul in the enormous, rooted oaken stump that was to be this year's Yule log. Now a roaring blaze brightly illuminated the hearth.

People gathered in small groups about the room, talking and laughing and a number of guests obliged the company by singing and playing the piano. Spiced wine was plentiful and many a toast to health and prosperity was heard throughout the night. At one point a footman entered carrying a large silver punch bowl mounded high with brandied raisins. Rennie was first to espy the man's entrance and announced, "Ah yes. Now we shall have Snap Dragons!"

A crowd gathered round the table where the bowl was placed and the ripple of excitement that began to move through the room on Rennie's announcement grew as the raisins were set ablaze; their blue flames rising high above the bowl. Those who were faint of heart stood well back and watched as those made of more sturdy stock shot their fingers through the flames to retrieve the prized raisins. These were then quickly extinguished and consumed.

Georgiana stood fairly near the front of the crowd and Darcy asked her, "Shall I take some for you?"

She giggled and replied, "Yes please."

Darcy, Rennie and George together presented Georgiana with so many raisins that Lady Margaret felt the need to step in and put a stop to it, lest Georgiana should become ill. Once, while Lady Catherine was deep in conversation with a dowager countess whom she had known since childhood, Rennie somehow managed to convince timid Lady Anne to try taking a raisin for herself. Her outstretched hand crept ever closer and just as she was about to strike out, a raisin popped, causing her to jump back with a shriek of surprise that evolved into giggles. Her cousins now gifted her with a number of raisins that they secured for her. Eventually she tried once again and this time, was quite pleased with her success.

The evening progressed with one entertainment after another; the guests even enjoyed a riotous game of Bullet Pudding from which many emerged fairly covered in flour. It was a rather exuberant young boy who finally came up with the bullet; he then proceeded to romp about the room waving it round and proclaiming loudly of his triumph. It was long into the night, by the time all the guests had finally gone. Darcy and Georgiana stood beside their father as the family drank one last glass of spiced wine and Mr. Darcy offered a toast. "Here is to good family, good health, wonderful memories and sound future generations. And…" said he, motioning toward the hearth where the Yule fire shewed no sign of dying down, "I believe we are all to be blessed with good fortune in the coming year."

"Hurrah," was the general response and with no one but family members remaining in the room there could be warm shews of affection all about.

In the morning the family attended Christmas mass at the village church, returning home to break their fast on cold meats, souse, coddled eggs, coffee, tea and heavy bread with butter and jam. Later, any who were willing to brave the cold went for a walk in the park accompanied by Cali.

The rest of the hours till dinner past quietly, but the dinner itself had nothing of quiet about it. Pride of place on the table belonged to a very large roasted haunch of Venison. Among the various other dishes were, sheep's rumps and kidneys, pigeons comport, a small ham, pork griskins, French Pie, Transparent Pudding, kidney beans and haricots. The desserts were many but included sweet-meats under silver webs, Blanc-Mange of Isinglass, Damson Dumplings and at Georgiana's request, Lemon Syllabubs.

The meal was made especially filling for on Christmas night the Darcy Servant's Ball was held so the family would be on their own for a light buffet supper. This was the one evening of the year on which everyone from the house keeper to the grounds keeper shed the responsibilities of their workaday lives and assumed a life of finery, indulgence and pleasure; there was even staff from one of the neighboring houses on hand to be in service for the ball. The Family opened the festivities, each dancing the first dance with one of the head servants before leaving the revelers to enjoy their very special evening, undisturbed.

On New Year's Eve, the family toasted in the new year with a simple glass of wine at midnight. On New Year's day there was another exchange of gifts. Dinner was of mutton

&c. followed by a lively game of charades. For supper, the family was again on their own for today the Darcy servants were doing the reciprocal duty of being in service for the Servant's Ball at the neighboring estate.

Once the New Year dawned, anticipation was great throughout the shire for after five long years, there was to be a reinstatement of the Darcy, 12th Night Ball, which had always been Derbyshire gentry's most eagerly awaited event of the year.

The colours of a glorious dusk had only just begun to paint the sky when the first carriages turned in at the lodge gates. Now, some half an hour since, though the guests had not yet been seen by any of the family, they could easily be heard for a growing murmur of voices swelled from the front room to which the guests, upon arriving, were being ushered to recover from the chill of their travels with a hearty bowl of hare soup, fortified with negus.

At long last it was time to open the ball and Lady Catherine stood up with Mr. Darcy to represent the family. Throughout the night, the host was seen to dance a fair number of times, but his son, hardly at all. The younger Darcy danced one dance apiece with each of his female relations but above that he danced as little as propriety would allow. There were those with whom he must dance because the close ties between their families demanded it, else there was no one present with whom he wished to dance. Well did he know each and every lady there and his standards were far too exacting to render even one of them an agreeable partner. Rennie, who was constantly dancing, tried numerous times to have his cousin dance; Mr. Darcy tried as well, but neither met with even the smallest jot of success.

The day of the Epiphany brought with it fine weather that

would remain nearly a fortnight. Most in the family were quite tired from the excitement of the ball so this would be another rather lazy day. The mood was further dampened by the fact that the season was at an end. It had been a wonderful Christmas just as it always had been before, but it was nearly over; all would soon be leaving and they were sorry for that. The better weather drew the party out for a long walk in the park, which was followed by an excellent turkey dinner. In the afternoon they exchanged gifts and after supper, enjoyed a 12th Night cake and their last spiced wine till Christmas next. In the morning, the coaches would wend their way through the park and out at the lodge gates then quiet would once again come to Pemberley.

Returning to Cambridge, the rest of Darcy's freshman year progressed smoothly for he was by then well established at university and quite comfortable with the rigors of study. Very soon came the end of the Easter term and his journey home to Pemberley for the long, summer vacation.

In October of 1785 Darcy went up to Cambridge for his second Michaelmas term; that second year began in much the same vein as his first year had ended and it advanced quite uneventfully. Darcy continued to distinguish himself in his Senate House debates, he and Edmund continued to study together and there was always Cousin Fitzwilliam to ensure Darcy did not neglect any opportunity for divertissement. The seasons changed, the school year moved forward and soon it was time for Darcy's second long vacation.

In the fall of 1786 Darcy began his senior year. His third Michaelmas term came and went. The New Year dawned and the Lent term followed. One afternoon, in the latter half of the Lent term, Darcy set out for Deighton's Book Store. He was making his way up the High Street when he heard Wickham's voice call out from behind.

"Good afternoon, Darcy," said he in a cheery voice.

Darcy stopt walking only long enough to look back and with an almost imperceptible nod reply, "Wickham."

Wickham fell in step with Darcy as he said, "I haven't seen you about much lately."

Wickham's excessive pleasantness put Darcy on his guard. He would have none of the man's nonsense so he returned flatly, "Perhaps if you could find your way to lecture hall or chapel on a regular basis, our paths would be more like to converge."

Offhandedly, Wickham replied, "Possibly. By the bye, Darcy do you think you might be able to help me out just a little. I seem to be a bit short of ready money at the moment."

Darcy gave Wickham a withering look and said, "I have had a letter from father in which he sends you his regards. He also expresses his belief that you are benefiting from your time at Cambridge. You must know he has great expectations for you and if he knew that the large sums he regularly sends you were being spent on nothing else besides drink, women and gaming he would be grievously disappointed."

"Darcy, some may be content to lead sedentary, colourless lives, shut off from all form of divertissement, but I see nothing wrong with getting out from time to time and seeking a little enjoyment in life. It makes one so much pleasanter."

Directed squarely at Darcy, this insult fell wide of the mark but Darcy felt no need to disavow Wickham of his mistaken impression. Let him think as he pleased; no matter, but Darcy very ill brooked being spoken to in so forward a manner and in so public a place as a town road. "Take care what you are about Wickham. There is a limit to my patience."

Thinking quickly, as he always did, Wickham parried, "I have no wish to try your patience. I only seek to offer a little friendly advice."

Darcy brought the conversation back round to Wickham, "I have never advised that you should shut yourself away from the world. I merely suggest moderation. Come round to my rooms this evening at seven and you shall have your money." Though he thought, *"...I fear I should as soon throw it in the fire."*

"Thank you kindly Darcy; till seven then." He nodded politely and was off.

Meetings with Wickham in recent years demanded great fortitude and generally left Darcy feeling out of sorts. This instance was no exception, for it was not the first time Wickham had begged money from him and he knew certainly it would not be the last. Darcy's conscience always warred greatly with how to respond, but in the end he usually convinced himself that a small sum could not lead Wickham into serious trouble and might, on occasion, actually be put to good use.

One morning, barely a se'nnight after that High Street encounter, there came a rap upon Wickham's door. When he did not answer, the rap came again; this time louder. Yet a third time did the rap sound, even louder still, and still it went unanswered.

Late that forenoon Wickham awoke to a fearsome pounding in his head. As he tried to rise from bed, the room swam about him and his thoughts refused to assemble into any sort of comprehensible order. His mouth was parched, driving him to find his way across to the table, where he poured himself some small beer. Seeing upon the table the remains of a loaf of bread and some cheese he broke a piece of bread and stared off into the distance whilst he ate. Slowly pulling the cheese closer, he reached for the knife and tried to recall the events of the previous night.

"How have I come to be so addled?... I never go till I lose my wits; most dangerous, that!... I cannot think what the deuce I was doing last night?! The effort of just this small amount of thinking had exhausted what little energy he had and yawning loudly, he found his way back to bed.

Waking again sometime in the afternoon he wanted something better to eat than stale bread and cheese, so he headed for the door in search of a meal. Just there, inside the door was a letter that had evidently been slipped beneath it. The sight of the letter stayed him where he stood, making him go pale and weak. *"There can be nothing of good in this."* He knew not why, but he felt a sudden sense of dread. Slowly he reached down. Even more slowly did he break the blood red seal and open the letter, for his hands shook. The missive was quick and to the point.

Trinity Hall, Cambridge
March 18th 1787

Sir,

*Your insult relative to me last evening requires
my notice and compels me to defend my honour.
I, by this letter, demand you make a public apology; else you will leave me no other course but
to demand satisfaction, in which case Smyth and
Williamson shall act as my seconds.*

R Hopkins

Falling, more than sitting, on a trunk that stood next the
door, Wickham thought, *"I am challenged! Great God, I am
done for. I must find a way out. There has to be a way out."*

It would seem injury was to follow close upon injury, for
Wickham soon realized he knew but one man who would
feel obliged to acquiesce if asked for his assistance, and that
was the very man in whose debt Wickham least wished to be.
He thought harder, but there truly was no one else. Knowing
there was nothing for it, Wickham betook himself to Darcy's
rooms. He rapped loudly at the door and even as it was but
half way open he sprang in, letter in hand.

"I have been challenged." he exclaimed.

Still further injury was to be visited upon him, for Darcy
was not alone. He and his cousin had only just returned
from a day's shooting on the fens. Rennie, who had been
industriously cleaning his fowling piece at the far side of the
room laughed and without turning about he joked, "What
are you playing at Wickham? I do not doubt there have
been many occasions in your life when you ought to have

been challenged, but you are far too artful to ever actually get caught out."

Wickham certainly did not wish to tell his tale before Rennie, but he had not the luxury of awaiting a more opportune time. Despite the gravity of the situation he attempted to assume a bit of swagger and continued, "I would not joke about a thing like this. I have been challenged to a duel." Actually speaking the fateful words had affected Wickham severely. At the last, his voice had even cracked slightly.

Rennie, in some surprise, stopt what he was doing and turned round. To Darcy, who had been watching Wickham since letting him in, the man's distress had been evident. Handing Wickham a glass of wine, he said, "Here; this should help steady your nerves."

Wickham sat to table and drank the glass down, refilling it for himself when it was empty. Some time, and quite a bit more wine was wanted before he could recover the disorder of his mind. When he was no longer able to avoid the issue, he began again. "What has happened is certainly not as I would have wished... None of it is..." With a forced chuckle he concluded, "You see, I really have not much idea how it all happened."

Darcy's back stiffened and he replied, "How can you possibly, 'have not much idea how it all happened' when you have evidently embroiled yourself in some very serious affair. It would seem you have greatly overreached yourself." Wickham went again for the wine bottle but Darcy removed it from the table demanding, "Speak."

Rennie, who had been keenly observing the scene advanced, saying, "I'll take that." and accepting the bottle from Darcy, refilled his own glass as he walked to a chair at the edge of the room in which to settle himself for what promised to be some fine theatre.

Finally Wickham began, "Last night I supp'd at the Hall."

"*That is a credible start.*" Darcy thought. He did not have to ask which Hall, for of course Wickham should find his way – and often – to the one particular Hall at Cambridge which at that time had the misfortune to house students of a most riotous nature.

Ignorant of the unspoken censure he had elicited, Wickham continued, "I was playing at Loo and I had been losing far more than I ought, whilst others kept winning more than they ought. After I had been looed for a second time I was in sad straits for somehow it seems to have been decided that we were to play at Unlimited Loo – or so it was said.

Well, that is when I started to watch more closely. Hopkins was always fiddling with his cards. He kept dropping them and having to pick them up again so that I was sure he was somehow switching cards. Smyth and the others said nay but how else could he have kept winning? I was convinced of it and I said so." Flinging the letter crossly onto the table, he concluded, "Now I find I am challenged for having defended my honour against a cheat! Hopkins has named his seconds, and now I must find seconds of my own."

The thought of Wickham as innocent victim was not particularly easy to comprehend but Darcy was willing to reserve judgment for the time being. "What sort of man is this Hopkins?"

"He can be pleasant enough when he is sober but drink changes him."

Darcy was determined to ignore the supreme irony of Wickham's words, but seeing his cousin lift up his eyes, it became difficult to school his features, "And what of Smyth and Williamson?"

"They are friends to Hopkins but I have had no quarrel with them."

"Were they playing as well?"

"Yes."

"And were they amongst those who kept winning?"

"They won, yes; but not near so much as Hopkins."

Taking up the letter, Darcy read and offered, "You are not challenged outright for it appears a simple apology will satisfy this Hopkins fellow. I beseech you to consider apologizing, for if you did publicly call the man a liar, you are lucky you find yourself with an option."

"But he cheated me. I am sure of it and if I apologize I will be taken for the greatest fool. I will not be able to shew my face in town again."

Darcy wondered at the absurdity of the whole situation. "George, are you truly willing to risk being sent down *now*? You are almost finished at Cambridge for it is already well into March of your Questionist year. At the end of the month we all leave for Easter vacation, after which you will have a mere three months left before you take your degree - if you have managed it. You have kept all your disputations, I hope?"

Rennie interjected, "Good question, that. There was no 'Wickham' entered on the backs of the first tripos papers. But then, perhaps you will pass on Thursday and make it onto the second."

Wickham replied simply, "That is taken care of."

Darcy looked askance at Wickham but not wishing to invite information he would regret being privy to, he simply proceeded, "Then you are soon to finish at Cambridge and need never find yourself back in it again; not in the university, the town or the county. Can you not resolve to keep to a smaller society for so short a space of time as three months?"

"I see no reason why I should." When buoyed by drink, Wickham could be intractable.

Rennie, swirling his wine and looking nonchalantly into space interjected, "You do know, I presume, that many gentlemen keep a fine Spanish blade and when one keeps his blade well oiled and polished, it can in one swift stroke quite easily slice through to the bone. I myself have actually seen a swordsman have a devil of a time to pull his blade free again... But then, I hear the preference these days is for pistols. How are you with a pistol?" Rennie knew full well Wickham was proficient with neither sword nor pistol and he certainly had carried his point for Wickham was now as pale as a corpse, but alas, sitting in the presence of two other young men, how was Wickham to back down?

"I guess I shall just have to take my chances." he declared.

Exasperated, Darcy tried a new tack. "You well know that in Loo, play moves forward largely as chance may direct; besides, things are not always what they appear, so it is possible you may have been mistaken. You said no one else saw things as you did. Are you ready to die in defense of what may be a false claim?" Wickham gave a start at the word *die* but he obstinately maintained his resolve. Clearly he would not be prevailed upon by logic so Darcy gave over the argument for the time being.

Thinking on how untoward a situation Wickham must have embroiled himself in Darcy was mortified, for all of Trinity, nay all of Cambridge more like, knew of his unfortunate connection with Wickham; it seemed the harder Darcy worked to preserve his family's good name, the more Wickham did that could besmirch it. Some of Wickham's past offences crossed Darcy's mind and this consideration compelled him to address the issue of propriety. "Wickham," he said, "I cannot begin to fathom how you can so far have insinuated yourself into the circles of a gentleman as to now find yourself in this situation."

More and more lately, the topic of Wickham's lower birth was become an irritant to him and thus baited he was quickly set off. "Your own father finds my company more than suitable. Why should not every other gentleman?"

"Take care what you are about Wickham. You may be tolerated and even thought amusing by my father; you may be suffered to move amongst some of his connections, but do not think it anything more than the extreme kindness of an extraordinarily good man."

Wickham smirked and said, "Your father is hardly alone in acknowledging me and finding my company agreeable. I have moved freely amongst the first circles since arriving at Cambridge."

"The sovereigns you place upon the card table will be just as welcome as the next man's coin, but it is folly to reach too far above yourself. If Hopkins has challenged you he must be a gentleman. If he *is* such, you very well know that if blood is shed over this matter *you alone* will find yourself held accountable by the law."

Wickham was now nearly beside himself. He wanted very much to refute anything Darcy could put forward, but here he was stymied. He had not considered this point, yet he did know it to be true and that angered him. Pride, that sometimes false friend, led him to respond, "Do not worry about me Darcy. I can take care of myself."

Darcy held his tongue but Rennie saw no reason to follow suit. "Excellent care you have taken thus far."

Wickham pursed his lips but thought better of responding. Rennie was not one with whom he chose to match wits.

Darcy asked, "Have you considered the likelihood you shall either be fatally wounded, else brought before a magistrate for having done harm to a gentleman?"

Wickham said under his breath, "I wonder which outcome would better suit you?"

Wickham could be so thoroughly vexing that it was difficult not to reply in high words, but Darcy managed to rejoin evenly, "I am trying to make you see sense! For all you know, Hopkins may be an excellent shot. If he is, there is a high probability you will be seriously injured and likely killed. If you kill him, you will be hanged; either way, what is there of good in it for you?"

"Should I die, there will be an end of it, *but* if I live, I will be raised up by having defended my honour against a gentleman."

Darcy now asked, "But at what cost? The odds are seriously against you."

"So have they been my entire life."

Darcy was speechless. *"Never in your life have you been denied anything. For heaven's sake, four years of a gentleman's education have just been lavished upon you. You ungrateful wretch! How can you dare make such a statement?"* Not only was it thoroughly delusional, it was supremely insulting to the entire Darcy family. It was at that precise moment that Darcy's disappointment in Wickham turned to outright indignation and his feelings warred within his breast for insincere and ungrateful as Wickham was, Darcy could not, would not, just throw him over. He had to support him; it was what his father would expect.

With artificial calm, Darcy asked, "Wickham, are you sure this is what you want to do?"

"It is what I am forced to do."

"Really?" asked Rennie. "I see no vise round your head."

"*You* may not see it, but *I* feel it."

Rennie replied coolly, "That is no vise you feel.   It is drink." Without giving Wickham time to respond, he continued matter-of-factly, "As the challenged party, it is for you to chuse the weapon. What is your choice?"

After some deliberation Wickham said, "Pistols, I think." for he felt he had a better chance of survival with pistols.

Rennie continued, "It is also for you to *provide* the weapons. Have you a set of dueling pistols, Wickham?"

"Do not make sport with me Fitzwilliam. You well know I have not."

Rennie said, "I am sure I can get my hands on a pair for you."

"Thank you, but you need not sound so gleeful."

Rennie replied in a most patronizing way. "Not gleeful; I am only pleased to be of assistance." Wickham deserved a barb after the insult he had thrown at Darcy and as Darcy had not taken the bait, his cousin was more than happy to step in.

By refusing to apologize, Wickham had officially accepted the challenge and so it was decided that Darcy and Rennie would act as his seconds. There was little left to discuss after that so Wickham soon took his leave. No sooner had his footsteps faded down the hall than Darcy observed, "This is grave indeed. He will be killed and I shall have his blood on my hands because I could not stop him."

"He does not wish to be stopt; or so he now thinks."

"Had I carried my points more effectively, could not I have made him think differently?"

"Not likely, but be not alarmed. He shall live."

"How can you be so sure?"

With a wry smile, Rennie said, "Because I shall see to it. We provide the weapons and decide the place… He will live. That I warrant you."

"I would not ever doubt your veracity Rennie, but I am afraid I cannot share your confidence. You know what a poor shot Wickham is."

Chuckling, Rennie said, "He is an abominable shot, but you must have faith in your cousin Rennie."

There was no logical reason why this statement alone should have brought Darcy such relief as it did but he trusted his cousin; implicitly. His spirits began to lift almost immediately. "By the bye," Darcy asked, skeptically, "have you truly seen a swordsman have to pull his blade free?"

"Of course not!"

Darcy laughed then and accepted the offer of his own wine that Rennie held out to him.

Four o'clock Monday afternoon found the seconds meeting to establish the particulars of the duel. Darcy, Rennie, Smyth and Williamson now stood in the osier-bed beside the brook; young men came shooting here all the time so it seemed a good place to inspect the pistols; never mind that the intended target was generally a partridge or a pheasant.

Rennie produced the mahogany case that held the pistols. Darcy took up the first pistol, skillfully inspecting and loading it. He then aimed steadily at a tree and fired. Missing by a large margin, he cocked a brow in surprise. Taking the second pistol he repeated the process. When this shot had no greater success than the first, he began to ponder his poor performance.

Smyth laughed, "You are lucky *you* are not the one facing the challenge. Give them me and I shall shew you how to shoot." Having much the same result as Darcy he became serious and said, "Whilst I do not claim to be an unparalleled marksman, my aim is sound. I can say with confidence these pistols are more than usually inaccurate. In fact they are pitiful."

Rennie said, "Precisely! and that is a problem why exactly?"

Darcy, having taken his cousin's meaning suggested, "Would not it be prudent to use these? After all, the ravings of a drunken man are hardly worth facing death over and given Wickham's condition when I saw him next day, I would say he must have been quite soused when he made his accusation."

Williamson recalled, "Actually, he *was* in quite a bad way, but I warrant you, he was master of his tongue when it came time to level charges at Hopkins."

"Master of his tongue, I do not doubt, but master of his senses?" Darcy reasoned.

Williamson replied, "Point well taken, but the room was full so Hopkins' honour was badly abused and he is a proud man. He will not back down."

Darcy replied, "Does Hopkins make a habit of issuing challenges then?"

Smyth laughed and said, "This is not his first, but he is a reasonable man."

"Reasonable enough to let there be an end of it without inviting bloodshed?"

"It is too late for that."

Pointing to the pistols Darcy asked, "Can you not, at the very least, join your interest with ours to limit the possibility of death?"

Incredulously Smyth replied, "Do you really mean to use these play things?"

When he saw in their faces that they did in fact mean it, he lifted up his eyes and reluctantly agreed. Shewing he was no stranger to discussions such as these, he quickly grew serious, "There is no need to prolong the matter any further; when do you wish the duel to take place?"

Darcy replied, "We had thought Wednesday morning at six o'clock. Have you any objection to that date or time?"

"None whatsoever; both seem reasonable."

"Right then, and what about Harston-Ham... or even Foulmire Mere if you like. Each has open fields hidden by trees."

Smyth acknowledged, "Both are sensible, for shots would probably attract no attention in either, especially as six will be just as the birds begin to stir. I think Harston quite far enough from town. It is what? Five and a half miles out?"

"Just about, yes." Darcy concurred.

"I propose ten paces."

Darcy thought, *"Anything under twenty and Wickham is dead, bad pistols and all."* so he said, "Wickham can agree to whatever you require but the nature of the offence demands no less than thirty."

"Thirty paces?!" Smyth laughed, "Surely you jest."

Rennie interjected, "I am sorry to say my cousin is incapable of crafting a jest."

Darcy pursed his lips and Smyth, shaking his head, compromised, "We will do twenty; no more."

"Agreed. Will you consent to one shot each to commence on mark?"

Smyth reluctantly agreed saying the whole thing was a

farce. They exchanged polite nods and Smyth said, "If you are lucky, Wickham will meet his fate Wednesday morning and stop ruining your family's name."

Darcy did not wish harm on Wickham but he could feel the blood rushing to his head. "Wickham is *not* of my family."

Smyth looked surprised, "Is not he a relation of the Darcy family?"

"He is the son of my father's steward."

"The son of a steward? Well. That is a shock... Then he is not a gentleman."

"I am afraid not."

Smyth laughed, "He is neither gentleman nor gentleman-like. You two have gone to great lengths to protect a worthless scoundrel." Thinking on it he saw the greater irony. "But if they fight, Hopkins will have raised him up. Wickham does not deserve to be raised up, even if he should be killed in the process. It is unfortunate Hopkins had not this intelligence earlier, but it is now too late to undo what is done."

On the Tuesday night Wickham sat alone in his room and wondered if this night should be his last. For the first time in his life he knew what real, cold, all consuming fear was, but he must work through it, for there where things he needed to do. He must pack a small box of personal items to be sent home if... Rennie had told him of the extreme inaccuracy of the pistols but that was small comfort. *"Life has never treated me fairly. Why should now be any different? Hopkins is a good shot; he will find a way to compensate for any inaccuracy and I shall be killed."* As he collected mementos and other items of value he thought back over his life and wished it had been different; very different.

When all was packed and ready, he moved slowly to his desk. There he sat, took up a quill and wrote:

Trinity College, Cambridge
March 21ˢᵗ 1787

Dearest Honoured Father,

If this letter has found its way into your hands, be proud, for your son has died honourably, defending the Wickham name. I have not always made the best choices in my life but I have always tried to be a good son. What has happened is regrettable, but it is all of my own doing. Darcy the younger acted as my second but he is not to blame. He actually did more than I could have wished in my aid.

As I go to join Mother, I thank you sincerely for your unconditional love and guidance and wish you to know it is my hope that you will soon hereafter find peace and happiness. May God bless and keep you.

Your loving son,
George Wickham

After this, Wickham wrote a quick note to the senior Mr. Darcy, thanking his good friend for his unmatched kindness over the years. When both letters were well folded and sealed Wickham sat back; the pain of fear so great he very much wanted to drink himself into oblivion but Darcy and Rennie had, earlier that evening, scoured his rooms and removed every drop to assure he would be equal to the demands of the coming morning. With nothing left that wanted his attention he betook himself to bed. It was but ten o'clock, far earlier than he would ever normally end his night, which made it very difficult to fall asleep. He lay abed staring at the ceiling, a multitude of thoughts flitting about in his head, till finally his thoughts came round to God. *"Funny that; I cannot remember the last time I thought to pray, not even in daily chapel, but dear God, hear me this night. If it please you to spare me to-morrow, I warrant I will acknowledge your glorious gift by living a very different life in future."*

The prayer gave him some small measure of comfort and he tried again to fall asleep but the idea that he might soon be sleeping for a very long time made this almost impossible; he lay awake and told the quarters past two, when sheer mental exhaustion brought on a fitful slumber.

Too soon, sounded the rap upon his door when Darcy and Rennie came to collect him next morning. Riding in the hired coach Darcy, Rennie and a doctor found the mid March air a bit chill, but to Wickham it might just as well have been the middle of January for he could not get warm. When the coach stopt he handed his letters to Darcy with shaking hands; then walking the half mile or so from the road to the appointed spot, his legs threatened numerous times to fail him.

Hopkins was already there with his seconds and his doctor. Rennie removed the case from beneath the cloak that had concealed it and with Smyth, he checked and loaded the pistols. They then paced off the distance and drove stakes into the ground to define the marks. Whilst they were so employed, Darcy stood beside Wickham and said, "Stay as calm as possibly you can for you will need to keep your wits about you. Take your time and be deliberate. When Hopkins is to shoot, stand to your side so as to make yourself smaller."

Wickham opened his mouth to reply but no sound came forth.

Williamson called out, "Gentlemen, it is time. Take your marks."

Having no idea how he had come to be there, Wickham found himself standing on his mark. Rennie, standing beside him asked, "Do you know what you are to do?"

Wickham nodded.

"Good." Rennie handed Wickham his pistol. "Take care; it is loaded."

Darcy said, "God's speed." but he could not tell if Wickham heard for he seemed to be staring right through Darcy.

When the field was clear of all but the duelists, Williamson called, "Fire when ready."

After a long pause, Wickham slowly lifted his arm into position.

Rennie with real concern, whispered to Darcy, "His hand shakes so much he might actually hit him."

All eyes turned to Hopkins who stood erect and seemed to stare Wickham down; in truth, his eyes were focused on nothing, for his thoughts were very far away. A shot rang out and birds scattered noisily from the surrounding brush. Hopkins flinched, then stood for some seconds without moving, but he did not seem to have been hit. Finally nodding to his seconds that he was unhurt, Hopkins began slowly to move into position. As his arm rose, Wickham turned ashen and took a half step back.

"Hold your mark!" Smyth called but Wickham did not move. Whether from fear or because his own gunshot still rang in his ears, no one quite knew, but Wickham seemed not to hear and Smyth was forced to call again, louder this time, "Wickham. Hold your mark!"

Reluctantly Wickham moved back into position. As Hopkins leveled his pistol, Wickham shut his eyes, heart pounding; legs barely able to support his weight; the acrid stench of his own nervous sweat suddenly accosting his nose. The world went strangely silent for what seemed an eternity; even the ringing in his ears had stopt. A multitude of scattered thoughts and impressions swirled round in his head, till an image somewhat clearer than the rest floated into the forefront; an image of himself as a small boy, playing on the kitchen floor whilst his mother cooked at the hearth; he could *smell* bread baking in the oven. At last the still was broken by the blast of a single shot. Quickly he opened his eyes. *"Am I hit? Am I dead?... I feel no pain. I see no blood... He missed. He missed. He has missed!"* Blissful relief flooded through him.

It was not long before relief was superseded by the conviction that he had just moved higher up the social scale. *"I have accepted and survived the challenge of a gentleman; I must now be considered as one myself."* It was this satisfying consideration that occupied Wickham's thoughts when Darcy came over to remind him, "You must now bring the duel officially to a close by offering Hopkins your apology."

Wickham could not like this little formality one jot. It still irked him mightily to give in to Hopkins but Darcy managed to convince him that protocol required it and by the time he made his way over to Hopkins anyone would have thought it had been his intent all along.

"Hopkins," he said familiarly, "it was never my wish to insult. I hope you will forgive any offense."

"Your apology is gladly accepted."

They bowed and as they moved to return to their respective friends Wickham said, "We should one day soon take supper together."

"I think not. Wickham, I hope you do not think me in the habit of becoming familiar with the sons of stewards." Immediately he turned and walked away. Wickham was mortified but it was difficult to say whether humiliation or resentment beat stronger in his breast.

Darcy had paid the carriage driver to await his passengers, so as to be off without delay once they emerged from the wood. Quickly donning his gown, Rennie drew from beneath the seat, a silver flask. Unscrewing it, he offered it to Wickham, saying, "Here, this is for you." Wickham rudely refused it, which surprised Rennie very much indeed but he cared not to comment. Just inside the boundary of the town, the carriage arrived at the doctor's front door. Darcy paid the man for his trouble and all said their adieus. So far the ride had been achieved in nearly complete silence but as soon as the doctor's house began to fade from view, Wickham addressed Darcy thusly, "You just could not bear to see me raised up, could you?"

There was an awkward pause for neither Darcy nor Rennie believed they had truly heard what their ears told them they had.

Thoroughly perplexed, Darcy replied, "I do not take your meaning."

"Truly Darcy? Do you truly not take my meaning?"

Believing Wickham must be suffering from the strain of the ordeal, Darcy said, "Wickham, you have been through a very trying experience. I fear you are now overwrought."

Nostrils flaring, Wickham parried, "Overwrought? Darcy, is that really what you think this is about? Either you are totally stupid or you are a complete and utter liar."

Darcy had no idea whence came this assault but he was not about to allow it to go unchecked. "Wickham, hold your tongue. Right now I fear you are like to say things you do not mean."

"I am fully aware of what I say. I have just risked my very life. My reward for which ought to have been that I now go higher, but *my Lord Darcy* just could not allow that I should be granted my due."

Incredulously, Darcy replied, "Wickham, you have risked your life because you were too proud, or too dense, to acknowledge your offense and offer a simple apology – which incidentally, *I* strongly advised you to do. As for going higher, though I do not think you worthy in the least of any such honour, it was hardly in my power to assist or prevent it."

"It was absolutely in your power and you saw to it that I should be denied my due!"

Rennie pronounced, "The jackanapes has gone mad!"

Now addressing Rennie, Wickham said, "Think as you please but tell me this. How is it that, of a sudden, there on the field, Hopkins should come to chide me for being the son of a steward? Till then, he had only seen me for who I am." Addressing himself to Darcy he continued, "Where but from my false friend Darcy, could he learn of my circumstances?"

So anxious was Rennie to respond, that it was nearly painful to maintain his silence, but as Wickham had addressed his accusation to Darcy, Rennie could but pray his cousin did not allow propriety to hold his tongue as Rennie must now hold his own.

Darcy said evenly, "Your circumstance *is* who you are. Furthermore, had you not insisted on parading yourself about Cambridge as a member of the Darcy family, there would have been no occasion for me to defend the honour of my father's name against the far less than honourable manner in which you have been accustomed to conduct yourself whilst at university." As Darcy spoke these words and thought of all the untoward circumstances Wickham had involved himself in, he realized his relationship with Wickham could never again be as it was and that pained him greatly for he had once thought Wickham a good friend.

The carriage was soon trundling along Trumpington Street. As it approached Trinity, Rennie, in an attempt to defuse the situation, motioned across the road toward St Mary's and said, "My dear sirs, all are still at Mass. If we hurry we can slip in so as to be seen leaving when it is over."

Wickham narrowed his eyes at Rennie and threw open the door even before the carriage had come to a complete stop. Jumping out, he lurched round on his heels and spat, "Give me my letters."

Alighting from the carriage, Darcy calmly reached the letters from his pocket and offered them up.

Seizing them roughly, Wickham said, "One day you will sorely regret what you have just done me."

"I have done you nothing but risk my own life by standing up for you as second; an kindness which you by no means deserved."

Wickham stood with his mouth ajar then seeming unsure of a suitable retort, stalked off in a huff. Rennie stood, looking after him and proclaimed, "The jackanapes has gone mad!"

The White Bear had an early patron that day, for that is where Wickham betook himself. Upon entering, he marched directly to the hearth, throwing his letters atop the burning logs. Two hours later, his ready money spent, he made his way back to his lodgings, gown bundled untidily beneath his arm. As luck would have it, he came under the watchful eye of Lynam, who upbraided him soundly for the disgraceful nature of his present condition. As an imposition for the offence of public drunkenness by a member of the university, Wickham was assigned to translate two pages of *The Spectator* into Latin and for walking about sans gown, another page. These were to be neatly written up and delivered to Lynam's rooms within two days time.

It was not long before the university year ended. Rennie, despite his constant quest for fun, was of superior natural intelligence and had been a particularly serious student. He graduated a rather high Wrangler, though as he put it, "Not quite so high as to attract inconvenient attention." Before he went back down to Greystone he pledged that he would delay his Grand Tour a year till Darcy finished at university so they might make their Tours together.

Wickham... well... no one ever did quite know for certain how it happened, but it was said that Wickham somehow managed to take a degree as well. The topic became the basis of some wagers amongst the undergraduates assembled at the coffee house, but the particulars were never made known. What is known is that after that year Wickham never returned to university.

Darcy once again headed home for the long vacation. As he was now one and twenty, it was time to have his portrait painted and to the satisfaction of all, Joshua Reynolds agreed to take the commission. Reynolds was getting on in years and his health was beginning to fail thus he had only accepted one other commission that year, but he gave the Darcy's to know he was very much honoured to have been sought out for this commission.

Darcy saw the whole portrait painting process not so much as a symbol of distinction, as a cross to bear, for it required him to stand still and idle many hours a day for what seemed an interminable number of days. Nevertheless, when it was complete, all including he, were most pleased with Mr. Reynolds incredibly accurate and lifelike interpretation of his subject.

At the beginning of September, Edmund Bingley came to visit at Pemberley and since Derbyshire was that much closer to Cambridge than were the Yorkshires, it was planned that he would travel back up with Darcy for their final Michaelmas term.

During Edmund's stay, Rennie came for a month complete and on his arrival the level of activity increased tenfold. There seemed never an idle moment for there was suddenly a surfeit of riding, shooting, swimming, fishing, fencing and archery. Even nine year old Georgiana was sometimes included in the fun for the young men would now and again carry her round on their backs or take her into town for treats from the confectioners shop.

One day Mr. Darcy was drawn from his library by the sounds of laughter. Stepping through the doors to the garden he saw Rennie wandering round the park with a neck cloth covering his eyes. He was trying to catch Georgiana whilst she tried, most unsuccessfully, to keep from laughing so as to avoid giving away her position. Rennie, at last, flung himself on the grass in mock defeat, to the hoots and cheers of all. No one had realized Mr. Darcy was watching till they heard him laughing as well.

All too soon, the time for happy noise was over, for Darcy and Edmund were headed back to Cambridge for their fourth year; the all important Questionist year. Before they went, Rennie made sure to tell them, "I shall be thinking of you as you toil away preparing arguments to defend your principles and to challenge each other's, whilst I toil away at… absolutely nothing… nothing but enjoying my leisure hours."

"If I never hear of Newton, Erasmus or Locke again once I leave this place it will be far, far too soon!" Edmund complained. He yawned deeply for it was very late one night when he and Darcy had just come to the end of a most intense study session. "I have read so much in Latin that I am beginning to dream in Latin and I assure you these are not pleasant dreams."

Darcy laughed heartily. "You need not dream in Latin, so long as you can think in Latin."

Edmund groaned and replied, "I have not yet learnt the words for what I am thinking at present, nor am I likely too; at least not here."

Chuckling, Darcy said, "Have patience; you are almost through. You have already completed your Opponency and you said Lynam told you he received a good report of your performance."

"That is true… It is surprising, and not at all a reassurance that I should ever have such success again, but it is true. Evidently I somehow managed to make some compelling arguments."

"Now you have only your Act to complete."

"Really Fitz. Do you mean to encourage me or to frighten me?" When Darcy merely cocked a brow Edmund added, "I suppose it could be worse. *You* are keeping two Acts, are you not?"

"I am."

"And you kept two opponencies as well."

Darcy said diffidently, "Actually, Lynam has asked if I would mind very much keeping a third."

"And you have agreed?"

"I have agreed."

"Well then I guess I really have not so much to complain of, but I tell you, I will be most grateful when this trial is over."

"It will be a relief to us all."

Lifting himself up from his chair, Edmund collected his things and after thanking Darcy for his assistance, made his way to his own rooms. During Darcy's fourth Lent term, hours spent together digesting and discussing the readings were nearly a daily event. Often there were others added to their circle but always, Edmund was there and always he was the last to depart. His diligence served him well, for he had been successful in his Opponency and soon he would be successful in his Act as well, arguing against his opponents with a fair understanding of the challenges they raised. This success he credited to Darcy, without whose assistance he was sure he would have been lost.

Soon the morning of Darcy's second, and final, Act arrived. As he ascended the stairs of the Senate House, it was with a strange mix of emotions for he thought, *My days at Cambridge are nearly at an end.* He had many satisfying memories of his time there. Aside from the anxiety of Wickham's escapades he really had nothing unpleasant to recall. Be that as it may, once he stepped through the door and into the Senate House, his reminiscences had to stand aside, for there was a serious matter that wanted his attention. Waiting upon the Fellow who was serving as moderator that week, Darcy handed over the paper on which he had written out his three thesis questions.

Scanning the paper, the moderator said, in Latin, for thus the entire exercise was conducted, "These are not the usual sort of questions respondents put forward for their Acts. These are quite complex. Lynam has spoken very highly of you and I begin to understand why."

"Thank you, Sir." Darcy replied quietly.

Once he and his opponents had acknowledged each other the Fellow asked, "Shall we begin?"

One by one, Darcy presented his theses and quite easily disposed of the arguments his opponents brought against them, with the whole of the disputation lasting a little more than an hour. Upon its completion, the moderator gave Darcy very high praise for his performance and then it was *over.* The intense examination for which one spent the better part of one's university career preparing, was over. Darcy accepted the realization with a mix of relief and purposelessness, for what was he now to strive for?

Edmund came to Darcy's rooms a few days hence, examining a sheet of paper and said, "I will treasure this for the rest of my life. Who would ever have thought to see the name Bingley emblazoned on the back of a Tripos paper."

"You have done well indeed."

"*We* have done well, both of us. I am an Optime but *you* are a Senior Wrangler. When first I arrived here I would not have thought it possible I should do so well. I owe you a great deal of gratitude for taking me into your care."

"I do not see it that way at all. You wanted to learn and I respected that very much; besides, I too benefitted from always having someone to study with."

When the university year was over, Darcy had the excitement of his upcoming tour to look forward to and Edmund, his return to the North and his education in the responsibilities of his father's business. In future, there would be few opportunities for these now good friends to meet but there was always the post and soon would begin an earnest correspondence.

Chapter IX

THE GRAND TOUR

1788-1789

WITH the sun low on the horizon and the spray of salt water in the air, a gleaming coach and four came to a stop before the Royal George in Dover. Hours earlier on a perfect July morning, barely a se'nnight after the last day of Darcy's Cambridge experience, he and Rennie had left their family's London townhouses and travelled east, through Kent. Tonight they would lodge at the George and in the morrow they would make the crossing to Calais. Immediately the footman opened the door, the gentlemen emerged, excitement evident in their step.

They knew the tremendous thrill of anticipation, for the journey that lay ahead was to be, not only a journey through new lands, but a journey through life, for this was their "Grand Tour," that time honoured rite of passage into manhood. It was intended to teach one responsibility and provide the knowledge and refinement that made one decisive; confident; strong. In short, it was designed to make one a *complete* gentleman.

After a sponge bath and a change of clothes, the cousins met to sup in a private dining room. Sitting to table, Darcy mused, "To think, Rennie, that to-morrow next we shall be to Paris. I can hardly wait to see the beautiful architecture and to be immersed in the culture of France."

"Yes." Rennie clarified, "The most important part of that culture being the exceptional ladies of France, and of course the fine food and wine."

"Certainly we must indulge in all the fine pleasures that come our way, but we cannot lose sight of the fact that this will be our one chance to experience for ourselves, the incredible achievements and discoveries of those on the continent and to learn from the finest masters and tutors Europe has to offer."

Rennie countered, "Yes. Yes. I fully intend to apply myself to studying the music; the art; riding; fencing, dance and all the rest of it, but I plan to expend at least an equal amount of energy entertaining the ladies. It has been three years since my brother's tour, yet he still cannot stop talking of the charms of the beautiful ladies with whom he associated on the continent. Now it is our turn to feast."

Darcy laughed. "How ever did you come to chuse that particular analogy?"

"Darcy, the ladies in the cities we are about to visit are known to be beautiful and extremely *friendly*. Clearly, you are not likely to find there, the future mistress of Pemberley… though you might find a mistress for yourself. This is our time to enjoy ourselves and leave our hearts out of it."

"Rennie, I know you too well to believe you so very unfeeling as you sound. Still, your point is well taken." Raising his glass he said, "Let us drink to the ladies of France."

"And of Italy." replied Rennie.

"To the ladies of our tour!" Darcy said.

The cousin's excitement was dealt a swift blow when before daybreak, they awoke to the sounds of a windswept rain. So far, it had been the driest summer anyone could remember, yet on that particular morning it had chosen to rain. By noon the sky was clear but it would be another two days till the winds shifted sufficiently to allow of a Channel crossing. With new travelers bound for the continent arriving daily and existing ones stranded, rooms and tables at Dover grew scarce. Having overstayed their accommodation, the cousins had to give up one of their rooms and they considered themselves lucky at that.

Finally, three days after leaving London, the cousins, their servants, tutors and baggage set sail. The waters roiled as they advanced across the Channel, but at least they could cross. When at last they neared the harbour at Calais, low tide prevented the boat from approaching the pier head and they were forced to disembark with the aid of small rowing boats and the strong men and women who, on their backs, carried passengers and their belongings from the row boats to the steps that led up to the quay.

Once Darcy and Rennie were ashore at Calais, the expertise of their servants began immediately to shew its worth, for within the course of two hours, those excellent men had obtained passé-avant for the entire party, thus assuring they could travel about the country with relative ease; they had been to the customs house to see the baggage searched, corded and plumbed, ready for its journey to Paris; they had purchased rather comfortable carriages and four with drivers and footmen; they had secured rooms for the night at an excellent hotel; and arranged for baths to be drawn and a light repast provided.

Their rooms at the hotel proved to be quite comfortable. Surprisingly, there was even a small sort of parlour that adjoined their two bed chambers. They were exhausted from the crossing but thankfully, rather than feeling sick, they instead felt extremely hungry. Much refreshed after a bath,

Darcy strolled to the parlour to find his cousin already there and quite comfortably sprawled in an upholstered chair.

"Sorry cuz." Rennie offered; his mouth full, and a half eaten brioche in his hand. "I was feeling quite peckish and simply could not wait for you… but do sit down. The fricassee de poulet smells most inviting; there is champagne and I can already attest to the excellence of the bread."

"That I can see."

Coming now to the table, Rennie continued, "Moreover, I have the most interesting tale to tell. Smyth has given me to understand why, on our way to our rooms, our worthy host behaved so abominably as he did."

"*Really…* and I take it from your tone that you find his incivility amusing?"

"Very much so, indeed. It seems Smyth and your man, Wilkins caused something of a kerfuffle by demanding the mattresses be removed from the beds and taken away."

"What? Whatever for?" asked Darcy in astonishment.

"Apparently it is generally to be found, when traveling in Europe, that the mattresses are infested with armies of fleas!" With a chuckle, he continued, "Evidently, part of the over large store of supplies we have in tow consists of traveling mattresses and doe skin linens which Wilkins was convinced we ought to begin using immediately, despite the superior reputation of the Hôtel d'Angleterre. Needless to say, Msr. Dessien was none too pleased."

Shaking his head, Darcy said, "I can well imagine he might not be." Chuckling, he added, "I dare say we shall want for nothing during our away; those two have left not one thing to chance."

"No, it would appear they have not, but if they *have*, I shall find it. I would dearly love to be able to rib Smyth about some deficiency or other. The man is too near perfect."

When they had finished eating, Rennie said, "Fitz, after the hours spent confined to the ship, I rather fancy a walk to stretch my legs. What say we see the town? We leave to-morrow, so there is tonight alone."

"That sounds an admirable idea," came Darcy's ready reply and the two struck out, anxious to begin their exploration. It was a perfect evening. The weather was fair, with a breeze off the Channel and their spirits were high. As they walked, they were struck by how very different everything seemed. The buildings looked different; the general appearance of the people and strangely, even the way they carried themselves was different. In every street they noticed monks; some walking singly, some severally; the great variety of their habits attesting to the large number of orders represented in the town. Some wore sandals whilst others trod bare foot.

"Fitz, we are but twenty-one miles from England, yet I feel I am got into a completely new world."

"And so we are."

"To actually be here is so very different from what I had imagined."

"Rennie, I dare say we shall see and do enough to fill volumes of journals."

"That is quite true."

When they returned to their rooms, the cousins chatted a bit longer over glasses of cognac before taking to the solitude of their chambers where each would close his day writing letters to inform his family of their safe arrival in France.

Next morning their party made an early start for Paris. For the sake of expediency, they followed the post route through Boulogne and Etaples to Abbeville where they stopped to dine and to tour the famous cloth factory.

The workings of the factory, they found most illuminating indeed, for neither had ever seen anything such before and they wondered how like it was to their friend Edmund's factory.

Their meal, being of a simple yet filling, provincial sort included chicken roasted with vegetables; cheeses and breads; custards, tarts and burgundy. Resuming their journey without delay, they pressed on. Anticipation was great in the carriage those last few miles for the gentlemen's heads were full of Paris.

Arriving in Paris, the city greeted them from beneath a crepuscular sky, for day was then fading into night. Little chance had they to take in its beauty for they were conveyed directly to the Bureau du Roi. It, like any customs house, was indeed the cause of some consternation, for just when their exploration of life was truly about to begin, they faced this delay. There was moreover, the unpleasantness of being surrounded by individuals who hoped to attach themselves to travelers as valets during their local stay. For a young gentleman to find himself in the position of having to fend off such advances was indeed a rude introduction to the realities of travel.

Thankfully, their passé-avant significantly eased the process and in due time, all was put to rights, allowing the cousins to make their way to the western end of Le Boulevard and the Paris home of Msr. Desjardins, an exporter with whom Mr. Darcy conducted regular business. Msr. Desjardins was currently in residence at his estate in Versailles, so the young gentlemen would not meet him til they traveled thence. For now, he had been only too glad to make his Paris home, servants, horses and carriages available to

Mr. Darcy's son and nephew.

Wasting no time, their first morning in Paris saw the cousins in a clothier's shoppe being fitted for the latest in French fashion.

As Darcy stood for the tailor to take his measurements his cousin strolled about the shoppe surveying the many bolts of fabric and accoutrements on display. Rennie, speaking in his own native tongue, said to the tailor, "I believe this may be the very shoppe my brother shopped in three years ago."

"Excusez-moi? Je ne parle pas anglais."

"Not even a little?"

"Non, désolé. Pas un traître mot."

Rennie thought, *"I see; Not one word."* He gave the man a slight bow and easily switched to French, "Not to worry. I was simply complimenting you on the fine establishment you have."

"Ah Bon. Merci, merci." Smiling broadly the man continued with his fitting.

Rennie now addressed Darcy in English, "Cuz, We must be on our guard, lest we be tempted to buy something we shall later regret."

"Whatever do you mean?"

"I mean precisely what I say. I am seeing a great many laces and shockingly coloured silks round about this place. All these frills and lace remind me of some suits of clothes my *dear* brother brought home when he came away on tour.

He professed them to be quite the thing in Paris fashion. I remember one in particular. When he put it on, he looked so ridiculous I could not help but laugh. Still, he took that monstrosity to London for the season and wore it to an important dinner party. Funny, I have never seen it since."

Darcy laughed heartily and said, "Duly noted."

Once both had been fitted, the tailor's apprentice brought from the store room, some of the finest and most fashionable cloth available. Some of the fabrics included in the offering were even more shocking than those Rennie had previously seen. Immediately he spotted these, he gifted his cousin a look of caution.

That morning saw the cousins give orders for a good many examples of the latest in French fashion; or at least such of it as suited their taste.

Returning home to dine, the gentlemen found a considerable sheaf of correspondence awaiting their review. Rennie, being the first to espy it, leafed through the pile noting, "There is one here from Madame Helvétius." Quickly breaking the seal and reading the letter he said, "She has invited us to her salon to-morrow."

"That is excellent." Darcy replied. "Her salons attract the brightest and most interesting minds in France but I wonder who they have now that Voltaire and Rousseau are gone?"

Rennie replied that they should soon find out. He went on to say, "There is another here from Suzanne Curchod. Is not she the wife of Necker, the former French finance minister?"

Darcy replied, "I believe you are right."

"He is now in exile; is he not?"

"I believe he is. There will likely be talk of his situation at her salons."

Rennie smiled, "The thought of the controversy certainly does appeal to one's sense of adventure."

"Yes. It certainly does." Darcy agreed.

The following evening saw the gentlemen announced at the home of Madame Helvétius. It was a grand home. The rooms were large and ornately decorated, with gilded furnishings and incredible statuary. Fine paintings and tapestries covered the walls and the painted ceilings depicted scenes from classical mythology. The lady was in her sixties; she wore an exquisite, flowing, silk gown and a large powdered wig. Coming to greet them she said, "My dears, I am ever so glad you have come to grace my little gathering."

Falling easily into French, Rennie said, "It was kind of you to include us."

Their hostess replied, "Think nothing of it. I am only too happy to have you. You are in Paris for how long?" she asked. Though she spoke quickly, her diction was perfect so the gentlemen had no trouble understanding what she said and the soft quality of her voice, together with the rhythm of her French tickled their ears.

Also speaking in French, Darcy replied, "It is not absolutely set, but as our host is now in residence at Versailles, we had thought to remain only two or three months now and to spend a longer stay on our return home."

"Mais non, stay long now and later; I am sure Desjardins cannot object. You need much time to appreciate the attractions of the city. There is so much for a young man to do here. To learn what it is to be a Parisian, you must attend many more salons, the opera, the balls..."

Rennie said enthusiastically, "We intend to go abroad every day and every night Madame. We shall be always busy."

"I am glad to hear it, and you will fit in perfectly for your French is excellent. You both sound as though you were born in France."

Darcy said, "I thank you, Madame; French is a beautiful language."

"Come, let me introduce you to some of my other guests."

Linking her arms with theirs Madame Helvétius led them in. They were more than a little taken aback by her familiarity. No! they certainly were not in England any more.

"We are most obliged, Madame." Darcy replied.

"Yes, most obliged, indeed. Thank you Madame." seconded Rennie.

"Please, please. I will have no more of this Madame nonsense; I am called Minette." She had taken them into a room where tall French doors ran the entire length of the outside wall. These all stood wide, inviting in the pleasant evening air. In here, she led them to a settee, on and about which were gathered a small group of men and women who looked to be having a rather friendly and intimate conversation. Minette addressed the group, "Friends, please let me introduce to you, Mr. Fitzwilliam Darcy and Mr. Reynold Fitzwilliam. Both are accomplished Cambridge men, here on their grand tour."

As general pleasantries were exchanged, Minette went to the handsome man seated at the centre of the group. "This," she said, "is a dear old friend of mine; Nicholas Chamfort."

"Ah Minette," said he with a fond look in his eyes, "*You*, mon cheri, are my very dearest friend."

"I am glad to hear you say so," the lady replied, "and now I should like to make you acquainted with these two young gentlemen."

"How very nice to know you both," Chamfort said sincerely."

"Thank you sir." Rennie replied.

Darcy added, "You are most kind. We have read your plays and enjoyed them immensely."

Chamfort replied, "Now it is I who must thank you."

Darcy nodded his acknowledgement. Rennie did as well, adding, "You are most welcome."

Minette soon excused herself, inviting Darcy and Rennie to feel at home and move about to hear all there was to be heard. Conversation began again as someone said he had heard the King was going to convene a meeting of the Estates-General. This set off a great debate, for immediately someone replied, "It has been well over a hundred years since France relied on that mistaken view of governing. What would make the King think the three estates will be any better able to come to a consensus now than they were before?"

A third voice said, "That is a very good question for what do peasants know of running a country?"

From somewhere else in the group rose still another voice, "The third estate should have no place in deciding the future of France. No good can come of involving them."

"But they are a large part of the citizenry."

Now someone slapping the back of his hand in his other palm, exclaimed passionately, "The important issues of the day must remain in the hands of the noblemen and the clergy. We need none but the first and second estates."

Voices for and against rang out, then one sounded more clearly than the others, "What value can the third estate possibly provide? They have nothing to offer!"

Chamfort, swirling his wine glass, cleared his throat and the conversation stopt. "The third estate," he said, "is *everything*, yet it has accomplished *nothing*... Perhaps now it will finally *be* something."

Darcy, fascinated to be listening as France's greatest minds discussed the issues of the day, looked to his cousin expecting Rennie to be equally enthralled. Rennie was indeed enthralled, but not with any discussion of the Estates-General. His person may have stood beside Darcy, but his thoughts were far away indeed and following Rennie's intense gaze, Darcy understood why. At the other side of the room was a somewhat larger group of men and women, engaged in what seemed a most congenial conversation. Amongst this group were a number of exceedingly handsome ladies.

Darcy suggested quietly, "Perhaps you might agree it is time we begin to move about the room?"

Not realizing he had been caught out, Rennie replied, "Indubitably." which caused Darcy's lip to twitch slightly. At the first appropriate lull in conversation they politely made their excuses.

As they made their way slowly yet steadily across the room, they happened upon Minette who, thinking them in search of a new voice to enlighten them, took it upon herself to once again shepherd them in the direction of an influential group. When she began to steer them toward the far end of the room, Rennie was crest fallen, but how was he to politely refuse?

Minette explained, "One of France's greatest treasures is the Marquis de Condorcet. He is at once philosopher, mathematician, and master of political thought. Many say his is the most important voice of the Enlightenment." Coming upon a very large group of men and women, who were engaged in a most animated discussion, Minette walked directly up to the marquis. Waiting for a slight pause in the conversation she placed her hand on the man's shoulder saying, "Condorcet, I have brought you two bright, young, English minds, to instruct so that they may take your noble ideas back to England and spread them through that realm also."

Clearly taken aback by this pronouncement, both Darcy and Rennie felt considerable disquiet. Having the attention of the group directed at them did not help matters at all. After making formal introductions, Minette left them, and moved again to mingle with her other guests.

"Welcome gentlemen, welcome," Condorcet greeted them in a confident and genuinely friendly manner. The cousins nodded politely and Condorcet went on eagerly, "You are on your tour, I presume?"

"Indeed we are sir." Darcy acknowledged, though he was not best pleased to be so offhandedly characterized as yet another colt loping about to find his legs.

"It is a very wise thing, the tour. One needs to know the world to understand what part one plays in it."

"Quite true." voiced many in the crowd.

Condorcet explained to Darcy and his cousin, "We have been discussing the troubles of the under-classes and I was explaining how I believe most of their difficulties are due to their complete lack of education."

"But," someone questioned, "the peasants have never been educated. Why should it now suddenly matter?"

"It matters in that there are every year, more and more people at the bottom and the distance between the bottom and the top seems ever to increase. The lot of the poor is not good, and when those of us who have, flaunt our wealth, it is like waving steak before a pack of hungry dogs. You cannot expect that they will forever lie quietly down whilst you eat before them."

Someone laughed, "They will if they have been properly trained."

Another voice said, "But what do you propose? There are many who do not *want* to work."

Condorcet replied, "True, but there are far more who very much *do* want work, but can find none. Even if there were work enough, without knowledge, a person will never have the ability to rise to a higher level of existence."

"Numerous voices offered decent, "No, No. That is not sound."

"What can you mean by this?"

"Why should you advocate pushing people beyond their station? They would not know how to conduct themselves."

"It would cause uprisings."

Holding up his hands to quiet the discordant group, Condorcet explained, "*I* believe there will be uprisings if we do *not* provide a means for our people to advance. They are not blind. They see that the few *have* whilst the many do *not*. Moreover, they see that no amount of hard work can ever bring them amongst those who have."

These ideas were in direct opposition to all that Darcy and Rennie had learnt of the French system and they were shocked by how forcefully and openly these people were challenging the principles of their government.

By this point Condorcet was saying, "It also stands to reason that the more knowledgeable your citizenry as a whole, the stronger your society must be. Who knows what invention or discovery or medical advancement we are now deprived of because it is a kernel in the mind of one less fortunate. We must provide a free and equal, public education, and give all people a chance to better themselves."

By now the discussion had turned quite boisterous and the cousins, having been forgot in the crowd, thought it wise to extricate themselves from a discussion fraught with pronouncements that in their estimation bordered on treason.

As they turned to move away, a young lady who too had been at the edge of the crowd caught their eye. To their bows, she returned a curtsy and moved with them to a quieter part of the room. She was of about their own age, or possibly a little older and was really most striking. Her skin had a flawless, creamy glow and her soft features were like those of a goddess; her eyes, large and round, were a deep, almost violet blue and her dark hair was not pinned up or hidden beneath a wig, the way most ladies wore it. It was allowed to spill from the centre of a single arrangement at the back of her head and flow past her shoulders in rivulets that shimmered in the candle light.

Exchanging introductions and pleasantries, they learned their new acquaintance, Mlle. Sabine M— was a ballerina with the Paris Opera.

She asked, "Is this the first salon you are attending?"

"It is." Rennie said and he laughed, "Is it quite so obvious?"

Sabine smiled and said, "It is the looks of shock upon your faces that have given you away."

Darcy replied, "If I might say so, some of the Marquis' ideas do seem rather..."

"Disquieting?"

"Well... yes... you could call them that."

She gave a small giggle that delighted them both and said, "*Some* of his ideas, you would probably find downright scandalous, but the marquis is a very intelligent man and a very great man. He loves his country and truly he has only her interests at heart."

"I do not doubt he does," Darcy assured her, "but why then does he seek to stir up discontent?"

Sabine continued, "I can assure you that is not his intent. You must understand that France is not England. What the English royalty and nobility have is indeed magnificent, but for the most part it is not any more *grand* than it need be.

Our royalty and nobility think nothing of spending great sums of money on obvious extravagances; on frills and baubles that serve no useful purpose and they flaunt it before those who have nothing. The bourgeoisie are become disaffected and the peasants, poor creatures are starving and they are getting restless."

Darcy and Rennie were already having a difficult time determining how they ought to conduct themselves for they were not accustomed to the fact that men and women so openly interacted at these social gatherings, but for a lady to be so aware of serious matters and to have so strong an opinion, then to so decidedly express her opinion, was a shock indeed. They of course had, neither of them, ever seen anything like it at home. Rennie, finding this just as stimulating as it was disquieting said, "That is a point well taken, Mlle. I had not considered it from that point of view." Deciding to test the limits of the lady's conversation, he continued, "Still, such a drastic change as education for all would be like to completely unhinge society as you now know it."

Sabine quietly replied, "Many of us believe the pins have already fallen from the hinges."

Rennie wanted to cry, "touché." Darcy was simply stunned by the whole exchange. For the next little while the three debated the practical considerations of this education scheme. Who would do the peasant's work whilst they were off at school? Where were all the teachers to be found and how should they be paid? The longer they deliberated, the more enthralled Rennie became with Sabine. He would make it a point to know her better.

Over the course of the next few weeks the cousins were always busy. During the day there were lessons in French style and etiquette; and in the culture and history of France;

they attended lessons with grand masters in fencing, dance and violin, there were visits to private collections of art and sculpture; tours of architecturally significant buildings; additional visits to the clothier's and of course they had begun to amass the requisite collections of art that one sent home as a remembrance of one's tour.

By night there was an endless round of entertainments but Darcy usually found his own way for Rennie spent every possible evening in the company of his goddess, Sabine. They attended the opera and sometimes visited the theatre, but always when they met, they spent long, blissful hours in each other's company.

Darcy had been gently advising discretion all along; still, near the end of the second week, he found it mildly amusing to hear his cousin whistling as he stood before the pier glass straightening his collars and adjusting his neck cloth before an evening abroad.

Darcy said, "I shall be attending Msr. et Mme. Cherubin's dinner party tonight. Is there any chance I might see you there?"

"Sorry, no. I will be visiting the theatre with Sabine."

"Beg pardon but did not you advise we should leave our hearts out of our associations whilst on tour?"

"Yes, of course. That is the only reasonable course."

Darcy simply looked askance at his cousin, which caused Rennie to laugh uncomfortably and possibly he was trying to convince himself when he said, "Not to worry Fitz. I shall be fine."

Darcy verily hoped that was true, though he could not feel any conviction that it was. Still, he would say no more and within minutes his cousin was through the door, not to be seen again till morning.

One afternoon a few days later, a messenger came to the door carrying a note for Rennie; he awaited no reply.

My Dear Reynold,
It will not be possible for me to see you this evening, as planned. I shall send word when and where next we can meet.

Adieu,
Sabine

"Well!" said he. "This is certainly a most unwelcome correspondence. I hope she is not ill." After a few days silence, Rennie posted a note to Sabine. When the messenger returned with the news that the lady had not wished to reply, Rennie had been not a little hurt.

That very night there was to be a formal masquerade ball. Weeks earlier, the cousins had received invitations to be amongst the guests at this gala affair, which was to be attended by a great many foreign dignitaries. With a bit of coaxing, Darcy was, able to convince his cousin that the noise and frivolity of such an event would be a welcome diversion.

They had been at the ball nearly two hours and Rennie had danced a number of dances. He was just then standing at the edge of the room drinking champagne whilst Darcy was off dancing with a princess connected with the royal family of Sardinia. Offhandedly observing the proceedings, Rennie's gaze happened upon a man who must have lately arrived, for he was just then being introduced round by the host.

The gentleman, who looked to be in his sixties was rotund, his coat unable to fully hide the protuberance of his stomach. He wore a large powdered wig, and his attire pronounced him to be a personage of some import. His white, silk waistcoat was embroidered all over in gold and the coat he wore atop it was of a deep indigo velvet with crested buttons to it. Rennie could only see the man's profile but he clearly saw the great puff of ruffled lace at the man's neck and he really could not like it for it looked very like those he had lately rejected at the clothier's shoppe.

In the ebb and flow of the crowd, Rennie soon lost sight of the man, who was just as soon forgot. Some short time later when deciding to take a turn about the room, Rennie happened into the path of his host and the large dignitary. Only now he could see what before he could not; on the man's arm was a lady, but this was not just any lady; it was Sabine! Mask, or no, it could be no other; he knew her far too well to doubt.

So stunned and sickened was Rennie that he blanched. Having come face to face with the threesome, propriety forced their host to make the introduction. He said, "I should like to introduce to you, his Excellency, the Ambassador from — in the Low Countries."

Rennie's mind was numb but he instinctively bowed and the Ambassador replied in kind. Then the Ambassador held out the lady's hand and said, "This is my lady Mlle. M—."

If Rennie could have dropt through the floor just then, he surely would, but having been offered up the lady's hand, he must buss it and politely say, "Madame."

It was still a further blow when she nonchalantly responded, "I am pleased to make your acquaintance, sir." Nothing in Sabine's voice or manner acknowledged that she had ever once seen Rennie before, and as the three moved on, she made no attempt to catch his eye.

Feeling physically ill, Rennie needed to be away from that place. The music, the voices, the swish of skirts, the tick of heels on the marble floor, the clink of glasses all suddenly melded together into a raucous noise that pained his senses. He needed air. He needed peace. Where was his cousin? It seemed ages but finally the dance ended and Darcy appeared.

Even before Rennie announced that he must leave, Darcy was alarmed for clearly his cousin looked most unwell. Darcy, immediately and unequivocally rejecting the suggestion that *he* should remain the rest of the evening, they left together. In the carriage, Rennie soon apprised Darcy of what had transpired.

"What a fool am I."

Darcy replied, "I feel this is partly my fault, for I have found it odd that she could live in the splendor you have described. She is not a principle dancer at the ballet thus her pay cannot be much, but I thought surely you could not see any possibility of a future with her so I said nothing."

"Yes, when first I visited her home *I* wondered about that as well, but I suppose I chose to overlook it… Thinking back, you did try to warn me. Had you said anything more, I should not have listened. I saw what I wanted to see and believed what I wanted to believe."

"Surely you are neither the first nor the last to do so."

"In my heart of hearts I suppose I always knew there could be no future with her. I would not want to live away from England and I dare say she would be none too happy to leave France. Besides, she is a ballerina, she is a Catholic, and she is used to behaving after the French manner." He chuckled as a thought came into his head. "Can you imagine how Lady Catherine would have reacted, had I come home with

Sabine on my arm?"

Darcy laughed and said, "Yes and *I* should have chosen to remain at the distance of a hundred miles of poor roads till the storm had blown over."

Rennie laughed heartily. "Fine cousin you are."

"Rennie, we always knew we weren't going to find our wives on this trip; we are here to enjoy ourselves. We can only ever hope to meet the sort of ladies we should seriously consider taking to wife amongst London society. There, and only there, shall we find the proper combination of breeding, beauty and refinement."

The last few minutes of the short ride were completed in silence. Once the initial shock had worn off, Rennie seemed quickly to be regaining his usual poise but Darcy's conscience could not be clear. His cousin had been deeply hurt by this experience and perhaps he need not have been. Darcy felt he had been very wrong not to have spoken more earnestly of his concerns and he determined that in future, if ever a similar situation should arise, he would be sure to carry his point forward. He would not stand by again and let someone he cared about get hurt as a consequence of choosing poorly.

Next morning a messenger delivered the following:

Dearest Rennie,

Please believe I cannot begin to tell you how grieved I am to have met as we did last evening but it was not in my power to know you would be in attendance at Msr. Richelieu's ball. Possibly I should have written to inform you that I would be there but sadly I did not think to do so; neither should I have known what I might say. Now it

*would appear I must find the words, for I owe you
the courtesy of an explanation.*

*My presence, at the ball, was required for the
Ambassador was expected to be there and when he
is in town, I make myself available to him. He is
generous and treats me very kindly; so much so,
that he wishes me to understand that when he is
away, my time is completely my own.*

*Early next week, he leaves again on a diplo-
matic mission to Brussels and shall be away at
least a month. If it please you, I should very much
like to see you then, for I have delighted in our
time together and hope you have as well.*

Adieu,
Sabine

Having read through his letter, Rennie's mind went from
mild surprise, to disgust, to offense and lastly to amusement
for he realized the lady's view of their situation was exactly
equal to his own; or rather it was equal to what his ought to
have been. Suddenly the absurdity of the situation became
quite clear in his mind and he had to laugh. Having come to
this realization, it was not long before he moved on, regaining his characteristic buoyancy, but he would be more careful in future; much more careful. Later that day, when the
gentlemen's coach past over the Pont Neuf, Sabine's crumpled letters flew from the bridge into the Seine.

By now it was late in the gentlemen's stay so they must
make the most of what time remained. True, they would return, but this was Paris and now was now. By the time they
left they would each have experienced many of the city's var-

ied entertainments. Both had been to the opera and the theatre a number of times; they had attended brilliant dinner
parties; had danced at numerous balls and had dared, at least
four more times, to visit various salons about the city; even
those of Mme. Curchod. These salons, interestingly enough
seemed less and less disconcerting each time they attended;
so much so, that they had even begun to participate, asking
questions and familiarizing themselves with different points
of view. Some of what they heard, they were still convinced
could not be sound, yet they acknowledged that not everyone shared the same views and that just possibly, a different
society might require a different social structure.

Clearly these lessons were all of the utmost importance
in establishing one as a true and complete gentleman, but
there was another sort of education equally important to be
had as well. It was universally acknowledged that the city
of Paris had been designed for the pleasure of the senses
and what grand tour would be worthy of the name if it did
not provide an education in that greatest of court arts, the
giving and receiving of pleasure to one's every sense. For
this specialized instruction, the gentlemen had the privilege
of being tutored by true masters of the art d'amour. Their
connections allowed them access to Madame du R— and
Madame de E—, thus the gentlemen had received tutelage in
the French art of intimacy, from which nothing was lacking.
All was explored; all was perfected. Paris had, as expected,
proven to be a diverse and most illuminating experience for
the gentlemen.

"Rennie, it is more than time you rise, for we have a full day
before us."

Quite surprised to hear his cousin's voice, Rennie forced open his eyes and looked toward the looming figure standing at the foot of his bed. "Fitz, it cannot yet be morning. I have just lain down my addled pate."

"It is well-nigh six o'clock and if you do not ready yourself with dispatch, we will be behind hand in our departure."

"Ah, Fitz, what can be the rush? Notre Dame has stood for hundreds of years. I should think it might remain a few hours more."

"True, but we have much to see and learn once we get there. As you say, it has stood for hundreds of years; therefore we have hundreds of years of architecture and religious history to study. As *you* desired to do it all in one day, we must have one *full* day, and as we leave Paris to-morrow, it must be today."

"Oh, we can stay an extra day, or let us see it when we return. We shall have far more time then." A second or two later, Rennie brightened, "Now that I think of it, I did want to climb to the top of the tower to see whether Paris or London is larger. Young Marlsbury claims Paris is larger but I do not believe it."

Completely ignoring this frivolous line of discussion, Darcy advised, "We *must* leave to-morrow. Do not you remember that Msr. Desjardins has planned a supper to welcome us to his chateau at Versailles?" Receiving nothing more than a grunt in reply, Darcy persisted, "He has been so gracious as to afford us the use of his Paris home; we cannot miss his supper to-morrow. He is also to shew his private collection of art and I am anxious for the privilege of viewing it."

"That last, I dread!" lamented Rennie. "Nothing is so tiresome as hearing someone describe and praise a painting or sculpture that he owns. He will spend half the evening congratulating himself on his achievement in managing to secure such a rare treasure for his own personal collection and the rest using all the grandiose verbiage in the world to try to convince you there is something to be seen in the blasted thing that the artist never even dreamt of."

Darcy replied drolly, "Surely Msr. Desjardins would find your diatribe most illuminating."

Rennie let out a deep, tortured groan, then turned over and burrowed deeper within the bed clothes. His muffled voice offered, "As for visiting here and there to look at paintings, let us come back in a year or two. I have heard there are plans to turn the royal Castle of the Louvre into a repository of art and call it a museum. If they do, we shall have only to venture to one place to see all we could ever wish to see."

With a sniff, Darcy answered, "I, for one, should hardly take promenading about the halls of a museum as a satisfying exchange for an actual, cultural tour."

Rennie, shewing a bit of forehead and a lone eye, acknowledged, "I suppose you do have a point, but at this hour of the clock, one quick, easy visit does sound rather appealing."

Darcy did not reply.

Finally throwing back the douvet and swinging his legs from the bed, Rennie queried, "By the bye Fitz, just how did you get in here whilst I slept?"

"Your man, Smyth let me in. I believe he was rather at a loss to know how to roust you from your bed this morning and I gather he was glad for the prospect of some assistance."

"Yes, well... I have to keep him on his toes. If he hadn't to look after me, he should feel quite useless, I am sure."

From the far side of the room came a muffled "humph" as Smyth continued to lay out his master's clothes for the day. With a broad grin, Rennie called out in the direction of the sound, "What is that Smyth? Did you say something?" "Nothing, sir. Nothing at all." With a still broader grin, Rennie said in a sentimental stage whisper, "Fitz, I would be lost without Smyth's assistance. We *understand* each other so well." "Yes sir." came Smyth's rejoinder."

Darcy cocked his brow, not altogether approving of the familiar manner in which his cousin bantered with his gentleman's gentleman. It amazed him that so far it had caused no real breach of the requisite level of respect a servant must shew his employer. But then, Rennie was hardly the usual sort of employer. Striding toward the door, Darcy said, "You had best make haste, for I have taken the liberty of ordering the carriage for seven and I shall be back to fetch you at five minutes of..."

"Fitz, you are developing into a regular martinet."

Not quite sure how to take this, Darcy simply nodded and said quietly, "Five of seven, then."

As the door closed noiselessly in his wake, Rennie was left to shake his head in wonder. He thought how providential it was that the responsibilities and expectations of first born son had not fallen to his lot for, "*I should not have liked the gravity of spirit required to do the thing right. No, I should not have liked it one jot.*" And what he did not intend to do well, he did not like to attempt at all. "*But you will do well cuz; that I can verily see. You shall do far better even than my brother, title though he will have.*"

Despite all this solemn contemplation, Darcy's closing salvo had awakened Rennie's competitive spirit and he bounded from the bed, barking orders to Smyth in a determined effort to be ready in a timely manner.

That evening, Darcy sat down to pen communiqués to his father and sister.

Château de Vie
Le Boulevard
Monday, September 1ˢᵗ 1788

Dear Honoured Father,

Received your letter of the 15ᵗʰ and I trust mine finds you in good health. We leave to-morrow for Versailles and as our stay in Paris draws to a close, I thank you yet again for having granted me the privilege of traveling abroad, for it has already proved most instructive. I feel I am got into a new world; I could never have imagined a place so near my home to have so little in common with it. Many and many a time have I seen something that is new to me and wondered if it was the same when you took your tour.

The profusion of art and opulence in one city is astonishing. There is exquisite ornamentation on everything, everywhere one turns; in truth, I think it rather too much for my own taste but I am the better for knowing of it.

We have made many new acquaintances, all of whom have been monstrous obliging and the ladies here are prodigious pretty and of superior understanding.

Much have I learnt that is wonderful, but much too have I learnt that disturbs me. Life here goes on in a comfortable, easy manner, much as I imagine it always has, but there is an undercurrent that seems not quite right. There is a thread of discord that runs often just beneath the surface of one's conversation that I cannot think benign. I can only hope my inexperience causes me to read too much into what I see and hear. If an appropriate opportunity arises, I think I shall make inquiry of Msr. Desjardins when we meet.

I have had a letter from him in which he advises that he and his family await our arrival with pleasure. Cousin Rennie and I already owe him much gratitude, for so completely did he anticipate our needs here in Paris that we have felt quite at home. So amply has he provided for us that I have had only to spend a mere £8 34s 12d against your credit upon Paris and much of that was for clothes. I have had a letter from H— & C— at London advising that you have ordered £100 credit upon Versailles. I dare say that shall go largely unspent as well for Msr. Desjardins advises he is determined to cover our all and sundry expenses at Versailles as well. He has made it clear that he will brook no objection for he says it is no more than is due the son of his estimable friend.

Rennie wishes to be remembered to you and Georgiana. I shall write soon again and I remain your loving and most respectful son,

F. Darcy

Château de Vie
Le Boulevard
Monday, September 1ˢᵗ 1788

Dearest Sister,

I trust this letter finds you well and in good spirits and that you continue to apply yourself both to your studies and your music. You are often in my thoughts, for much that I see, I believe would be to your liking. There are roads which have walkways lined with orange trees planted in boxes and it is quite pleasant to smell their scent in the air as you walk by. The gardens of the Tuileries remind me much of Mother's garden, that you have so lovingly made your own. The profusion of colour and fragrance there would delight you.

Cousin Reynold and I have been to the Palais Royal which is a square lately built by the Duke d'Orleans. The many shops in it are over-full with things I am sure you would like. We could, neither of us, decide which you would best like, so you shall soon find yourself in receipt of a parcel that includes a large assortment.

Last week we visited Gobelins and were appropriately impressed by the manufacture of tapestries. The dying of the silks is a messy business and the skill required for the delicate weaving is quite extraordinary. I shall now have an even greater appreciation of those we have at home; the which number shall be increased when those I have lately commissioned are completed and sent on to Pemberley.

There is, just outside Paris, Mont-Marte. When once we climbed to the top, the view was incredible. On the one side we saw spread out before us, the magnificence of the city with all its spires and pinnacles rising heavenward; to the other side lay completely flat, pastoral land, dotted only with a few low farms and here and there a wind-mill. The contrast was hardly to be believed. Perhaps someday, when you are grown and married, your husband will bring you to see Paris, for he will have seen it himself and will know where best to take you.

You are ever in my heart and the miniature you provided upon my departure keeps the memory of your dear, sweet smile always in my thoughts. Mind your Papa and God bless. I am as always, your affectionate brother,

F. Darcy

The distance from Paris to Versailles was traversed with speed and comfort for the excellence of the roads betwixt, matched that of the roads within Paris itself. The supper hosted by Msr. Desjardins was a lavish affair. There were upwards of sixty guests and the meal included twelve courses, which were followed by entertainments that ended in a magnificent display of fireworks. From the moment their carriage rolled onto his estate till they left Versailles weeks later, the cousins were entertained, constantly and in grand fashion. They enjoyed superb French cuisine; attended a dinner at court; were entertained by beautiful French women; were again scandalized at salons; studied French conversation, including gestures; took dancing lessons from prominent teachers of French dance; and received invaluable instruction from celebrated fencing masters & riding instructors.

Leaving the centres of court life behind, nearly three months after their arrival, Darcy and Rennie continued on to Switzerland. They travelled south through Orleans to Nièvre, which lay at the edge of a bois d'Arce. Their inn-keeper at Nièvre confirmed that from this area, many d'Arce men had answered the call to conquer and had, with William, Duke of Normandy sailed for England, never to return. Darcy knew his ancestors had originally sailed from France with William, and old family records indicated they had come from the vicinity of Nièvre so he could not but feel powerful sentiment, knowing this was likely the very place his family began. He imagined what life must have been in the eleventh century and what it was to embark on such a quest, sailing to England in one of those old boats. He thought of all the advancements since and appreciated even more how difficult it must have been for those who sailed with William.

After Nièvre they made their way south-east, following the most direct route possible. Still, their carriage trundled along at an interminable pace for the roads, once outside Paris, were intolerable. There were areas where part of the road had long since washed away leaving ruts and gouges so deep, at times they threatened to swallow the carriage wheels. At least thrice was their passage further delayed by some part or other of the carriage breaking down.

When at last they neared Genève, the two had been silent for quite some time and Rennie mused, "Do you think, Fitz, that traveling upon roads such as these shall instill in us much strength of character?"

Darcy replied, "It well might, but let us hope the roads will not be so bad in other countries for there is a limit to how much *character* a body can bear."

Rennie laughed and replied, "This really is not to be believed; the state of the roads is far, far worse than any that ever I have traveled in England – even in winter."

Darcy observed, "They are deplorable."

Rennie said, "Yes, it began just as we left Versailles. I am shocked that there could be so sudden and vast a change, immediately one leaves the cities." Looking out at some dirty children who seemed to have more bone than flesh and who played beside yet another ramshackle house with crude patches in its roof, both gentlemen were profoundly disturbed by what they saw. That there should be so much wealth and refinement in Paris and such utter wretchedness in the country was incomprehensible to them. Rennie observed, "I could not have imagined it to be so very bad as this. I now begin to understand why people spoke as they did at the salons."

"I too." Darcy concurred. "At home, even the poorest in a parish are far better off than this."

"Quite so." Rennie agreed. It was unfortunate their parting images of France were so unpleasant as they were, but those images became part of the collective experience that helped form their characters and transform them into the complete gentlemen they were to become.

They had bought copies of Rousseau's *Julie, ou la nouvelle Héloïse* whilst in Paris; if they were going to visit the birthplace of the father of the Enlightenment, they thought it appropriate to familiarize themselves with his writings. Reading throughout the journey, they were just done when the coachman gave them to know they were within sight of Genève. Darcy, having finished his book sat deep in thought as Rennie read to the end of his last page.

Sensing Darcy's eyes on him as he closed his book, Rennie looked up and said, "I had forgot how powerfully written this is. One can certainly understand why so many speak well of this book."

Darcy replied, "So it is; indeed Rousseau writes as one who has lived. Especially his telling of Julie's passing at the end, for the loss of one's mother is a pain that is never truly gone."

Rennie observed, "You can sense that in how he writes of its effect on her relations. I wonder that someone can have such a vivid imagination as to create a story so real as this."

Darcy said quietly, "I believe this part, at least, to be his own true story. I have heard that his mother lived little more than a se'nnight after he was born." Looking out over the countryside, he continued in a far off voice, "He never even knew her... much like poor Georgiana."

Since childhood, there had been virtually nothing Darcy and Rennie did not share, but his mother's passing was a subject of which they had never really spoken, thus Rennie ventured cautiously, "That is true, but there is one vast difference. Thankfully for Georgiana, Providence saw fit to give her a father and brother who love her deeply; didn't Rousseau's father abandon him to an uncle, who in turn sent him off to be taught in some little village or other? I do not think he was ever so fortunate as to feel any familial attachment."

They spoke on this topic only a short while longer before being interrupted by their arrival in the city, but Rennie that day saw what hither to he had only surmised. He now knew absolutely, how very deeply Darcy still felt and would always feel, the loss of his mother.

Passing along Genève's main road Darcy said, "So this is it; this is the birthplace of Rousseau."

Rennie commented, "It is quite a handsome city, to be sure, but do you not feel we have come too late?"

Darcy held that, "It must have been fascinating for those who could actually came here to visit with Rousseau and trade ideas."

The gentlemen installed themselves at an inn and were not long in finding great numbers of their own countrymen; some on tour, as were they and others in permanent residence. As guests of resident Englishmen, they sailed in three or four of the multitude of boats that coloured the lake; they dined at the homes of some of the more prominent members of Genevese society and attended a ball. Whilst in Genève, they were shewn the house where the great philosopher had been born and the places where he was apprenticed in his youth. There was indeed much to entertain but as this was not to be a primary stop on their tour, they stayed barely a se'nnight. The wonders of Italy awaited.

Standing beside their chaise on the morning of their departure, they took a last look about, still awed by the scale of the prospect before them. "Rennie, does not this place amaze you? It is like the peaks of Derbyshire and the Lakes together."

"Yes," Rennie agreed, "but each on an even grander scale."

Neither man was given to great sensibility, but nor was either insensible. Darcy, still looking about said, "No picture that ever I have seen has come at all close to doing this place justice. The enormity of it staggers the imagination."

Rennie mused, "I hope the image of this glorious lake before the majesty of these incredible mountains shall remain always as vivid in my mind as it is today."

Over the course of the next week they made their way to the bustling town of Lanslebourg, and the foot of Mont Cenis.

As their carriage entered Lanslebourg, Rennie looked about and said, "Ah, so this is where all the people are."

Darcy replied, "I still am not become accustomed to how suddenly we can happen upon such a thriving town, when for miles we have seen nothing but a hovel or two with a few ragged, barefoot peasants about them. Are we to be met with stark contrasts throughout the entirety of our journey?"

"So it would seem, Fitz."

Coming to a stop before one of the many inns, they alighted and were immediately swept into the bustle of the town. Travelers and locals moved about in every which direction, some engaged in jocular banter, some in quiet conversation, still others moving swiftly in determined efforts to achieve their varied purposes.

The cousins were shewn to their rooms which were comfortable, tastefully appointed and which had excellent views of Mont Cenis, yet hardly did the cousins notice the grandeur of it for they could think of little else save for the fierce rumblings of their stomachs. Having rid themselves of traveling dust, they headed back downstairs to the large dining hall for a late mid day meal. The interior of the Inn proved to be as much a centre of activity as the street had been, for there seemed not a single table to be had. Scan-

ning the hall Rennie said, "It is a good thing we sent ahead
or we might not have had a place to sleep tonight."

"It rather looks like Tattersalls on auction morn."

Laughing, Rennie said, "Sounds like it as well," and pointing with his chin he said, "There is a lady just there who
completes the illusion, for her laugh puts me in mind of a
whinny."

Their joking (perhaps not so discrete as they had believed) drew the attention of a nearby group of fellow English tourists, who were of about their own ages, and the
cousins were promptly invited to dine with them.

The idea of having to sit to table with people wholly unknown to him, and to have to try to carry on conversation
whilst he ate, Darcy could not like. Espying no vacant table, there seemed nothing for it, so when Rennie happily accepted the invitation and gave Darcy a *'What else can we do?'*
look, Darcy resigned himself to follow. The most outspo-
ken of the group raised his wine glass and said, "Welcome,
gentlemen, I am Richard Westfall and these are my friends
George Randolph, William Marston and Henry Lenox."

After pleasantries were exchanged, Westfall stood and
called loudly, to no one in particular, "Bring more dishes
for our friends. We want more dishes here." Darcy was most
embarrassed.

Soon he and Rennie were set to work pacifying their
abused stomachs. Someone suggested the pickled salmon;
someone else, the poached figs. They tried everything and
finding all to their liking, were quite sure it was not simply
because they had been starving.

Hunger abated, Darcy could now direct more attention
to the conversation, which had continued without interrup-
tion the whole of the time they ate. By now the cousins had

learnt their new acquaintances were from Warwickshire and though their families lived on neighboring estates and travelled in the same circles, they had only come to know each other so well when they were boys away at school. Westfall was destined one day to be the fifth Duke of B—. The only reason the four were braving the mountain crossing rather than taking the sea route from Marseilles to Genoa was because Randolph had nearly drowned as a young boy and was determined to keep his feet on dry land at all times. Westfall was now saying, "…so you see, as we are all named for Kings we thought if we were friends, there should always be peace amongst our kingdoms. We were eight at the time and clearly subject to wild imaginings but we have remained good friends ever since."

Lenox added, "And we take our play quite as seriously now as then."

Rennie heartily joined in their laughter whilst Darcy gave a slight smile and a quick raise of his glass. An hour and a half later, as desserts were consumed and wine continued to flow, conversation that had already run the gamut turned to the anticipated delights of Italy.

"I hear," Marston proclaimed, "the ladies of Italy are all starved for the attentions of young men – particularly young Englishmen and I intend to do my part to sate their hunger."

"Just see that you do not take more than your share." Randolph laughed.

Feigning great deliberation, Marston said, "I shall try, but it shall be hard."

Darcy hoped the double entendre had been accidental for there were refined ladies sitting well within earshot; alas the answering round of hoots and bawdy laughter quickly told him otherwise.

Westfall added rather loudly, "It is said that a man has not done a proper tour if he has not bedded at least one Italian Comtesse."

Randolph said, "And I hear they are so ripe for the picking that it does not even signify if she is married. I think I shall offer myself up as a cicisbeo. I very much like the idea of having the husband secure my services; hardly any chance of a challenge then."

At this, Darcy's discomfiture increased tenfold; he was mortified to be associated with so very public a display of ill manners.

Westfall continued, "I plan to make myself known to the Comtesse di San Gillio immediately I arrive in Turin. Casanova himself named her as the one who orchestrated all the intrigues in town and I hear she still does. I have a letter of recommendation to her for myself and my friends. I can add your names to it if you like."

Before Rennie could reply, Darcy said in a humourless tone, "Thank you; no. We shall be able to find our own way."

With a quizzical look Westfall shrugged and said, "As you wish."

Lenox, being the most serious of the four, picked up the thread of Darcy's comment and changed the subject, "I wonder how things are going upstairs. When we came down there was still so much left to be packed."

Westfall, the clear leader of the group, rose and directed, "Perhaps we had better go and check." To Darcy and Rennie he said, "We must see to the arrangements for our crossing. We leave to-morrow morning for Turin. Perhaps we shall see you there."

The cousins offered that they expected to follow tomor-row-next and that as Turin was not large, it was likely they should meet there.

The next day, Wilkins and Smyth were devoted to preparations for the mountain crossing. They made remunerations for services rendered in Lanslebourg and paid for the crossing; they visited the banker to see to the dispatch of necessary correspondence such as the confirmation of their imminent arrival at le Bonne Femme Hotel at Turin and letters of recommendation to eminent members of Turin's society; they saw to the packing and cording of portmanteaus and to the delivery of these and the chaises to the porters whose task it would be to dismantle the chaises and see everything into the hands of the muleteers for transport over the mountain.

Rennie, in a mischievous frame of mind, chose to hang about, getting in the way for the better part of the morning, for he thoroughly enjoyed watching the constant whirl of activity, knowing there was absolutely nothing in it that required his attention. Not till it was time to dress for dinner did he manage to pull himself away from this divertissement.

At five, next morning he presented himself in Darcy's room carrying what looked to be a large dead animal. Dropping it in the middle of the bed he asked, "What the deuce are we to do with these?"

"As I understand it, we are to wear them." Darcy replied with a smirk.

"You cannot be serious. We shall be carried off by some wild creature that thinks we are of its own kind." Holding up a very bulky, dark brown, fur coat, Rennie said, "Wilkins, have you ever seen the like?"

Continuing industriously to brush off his master's shoulders and straighten his neck cloth, Wilkins replied, "No sir,

I cannot say that I have."

Rennie observed, "I do not know whether to wear it or shoot it." Placing the coat over Wilkins' shoulders and the bulbous fur hat cockeyed on the forbearing man's head, Rennie stepped back to consider the effect and pronounced decisively, "Shoot it, I should think."

Wilkins, removing both and laying them neatly in a chair said, "Very good sir."

Laughing, Darcy explained, "Evidently you cannot be sure what the weather will be in the mountains in October. According to Wilkins' information, by next month these skins will be an absolute necessity, but apparently we may find we are glad of them even now."

Not particularly convinced, Rennie gathered up his skins and left the room saying, "Well if I should see any wolves whilst wearing these, I shall roar and run at them so they think me a great bear and hie away."

An hour later, the gentlemen were faced with yet another curiosity of the crossing. Gentlemen and gentlemen's gentlemen were assembled at the foot of the mountain (their chaises and the bulk of their belongings having preceded them by a day). Looking askance at the preparations before them Rennie said, "When our friend Westfall told us of his 'Alps Machines' I truly believed he was simply having sport with us; now I see he told truth."

Darcy replied, "I cannot say I like the idea of being conveyed over the mountain in such an odd contraption as this chair."

"Well," offered Rennie, "at least the bearers are all nearly the same height, so we shall have a fairly level ride."

Darcy simply looked askance at his cousin, for truly it was a strange sight to behold. The *machines* were actually large skins fashioned into the shape of chairs. These were slung between pairs of poles, long enough to serve as handles; front and back. One sat in a chair to be borne over the mountain by four strong men, with an additional pair of bearers who switched off now and again in relief.

Once they got underway, the ride proved to be far more agreeable than either Darcy or Rennie had dared to hope. Darcy was excessively impressed by the ease and speed with which the bearers maneuvered from stone to stone, never losing their footing or their balance. So easy was the ride that he could devote much attention to the prospect before him, watching chamois nimbly make their way along the slopes; noticing masses of purple and yellow flowers waving in the breeze; considering how some of the mountain tops were lost in the clouds. Sometimes he heard the shrill whistle of a marmot or the raucous caw of a crow. When the sun was high in the sky they were warmed and even betimes lulled into a somnolent state, but as it began to sink lower, the air cooled rapidly so that the skins they carried did in fact prove their worth. A little way beyond the summit of the pass they reached the hospice where they would spend the night. They were now about eight miles out from Lanslebourg with another thirteen still to go ere they reached Susa, but the ascent was now behind them. Passage would be swifter when they resumed their journey in the morrow.

On their arrival, the Reverend Father welcomed them warmly and his servant girl provided for them an excellent meal of cold capon, white partridge pie, heavy bread and a very good wine. Next morning they attended mass and broke their fast with the priest before continuing on their way. The descent through the Cenis valley, into Susa was an easy one, and by early evening they were seated in their reassembled chaise and heading into Turin.

At Turin, their letters of recommendation to the minister from the English court secured them gracious welcomes from the local dignitaries. They were presented to the King of Sardinia, also the French Ambassador and his Excellency's lady. Here they spent about two months making the usual rounds of dinner parties, balls, the opera and the theatre; now and again they came across their Lanslebourg acquaintances at these functions.

The rest of their journey through the kingdoms of Italy progressed in much the same vein. From Turin they took the eastern road to Milan where they past a pleasant fortnight; thence traveling south to Florence. Arriving in mid December, the gentlemen past their Christmas in Florence and stayed till early April studying Renaissance sculpture & painting. From Florence they moved on to Rome for a neoclassical experience amongst its many ruins. Arriving on the 9th April, their route had been planned to allow of Holy week and Easter spent in Rome witnessing its hallowed festivities.

In June, when it was time to travel on to Naples, Wilkins and Smyth set to work procuring the most experienced guard of soldiers they could find to accompany them on their journey. One did not travel the road from Rome to Naples without protection from the banditti, whose ruthlessness made the passage incredibly dangerous.

At Naples the gentlemen were to be guests of Sir William Hamilton, the British Ambassador. They would see his extensive private collection of art and study the music of the masters, but the great attraction was the newly excavated ruins of Herculaneum and Pompeii, and the thrill of ascending the smoking Mount Vesuvius; who better to direct their expedition than Sir William, volcanologist that he was.

On the evening of the day Darcy and Rennie first climbed Vesuvius, the ambassador and his wife were from home, attending a state affair, leaving the cousins to supp alone. They remained at table long after the meal, finishing a bottle of very fine burgundy and discussing the incredible sites they had just seen.

Darcy commented, "I cannot imagine anything so humbling as the feeling you are looking down toward the center of the earth."

"It is particularly humbling as it still smokes. It is at once exhilarating and menacing."

Darcy considered for a while and observed, "...when you see what it did to the humanity living in its midst, it is hard to reconcile that truth with our faith."

"It is yet another evidence of how fragile life is."

"It makes you feel your every action should be one you can be proud of."

Rennie exclaimed, "I should not go nearly so far as that, but it does make you think more seriously; though as first born son, the weight of responsibility will fall much more heavily upon your shoulders than mine. *I* will have only to look after myself but *you* will one day have charge of a small empire."

"Yes," Darcy agreed, "Duty and responsibility await." The gentlemen grew quiet for a time, having both drifted into deep reflection till Rennie broke the silence.

"Now that we have grown so sober, this might be a good opportunity to speak to you of something that is in my mind. I have been considering the prospect of joining the military; perhaps a mounted regiment."

Very much surprised by this pronouncement, but knowing his cousin far too well to suspect a jest, Darcy replied, "I know you love to ride and you have an excellent seat, but a mounted regiment… the military? I had not thought you so serious as that."

Leaning back and swirling his glass, Rennie expounded, "As a second son, it is important to me that I make my mark in society. True, all that is *required* of me is that I not disgrace my family, but it is not enough for me simply to maintain a quiet existence; I so loathe being idle."

"Well do I know that."

"Besides, you know I have never shied away from confrontation and in the military I might be of use not only to myself, but to crown and country."

"If that is truly your goal, it is an admirable one."

"I have other motives as well. Having no property and no real money of my own, you very well know I shall have to marry with an eye toward financial security. How much more palatable that, if the lady is someone I actually admire, but how high can I reach as I am now?"

"Rennie, you have much to offer indeed. You are amiable and intelligent; you are honest and loyal…"

"Yes. Much like a good spaniel."

Darcy could not help but laugh. "You are also of an old and highly respected family."

Not in the least appeased, Rennie forged ahead, "I should fare much better in the marriage mart if I were a man of accomplishment, and the married state would be much more agreeable, were I afforded the dignity of feeling *I* had brought some value to the union."

"Those are points well taken. I cannot argue against them, but just as we speak of the fragility of life, you begin to consider risking your own. Are you determined to put yourself in harm's way?"

"I am determined to make something of myself. Perhaps if I were a different sort of person, I could be content with a more sedentary sort of pursuit but as I am, I cannot. If I were to achieve military honours I would indeed feel most worthy..." Here his words gave way to exceedingly solemn contemplation.

"Rennie, I have always respected you for your judgment and candor but never had I realized the depths of your sagacity."

Leaning far back in his chair, Rennie said, "Oh 'tis nothing, Fitz; be not concerned. The military 'tis all just a consideration; I have made no decision."

Seeing his cousin in a new and different light, Darcy thought, *"just a consideration.' Nay, this is hardly a mere consideration. Ah cousin, we are both much changed since we left home; much changed indeed."*

Some weeks later, having just alighted from one of Sir William's carriages, the gentlemen were walking to his front door when Rennie asked, "Does Sir William never tire of studying that wretched volcano?"

"It would seem not." Darcy replied with a dry laugh. "He is quite a singular man."

Rennie observed, "It was quite thrilling the first time or two we went up it, but really! having spent the whole day together going up, down and round that thing, I rather wish it had just blown itself into oblivion and been done with it."

Rapping at the door, Darcy replied, "You and I never do seem to be in agreement regarding what constitutes the whole of a day, do we?"

Looking exasperated, Rennie said, "Is that really all you got from what I said?"

Laughing, Darcy replied, "No, I fully agree it was too much. All *I* want right now is to lie in a hot bath."

"He is more than both our ages together, yet here we are exhausted, whilst he has stayed behind to collect more rocks... or minerals or whatever it is he is after. Oh! that reminds me; I left the satchel he sent along in the carriage. I suppose I had better go round and fetch it. "

Just then, Rafaele, Sir William's servant opened the front door. Rennie said, "You go in. I shall follow directly." and he trotted off round the side of the house.

When Darcy entered, Rafaele brought forward a salver baring two letters that had been delivered during their away. The letters were bound together with string. Taking them up, Darcy observed the binding and thought, *"This is rather peculiar."* He untied them as he headed for an adjoining sitting room. One letter was addressed to Darcy, in his father's hand, the other to Rennie, in *his* father's hand. They had been posted from Pemberley. *"Uncle must have been visiting."* Darcy thought as he broke the seal and began to read his letter.

Rennie, soon joined Darcy saying, "I hear we have mail."

Darcy, without looking up or even pausing in his reading, pointed to the unopened letter on the table before him.

Rennie, perplexed by Darcy's odd response asked, "What is it? Has something happened?"

Darcy simply said, "A moment." and continued to read, leaving his cousin to watch in wonder and concern; his own letter held unopened in his hand.

As Rennie watched, Darcy drew a very deep breath.

"Fitz. What is it?" Rennie asked.

Now Darcy swallowed hard and began to read again from the middle of his letter. When finally he had done, he remarked half to himself, "This cannot be. Their intelligence must be faulty."

"What cannot be? What intelligence?"

"Father and Uncle are calling us home! They have heard of the events in France and believe we are in danger."

Rennie exclaimed "No?! You cannot be serious. France? We were just there. It was not bad at all. The business about the tennis court oath was just a squabble. The Bastille was bad, yes, but surely that was an isolated incident. You must have misread your letter."

A little miffed, Darcy replied, "I have misread nothing. They feel that what is going forward in France makes it exceedingly unsafe for us to remain on the continent and they wish us to return home at once."

"At once? Not that! Not now! How can they ask us to leave this place. Do they not know of Lady Hamilton's divine dancing? Oh this is not to be borne." Convinced there must be some error, Rennie began roughly to open his own letter, reasoning all the while. "Reports reaching England must have been exaggerated. Perhaps if we write and explain how calm it truly is here... For Heaven's sake, we are not even in France!"

"No but they feel the French problem could quickly and easily spread through the continent and that if it should, we would be caught in the middle of it."

"There must be something we can do." exclaimed Rennie

"It may be too late. Evidently Father has already sent word to Sir William, asking that he arrange everything."

Rennie replied, "It is not too late till we are packed and on our way." Holding up his own letter he continued, "Immediately I read this, I shall write and you must write as well, for there is strength in numbers."

"Rennie," Darcy queried, "how can we oppose them?"

"It may very well be a simple matter of helping them to see that things are not so very bad as they believe. Fitz, we cannot give up without a fight."

"But if it should come to pass that their intelligence is correct whilst ours is wanting – what then? My father has pointedly reminded me of my duty to Pemberley."

"I still think it may be possible to convince them an immediate return is not necessary, in which case, *they* may reconsider. That is not the same as opposing them. Just give me a moment to read." As he said this, he plopped himself into the nearest chair.

> *Pemberley*
> *Monday July 27, 1789*

My dear Son,

> *Your mother joins with me in sending love and prayers for your continued good health. Your brother also wishes to be remembered to you. The letters you have been kind enough to send along tell me you are, as I could not but expect, eking every possible ounce of pleasure from your tour. I am glad of it and trust you are gaining an amount of knowledge and refinement equal in measure to your enjoyment. I must however, ask you now to cast aside your usual ebullience in favor of the gravity I know you to be equally capable of, for there is a very sober circumstance that begs me write this letter.*

Your cousin has, by the same post, received word that he is being called home, which command would of course include you. The reason is ostensibly the instability of the situation in France. Certainly, your wellbeing is our utmost concern, but if our intelligence is correct, the situation in France is not nearly so bad as to require your immediate departure from that region; I say this cautiously, knowing it possible things there can degenerate without a moment's notice. As you are on the continent, you will probably know even better than we, how things truly stand, so your cousin is likely up in arms at his father's request. Before you join with him in protest, you must know the true reason for the summons.

Your uncle has authorized me to take you into my confidence regarding a family matter of the utmost importance. This I do, knowing full well that I can wholly depend on your discretion. He has delayed taking action for months, but the truth is his health has been failing the whole of the time you have been away and as he lately grows much worse, he believes now that he has no choice but to request Fitzwilliam's return. I ask you to join your interest with ours by shepherding him home as quickly as reason will allow.

None of this has been communicated to your cousin, for your uncle believes that were he privy to this intelligence, he would move heaven and earth to make a hasty return home, likely jeopardizing his safety and yours as you travel.

I am heartily sorry that you must so severely

truncate your tour, though I cannot honestly deny it will be a relief to see you safe home. God willing, you may find opportunity again in future to live in the world. You are ever in my thoughts and prayers. E'en now I pray Providence to keep you as you journey home. I am, my dear son, your affectionate father,

Edward Fitzwilliam

Rennie may not have particularly cared about social convention, but he assiduously followed it and now he clearly saw the value of one such, for as he read, his features had not once betrayed the utter shock and great apprehension he felt. Feigning that he still read, the gears now turned furiously as he determined how best to proceed. When finally he looked up Darcy asked, "Has your father said anything different?"

"Nothing to add to our negotiations. They send their blessings and regret the disappointment, but feel we must return. Whatever reports they have heard must be completely different from those that reached us."

Darcy offered, "We can write, as you say, but I cannot see how it will help."

"Fitz," Rennie began quietly, "We shall speak with Sir William upon his return. If *our* letters have just arrived, *he* may not even know of this yet, but if he has already made any arrangements, how difficult can it be to undo whatever he has done?"

Darcy replied, "That is hard to say."

Rennie said, "But it *can* be undone."

A pensive Darcy said, "Yes. I would suppose it can…

But if he has gone to the trouble of making arrangements on our behalf, would it be right for us to ask that they be undone?"

"Probably not."

"Besides, this is what our fathers want and it is through their generosity that we are here at all."

Pausing a few moments before his reply, Rennie acknowledged, "That is true… I suppose we can be satisfied with what we have already seen and done for we have seen much… It is a great blow, but I expect we will both feel tremendous guilt if we do not comply."

Darcy replied, "I am sure you are right."

Rennie's calculations had been correct. He knew his cousin well enough that he had managed to steer Fitz' conscience precisely where he had wished it to go.

In two days time the cousins were on their way from Naples, but not before Lady Hamilton had entertained them with one last dance upon the table. The ambassador saw no harm in sending them away with smiles upon their faces, though Rennie bore a forced smile; the burden of his intelligence weighing heavily upon him. They were to travel north by way of Venice for Sir William had reliable contacts there. Though it would take them farther east than need be, it kept them from the dangers of the banditti. Besides, Sir William had been young once too and he thought a short time spent enjoying the pleasures of Venice was better than no time at all. From Venice, their route took them through the County of Tirol with a brief stop in Innsbruck. They continued their journey, travelling through Switzerland, and Germany, before reaching Belgium. At Bruxelles, an express was sent direct to a contact at Calais, alerting of their imminent arrival and assuring that passage would be arranged for them on a packet boat to Dover.

Their altered plans brought them to Calais on the morning of the day they were to sail so Msr. Dessien was deprived the pleasure of their company at his hotel. This, of course was a bit of a disappointment to Rennie, who promised himself that he should one day return – with or without Darcy, but surely with a travelling mattress and linens.

Whilst most of the passengers sat along the sides of the ship where its high walls blocked much of the wind, this mid August day, saw Darcy standing alone, looking toward the peaks of Dover and the Castle. Its towers and parapets shewn gloriously, burnished by the setting sun, but the sight was of little consequence to him. He could not explain why, but he had a niggling feeling something was amiss. His mind passed over the events of the preceding month. He and Rennie had barely seen the lands through which they travelled, for they journeyed at a pace better suited to fugitives, than young men on tour. *Was it Rennie? Was he somehow different? More reserved perhaps? Was it the situation in France and what it might mean for England? Could it somehow affect Pemberley and her business dealings? Was that the true cause of father's summons? Why had father been so insistent? He could not have received intelligence so vastly different from what we knew to be the situation, could he?*

"There you are, Fitz!" From a slight distance behind him came the jovial tone of Rennie's voice. Grateful for the opportunity to school his features before coming under his cousin's perceptive eye, Darcy bore a placid expression when he turned about to face Rennie. Soundly clapping

Darcy on the back his cousin said, "Abbreviated as it was, I still say we have done our tour in grand style. What say you, Fitz?"

Smiling slightly, Darcy looked again toward the peaks of Dover; this time granting them his attention. Quickly redirecting his thoughts, he replied with some amusement, "I do not know that it was done with any extraordinary style Rennie, but it *was* done in memorable fashion. There were times I thought I might be forced to leave you behind."

"Ah yes. It might have been well if you had. France ... Italy... Switzerland... What beautiful countries."

"Oh, then you *did* notice the beauty of the *countries* as well?"

"Why Fitz, whatever do you mean? How could I not notice? Every city was magnificent; every town bucolic. Do not you agree?"

"Oh yes, I do; wholeheartedly, but I had not believed you to be so aware of your surroundings. I rather thought your mind too fully occupied admiring the beauty of the local ladies."

Cuffing Darcy roughly on the arm, Rennie feigned great affront before smiling broadly and musing, "We did meet some *very* lovely ladies, did not we?"

"Yes, quite so, but do you not think your mother would have been thoroughly put out, had I not managed to drag you home again?"

"Fitz, you give me no credit at all! To think that I could really do such a thing to my poor dear mother! Nevertheless, in my stead I could have gotten one of the grand masters to paint for her, one of those larger than life portraits of her son. Mischievously, he added, "In fact, I *have* had one such sent on, so perhaps I need not have come home after all."

The hearty laugh that followed was reminiscent of many they had shared during their time abroad. Similar in age and understanding, if not temperament, the two cousins were in that moment, struck suddenly and forcefully by the realization that this journey into life had forever cemented the bond that had been growing and strengthening between them since early childhood. They both knew there would be nothing *ever* for which one could not completely rely upon the other. Indeed, they had changed much, during their away but their mutual regard for each other had only grown stronger.

Disembarking at Dover, Darcy and Rennie scanned the crowd, searching for familiar faces. Soon they espied Lord Fitzwilliam and Lady Margaret. Darcy continued to look about, for surely *his* father must be somewhere close by and possibly Georgiana. When it became apparent that the Fitzwilliams were alone, Darcy began to be concerned, *"Has something happened? Why should Father not be here? True it was Uncle who wrote to say they would be here but I had thought Father was to accompany them. Perhaps I misunderstood."*

Heartfelt greetings were exchanged all round and Lord Fitzwilliam said in an even tone, "Fitz, my boy, we are here, not only for our Rennie, but also in your father's stead, for he could not make the journey with us. He and Georgiana are at Pemberley, where they anxiously await your return. Come along and I shall explain fully once you are settled at the inn."

The party moved across the road to the inn where Lord Fitzwilliam had already made arrangements. Ordering refreshment, he took Darcy ahead to their private dining room and answered the unasked questions writ' large in Darcy's eyes.

"Fitz, over these last few months your father's health has not been what it should and the rigors of traveling so far on the road would have been too great a strain on him. He suffers from weakness of the limbs and he tires easily. He also finds little pleasure in eating now so he is of late not quite so broad as before."

Darcy asked, "But what is wrong with him? What has the doctor to say?"

Lord Fitzwilliam replied, "The fact is, no one can rightly say. Doctor Braxton has tried whatever methods he knows and he has brought in specialists from Edinburgh and even one from Austria but they are, all of them, perplexed as to the cause."

Almost to himself, Darcy asked, "How can he have come to be so sick and I have heard nothing of it, yet Rennie and I have received regular correspondence."

"Apparently your father first noticed something was amiss even before you finished at university but it was hardly noticeable then and he paid it no mind. When it began to grow worse, he believed simply that as he was not so young as he once was, he had just been trying to do too much. He was sure a little rest would make the weakness abate, but it did not.

That was about four or five months into your tour." Holding up his hand as Darcy opened his mouth to protest, Lord Fitzwilliam continued, "That is when he first acknowledged it to the family but he forbid any of us to inform you, for he knew you would have been determined to return home at once. You see Darcy, your tour was a rite of passage your father dearly wanted you to experience to the fullest. He said you would find out about him in due time and that your knowing sooner rather than later would serve no good purpose. You can well imagine how he warred with himself over calling you back even now, but at last he knew he must." Reflecting, Lord Fitzwilliam added, "He has many good days. We left Greystone on Sunday last and stayed two days at Pemberley before coming on to Dover. Your father was well enough whilst we were there and I can tell you he most anxiously awaits your return."

"And Georgiana," Darcy asked, "how does she fair?"

"She senses the gravity of the situation of course and I believe she feels it keenly, though she will not shew it in your father's presence. She has grown much since you went away; both in *stature* and *character* and she is beside herself with anticipation of your return. Your father was most amused to tell us that she has been worrying poor Mrs. Macey to distraction with suggestions about what you might like for your first repast upon your return. Every favorite has been fondly remembered and duly noted. Had it been left to her, I believe you could expect to be presented with a meal sufficient to feed half the kingdom.

It is not always the case that an elder sibling inspires such genuine regard in a younger one; I can assure you that! You have ever been a dutiful and loving brother and I am much mistaken if Georgiana does not recognize her good fortune." The hint of a smile did then soften, somewhat, the lines of worry and concern that creased Darcy's brow.

Whilst he and Lord Fitzwilliam spoke, Darcy had not realized that his cousin and Lady Margaret had stayed behind, but as they now entered, it was clear that Rennie too, was aware of just how matters stood. Coming across to Darcy, the strength and comfort their faces expressed, said more than any words they could have spoken. He found solace in knowing how deep a bond existed between these two branches of the family. Much out of character, the very staid Lady Margaret gathered Darcy into a firm embrace and said quietly, "Fitz, please know we are here to help you in whatever way we can, just as we hope we have already begun to be of assistance to your father and Georgiana." She quickly relinquished her grasp and Rennie said sincerely, "So say I, as well. You are more a brother to me than my true brother ever has been."

"Reynold!" chided Lady Margaret

"I am sorry Mother if it pains you, but it is true."

"Thank you," Darcy replied earnestly. Meeting the eyes of all three in turn, he continued, "Thank you all, very much. I know I can always depend on you and I am truly grateful."

In a determined bout to change the tenor of the conversation, Lord Fitzwilliam directed, "Now let us eat. Heaven knows what you two have been eating on the continent. A good, lean roast of beef is just what you both want to feel at home. There is nothing like a solid English supper to warm the heart and sooth the soul."

As they sat to table, Darcy's mind was numb from the shock of his news; he was in no humour for conversation, still propriety demanded that he ease the tension for the others, so barely knowing what he said, he quipped, "Lord Fitzwilliam, from the great assortment of this offering and the size of the roast, I wonder that Georgiana did not have a hand in these arrangements as well." Rennie was the only one who seemed not to appreciate the allusion. He simply asked, "How is Georgiana? She must be much grown since last we saw her."

Lady Margaret eagerly offered that Georgiana was become quite the young lady. "She is nearly five feet tall and she looks more like her mother every day. She sounds like her too, both in voice and manner. Darcy, you will be astonished when you see her; you will hardly know her."

The rest of the meal passed pleasantly enough with stories told of the young men's experiences abroad. It being too late to begin their journey that day, they were to stay the night in Dover. On the morrow, they would journey to London and spend the night at the Fitzwilliam townhouse. The following day, they would strike out for Pemberley. Lord Fitzwilliam ordered his coach to be ready at first light so they could make an early start for London and Lady Margaret retired, leaving the gentlemen to their brandy and manly talk. In her absence, Lord Fitzwilliam brought his son and nephew up to date on news they might have missed whilst on the continent.

"I should not wish you to think," he began, "that everything of note that happened in the world during your away happened in your midst. We too have had our share of interesting events. Probably of most interest to young bucks like you is that last month the *London Chronicle* printed the complete laws of the game of cricket. Rennie I have kept a copy for you and Fitz, your father has done the same for you."

"The rules printed out in full?" Darcy queried.

"In full; there is even a section that addresses wagering on the game."

"How convenient."

Rennie concurred, "It is that. How I long for a good game of cricket. That is one thing I have missed."

Talk of cricket continued for a short while, then moving

on, Lord Fitzwilliam asked, "Do you recall hearing a couple years ago of HMS Sirius and the expedition to establish a colony of convicts in Australia?"

They did vaguely remember and Lord Fitzwilliam said, "There have lately been printed some letters written by one of the officers on board that give a more positive account of life there than what was originally thought to be the case. It seems they have been successful in their quest, for they now have expanded their stock of animals to a sufficient number and have used an entire outlying island to plant a large garden that is thriving so that it provides all the vegetables they need."

That this experiment had proven such a success was a surprise to the cousins.

"Then there are the Americans. I had truly believed the separate colonies would begin to fight amongst themselves, but that does not appear to be the case; at least what fighting there is, has not been severe enough to divide them. Fitz, I believe your father wrote to tell you the Americans had elected Washington, their most celebrated general to be their president. Rennie, I am sure you remember me writing to tell you of it."

Both answered in the affirmative and Lord Fitzwilliam continued, "His inauguration was held last month and what a ceremony it was. It had nearly the pomp and circumstance of a coronation; it lasting all day, beginning with prayers in the morning then a procession from his home to their Federal Hall. His oath, he took in the gallery of the Senate House, before an immense throng of citizenry."

The young men agreed that indeed it did seem rather equal to a coronation.

"The latest we hear is that the states, for so they now call themselves, are one by one ratifying a document which they call the Constitution. Evidently it takes its inspiration from Magna Carta for it defines three separate bodies of government. An American constitution; can you imagine? Who could have foreseen such an end to the establishment of English colonies in North America? The whole thing was very poorly played on our part and I am sorry for it."

The exchange of news continued till Darcy felt the passage of time had been long enough for him to graciously excuse himself and retire to the solitude of his room. Finally alone, he could reflect on the painful revelation of his father's condition. It was blatantly obvious that there was little hope of improvement and Darcy knew not what to expect when he reached Pemberley. He remembered how strong and perfectly healthy his father had looked last July, when he and Rennie had left London. He remembered his father laughing with them, in the best of spirits and seemingly in the best of health, as he expertly conducted the activities of the entourage of servants and tutors that would escort them on their journey. He thought then of Georgiana and what she must be going through, having to experience this alone. *She is but eleven years old. It is no wonder Lord Fitzwilliam says she has matured so much; she has had no choice.* He thought of how very much she had already lost for, *She never even knew her mama; now after barely a decade, her papa is ill as well.* Darcy thought then of his mother; of how close he had been to her and how terribly painful it had been for him to lose her, but he had had his father and they had eventually helped each other through it. His father's strength was something he had counted on all his life. Now it seemed his father would need to draw strength from him.

In many ways, so very similar were they, his father and he, that they had always been very close. Their compatible temperaments and shared interests had made their relationship almost as much one of friendship as of paternal duty and filial respect. His father had taught him much and now, as he was just reaching the point in his life when he would be called upon to apply those teachings, it seemed he might not have his father to guide him. *"Yea, duty and responsibility await... but they come much faster on than I would have hoped, and in a most unwelcome manner."*

The days spent on the road seemed interminable. Fully determined to keep his unease to himself, Darcy carried on cordial conversation throughout, but within, he very ill brooked the suspense of what should otherwise have been a joyous homecoming. Lord Fitzwilliam had sent word ahead from Dover of the ship's safe landing and of the party's expected arrival at Pemberley two days hence, so all would be at the ready when at last they did arrive.

At the final coaching stop before Pemberley, the servants coach had stayed only long enough for a change of horses, thus the lodge gates were swung wide in anticipation of the Fitzwilliam carriage's imminent arrival and when it made its way along the final approach to the house, the forewarning had allowed for the assembly of a welcoming contingent that included nearly every servant and representatives of every tenant family. The end of the carriage drive and the tall staircase leading to the front door were awash with people, save for a generous path up the center. Though Darcy knew this was to be expected, it still touched him deeply. Of course he should not, would not shew it, but touch him it did. Sooner than he would have liked, the well being of each and every one of these people would rest on his shoulders.

Whether or not they had formally been told how things stood, he knew not, but they were aware; from what Lord Fitzwilliam had described of his father's condition, they must be aware. From his earliest days, the young master's comportment and sincerity had led him to be held in the highest regard by the people of Pemberley, but now they would be seeing him differently.

Lord and Lady Fitzwilliam had insisted that Darcy should be first from the carriage. As he alighted, he looked round quickly, nodding a general acknowledgement to all; he then directed his attention to the top of the stairs, where the family awaited. Midmost of the assembly, his father sat in a chair; Georgiana stood to his right; Mr. Wickham and George to his left.

Georgiana, fidgeted incessantly, as she tried valiantly not to forget herself, but she soon lost the battle and ran down the stairs, meeting Darcy before he could ascend. So vigorously did she jump up into his arms that he was forced to take a step back. Clutching her in a tight embrace, he chuckled and swung her round a full revolution. When he let her down she would not yet quit the embrace. Face buried in his chest, she said quietly, "Oh brother, I have missed you so very much."

"And I you." he replied.

"Brother, you know not how good it is to hear your voice." When finally she looked up at him he saw that tears were about to spill from her eyes and his words caught in his throat.

Looking away, over the top of her shining, golden head,

he cleared his throat and said, "I am home now Georgiana; I am home and we will face our trial together." Smiling at her and lightly bussing her hand, he added, "But now I must go to father." Still holding her hand, he led her up the stairs, acknowledging all as he past, yet making his way quickly up the long flight. Nearing the top, Darcy saw that whilst his father was smiling, his eyes looked sad and weary.

Determined to meet his son standing, Mr. Darcy strained to rise from his chair. Mr. Wickham and George helped him to his feet and supported him once he was there. The sight sliced at Darcy's heart. He had not known in what condition he would find his father, but he had not expected this. To be sure, he had not imagined his father could have changed thus much. Quickening his step even more, Darcy reached the head of the stairs and nodding to the Wickhams took hold of his father's arms. "Father," he said as he looked into Mr. Darcy's sunken face. It was all he said; it was all he could say, so shaken was he by the vision before him.

"Ah my boy; *welcome* home." his father said in a voice that retained little of its original timber.

"Thank you father; it is good to be home, but would that you had called me home sooner."

"None of that, Fitzwilliam. None of that. This is not the welcome I would have hoped to give you on your return from such a significant venture as your tour but alas…"

"Do not concern yourself father. We need not stand on ceremony. There are none about who do not understand." Helping his father back into his chair, he added, "I am just glad to be back. I require no fanfare." Looking now to the Wickhams, who had been silent during the whole of Darcy's exchange with his father, Darcy acknowledged them with a nod. "Mr. Wickham," he said.

Mr Wickham replied, "I wish you a very warm welcome home."

"Thank you, sir. That is most kind of you." Then he addressed George. "Wickham." he said.

Donning an unctuous smile, Wickham replied, "Darcy. How good to see you. It has been ages. I trust you enjoyed your time abroad?"

"What utter, fawning, insincerity," Darcy thought, *"I see things have not changed a whit."* but he simply said, "It was most instructive Wickham. Thank you for your kind wishes."

By now Georgiana was kneeling before her father whose hands each clasped one of his children's hands. *"There is still strength in your grip father,"* Darcy assessed, *"but it is hardly as it was."*

The Fitzwilliams had long since alighted but had watched this scene unfold from below. Even at that distance, the change in Mr. Darcy was evident and Rennie was shocked. If *he* was so strongly affected, he could only imagine what Darcy must be feeling. Lord Fitzwilliam took his wife's arm and led the family up to meet the others. After brief greetings, all retired into the house where the travelers disbursed to their rooms for a much needed respite after their journey; baths had been drawn, fresh clothes set out, pillows plumped. There was now time to reflect in solitude till supper.

Refreshed after a bath and a change of clothes, Darcy stood by his bed chamber windows surveying the grounds that were the fabric of his life.

"Will there be anything else, sir?" Wilkins inquired.

"Thank you, no. That will be all." He watched as Wilkins left the room, pulling the door shut noiselessly as he went. In the quiet of his chamber, Darcy leaned against the chimney piece and reflected on the revelations of the last few days. *"Father's condition is grave indeed."* he thought. *"That is all too painfully clear. But how can he have come by such an illness as this and no one have any idea how it happened, or even what it is? Oh, my dear Father. Nay, more than father; you have ever been my mentor and my friend. And poor Georgiana, having to watch alone, for so many months, as her father withered away beside her; no Mama to help her... no brother either. Mother you are gone these eleven years and it would seem we are now to lose father as well. I only hope I will be ready when the time comes for me to serve as master of Pemberley."* His cousin's words then found their way into his consciousness, *" '... as first born son, the weight of responsibility will fall... heavily upon your shoulders. You will one day have charge of a small empire.' Rennie,"* thought Darcy, *"you could not have guessed how near the mark you struck for that day is nearly upon me."*

Chapter X

MASTER-IN-TRAINING

1789

I⊤ had been a se'nnight since Darcy's return and he had easily fallen back into the routine of life at Pemberley. He drew strength from his home. That strength had helped him through his mother's death and now, at the age of three and twenty, it appeared he would need to draw on it to see him through both the loss of his father and the monumental task of quickly becoming a worthy master of Pemberley.

It was near on ten in the morning and Darcy had, as usual, been up since dawn. Having already changed his clothes after a brisk ride, it was time to break his fast. Upon entering the breakfast parlour he came up short, for there was Wickham, deep in conversation with Mr. and Miss Darcy.

During Darcy's away, Wickham had somehow managed to so far recommend himself to Mr. Darcy that he was now welcomed on a regular basis, to break his fast at the Darcy table. Darcy could not begin to imagine how such could have come to pass, but so it had and he could not like it. Mr. Darcy still saw in Wickham a worthy young man, full of compassion, good humour and good sense. He did not at all see in him, as Darcy had long since learnt to see, someone completely insensible to the needs and wishes of others.

Alert to Darcy's entrance, Wickham stopped mid-sentence and addressed him, "Why Darcy, my friend, how *are* you this fine morning?"

Darcy replied, "Quite well thank you. I trust you also are well."

"Very much so. Never better." Wickham said.

Darcy greeted his father and sister and headed for the viands arranged on the side board. As he served himself from the assortment of excellent dishes displayed before him, he noted what a change this was from their university days for Wickham, being one much in harmony with the small hours of the night, had not been one to rise much before noon. When Darcy sat to table there followed a few minutes of strained conversation betwixt himself and Wickham, who soon rose from his chair, dabbed the corners of his mouth with a great flourish of his napkin and said, "I think I shall be off. I must to Lambton this morning for I have some business to attend." With slight bows he addressed them all, "Mr. Darcy, sir... Darcy... Miss Darcy." and quickly he left the room.

The rest of the meal past most pleasantly, then Georgiana excused herself, as it was time for her French lesson. Once she had gone Darcy earnestly deliberated, *Am I right in my thinking. Is it time I begin to learn...?* He asked, "How do you feel this morning Father?"

"I think it will be a good day, my boy. I have a bit of strength this morning." Mr. Darcy smiled and added, "*Ah, but now that you have had your tour, I must no longer call you *my boy*. You are now a man in truth as well as in name."

"Father, you may call me as you chuse."

"Then I chuse to call you Darcy, as befits a grown gentleman for it is time you get used to it. Else I shall call you by your Christian name, but I shall refrain from calling you *my boy*... At least, I shall try."

Darcy laughed, "As you wish, father." He just caught that mischievous twitch before it receded from the side of his father's mouth. It was such a subtle characteristic; one a less observant person could easily miss, but it was one Darcy had been familiar with for as long as he could remember and somehow seeing it *now* caused a great lump in his throat. Darcy watched his father intently. He discerned both tremendous pride and great pain in those strong, wise, caring features and he thought, *"It is for me, and me alone, to ease your pain, for it is I who am the source of it. It is for me to shew you father that I will be fully prepared and wholly willing to take on the duties of Pemberley and the care of my sister... no matter how soon that need should arise."*

They began synchronously with, "I believe it is time..." Mr. Darcy yielded, refusing to continue, so Darcy said, "I was about to say I think it is time I learn specifically, all that is involved in running Pemberley."

"That," said his father, "is precisely what I was about to say. I am sure you know more than you realize, just from your observations during our rides out and from your part in our conversations over the years, but all the same it is well you gain practical experience, dealing with those entrusted with actually running the estate. I thought you might begin today by riding out with Cooper."

"Yes... Yes, if you wish it."

"Good. I have instructed him to await you this morning."

"That would be excellent father. I shall require an half hour to ready myself, no more."

His father nodded then said with conviction, "You will want for nothing with Cooper. He has been my overseer so long there is nary a thing he does not know about Pemberley."

"Understood; I am glad of it, but I am not surprised."

Four hours later, Darcy and Mr. Cooper began making their way back from a thorough and most instructive tour of the estate. Darcy had absorbed facts and figures of their wheat, barley, flax and hay production; these had been compared with the yields of prior years. He had learnt of this year's lambing and foaling, and of how successful had been the recent introduction of the short horn cattle. During the course of the week, he toured the stable block with Mr. Cooper and the stable master, Mr. Abbot. The horses were of particular interest to Darcy for not only was he an avid rider, with an excellent seat, he also had inherited from his parents, a keen eye for the characteristics of a fine animal. There had been a number of new horses and mares added during his away at university and still more whilst he was abroad, thus his attention was quite captured. They discussed in minute detail the lineage of each of the hunters; they inspected the brood mares; walked through the stable of carriage horses; even that of the plough horses. All naturally were kept clean, comfortable and well supplied with grain and fresh water.

By week's end, Darcy and Mr. Cooper had visited at least a quarter of the eighty odd tenant farms and spoken with many of the farmers; before they were through, they would visit them all. They had seen some of the shepherds driving their flocks between pastures; explored the areas worst plagued by foxes and those most prone to poaching.

Just as the Darcy family allowed of a reasonable amount of poaching; likewise, nothing was said if people came along after the harvest, to scavenge for what crops had been left behind. People throughout the shire knew that anyone truly in want would meet with kindness at Pemberley. The Darcys were well aware it was difficult for many to support their families, and if it did not hurt them to share their good fortune, with honest, hard working people who chance had rendered less fortunate, they saw no reason why they should not.

As for the foxes; well, that was another matter entirely. "Mr. Darcy, sir," began Mr. Cooper, "with the foxes left in peace, the lambs have been hit hard this year. The ewes were doing their part just fine, but we were losing the wee ones near just as fast as they were droppin' em." With Mr. Darcy being ill, there had not been a hunt organized in well over a year, so the lambs had fallen victim in record numbers and this was Mr. Cooper's way of asking that the situation be remedied.

Darcy chuckled and said, "I see, Mr. Cooper, you have saved me the trouble of identifying for myself what first wants my attention."

"Well sir, I would not have put it quite so plainly, but it would be a good thing for Pemberley if we had a hunt."

"Then it shall be done and I thank you for bringing it to my attention." Bowing slightly, atop his horse, Mr. Cooper said, "Your servant, sir." and Darcy knew these were not empty words." Cooper had been a fixture at Pemberley since Darcy was a boy. He liked the man's forthright nature and knew instinctively they would get on well together.

Over the course of the week, Mr. Cooper had taken Darcy to meet all the principle members of the outside staff and many of the under staff as well. From them, Darcy had gleaned a comprehensive understanding of how things stood on the estate. Now it was time to look to the business side of Pemberley affairs, so the following Monday morning found Darcy sequestered in the library with Mr. Wickham.

The two sat at a wide, mahogany chart table, laden with a great variety of neatly sorted vellum documents written in flourishing hand. The table was a sea of silver tax stamps and bright red wax seals. There were notes and receipts; obligation bonds for monies lent; lease indentures for tenant farms; government notes; stock certificates &c. Added to these were a multitude of ledgers filled with detailed entries of monies collected and monies spent.

Whilst perusing the leases, Darcy commented, "I see that all the tenant farmers have life interests."

Mr Wickham replied, "Every last one. Your father will hear of nothing else."

"I recall a letter he wrote to me while up at university in which he spoke of the leases. Evidently fixed rent contracts were then lately become quite popular, but father very much questioned the logic of them. He said it was, 'Blamed foolishness entering into an agreement that was, from its very creation, destined for dissolution.' "

"Quite so. Your father never liked the fixed rent scheme; never trusted it. He thought a man far more likely to take a genuine interest in maintaining the value of the land if he knew his living would depend upon it for the entirety of his life and I believe he was right. From the first he heard of fixed rent, he thought it a nonsensical idea."

The two went on to discuss arrangements for the sale of barley and wheat to various millers and granaries; wool to Scottish worsted mills and flax to Devon and Norfolk linen makers. Darcy thought of Edmund and of how good it would have been if their crop was what he needed.

True most of the Darcy's wealth came from the fruits of their lands (both that which was tended on their behalf and that which was in the care of tenant farmers) but the elder

Mr. Darcy was an astute and well informed man; he was very much aware that change was afoot in England and he sought actively to protect his wealth by broadening his financial interests. His son was now made familiar with their investments in government bonds and their interests in various import and export concerns.

These last Darcy knew had begun strictly as imports of French wines and brandy, but then whilst he was away at university he remembered his father mentioning in some of his letters that the situation in France had begun to deteriorate and that he thought it wise to vary his investments. Still, Darcy was much surprised to see just how widespread were his father's concerns, for they now included interests in trade not only with the continent but with the Americas and the West Indies as well.

It was now midday Saturday and a multitude of issues had been covered. All the principle matters of business had been touched upon and many had been considered in minute detail. "I think," said Darcy, "we have both earned the right to some relaxation for it has been a very full week."

"It has indeed sir." Mr. Wickham concurred.

"Then let us stop here till Monday morning."

"Very well sir."

As Darcy left the room, he considered how impressed he was with Mr. Wickham's thorough knowledge of his father's business arrangements and his genuine understanding of the concepts upon which his business decisions were made. Darcy had known Mr. Wickham all his life and had always thought highly of him, but never had he realized just how astute a man Wickham truly was. Once again he marveled at his father's ability, always to find and secure the most perfect person for every responsibility.

There was much information to digest, but first Darcy needed to rest his head so he sought a few minutes quiet in his chamber. Reaching the head of the stairs, his progress was arrested by the faint sound of muffled sobs. Recognizing full well whose sobs they were, he headed in the direction from whence they came. Finding the door to the music room slightly ajar he stepped quietly in. At the far side of the room Georgiana sat at her pianoforte. Alone in the very middle of the bench, with her head resting upon folded arms she looked, Darcy thought, *"so very small and fragile."* Softly, he called "Georgiana?"

She gave a start and without lifting her head, sobbed, "Dear brother, I am truly sorry you should find me thus. I have so not wanted to burden you."

Striding swiftly across the room, he sat beside her and placing his hands so they completely cradled her shoulders, he gently coaxed her to face him.

She sobbed, "I thought it would help to come and play, but once I got here I found I could not. It has been… I feel so… Oh dear brother, I am so glad you are come home."

"As am *I* glad to be home; I should not have liked to miss the opportunity of knowing the continent, but I am always happiest at Pemberley."

"So have I always been… until…" Georgiana's voice faltered and she stopt, but she managed not to weep. Darcy looked at her for a long time and what he saw was a sister so changed he barely knew her.

"Georgiana," he softly said, "you must not let what is happening now influence your feelings for your home. You have spent many happy years here, have not you?"

"Of course I have brother! All my years have been happy ones."

Nodding, he continued, "If you see Pemberley as the source of a Darcy's strength and of everything that is good in our lives, it will be easier for you to find your way." Georgiana was listening, he knew, but she was far from being comforted. "Think of what it means to be a Darcy of Pemberley."

"Is that what *you* do?"

"Yes. It is what I have done most of my life. It is what I learnt from father one time when he and I rode out together and he taught me of how Pemberley has been home to the Darcys' for hundreds of years. Do you know, Georgiana, when the first D'arcys came over from France, in Norman times, some of them settled here on this land. That means much of Pemberley has been Darcy land since the eleventh century. I believe father must have told you this. Did not he?"

Georgiana nodded her head but said nothing so Darcy went on, "Each of us is here for a certain length of time and whilst we are, it is our duty to appreciate the great gift that Pemberley is and to care for it so we may pass it on to future Darcys' in the same, if not better condition than when it was given us. What is happening now is certainly not as either of us would have wished, but Providence has willed it and we cannot change it. If the worst should come, you and I will have to carry on." With this Georgiana lost the composure she had been trying so valiantly to maintain and fell against Darcy's chest; her shoulders heaving in despair.

He was not sure what reaction he had expected, but surely not this. *"I see,"* he thought, *"I shall have to hone my skills if I am to be of any use to my sister."* Soothing the pained sensibilities of a bereft female was clearly not something one learnt at Trinity. Enfolding her securely in his arms and placing his cheek gently atop her head, he heaved a sigh and began again. "I am sorry Georgiana. I did not mean to upset you. I only meant to assure you we would find our way... together."

"Do not apologize brother. It is I who should be sorry. I know you could not have meant anything but good and I am behaving foolishly."

"No Georgiana. There is nothing foolish in loving your Papa so deeply as you do. It is something to be proud of. It is one of the many qualities for which I admire you."

Georgiana looked up then and tried to focus through tear filled eyes. "*You* admire *me*, brother? You are so much older and have lived in the world. Why ever should you admire me?"

For the second time in this single encounter, he was taken aback by his sister's reaction. "Georgiana, there are many reasons why one may be worthy of admiration. I admire you because you are kind and honest; because you take your studies very seriously; likewise, because you are determined always to do your best at every endeavour; but I think most of all I appreciate how deeply you care for those you love. I am truly proud to call you sister and I will always be here for you."

"Truly brother?"

"Yes, *most* truly."

A small smile then appeared behind her tears and she whispered, "Oh, then I shall not be so alone as I had thought."

"Georgiana, whatever would have made you think you would be alone?"

"Well, Mr. Wickham said if Papa should... you know... that you should not have much time for a younger sister for you will have to put all your energies toward being master of Pemberley. I thought it would not be fair to expect you to look after me as well and I knew I should not ask Mr. Wickham to look after me."

"Georgiana, you are my sister and family is even more important to me than Pemberley. As long as I breathe, which I expect to do for many years to come, I promise you will not be alone."

She smiled, reached up to salute him on the cheek, and said, "Oh thank you. I had been so afraid, but I am not afraid any longer because now I know I have the very best brother who ever lived."

Darcy was not so sure he concurred with her assessment but he was glad of it just the same. "Georgiana, if ever you are unsure of anything concerning me, ask *me*."

She smiled fully and said, "That I shall."

"Do you think you might play something for me?"

She smiled again and said, "If you wish." He nodded and began to rise to give her room but she held his arm and said, "Please stay beside me." She played three pieces before he escorted her, on his arm, to her chamber door so she might ready herself for supper.

Completely insensible of the turmoil he had created, Wickham himself was at that very moment dressing for the evening; difference was *his* plans did not include a quiet family supper. His was to be a late night abroad, filled with revelry of whatever sorts he might happen upon and the more, the better. Any habit, profligate, immoral or lascivious, that George had practiced whilst up at university, he had assiduously honed since coming down. Keeping his proclivities from the notice of his worthy benefactor, and to the extent possible, from his own father, was a feat that required considerable skill; George Wickham was a man of many skills.

"Father," George said as he came into their parlour, "You recall, I am sure, that tonight I am to supp with friends in Lambton."

"Yes, you had told me so."

"After supper I should think we will play at cards and you know what it is like once we all begin talking."

George laughed at that and his father chuckled mildly too, "Yes, I can well imagine what that must be like. I hope your friends will not be playing high."

"Not to worry. I am sure the wagers will be small."

"I am glad of it."

Not wishing to invite any further discussion, George said quickly, "Well good night then, father. It will be late when I return, so I shall see you in the 'morrow."

"Good night son and God's speed."

"Thank you father. To you as well."

Consulting the pier glass ere he left his house, George was quite pleased with the fine aspect that gazed back at him. Making a final adjustment to his neck cloth he thought, *"Yes, this is going to be a very good night."* Quickly passing through the door, he strode the few yards to a small, but very well equipt stable, the construction of which had been commissioned by the senior Mr. Darcy, for the Wickhams' own use. All the while, George smiled contentedly for everything was right with the world.

Passing through to the tack room, he lifted a bridle down from the wall and moved quickly to the saddles. He was thinking which to chuse when of a sudden, he cried out, for in the shadows that separated him from the entrance, there emerged a human form. In the dim light, he could not make out the specter's features but that was of no consequence for there was no mistaking the tall figure.

"Darcy! What the devil are you doing lurking in the dark?"

"I have been waiting to speak with you and I would have thought to find you here long before now."

Wickham had no idea what Darcy was about, but he could not like it. Shewing far more pluck than he felt, he grabbed up the nearest saddle and said, "Darcy, I should love to stay and chat but as you say, I have had a late start so I really must be off." Carrying the saddle, he made to pass through to the horses but Darcy blocked his way.

"I think not. There are serious matters we must address."

"I am sure they can await the 'morrow."

"They cannot. It would seem that in my father's illness, you have managed to creep much further into the fold than you have any right to be."

Knowing full well there was any number of circumstances that might have led Darcy to this conclusion and wishing them all unknown to him, Wickham smiled uncomfortably and replied, "Darcy, I truly cannot imagine of what you speak." Darcy moved closer and Wickham backed away.

Nostrils flaring, Darcy explained, "You have caused Georgiana the greatest distress by leading her to believe I would not have time for her once I am master of Pemberley."

"Darcy, where ever should you have got such an absurd idea?"

"From my sister."

Forcing a chuckle in a vain attempt at levity, Wickham

offered, "You know how young girls are. They are subject always to such flights of fancy. Clearly she has just mistook some little something or other..."

"Wickham, you are pathetic." spat Darcy.

Laughing uncomfortably, Wickham said, "Darcy my friend, you do me an injustice for I am a man of great compassion. I was merely trying to offer solace, for your sister had nowhere else to turn."

"This is not to be borne! Wickham, with passing acquaintances, I do not doubt that such condescending drivel must serve you well, and possibly my long away has made you forget how well I know you, but devil take it; do not try anything like on me again. It will not end well for you."

"My father and I have always shewn your father the utmost loyalty, so I really think I deserve a bit more civility from you." Roughly replacing the saddle he spat, "You think just because you are Mr. Darcy's son, you are above everyone! What makes *you* so special?"

Darcy felt his muscles go rigid and his fists clench, but Wickham's mention of the senior Mr. Wickham served to hold his rage in check; if only just. Maintaining command of himself was a mighty effort, but he managed it as he said, "Your father is the model of integrity and loyalty. *You* are a different matter altogether. You have ever taken liberties where the Darcy family is concerned, but this time you have too far overreached yourself."

Wickham's brow knitted and he opened his mouth, but before he could make address, a deep voice, brimming with controlled rage, growled, "Have you no decency? During my away, you have contrived to bring a great deal of disorder into my home."

Aye, there it was; the most recent sore to fester in Wickham's innards. His feathers exceedingly ruffled, what little reason and caution had remained, were now lost to him. "Oh but of course; your home tended for you during your away! It must have been a magnificent adventure, flitting about, living in the world at your father's expense, whilst the rest of us stayed behind to maintain for you your prize. What have you ever done to deserve all that has been handed to you?"

Darcy's blood boiled so that he could barely speak. "*Nothing* has ever been handed to me or to any Darcy! My family *built* what we have and each generation is entrusted with the responsibility of preserving it. It is because of *us* that you have always lived so well as you do. For your *father*, I have the utmost respect. He is a most honourable man who works hard and has much to shew for his labours, but he would not live near so well if not for the Darcys. You, with your continued extravagances would long since have made him poor."

Wickham suddenly lashed out at Darcy, who blocked the blow and with his other hand grabbed Wickham by his neck cloth and drove him hard against the wall. "You will not ever! do such again, and for your father's sake alone, I shall forget you have done so now." He paused ominously then said, "See that you mind what you are about, for you shall suffer the full extent of my wrath, should you ever again try to insinuate yourself into the affairs of my family."

So tight was Darcy's grip that Wickham could not have replied, had he chosen to. Eventually Darcy loosed Wickham from his stare and his hold, and walked quickly from the stable. Once the sound of hoof beats could no longer be heard, a much shaken Wickham brushed himself off, saddled his own horse and rode away. In the shadows of the stable, a great sigh of sadness and disillusionment shook the frame of an utterly disconsolate father.

Chapter XI

A PAINFUL LOSS

1789

D ARCY's rigorous instruction progressed quickly and one afternoon during the third week of September, whilst he and his father were taking tea he said, "Father I am undergoing a most careful tutelage at the hands of your very able staff."

"Yes. I am well aware of the fact." his father said with a chuckle. In response to Darcy's quizzical expression he continued, "Could you think for a moment that I would not be closely following your progress?"

Darcy laughed and said, "I must admit I had been too focused to consider that point, but now that you mention it, no, I would not think you desirous of anything less than a complete daily report."

"Ah well, that might be a bit much for me these days but I am following as closely as my strength allows and I am best pleased with what I hear; not *surprised* mind you, pleased... best pleased."

"Thank you father, I am gratified to know I have earned your approbation."

Mr Darcy did not answer; he just looked on, his eyes tracing every line of his son's face. After what seemed a very long time, he said wistfully, "Son you have ever earned my approbation. You are three and twenty years old and I remember with good opinion, everything of your life; everything from the day you were born... which seems as 'twer' yesterday... Indeed it practically was yesterday." With a catch in his throat he continued, "Son, I cannot begin to make you understand how very much it pains me to know that having barely lived, you must now give over so much of your life to the care of Pemberley."

"Father, I hardly consider it giving over my life, for Pemberley is my life."

"Ah son, that is a mistake you must be careful not to make. I should hope you will always see Pemberley as a very important *part* of your life, but it must not be the whole of your life. You cannot let it consume you, for then you will lead a hollow existence and in time even Pemberley will cease to matter."

"Father, I do not understand."

"No... I fear you do not. You have not yet lived long enough... have not known sorrow enough to truly understand."

"That is not so. I have known deep sorrow."

"True, but not deep enough to understand of what I speak. Fitzwilliam, find a wife and have a family. Then you will live not for Pemberley alone. Only then will you understand what I have said to you this day."

Father and son spent a while longer in deep conversation but only a short while for of late conversation drained Mr. Darcy's strength.

Darcy's education continued and as he took an increasingly more active part in the affairs of the estate he steadily gained

confidence in his ability to meet the challenge of his forthcoming duties. Mr. Darcy became less and less involved for
his strength ebbed quite as quickly as his son's proficiency
flowed.

It was now early October; not two months had past since
Darcy's return from abroad and his father had taken to
spending much time abed for he now often felt weak and
when he stood he grew lightheaded. On this morning father
and son talked in the former's bed chamber.

"It shall not be long now." Mr. Darcy said.

Darcy very much wished he could refute this assertion,
but he could not. His father knew the end was near and so
did he; to say otherwise would, to Darcy's mind, have been
an outright lie and border on disrespect. He knew not what
to say, so he said nothing; he simply tightened his grip on his
father's hand and looked steadily into his sunken eyes. *Your
eyes once shone so brightly. Now they are but shadows of their
former selves.* he thought. *They are dead already.* So little
did his father eat of late that he had become gaunt. Illness
had caused his drawn face to darken round its perimeter
making it seem even thinner still.

"Find a wife Fitzwilliam." said his father at last. "It will
not be easy to discharge your duties to the estate if you feel
you are as an island."

"Father I had not thought to take a wife for quite some
time to come. Besides, I cannot begin to think where I
should ever find a wife to suit me."

"Then you do not intend to marry your cousin?"

"Father," Darcy began uncomfortably, "Please understand; I have the greatest respect for Lady Anne, but it
would be a grave mistake for us to marry. Our temperaments are so vastly different that neither of us could ever

hope to make the other truly happy."

"I am glad to hear you say so for I heartily agree, and so did your mother. We could, neither of us, imagine any two people more unlike than the two of you; besides, I seriously doubt Anne is strong enough to give you an heir. And do not think you must allow your aunt to bamboozle you into marrying her daughter. That may be your aunt's favorite wish, but if it be not yours, it does not signify."

"You say mother too realized? Even all those many years ago?"

"When you both were very young, your mother did hope it would come to pass, but as you both grew and your characters began to develop, she came to realize it would be a very unfortunate match for you." Mr. Darcy smiled as he said, "For all the times your aunt has spoken of it, have you never wondered why your mother never did?"

Darcy said, "I suppose I did not think on it at all."

Now his father laughed, then for quite some time he said nothing. He considered his son and heir, taking in every detail of Darcy's face. At last he said again, "Find a wife. She must be someone worthy, yes, but let her be someone you can love and respect so that you feel always proud and content knowing she is yours."

"The only lady in the whole range of my acquaintance, who could tempt me to marry, lives in India and she has no desire ever to come back home to live in England."

Thinking on this briefly, his father replied, "Ah yes, Casterley's younger girl; you two did seem to get on quite well together. I had forgot that."

Darcy's countenance did not at all betray his thoughts just then but as he reflected on a time that seemed ages ago he thought, *"Indeed father, you could not begin to imagine how very well."*

"That is a match of which I would wholly approve, but you are right; she has no feeling for the land of her birth. Pity that. You well know Casterley is, to this day, my dearest and most trusted friend, and *never* have I questioned his judgment except on this one score. I really do believe he did his girls the greatest injustice removing them so completely from their home before they were old enough to realize and appreciate what a tremendous gift it is to be born English. For heaven's sake, they have only ever known two short visits back."

"I could not agree more, but the past is gone and only Providence knows what the future holds, so it is for me to focus on the present, and my present requires my complete devotion to discharging my duties to Pemberley. For all that entails, I verily think I shall go little into company for quite some time, thus any thoughts of marriage will have to wait."

There was great sadness in his father's eyes as he replied, "Would that you could have lived more of your life before having the responsibilities of Pemberley thrust upon you. I feel I have failed you by forcing this upon you so soon and for that I am heartily sorry."

"Father I will not hear this. Never have you failed me."

Mr Darcy gave a faint smile and for a long while looked intently at his son; the years passing through his mind. At last he said, "There was at least one time I can remember when I failed you very much indeed. That was when your dear mother left us. So severe was your grievance that you even tried to run away from me."

Darcy caught the quick, mischievous twitch of his father's lip but nonetheless felt the need to defend his honour. "Father, I most certainly was *not* running away; I simply needed to distance myself so that I could think and try to understand what had happened... what was then happening. Even there you did not fail me for to be sure, had you not reacted as you did to mother's death, I would never have fallen upon what has to this day been one of the most valuable lessons of my life."

Thinking back, Mr. Darcy laughed, "That is true. Come to think of it, I do not believe I have ever known a single drop more of strong ale to pass your lips."

Darcy coloured slightly and replied, "Yes, well, there was that also; I cannot say I own any great affinity for strong ale. Associations do sometimes influence one's tastes, but I was referring to my having come to see people and events more fully since that day."

"If you mean to say it gave you a better understanding of what drives people and what their lives are about, that is a good thing for that will be of immeasurable value to you as you discharge your duty to Pemberley; but, as that experience taught us both all too well, we must be careful lest we allow our sensibilities to cloud our judgment.

There are many different responsibilities in want of discharge and many different people charged with each of them; if even one forgets his place, things will not go as they ought. Be kind, yes, Fitzwilliam, but at the same time, see that you remember who you are.

If there is any one thing I have ever taught you that is of paramount importance, it is that you must ever and always remember who you are. Remember, not only for the sake of Pemberley, but for your own sake as well. Remember that it will be you, by your actions, who will determine the fate of Pemberley and you who can bring comfort or pain to the countless lives that depend upon her. You are a Darcy of

Pemberley. Do not you forget it and do not let anyone else forget it either."

The conversation did not last long past this point for it had drained a great deal of Mr. Darcy's strength and he was fast growing somnolent. Darcy, as he left the room, was struck by the sudden speed with which his father's condition was deteriorating. He thought of all that had been revealed and all that had happened in the short time since his return from abroad and he was beset by the magnitude of the alteration that had befallen the house of Darcy. He thought of all that had to be done; that *he* now had to do. With each successive item in his mental tally, his respect for his father's unerring command of Pemberley increased and he prayed Providence to guide him as he carried on.

About a week after this conversation with his father, Darcy was in one of the stables, discussing with Mr. Abbot, the progress of the three mares, bred that summer, when a coach was heard entering the court yard. As no visitors were expected Darcy was surprised when he emerged to see that the attendants wore the Fitzwilliam livery. Cousin Rennie alighted and came toward the stables calling, "You never rest, do you Fitz?"

Darcy replied, "I really have not that option, have I?"

"Of course you have. What you do not finish to-day will happily await you to-morrow. I can assure you, on good authority, it will."

"I am afraid I cannot share your confidence that such would be wise."

"No. I should think you could not."

"I am full curious to know to what we owe the honour of this visit?"

"I have come on a mission. I am here to see that you do not so far lose yourself to your duty that you forget you have a life to live. You were once quite pleasant, in spite of yourself, but lately it would seem you… shall we say, need a little encouragement."

"Reynold I cannot like what I am hearing. You speak as though I had chosen the circumstances I now find myself in. What are you thinking?"

Flashing his signature grin Rennie parried, "Cuz you take yourself far too seriously."

Darcy was not amused; perhaps he was a bit more easily riled of late, but he was fast moving from disbelieving irritation to outright resentment and he cared not that his features plainly shewed it. *"Rennie, you are no fool. What can you be playing at?"* he wondered.

Rennie had always been one to push his luck but he was likewise quick to recognize when a limit had been reached so he now deftly steered the conversation into calm waters. "Cuz, I have not come all this way to joust – verbally or otherwise. I have come, as I have said, on a mission. Actually it is really rather a mission of mercy."

At this point he paused to assume a comical look of piety and only when at last he saw Darcy's lip twitch did he continue. "You see, Fitz I cannot like the tone of your recent correspondence. It is become quite stoic so I have taken it upon myself to come and remind you (lest you forget) that one of your duties is to yourself. As you are now, you are far too likely to lose yourself to the needs of Pemberley. If that should happen you would become as big a bore as my brother and that will not do."

"Have you been corresponding with *father*, as well?"

Comprehension not his, Rennie said, "No... I fear that is really most remiss of me, but I have not."

"It quite sounds as if you had."

Now quickly taking up the thread Rennie parried, "Ah, so I am not the only one to have seen what I see." Not able to resist, he added, "I have heard that the greatest minds are oft' like to think in concert."

"Be that as it may, Rennie the fact is, you take an overly simplistic view of things. One that takes not adequately into account the multitudinous responsibilities involved in running an estate. Perhaps if you were destined to inherit your father's estate you would understand."

"I should hope I would understand; understand that an estate needs not only to be run effectively and efficiently but also to be nurtured. Has it occurred to you that just possibly I might be able to see things *more* clearly *because* I am one step removed? Greystone Manor and Pemberley are both models of proper estate management but they cannot always have been such models. They are now, for they are so well established that everyone and everything is in place to allow them to operate as smoothly as day turns into night into day. One would have to consciously work at making things go amiss... or lose one's money till there was nothing left to put back into the estate and really Fitz, I just do not take you for someone in danger of doing either."

"Certainly not."

"Fitz, I see how my father is and I see how my brother is; you well know they are nothing alike. To the point, I see that whilst Greystone flourishes it seems almost to have taken on my father's characteristics just as Pemberley has taken on your father's. They are both nurturing cheerful, restorative places in which to live. I truly believe that will change for Greystone when my brother becomes its master. He has not those qualities in him," smirking he proceeded, "but I cannot change him; he is incorrigible. Besides, an elder brother will never take advice from a younger; no matter that the younger is of superior understanding." Now he did make Darcy laugh but he would not miss a beat. He merely lifted up a brow in feigned surprise and continued, "*You*, I believe, can still be helped and who better to help you than your willing, able and perfectly affable cousin Rennie?"

Again smiling, Darcy could but shake his head for he truly did not know what to make of his cousin's discourse. He wanted to take offense but something told him there was sense and truth in what Rennie said; besides it was difficult to be truly offended by Rennie. It was true; he had been approaching his duties more procedurally than reflectively. Had his own father not said the same thing? And he had thought of little else really, since returning from the continent, but then, was that not to be expected of one who suddenly needed to learn very quickly to shoulder so enormous a responsibility as Pemberley?

"I cannot say I fully agree with your assessment but I will allow there is merit in it."

"That is all I ask. We shall start tonight with some small diversion or other... such as... oh perhaps a ride into town to buy a few rounds at the inn."

"No need. We have spirits aplenty right here. You know that."

Rennie sighed, "Yes I do know that and yes there is a need. My purpose, dear cousin, is not to ply ourselves with spirits, though that might serve a useful purpose, it is to make a small start at getting you out into society."

"A very small start, that. What society can we possibly find at the inn to which we should wish to be known?"

Shaking his head, Rennie replied, "Honestly, Fitz. How do you live when I am not about? You really are very lucky I came when I did for you are much worse than I had imagined; besides, as I have only just arrived, I have not had time to arrange any formal entertainments." Anticipating a parry, he changed course, "Never mind that. I am quite parched from my long journey. Will not you offer some refreshment to a weary traveler?"

"I hardly consider the distance from Greystone to Pemberley a long journey, but of course you may have some refreshment. Let us go in."

"Why thank you. What a very fine host you can be once you set your mind to it."

Darcy lifted up his eyes but he had to chuckle as he led his cousin within.

"How is my uncle?"

"You may well be surprised at the change since last you saw him for truly correspondence cannot adequately describe the alteration. It is all very difficult for him. He grows frustrated when he finds he cannot do as he feels he ought."

"Do they still not know what is to be done for him?"

"Nay, the doctors keep trying various draughts and elixirs but it would seem these do more to appease their consciences than relieve my father's malady. One specialist said he had, some time ago, seen something like, but if truth be told they, none of them, know even what it is, let alone how to go about treating it."

"Uncle's frustration must be great indeed with so many attempts and still no cure."

"Last week, another of the specialists wanted to try bleeding him again but he would not hear of it. He said he did not believe in it; that it seemed always to make him worse rather than better and that whatever blood he had left, he was determined to keep."

Rennie laughed, "That does not sound like Uncle."

"It was not a moment of great diplomacy, I can tell you that, but I cannot say I blame him. This lingering helplessly has been a torment for him. Had father been struck by something that took him quickly, it would have been much better for him."

"But much harder on you and Georgiana."

"Quite true."

"And Georgiana; how does she fare?"

"She is doing as well as can be expected. She is very sad of course but she does not shew it before father and she is resolved to accept with dignity what is inevitable."

"She is a rare treasure. I hope you will look after her well."

"You know I will do my best."

"I am sure you will; I only hope your best is good enough. I have never known you to be anything resembling *jolly* but lately you have grown so completely somber that you must be careful lest you crush her spirit."

Again, Darcy might have wanted to be cross but he could not, for here too he knew there was truth in what his cousin said. Words that would have been caustic spoken by anyone else were not so, coming from Rennie and Darcy replied evenly, "Somehow I think you will be there to check me long before that can happen."

"That I most certainly will!"

Rennie stayed a fortnight complete and arranged entertainments not only for Darcy but for Georgiana and Mr.

Darcy as well. He and Darcy did go into town that night and a few other nights as well; some acquaintances came round for dinners followed by card games with wagers; and of course he and Darcy rode out over the Pemberley lands countless times. On the last of these rides, the day before Rennie was to leave, Darcy brought up the subject of Georgiana, asking whether Rennie had meant what he said about helping to look after her. When he confirmed that he very much had meant it, Darcy offered that Georgiana's care was the one responsibility he was not confident he was yet quite equal to and that having shared with his father some of what Rennie had said they had decided together to ask if Rennie would be agreeable to shared legal guardianship. Rennie was, for the first time Darcy could ever recall, rendered speechless. He was no less than five seconds before replying very seriously, "I would consider that a very great honour."

Somewhere about the middle of his stay, Rennie had taken Georgiana for a spirited drive round the park in a curricle and of course he chose to explore some of the less travelled paths. Had he known then of his future guardianship, the drive *might* have been a bit different than it was, for responsibility *might* have compelled him to be more sober, but that knowledge was not yet his, so it could not interfere as they happily bounced over protruding roots and swung hard round curves. During the drive he advised her that he had waited till Darcy was gone into town for, "Your brother certainly would not approve of my taking you on such a wild ride. He would have insisted that I drive as slowly as a parson making his Sunday rounds."

She could hardly reply for all her giggles but she did manage to say, "I shall not tell." Holding on to her hat she added, "It really is not so very wild a ride, but it is most exhilarating! I thank you." Also during his stay Rennie twice or thrice took her into town and when she had admired material in the draper's window he had bought some for her to have a dress made from it.

Mr Darcy, Rennie regaled with stories of his adventures at Greystone Manor as a child and some of the many harmless pranks he had played on his brother who as he said, seemed to have been born thirty years old. Most of these stories Mr. Darcy had never heard before and finding them thoroughly amusing he wondered that Lord Fitzwilliam had never shared them with him. Rennie gave him to understand that was because, much to his relief, most of his antics had never reached his father's ears. "I owe the preservation of my hide to my pompous elder brother's over large ego. Richly would he have enjoyed seeing father take a switch to my bared bottom, but such entertainment would have come at the price of his having to admit being bested by a younger brother and that just would not do. So you see, much to my advantage and his regret, I early learnt that he valued pride over pleasure."

Rennie recalled too, particular events during the summers he had spent at Pemberley and those Fitz had spent at Greystone Manor.

For the first time in months, laughter found its way into the halls of Pemberley. True to his nature it had been Rennie who recognized the good sense in making his uncle's last days a time of happy memories rather than a solemn wait for the inevitable. When Rennie left, the house grew quiet indeed but he left behind an air of hope and a feeling of comfort and serenity.

Barely a se'nnight after Rennie's departure Mr. Darcy's condition had worsened dramatically. He would not eat at all and both day and night he began to sleep long, long hours at a time. One morning early in November, a glorious sun rose over the hills, but Mr. Darcy rose not.

Just gone five in the morning, Darcy awoke, for he had heard his father's voice call, "Anne." Seated in a chair next the fire in his father's room, Darcy had been keeping watch throughout the night. He could not have been asleep long, for he had heard the clock in the hall strike three quarters. He walked to the bed side to find his father was gone. Having known for months this moment would come, he thought he would be prepared. He was not. He knelt beside the bed, took his father's warm hand in his and cried.

There had been no sorrowful, death bed scene; thankfully, for Mr. Darcy would not have wanted it so. He just fell asleep and quietly went off to find his dear, dear Anne whom he had never stopt loving and never stopt missing.

For Darcy and Georgiana, having watched the progression of their father's illness helped them accept that this was for the best, but of course such understanding did nothing to ease the pain of their loss. They could take solace in the knowledge that their father was now beyond the emotional torment of knowing himself helpless; still that was little comfort when anything arose that they found they would have wished to share with him or consult with him about. Eventually they both began to heal and thought they would never stop loving their father, or missing him, they learnt to live in his absence.

Darcy, having been down this path before, was able to help his sister a great deal. The pain of loss was more than enough to bear, thus he was determined that Geor-

giana's suffering not be compounded by the isolation he
had felt when their mother died. He took great pains to be
ever present for Georgiana during the time it took her to
be whole again; the time it took *them* to be whole again.
Indeed, Georgiana ever after grew misty when her father
entered her thoughts. Even for Darcy it was many, many
months before he could think of his father with complete
equanimity, but death is a strange sort of thing, for those
you love are never truly gone. They remain with you always,
if you chuse to hold them near. For Darcy, the scent of a
wheat field always brought his father near, for how very
many times over the years had they ridden out together
to inspect their lands? A gloriously coloured evening sky
would do it as well, for on those occasions when the sky was
particularly resplendent, his father would stop what he was
about to take in the sight.

It was always this way with his mother's memory as well.
When the delicate scent of wisteria wafted through the windows he could feel his mother's presence for she had so
dearly loved the canopy of lavender flowers hanging from
the trellised vines in her garden and the white flowered
vines that, by now, covered nearly an entire wall of her conservatory. The flowers lasted nary a week so the scent was
fleeting, but each spring Darcy awaited their appearance
and took note. Slight as the fragrance was, he recognized,
as his mother had taught him, the ever so subtle difference
betwixt the fragrances of the two varieties.

No, they were not alone, he and Georgiana. Their parents
would be with them always, though they had now joined all
the shades of Pemberley who looked on proudly from their
portraits in the gallery. From the understanding that they
had been deeply loved and the conviction that they were

an integral part of something much larger than themselves, came the strength to move forward.

Chapter XII

FILLING THE VOID

1790-1793

THE year Mr. Darcy died, Darcy and Georgiana spent Christmas with the Fitzwilliams. Clearly neither of them had any feeling for festivities, but Lord Fitzwilliam would not hear of them spending the Christmas tide alone. Celebrations at Greystone were kept simple and quiet; what mattered was that the family was together. For Georgiana, this time spent with Lady Margaret, who she had always seen as something of a mother, was of great comfort. They talked together, cried together, laughed together and when it was time to leave, Georgiana felt much better able to see her way through her sorrow.

Darcy's discomfiture was borne not only of grief but also of his anxiety to do well in his new role; a role he did not feel quite up to just yet. At this pivotal juncture in his life what better place could he be, and in what better company than with his "brother" cousin Rennie.

During the exceptionally warm month and a half Darcy and Georgiana stayed, Darcy and his cousin took many rides out over the Fitzwilliam lands. During one of these rides they had stopt to water their horses and Rennie asked, "Fitz, do you recall me telling you I was considering a career in the military?"

"I remember it well. I also remember believing it to be far

more than the mere consideration you claimed it to be."

Rennie laughed, "We know each other well, do not we?"

"Very well indeed."

"Then you may easily imagine what I am to say next."

"From your tone it does seem quite obvious, but I shall wait to hear, just the same."

"Very well then. I have purchased a commission in the _th —— Guards. As of the 23rd of March you may call me Colonel Fitzwilliam."

"Rennie I am immensely happy for you and I am ever so proud to call you cousin for I know how seriously you will take your duties."

"Thank you Fitz. It means more than you can know, to hear you say that."

"In March you say; that is not at all far off."

"No, it is not. No time to rethink my decision and find I have made a terrible mistake."

"I dare say you have thought and rethought your decision a thousand times since returning home; nay even whilst we were away, so there can be no chance you acted rashly in seeking your commission."

"You are quite right and I feel very lucky to have got this particular commission. From what I understand, the men are all highly skilled and very professional. From the lowest up, there has not been a disciplinary issue amongst them in the ten years they have served under their present colonel. The regiment is currently quartered in ——shire so I shall not be far from home either."

Darcy said, "I am glad to hear it, for though I am most happy for you, I was beginning to feel a bit sorry for myself."

"How so?"

Shooting his cousin a side long glance, Darcy said, "It has

occurred to me that when my pressures are great, I should sorely miss being cheered by your ready wit and nonsense, but if you are so near, I should think now and again I might see something of you."

"I take it that is meant to be a compliment?"

"The very best kind, Rennie!"

During some of the few spare moments Darcy had had in the weeks immediately following his return from the continent, he had reviewed what correspondence had collected for him at Pemberley since last his mail had been forwarded abroad. Amongst these was one note edged in black, which read as follows:

> *Bingley, West Yorkshire*
> *August 1, 1789*

Dear Sir,

> *It is with unspeakable sorrow that I write to inform you that our dear brother Edmund departed this life, on July —, when the coach in which he was riding overturned in the road.*
>
> *All his family, especially our Papa, wish you to know how very much we appreciate the great kindness and friendship you shewed Edmund whilst up at Cambridge. I can tell you with certainty that he valued your friendship immensely and remembered always the great part you played in his success.*
>
> *With heavy heart and sincere gratitude,*

Louisa Bingley

One can well imagine the shock and melancholy this intelligence visited upon Darcy whose spirits were already so low. He had dispatched a prompt reply and promised himself to seek out the family personally once his own circumstances were more settled. It seemed such a cruel turn of fate this, for Edmund had just spent four long years working uncommonly hard at university and now, when he should begin to enjoy the benefits of his achievement he was dashed from this world.

Seven months had past since Darcy read that letter. His circumstances were very different now from what they had been then and today the post brought another missive.

Bingley, West Yorkshire
March 10, 1790

Dear Sir,

I hope this letter finds you enjoying the most excellent health. I dare say you may find it a very odd sort of letter, for having rejected many drafts of it, I still find it so myself. I am Charles, younger brother to your late friend Edmund. Quite possibly you know little of me, so I beg you will forgive my impertinence in thus applying to you.

As you can well imagine, the shock of my brother's death was such that it threw our family into utter turmoil. My father, it affected most grievously for he was inconsolable. So much so, that in the afternoon of the Epiphany, his broken heart gave out and death visited upon our house once again. Hardly having learnt to accept the passing of our brother we have had to face another great sorrow, the significance of which is twofold for it threatens to topple the house of Bingley.

You see, it was always Edmund who was to follow after Father, never me, and now here am I, in possession of my father's businesses and interests and having not the foggiest notion what is to be done about any of it. So far, everything has been moving forward quite on its own, but I am not so foolhardy as to imagine it can continue so for long. Father devoted his life to building up his business, and ill prepared as I am for the challenge, I must at least make a genuine effort to preserve what he created.

Now I come to the heart of the matter. Edmund credited his success at Cambridge largely to the assistance you afforded him there. He oft' wrote of things that shewed how even whilst at university you had some understanding of how things were done on your estate. I suppose you will think I ask far too much, but I wonder if I too might now impose upon your kindness. If you would but give me some little direction, I should find myself very much in your debt. If it please you to grant me an interview when you are in town, I shall happily go thither and wait upon you when and wherever it might be to your convenience to receive me. I am sir,

Your Humble servant,
Charles Bingley

A month after receipt of this letter, Darcy betook himself to London. There were many reasons why he needed to be there. The season had begun and propriety demanded he make his appearance in town. More importantly, Darcy knew it was time he assume the reins of responsibility in earnest there, just as he had done in Derbyshire even before his father died. To that end he needed to establish a normal routine, whereby announcing to his London staff that though their world might have listed, it had not capsized; that all was indeed well.

Besides, now that Georgiana was beginning to grow into a young lady, Darcy realized he alone could hardly provide the proper environment for her at Pemberley. She needed the benefits of association with other females and the experience of living in town, so he thought it best that he place her in a school for girls. There were many excellent schools in London and having sought recommendations to the very best of these, he would go round, one by one, and determine which he thought the most exemplary establishment.

While it was true that Darcy devoted his life to home and family, he had also himself to consider. His father had advised that he marry, but marriage was not something to be rushed into. So exacting were his standards that it would take a great deal of time and forethought to chuse the ideal woman to take to wife. He was not even sure there existed a woman who embodied all the qualities he required, for not only would she be marrying him, she would become mistress of Pemberley and that was an incredibly demanding responsibility. Lady Evelyn had come very close, but even she would not do, for her lack of pride in home and country was intolerable. Only lately had he come to consider how very little they both truly had in common and what a completely wrong choice she would have been. If indeed one such as he required was to be found, he had not the faintest idea who she might be or when she was ever to be found. All he knew was that he would find her here amongst London society.

In the mean while, his comfort required that some other arrangement be made. Whilst he was in town, he would chuse from amongst his acquaintance, a respectable woman who was to his liking and who was the model of discretion. He would establish an understanding with her and set her up in elegant lodgings in a fashionable part of town. It would be a contractual agreement, like any other business arrangement; nothing more, nothing less.

Then there was Bingley's younger brother. From what Darcy remembered hearing Edmund say of his brother, it would take an exorbitant amount of teaching to bring Charles to a level where he could successfully run a business and clearly Darcy did not need a wayward gosling running about underfoot at this particular time in his life. Still, he felt he owed it to Edmund to do what he could to set the man on the right path. He would grant Charles the interview he requested, offer what advice he could and send him on his way.

"Jackson, I will be visiting with an acquaintance at the Heart and Crown for the afternoon and will return in time for supper. Please tell Mrs. Davis she need only prepare something light."

"Very good sir."

Taking the hat, gloves and walking stick Jackson held out for him, Darcy stepped, at a brisk pace, from his London townhouse and out to his waiting carriage. Asking after Bingley at the Inn, Darcy, rather than being shewn to the gentleman's private rooms, was directed into the tap room.

"The tap room?" he inquired.

"Yes sir. The gentleman is there now and he is expecting you."

As the publican led him within, Darcy thought, *"Edmund, how very different must your brother be than were you. Can he truly mean to discuss matters of business in a public tap room?"*

It was in general a noisy place but above the usual din could be easily discerned a group of gentlemen who were talking and laughing heartily at a table near the back of the establishment. Darcy noticed that midmost of the assembly was a young man, slim in stature, whose wavy, sand coloured hair and broad grin gave him a decidedly boyish appearance. He spoke and gestured in a most animated fashion and it would seem he alone was the party's source of divertissement. Darcy was being led in the general direction of this party so it was easy to watch the spectacle. He found that against his better judgment, his attention was quite arrested for he was much impressed by the easy manner in which the young man expressed himself; when they neared his table he was regaling the group with the account of his recent dealings with a tailor, in which every imaginable mishap had occurred. The subject of conversation was hardly of any particular interest but the manner in which the gentleman told his story was excessively diverting. To Darcy's great surprise and no little affront, it was to this boisterous group that he was led.

"Mr. Bingley, sir," said the publican, "the gentleman you await has arrived."

The jovial story teller fairly leapt from his seat, made a proper bow and said with much enthusiasm, "Mr. Darcy, sir. Thank you so very much for coming. I cannot begin to tell you how grateful I am." Much to the disappointment of the others at table, he quickly excused himself and made to shew Darcy up to his rooms.

On the way he explained, "I have never lived alone and probably never could because I feel a constant need for society. I tell you I was at sixes and sevens, awaiting the hour of our meeting. Finally I had to bring myself down to the taproom in search of company."

Darcy began a mental tally of this man's faults: *"impropriety; impulsivity…"*

So much did this young Bingley fellow talk that within twenty minutes of their reaching his rooms Darcy had already learnt that Louisa had just accepted a proposal from the brother of one of her school friends and was engaged to be married, after which she would be coming to live in London, and Bingley's other sister, Caroline, had begun at once to mourn the impending loss of Louisa's society.

He had also learnt how Edmund's accident had come about. The heavy rains of the prior spring had made the roads in the North almost impassible. Edmund had been travelling home from London and he was already to West Yorkshire, just shy of the Bingley sign post, when a part of the road gave way under his coach.

Bingley exclaimed that he could not ever have imagined how severe an affect Edmund's passing would have had on their father but the poor man had, for the rest of his life, walked about in a daze; as if half dead himself. He had so much vested in preparing Edmund to follow after him, but more than that, he missed Edmund's society, for father and son were as similar as two people could possibly be. The father's response was certainly well within the scope of Darcy's imagination; it was in fact most uncomfortably familiar for it sounded very like his own father's reaction when Darcy's mother had died.

Charles also explained that as second son, he had always been allowed to indulge his every whim; that all his father had ever asked of him was that he mind his manners and his tutor so he would not grow up to be an embarrassment to his family.

Finally Bingley had come round to discussing his father's businesses. It seemed that not only had his father purchased two cotton mills over the years, he had eventually purchased the coal mine that supplied his mills and since it produced far more than their mills required, there was profit to be had there as well.

Bingley went on to say, "My father was always looking to the future. The Bingley family has long been well respected in the north but it was Father's greatest wish to use the profits from his mills to raise the standing of our family even outside our part of the world. When my brother died, Father believed all his hard work and dreams would come to naught, for you see, I haven't much head for business. I am more naturally suited to enjoying the fruits of one's labour than actually taking part in the labour." Bingley had the grace to colour when he said this last. "When Father realized he would not live to see his dream complete, he charged me on my honour, to do whatever it took to carry forward his wishes.

I am trying hard to understand what goes forward in Father's businesses but I am having a devilishly hard time of it. Still, I am determined not to fritter away what he created if ever I can help it, so here am I, come to London to try to learn what I am about. Then perhaps someday I will be able to join society and convince some fashionable club to have me as a member. All this, of course would be done with an eye toward raising myself up so that I might purchase an estate and establish the house of Bingley; my father's house of Bingley."

"*Great heavens,*" thought Darcy, "*this man's candor must be checked or he will surely find himself cast out by the very people he wishes to become associated with.*" Though Darcy had lived in the world, never had he met with anyone so wholly unguarded. "*Impetuosity seems clearly a fault as well.*" he observed for at that moment a thought popped into Bingley's head and he of a sudden exclaimed, "Possibly I ask too much, but I wonder if I might beg an introduction to your tailor? I am very much in need of assistance on that score. To tell truth, I am in need of assistance on any number of scores, but I must admit, as I sit here I am struck by the impeccable cut of your clothes."

Though completely taken aback by Bingley's forward line of address Darcy found he really could not be affronted. The more he watched and listened, the more he realized that Bingley's nature was too guileless to cause offense. Darcy observed, "*He is so open, so genuine and unaffected. It is clear this man is every bit what he appears to be. Seldom does one come across anyone like this; especially amongst the quality.*" Recollecting himself, Darcy replied, "I use Josephson's in Cork Street and I shall be glad to send round a note advising him to expect you."

"I thank you most sincerely."

Darcy said, "When I arrived I did overhear part of the rendition of your tailoring disaster."

With a bashful grin, Bingley returned, "As you know little of me, you may well doubt the veracity of so ridiculous a tale. My father used to say he often wondered when I spoke, how much was real and how much imagined, but I tell you, my stories are complete truth."

"I can quite believe that." Darcy replied, for he was then thinking, *"Somehow I sense a falsehood would be foreign to your nature."*

Laughing, Bingley said, "Edmund was never so good at telling a story till he went up. The stories he wrote to us from Cambridge made it seem such a very diverting place. You probably are unaware of how often Edmund's friends (especially you and your cousin) figured into his stories but you did. Wasn't there once a good joke about your cousin and a lecture on Locke."

Darcy laughed and said, "Diverting is hardly an adjective that comes to mind when I think of Cambridge but yes there was a very good joke about Rennie and he is to this day pleased with how it went off. Rennie and George, a connection of ours, took their lectures in philosophy with Lynam, the Fellow on whose side we had all been entered. On the occasions when George actually deigned to attend lecture, he generally came ill prepared and often applied to Rennie for assistance.

On that particular day, I suppose Rennie's patience had worn thin. Lynam was quizzing the students regarding the lecture which he had given on the previous day. He asked George to explain the theory of tabula rasa. When George applied to Rennie to shew him his notes, Rennie opened his book and placed it before George, who confidently announced that it was the concept that upward buoyant force exerted on a body immersed in fluid is equal to the weight of the fluid that has been displaced.

The room erupted in laughter and when Lynam could again be heard, he said, 'Sir, that is Archimede's principle and it is a *law* of physics, not a concept. *This*; however is not a lecture in physics.'

Someone else then correctly explained, 'Tabula rasa is the theory that when we are born, our minds are blank and all knowledge comes from experience and learning.'

Lynam said quietly, 'For some, *blank* does the mind remain.' Again the room filled with laughter. George did not speak to Rennie for upwards of two months."

After at least an half hour more of easy and companionable conversation, Darcy realized that in spite of his many misgivings, he had found Charles Bingley to be a genuinely pleasant and agreeable fellow. Darcy still had no idea what to make of this singular man, but somehow he felt instinctively that he could come to value his society very highly. He asked, "How long do you plan to remain in town?"

"I had thought to return home in a month's time, but I have no specific plan at present." Chuckling, he added, "I seldom ever do have any specific plan."

Darcy pursed his lips but managed to suppress his disapproval, "Have you many friends here?"

"Not a one. I have spent all my days in the north so I know no one in London."

"In such a case as that I should imagine one can feel very alone amongst all the people in town." Something deep within (almost against his will) directed him to add, "If you would like, you are more than welcome to stay with me whilst you are here."

Surprise writ large upon Bingley's face, he said, "That is a very generous offer, Mr. Darcy, but I am sure I would be in your way? I should not wish to be a bother to you."

"You would be no bother at all. There is space enough to accommodate any guests I should wish to invite."

"If that is the case, I would be very glad indeed to accept your offer."

It was decided that Bingley would quit his lodgings and join Darcy the very next day. Riding home, Darcy reflected on how easily he and Bingley had conversed. To speak with someone he did not know was no less a trial for Darcy now than when a child, yet somehow, this man whom he had never seen before to-day had him talking as easily as if they had been acquainted for years... then actually to have offered up his home to the man! He was still perplexed as he entered his townhouse.

Jackson relieved him of hat, gloves and stick, inquiring, "When should you like to take supper sir?"

"I think eight will be fine, Jackson. Thank you. I shall be in the library till then." As he started for the stairs he added, "Oh and please see that a room is prepared; a guest shall be joining me in the morrow."

"Very good sir."

Darcy had planned on spending the evening writing the letter he owed to his sister and now he would have an interesting new development to add to it.

Over the next fortnight, Darcy and Bingley tended to their own separate affairs but they dined and supped together often, with much of the conversation devoted to Bingley's business arrangements and future plans. Darcy took Bingley round to Josephson's, where on their arrival, Fraser, a friend of Darcy's happened to be just leaving. Fraser had been at university with Darcy and Edmund. Having known Edmund well, he was saddened to hear of his passing and was more than happy to extend to the younger brother, the invitation to a dinner party he was hosting the following week.

On the night of that gathering, Bingley had not been able to sit still in Darcy's coach. When they entered the Fraser townhouse and Bingley considered where he was, he looked very much like a child who had just received the gift of his heart's desire. Nearly all in attendance were known to Darcy, but not a one was known to Bingley. After a time Darcy became engaged in a rather lengthy discussion of a new tax that some in Parliament wished to propose and Bingley took the opportunity to begin moving about on his own. He conversed and laughed as if these were his own lifelong best friends.

When Darcy noticed Bingley's absence, he scanned the room with concern, convinced he should be required to extricate his friend from some socially awkward situation. On spotting Bingley in the centre of a lively group, Darcy feared those with Charles might be laughing at him rather than with him. Continuing to watch, Darcy saw that Bingley's comments were being accepted with enthusiasm and what looked to be genuine interest.

As he moved about the room, Bingley mingled easily, bringing with him a constant air of fellowship and good cheer. Every so often Darcy would look round to check on Bingley, till he realized Bingley was quite capable of conducting himself appropriately in this environment, new though it was to him.

At table, Darcy was seated near enough to observe how much admired Bingley was by the ladies, for though he spoke with everyone, throughout all the courses of the meal he was engaged in a constant chatter with the ladies either side of him and one across as well. When the gentlemen had retired to the library after dinner a friend of Fraser's named Stevens approached Darcy and Bingley, and addressed Bingley thusly, "I have heard you are in the textile industry. Is my intelligence correct?"

Darcy stiffened for he feared the man might find fault with Bingley for being involved in trade.

Bingley replied, "Yes sir. It is quite correct. I have lately inherited my father's cotton mills."

"May I ask where you get your cotton?"

"To speak truth, I do not yet know the whole of it, but some comes from the West Indies and some from America."

"Do you happen to know if it is the long staple cotton you are importing from America, sir?"

Charles replied, "It is. That much I can tell you with certainty for I recall hearing my father speak of it more than once. He called it Sea Island cotton and spoke highly of its fine texture. I never knew what a long staple was but I knew it must be something good."

Laughing, Stevens said, "Quite so. Long staple cotton is the very best kind to be had. That is why *I* have chosen to grow it exclusively. I own large holdings of land on the Sea Islands off South Carolina which produce great quantities of just that cotton. If you are agreeable, one day soon I should be very much interested in meeting with you and whomever you have to run your business. Possibly we can be of mutual benefit to each other." Reaching into his watch pocket, he asked, "Would you be so kind as to accept my calling card?"

Happily complying, Bingley exclaimed, "Why certainly, sir!"

Stevens said, "And I should very much like to have yours."

"Of course, sir. Here it is."

Later, Darcy told Bingley that while he had not been in touch with Stevens in quite some time and had not known of his land holdings, he had known him well at Cambridge and personally knew him to be a man of high moral character. Still, he advised Bingley, "Be ever cautious in your business dealings, for not every arrangement you are offered will necessarily be in *your* best interest. Until you know what you are about, and even after, it is best to have the man who runs your business verify that whatever price you are offered is a fair market price and that whatever terms you are offered are beneficial to you."

Bingley had made a connection that would prove most valuable in the coming years. In fact, he met with a number of gentlemen that evening who had known Edmund well and had thought highly enough of him to now readily offer their friendship and assistance to Charles.

Throughout the night, Charles' easy manners continued to astound Darcy. He even saw two gentlemen join a group with which Bingley was conversing, simply to convince him to be of their party for a game of Hazard once the gentlemen rejoined the ladies in the drawing room.

It was very late when the party finally came to an end but Bingley seemed to have just as much energy then as when he had arrived and he had much to speak of during the short ride home. "This night has made me feel it possible for me to keep from shaming the Bingley name after all. I had rather thought I would not be able to live up to everything that is suddenly expected of me, but now I see that I *may* actually have a chance and I owe it all to you."

"I believe you are affording me far too much credit. It is you who has proven yourself worthy of regard."

"That may be, but Darcy, you are the one who has made it

possible. I would not have known how to behave in society if not for your instruction, nor would I have had the chance to attempt it if not for your introduction."

"All I will take credit for is chancing to have been the source of your introduction. Bingley, you come from a respectable family. *Clearly* you have been taught how to conduct yourself properly, so there is no reason why you should not be able to gain acceptance into society."

"I am not nearly so inclined as you to see my acceptance as a certainty, but I am incredibly pleased with how things have gone thus far and despite your protestations I credit any success I have had largely to your example. You probably do not know it, but these past weeks, I have been observing how you conduct yourself and it has been most instructive. For that I am immensely grateful."

Later that same week, the gentlemen found themselves attending a ball. As far as Bingley was concerned, the only reason to attend a ball was to dance. He was not about to stand round talking and observing, thus it was inevitable that he should here too strike out on his own. Nevertheless, every so often he would find his way round to where Darcy was, for he realized it was, after all, through Darcy that he was here at all. On one such occasion Bingley announced, "This is the most pleasurable evening I have had in… possibly ever. There are so many beautiful ladies here, and they are all so amiable that I am always at a loss to know which to dance with next."

"Then your standards are not very exacting Bingley?"

Laughing, Bingley replied, "Whatever do you mean, Darcy?"

"I mean simply that there are here, in my estimation, no more than five or six who truly deserve the appellation of

beautiful. Besides, you must know with whom you are dancing, for once you ask a lady to dance, immediately she begins
to imagine your interest goes far beyond that one dance. If
it does not, you can find yourself in a most awkward situation."

"But I have seen *you* dance tonight. Have you really been
so calculating in your choice of partner?"

"Indeed I have. I have asked but two ladies to dance thus
far and may or may not ask a third. The first, in addition to
her beauty and grace, is the daughter of an Earl and known
to be of the highest moral character; the second, though not
of noble birth, is of an ancient and well respected family.
She is good natured and has a lively disposition. The third,
if indeed I should chuse to ask her, has beauty and grace, yes;
she has also a cultivated mind, though not the advantage of
such very high birth."

"Darcy, you are incredibly fastidious. I, on the other
hand, am not nearly so hard to please. Why, it may very
well be that I am in love already."

"Bingley, when one has the interests of a large estate to
consider, one needs be fastidious."

"If that is so, I am grateful I have *not* so large and important an estate to consider. There is one lady… just there,
whom I have danced with twice already. Is she not a beautiful creature?"

"I will allow she is quite pretty, yes, but Bingley have a
care; if you dance with her a third time, not only will *she*
have expectations, so will everyone else of the assembly. In
this, as in all things, you must know what lies beyond the
paling before you take the jump."

Looking terribly wounded, Bingley acquiesced, "I suppose I can see your point…" Then looking about, it quickly

occurred to him, "…yet there are many others with whom I have danced but once or not at all." Just as quickly he was off in search of a new partner for the next set.

There were so many guests in attendance that supper was served in the picture gallery, where a number of long tables had been set up for the evening. Throughout the meal there was far more chatter and laughter at Bingley's table than anywhere else in the room. So noticeable was it that at one point, the host exclaimed he felt slighted not to be a part of it all and came over to see what could be the cause of so much levity. When everyone was leaving Bingley received many assurances that his name would be added to the guest lists for future entertainments. The ball had lasted till nearly four in the morning and again Bingley shewed little sign of fatigue at its end. In fact, he expressed great surprise when the orchestra stopt playing and no little disappointment that the dancing had not lasted longer.

Next morning, whilst the gentlemen were breaking their fast, Bingley of course wished to extend the enjoyment of the ball by talking of it at great length. As they spoke, Bingley's mirth and exuberance were such that Darcy was unable to refrain from putting forward the question that had puzzled him since their first meeting. "Bingley, forgive me, but I feel I must ask how it is that you can go on in such a happy manner when you have so lately lost two so near to you?"

Bingley may have been surprised by the question, or he may not, but he did not miss a beat in issuing his reply. "True my father and brother are gone and the fact that I shall never see or speak with either of them again is a very great loss to me, but *I* still live. Neither of them would want me to stop living because they have. Besides, it is not in my nature to be melancholy; that is what killed my father. In a way, it is as if I must now live for *them* as well as for myself; especially for Edmund, who had lived so little of life."

Such serious contemplation did this reasoning elicit, that Darcy could not immediately respond, then slowly and quietly he said, "That is a unique point of view; one that never would have occurred to me."

With a sad little smile, Bingley replied, "Nor would it have occurred to Edmund. He and I were nothing alike so it is rather surprising that we were always very close. Where I have always looked for pleasure in life, he was always the sober one... much like you actually. Just the same, I cannot remember a time when we did not get on very well together.

Do not suppose I do not miss them. Not a day goes by but there is something I would wish to share with one or other of them... sometimes both... but for whatever reason, Providence chose to take them and leave my sisters and me to muddle through on our own. I cannot change my past, but I can direct my present."

Darcy now reflected on his own grief and on how it was influencing his actions; he thought too of his sister and of what effect his sorrow might have on her. To Darcy's immense surprise, he had to acknowledge there was great wisdom in the words of this buoyant man who seemed not to have a serious bone in his body.

In the end, Bingley stayed on in town for two months complete, enjoying everything London had to offer. After that he and Darcy began an earnest correspondence; Bingley's letters often raising new questions or concerns about his business; Darcy drawing on his own experience to offer advice. Louisa's marriage took place in the autumn of that year and Charles, in his next letter, gave a rather detailed description of the festivities, adding that he had never in his life heard so much noise and commotion as in the weeks preceding the nuptials. He was as happy for Louisa as she was herself, to be Mrs. Hurst. He wished her well indeed; still if truth be told, once the day had come and gone he had been much disappointed with the sudden and complete return of quiet in the Bingley household. It seemed Louisa and her new husband had taken all the life with them when they went away to London. Even at so great a distance, Bingley could make Darcy laugh.

These most unlikely of friends did not meet again until the following year when Louisa had her sister and brother to spend the season with her in town. With Georgiana now living at school, Pemberley had become a rather lonely place, which made it much easier for Darcy to carry himself off to town. When he brought Georgiana back to London after Easter he had remained in town himself and save for short trips home to tend to business affairs, he planned to spend the entire season in town. Within days of his arrival, he received an invitation to dine at the Hursts' townhouse. When he read it, the thought occurred to him that he quite looked forward to seeing Charles again; this very much amused him for he still could see nothing they had in common. He would also, for the first time, have the opportunity of meeting the rest of Charles' family.

Arriving for the dinner, Darcy was greeted by Charles who came out to meet him on the door step.

"Darcy! It is really good to see you again!"

"And you, Bingley." Darcy heartily returned the greeting whilst making a mental note to explain to Charles that it is proper to wait inside and let one's guests be shewn in to you.

Charles said, "My sisters have been most anxious to know you Darcy. At last they may put a face to the name which they have heard so many times over the years."

Introductions were made quickly and the party moved into a bright, cheerfully decorated drawing room. Louisa explained how her husband had inherited the townhouse from his father and how they had just redone all the decoration and furnishings to suit their own taste. Darcy expressed his appreciation for the quiet sophistication of the design. Thus complimented, Louisa giggled much like a school girl, "I am flattered indeed Mr. Darcy for I have heard *your* home is beyond compare."

"I am sure it is not that. I am very proud of my home but there are many others more worthy of such praise as you offer."

"I wonder?" Bingley mused. "When Edmund recounted his visit to Pemberley, he said it was clear Henry VIII had never seen or heard of it for surely he would have taken it for his own."

Darcy laughed, but he was most flattered.

Caroline, who had been silently observing their guest throughout this conversation now asked, "Is yours one of the great houses that is open to visitors in summer? Possibly the Bingley family can plan a trip to the peaks next summer to see it for ourselves."

Darcy could not like the subterfuge, transparent though it was, but he allowed that politeness must have prevented Caroline from being more direct and in the end her query had precisely the desired effect for Darcy replied, "There is indeed a section which opens to tourists, but surely you would do me the honour of coming as my guests."

A frisson of excitement gripped the sisters as they said in

unison, "Oh Mr. Darcy!"

Louisa added, "That would be ever so gracious of you."

Caroline held that she could not imagine anything so wonderful.

Darcy replied, "Then so it shall be; perhaps in August, after the season is over. Hurst, do you shoot?"

"As I am rarely in the country, I have not much chance to practice, but I am a fairly decent shot."

"Very well then; it is settled. My cook knows any number of excellent ways to prepare grouse; Hurst, Bingley, you will have to do your part to supply her."

"Excellent." cried Hurst. "I long for a well done dish of Red Grouse."

"What a perfect plan." chimed in Bingley. "On behalf of us all, I thank you kindly."

Almost as if on cue, when the conversation came round to food, the butler entered the room to announce that dinner was ready. The table had been set in the breakfast parlour, for their party was small and as they were an odd number, the round table in there would suit very well. At dinner, the conversation continued just as cheerfully with talk of life growing up at Pemberley and at the Bingley family home. Darcy spoke of Georgiana in such glowing terms that one might have thought her his daughter rather than his sister.

It was well into the evening when Darcy's carriage was finally called for; he rode home with a happy sense that his circle of friends had just expanded. Bingley's sisters were educated and polished; Hurst seemed a pleasant enough sort of fellow; and with Bingley's happy manners he had been as agreeable as ever. It would not be a chore for Darcy to spend time in the company of people such as these. In fact, he rather thought he should enjoy their society. That autumn the Bingley family visited Pemberley for a month complete, cementing the bond that had begun that summer day in London.

Darcy and Bingley took many rides out over the Pemberley lands, during which they discussed all manner of topics; business, current events, family, aspirations and whatever else struck them as relevant at the time. The more they spoke, the more they found they had in common. During one of these rides, they heard hoof beats cantering up behind them. Upon their looking round, the rider called, "Afternoon gentlemen."

As the man came along side them, Darcy greeted him, "Tenor, how are you getting along?"

"Oh, very well sir; I thank you." Gesturing confidently he continued, "The fields beyond that stand of elms are ready and will be harvested within the week."

"Glad to hear it, and how about you? Are you settled and well familiar with the estate?"

"Mostly sir. It wants some time to learn the whole of it, but no matter. Now and again I take a wrong turn, but hardly ever anymore."

"Excellent." Darcy replied. "I have no doubt you shall do well. If you want for anything, do not hesitate to ask Mr. Cooper or me."

"Thank you kindly, sir. I appreciate that. I have been well supplied already and can want for nothing more." At Darcy's nod Tenor concluded, "I had best get back to work. Good day to you, sir."

Darcy returned the civility and Tenor rode off.

Bingley, who had been observing the scene, now questioned Darcy about this obviously new employee.

"He is my new overseer." Darcy explained that Cooper,

had lately been raised to steward, following the death of the
elder Mr. Wickham and Cooper had recommended Tenor
to take his place. "The recommendations of an exceptional
employee," he advised, "are invaluable and this one has
proven particularly so."

In the spring of 1792 Darcy travelled north, to the Yorkshires
to see the Bingley mills and mine. During his stay, Charles'
had requested Darcy look over the financial side of the operation and he had been able to make some useful suggestions.
He shewed Charles, how recording credits differently would
make it much easier to quickly identify payments that had
not come in or that had been made for an incorrect amount.
Additionally he recommended renegotiating a couple of the
contracts for raw materials, the terms of which were heavily
weighted in favor of the supplier.

That summer, the friends met often in town. Darcy introduced Georgiana to the Bingleys and soon after, she was
invited to take tea at the Hursts' with Louisa and Caroline.
She was later invited to dine of a Saturday when she had no
lessons to attend; then the sisters, one afternoon, took her
shopping at the drapers and mantua maker's shoppes.

Whilst the Bingley sisters entertained Georgiana, Bingley himself, took advantage of every possible opportunity to
learn from Darcy's experience. During the course of the season he came to depend more and more upon Darcy's judgment. By no means was Bingley deficient; he was simply inexperienced and it satisfied Darcy to feel he could help Bingley meet his potential. So easy did they all become in each
other's company that by summer's end, Darcy had come to

regard the Bingleys with something nearly akin to a familial attachment.

Charles and Caroline went again to stay with Louisa at Christmas. Drawn to London's steady flow of divertissements, they had arrived in early November. As Darcy would not be travelling home till St. Nicholas' Day, he was still in town at the start of December and happened to be visiting at the Hurst's when Bingley discovered what he considered to be the most excellent news. Perusing the adverts in the morning paper he said, "Darcy, it says here the Prince of Wales is to sell all his horses."

"Again? I believe he has done so once before."

"Evidently he is doing it again for there is to be a sale by auction on Monday the 10th of December. It says here, 'All the STALLIONS, MARES, COLTS, FILLIES, Horses in training &c.' are to be sold by Messrs. Tattersalls."

Chuckling, Darcy commented, "The Prince has been most instrumental in swelling 'Old Tatt's bank account over the years. It will be a great disappointment to him if this is truly the end of it."

Bingley offered, "I have been wanting to buy one or two really good horses; can you imagine me owning one of the Princes horses?"

"That is not so very hard to imagine. If you have the funds, you may purchase what you will; but do not be overly impressed by the source of these horses. I have heard the Prince does not have any stock of great value… Bingley, I do not suppose you are planning to enter upon the Turf. Are you?"

Laughing quietly, Bingley replied, "Hardly that! At least, not at present; I should barely know where to begin."

Darcy gave a side-long glance but leaving well enough alone, did not address that particular comment. "For what purpose exactly do you wish these horses?"

"What I should most like at present is a spirited horse, good for rides in the country and for hunts. If truth be told, our entire stable is rather a sad collection of misfits. You see, my father never would spend a farthing if he did not absolutely need to."

"That is not an unsound principle, but perhaps his idea of need was not the same as yours."

"In this matter at least, it was far different. To him, if a horse could support a reasonable weight for a reasonable distance, that horse was good enough, but I should like to be able to get some enjoyment from a ride. I certainly do not hold myself out to be any sort of accomplished rider, but I am not bad."

"From what you say, I would strongly advise against considering the Prince's horses for I should think them poorly suited to your purpose."

"But it would be quite the thing, would not it? Just imagine a Bingley owning a Royal horse."

"Or rather, a horse that happens to have once belonged to a Royal. I should sooner hope to see this particular Bingley acknowledged for his achievements than for his possessions." With Bingley looking rather like a child who had just received a set down, Darcy changed course. Indicating the paper, he asked "May I see that?"

Perusing a full column of entries he said, "If it is a hunter you are after, might I suggest this second listing; there are a number of hunters included here." Continuing down the column, he commented, "The one following simply states, 'Five capital, well managed...' so I rather doubt they are hunters; the fourth, again includes a hunter; the two next are likely turf prospects somehow connected with 'Old Tatt' himself, for I recognize some of the names..."

"Deciding will be quite a daunting task for I haven't any experience in choosing a horse. I would not know how to judge."

"Despite what you say of your father, he must have needed to buy a horse or two at some point. Did you never go with him?"

Shaking his head, Bingley replied, "Edmund always went with father, not I." Then a recollection came to him. "There was one time when Father and Edmund had to go off to a farm to see about buying some plough horses. Mother and my sisters were away visiting my aunt and Father knew not what to do with me so he packed me up and took me along. I suppose I was about six or eight at the time and I spent the whole of the afternoon up a tree with the farmer's son, picking and eating plums, which by the bye were incredibly sweet. All I learnt from that experience is that plums are to be eaten in moderation."

Darcy laughed heartily.

Reflecting, Bingley commented, "You must think me quite hopeless."

"Not in the least; if I did so, I should hardly pay you any mind; I have neither the time nor the patience to suffer fools. Bingley, though you have only lately become master of your own circumstances, already you have done much to alleviate your weaknesses."

"And many there are."

"You are making the effort and you are learning, but you

want time."

Bingley gave a mischievous little smile and replied, "I am glad to hear you do not consider me a fool." Darcy opened his mouth, but did not reply and Bingley continued, "Do you think I might impose upon you to attend the auction with me?"

"If you are set on attending the auction for the Prince's horses, I cannot attend, for I shall already be in Derbyshire for the Christmas by then, but if any of the others, I will happily join you for *they* are all to be held Monday next; Georgiana and I travel to Derbyshire Tuesday morning."

"I would appreciate that very much indeed. I *may* go on the 10th, if even just to know I was a part of it, for I admit I still rather fancy the idea of owning one of the Prince's horses, but as you say, the horses to be auctioned Monday next are far better suited to my requirements."

"I am glad to hear you say so."

Consequently, on the morning of December 3rd, a curricle bearing the Darcy crest departed the Hurst townhouse, conveying its owner and one very excited passenger to Hyde Park turnpike.

"The Corner" and its environs were alive with activity. Entering through the arched passage, the inclined drive gave the gentlemen an unobstructed view of the sea of humanity that was Tattersalls on a sale day. Looking about, Bingley said, "This is incredible. You cannot even begin to count the people."

"The same scene is repeated every Monday and Thursday."

"I cannot believe it. This far surpasses my wildest imaginings."

"Making their way slowly through the crowd they came at

last to the bottom of the drive, Darcy motioned ahead, "The Turf Tavern is just there. Perhaps when we are through we can go in to quench our thirst."

"I should enjoy that very much."

Darcy directed Bingley through a covered gateway on the right, which led into a large courtyard, and gave him to know the far end was where the auctions took place. Finding a groom who was not engaged, Darcy asked to be shewn any hunters.

"Yes sir. Right this way, if you please, sir."

Waving his outstretched hand, the groom led them along under the covered 'way' that ran round three sides of the courtyard. Coming upon a certain group of stalls, he said, "There are these five here sir and another round the other side that are to go today; then there is another pair I can shew you, but terms are not yet decided for those." As he spoke, he unlatched a stall door and swung it wide. Gathering up the bridle, he easily led the docile horse out. "This one be a mare." he said. Which of you be it for?"

Bingley replied, "It is for me but I rely on the advice of this gentlemen, my friend."

Darcy asked, "How old is she?"

"Eight year old, sir."

Darcy said to Bingley, "That is a good age; old enough to be calm, but not so old that she will not want to exert herself."

"And what do you know of her history?" Darcy asked the boy.

"These five belonged to a gentleman in Oxfordshire who is lately gone abroad."

"Did he ride much?"

"I cannot rightly say, sir."

Darcy began to inspect the horse, explaining his method to Bingley as he did so. "Her proportions are good; they are well balanced and her feet are a good size so they should easily hold her weight and yours. She has an ample girth which is good for if you were to sit atop a narrow horse, your legs would hang straight down and you would not look well at all."

Next he looked for temperament saying, "Bingley, as *you* tend to be a bit, shall we say, exuberant you will want to chuse a calm horse." He asked the groom to go round the horse lifting each of her feet so he could see their condition. Whilst this was being done he quietly said to Bingley, "Notice how readily the boy does this. If he were leery of the horse he would not have been so quick to oblige; and see how she lets her feet be lifted? If she were skittish, she would not so easily allow of that. You do not want a skittish horse, Bingley." After this, standing where the horse could not see him, Darcy made a loud noise and the horse calmly turned her head and looked at him as if to say, "May I help you?" Both Darcy and Bingley laughed and Darcy said, "She may be calm but she has a personality." Finally he had the groom walk her about a bit then trot round the domed pump house in the centre of the courtyard.

One by one the groom brought the horses forward for inspection. Some Darcy thought too spirited; one he thought too old; and one he suspected would develop trouble in one eye. In the end he would recommend but two horses from the whole of the three lots for Bingley to bid on. So much time did Darcy devote to carefully examining each horse that when the task was complete there was but half an hour left before the start of the auction.

Bingley went home a very happy man that day for he had

become the proud owner of a very fine hunter. He told Darcy that once the horse was delivered, the north should not seem so much less appealing than town, for then he should be able to go for excellent rides as often as he pleased.

By the following spring Bingley knew not how he had survived before he had bought his new horse. So exhilarating was it to go for long, hard rides through the local environs that life had grown infinitely better; better, *yes* but not quite good enough. Much to his surprise and tremendous disappointment, the horse had not added *enough* of excitement to life in the north for Bingley's taste. He still longed for proximity to the exhilaration of town and he began in earnest to look for a country house that was within an easy day's travel of London; less if possible. He was sure if it were so thrilling to race about the countryside in the north, it would be that much more thrilling to race about countryside that lay but a few easy miles of good road from London.

Chapter XIII

TREACHERY

1793

IN the library of Darcy's London townhouse, he and the now Colonel Fitzwilliam sat drinking port, having just partaken of their evening meal. The Colonel stretched and sighed deeply, "As usual, that was a fine supper. I can safely say that despite your less than hospitable manners, the superb achievements of your excellent cook shall continue to assure you the pleasure of your dear cousin's company whenever the Regiment should require my presence in town."

"Capital!" Darcy mocked.

"Quite so! Now that I think of it, your Pemberley cook is really quite accomplished as well and since we are quartered so near Derbyshire, I am close enough to offer you the privilege of entertaining me wherever you should happen to be residing."

"I might have been more inclined to be hospitable had you not caused me a day's delay in leaving for Pemberley. You know how anxious I am to be home."

With a goodly portion of sarcasm in his voice and a decided twinkle in his eye, Colonel Fitzwilliam replied, "I am *that* sorry Cuz, but I had a most pressing matter of business to attend last evening."

Matching his cousin's sarcasm, Darcy replied, "Please do

advise which tailor was so very anxious to produce new shirts for your men, that he was willing to consult with you in the evening?"

Most casually, Colonel Fitzwilliam corrected, "No no; the tailor was in the morning. I had another matter; one of most pressing urgency indeed that required my attention last evening."

"And nearly the whole of the day today as well, I presume. When was it you arrived? Not till two, I believe."

"Yes well. You know how it is. One's pleasures come always at a cost; it was rather difficult to lift my weary pate this morn."

"And of course you saw fit to put pleasure before obligation."

With a mischievous smile, Colonel Fitzwilliam laughed, "When opportunity knocked, it would have been quite impolite of me not to answer, and I dare say you would not have me act in an ungentlemanlike manner now would you Fitz?"

Darcy merely sighed.

Taking a different direction Colonel Fitzwilliam admonished, "Really Fitz, what can you possibly have awaiting you at Pemberley that a day or two's delay could materially affect? Your presence cannot be nearly so vital as you believe, for your steward is probably the best in the Realm; better than Dear Ol' Georgie's, I dare say."

"It is not the operation of the Pemberley estate which concerns me at present; it is the running of Pemberley House." Quite ready to refute this argument as well, Colonel Fitzwilliam could but part his lips before Darcy silenced him thusly, "As you know full well, I have been from home nearly a se'nnight. As you also well know, Bingley and his family await me there, so I am most concerned for the peace of my people."

To the Colonel's quizzical expression, Darcy replied, "As I have grown familiar with the Bingley family, I have come to realize Bingley's younger sister, Caroline can sometimes be a bit overbearing. With no one there to check her, it is quite possible she will be taking liberties and God only knows what mischief she can have caused. I would not wish to return home to an uprising amongst the under-staff."

"I see." Colonel Fitzwilliam chuckled with more mirth than Darcy could like.

"Incidentally," said Darcy, "I should very much appreciate you not referring to your King in that undignified manner."

"What, what?" parried Colonel Fitzwilliam for he was not at all ready to give in to gravity. "Ol' Georgie and I are on the very best footing. I am sworn to protect him and willingly would I lay down my life in his defense. He sleeps better at night just knowing that."

As Darcy's sole response was to purse his lips, Rennie admonished, "Ah Cuz, you dearly need a vibrant, quick witted, pretty little miss to bring you back to your own age, for you are seeming more and more like my father every day."

"I will thank you to withhold your advice on my personal life, if you please."

"Suit yourself, but I really think you would do well to heed it. One's pressures and responsibilities seem that much less when one has the benefits of domestic comforts as well."

Raising a brow, Darcy quipped, "The words of a true expert."

Colonel Fitzwilliam replied sarcastically, "I have never lived in ancient Rome, but I know Latin as well as the next man and I dare say better than most." Darcy only lifted up his eyes.

There was a knock at the door, to which Darcy called, "Enter." and Wilkins appeared, carrying a silver salver of what appeared to be the days post. As he moved to place it on the side board he said, "As you have a guest sir, I shall not trouble you with this now."

Darcy asked, "Post at this hour?"

Wilkins replied, "It would seem sir, the young boy responsible for accepting the post was unaware of the delay in your journey and set aside today's post to be carried to Pemberley in the morrow. Only now realizing his error, he has just given it me; he is in quite a state and offers his sincere apologies."

With a smirk, Colonel Fitzwilliam interrupted, "Goodness Fitz. You have your staff quaking in their boots. That is most unkind of you."

Ignoring his cousin, Darcy handed Wilkins a farthing from his desk drawer and instructed, "Give this to the post boy and assure him no harm has been done. His conjecture *ought* to have been correct." This last was stated in the direction of the colonel, who of course considered this an admirable opportunity to employ selective hearing.

"Very good, sir." Wilkins replied.

Colonel Fitzwilliam stood, having realized the lateness of the hour, "As you speak of journeys, I had better be off. We must both be up before dawn to travel and I am sure you will soon be wishing me gone; if the thought has not already crossed your mind."

"It had not..." Then the corner of his lip twitched and he added, "... but as you mention it, I do now have the additional chore of a day's post to go through ere I go to bed."

The Colonel laughed and clapped his cousin roughly on

the back. "Then I had best be off post haste." To Wilkins he said, "Do not bother about me. I shall see myself out."

"Thank you, sir."

"Good night Cuz and thank you for an excellent supper."

"Good night Rennie and God's speed on your journey."

"Thank you; and you on yours." he replied before taking his leave.

Darcy spent a few minutes going over with Wilkins the arrangements for the trip to Pemberley in the morrow. They would leave at first light, thus everything must be made ready tonight. Once Wilkins took his leave, Darcy walked to the side board. Leafing through the pile of correspondence he recognized his sister's hand on a rather thick packet. Breaking the seal and unfolding the missive he thought with a chuckle, *"Georgiana, you have not been at Ramsgate a week. Whatever can you already have to say that should fill so many sheets as this?"*

> *The Inn*
> *Ramsgate*
> *Thursday, July 11ᵗʰ 1793*

Dearest Brother,

Mrs. Younge and I are safely to Ramsgate. The weather being fair for the whole of our journey, we arrived early this afternoon, in time to dress for dinner and are enjoying ourselves immensely. The harbour is much grander than ever I imagined and there are gulls everywhere about. They are much larger than I had thought them from the pictures in my books. They land on whatever does not move and strike a pose as if they think themselves the

King, himself.

The town is quite lovely and there is a constant whirl of activity about. It is very funny to see people bathing in the sea. I hear it is the thing to do, but I do not think I should ever like to try it myself. It is the strangest sight to see the bathing machines transporting people into the water. I shall take lots of sketches to shew you what I see and shall write down all my impressions to share with you on my return to Pemberley in August. Am very tired from the journey, so shall to bed early tonight and will take up my pen again in the morrow.

Monday, July 15*th*

Since last I wrote, something truly wonderful has happened. So very, very happy is the news I have to share with you that I am fairly bursting with anticipation. Friday morning, whilst Mrs. Younge and I were out for a walk in the town, we had the most perfect surprise. Whom do you imagine we should espy coming from a coffee house but Mr. Wickham. He was as shocked as we to find that we should all happen to be visiting Ramsgate at the same time.

He was as attentive as ever I could imagine someone to be for he changed his plans and spent the whole day together with us, only taking his leave after supper. He returned Saturday and again yesterday, each day giving us the whole of his day.

Brother, we are having such a wonderful time for he is all goodness and consideration. He has told me stories about you, dear brother which made me laugh and which much surprised me indeed. We talked and laughed till our sides ached. Mr. Wickham did not come round today, which I must admit disappointed me. It would seem I am already grown accustomed to his happy manners and easy conversation. Mrs. Younge says I need not fear for he is so taken with me, now that I am grown, that she is sure he cannot stay away long.

Tuesday, July 16ᵗʰ

This morning dear Mr. Wickham came again and collected us for a walk at Pier Head. It was cloudy and he said if it should rain he would happily carry me over every puddle. He and I walked a little ahead and he told me our meeting in such a fortuitous way was a most providential coincidence indeed, for he has been thinking of me much during recent months and remembering happy times growing up at Pemberley.

You may well be surprised to hear this next, dear brother, for I certainly was. He says he has loved me forever, but never dared to imagine I could ever love him in return and that it is only my sincere smiles and decided approbation in these recent blissful days that gave him to hope there might ever be a chance of my returning his affection. He says his heart is overflowing with admiration for me. Can you imagine perfect Mr.

*Wickham so much in love with me and for so long?
It is too wonderful.*

*Brother, he is all goodness. I have known him
all my life, but never would I have dreamt how ro-
mantic he is. He said he is sure it must be Providence that has brought us together in this way and
he thinks that a sign we should be loath to ignore.
Is not this all most wonderful? Please write and
tell me how happy you are for me. I am your ever
so joyful sister,*

Georgiana Darcy

More than once, during the reading of his letter, Darcy
could feel his temples pulsing as the blood rushed to his
head. Coming to the close of the letter, his face red with
rage, he thought, *"The blackguard! By heaven, what is he
about? I must to Ramsgate immediately."* Darcy rang for
Wilkins. Checking his watch he calculated *"It is long gone
10 o'clock, but if I ride through the night I shall be there by
mid-morn."* Barely able to tether his wrath his mind raced,
*"I cannot be sure, but from what she writes, I do not believe
he has quite forgot himself; at least, not yet, at any rate. By
God, if he has even attempted anything, I shall surely run him
through."*

When Wilkins entered, Darcy directed him to send someone out to quickly secure post horses and the fastest, available, long distance carriage, and then to pack a single satchel
with naught but what was required for one day's away. Much
would Darcy have preferred the speed of traveling on horseback, but whilst travel under cover of darkness was inher-
ently fraught with danger, travel on horseback, over long

stretches of dark, lonely Kentish countryside, would have been utterly senseless. It would do Georgiana no good if he were killed on the road. Having issued his orders, Darcy tore off to his chambers to change into travelling clothes.

In less than an hour, Darcy was on his way, accompanied by Tom, his able coachman, and two footmen; all were armed to the teeth. The footmen each had a blunderbuss, all four had double barrel, revolving, flintlock pistols and Darcy had a fencing sword besides.

Trundling over Westminster Bridge, Darcy said the first of many prayers he would say that night. Whatever Providence willed, would be. He just prayed Providence would watch over his sister till he could reach her. He wished he had read Georgiana's letter before Rennie left, for his sister's whole future depended on his safe and timely arrival at Ramsgate and highwaymen would be far less likely to challenge one of the King's men. Now he prayed he *would* reach Georgiana.

Passing along Kent Street, he agonized at their slow passage through the still bustling London roads. Everywhere, there were private coaches, hackneys, people walking to and fro in the road; dogs too crossed in their path, roaming about in search of scraps. *"These are not the safest of times."* he thought. *"Why are all these people still milling about when it is near on mid-night?"*

They past swiftly through the New Cross and Deptford Gates for they had only to shew the ticket Tom had run in at the Green Man Inn to purchase; still it was not swift enough for Darcy, anxious as he was to get on with his journey. There would be other gates to clear as well; never before this night had Darcy considered just how much of an inconvenience the many tolls actually were. The obstacles were even more aggravating for Darcy knew his coach to be quite capable of maintaining speeds upwards of 12 miles an hour.

They traveled with relative ease on through Black Heath & past Morden College. Though it seemed an eternity to Darcy, Runnet Wood, Danson Hill & Bexley Heath were soon behind them as well. The town of Dartford really seemed a bit early to change horses but it had many large coaching inns in the High Street and at such a late hour, Darcy thought the more options the better. Besides, now that they had good, open road, he intended to drive the horses hard, so he readily accepted his coachman's suggestion that they make their first stop here.

Despite the lateness of the hour, the staff at the inn was most obliging and moved very quickly to get their hurried travelers back on their way. All told, they had lost about three quarters of an hour, but they had a new team and the men felt refreshed and ready to resume their journey. On the road once more, Tom quickly had the horses accustomed to his style of instruction and stepping in perfect unison.

All of Kent, it would seem, was asleep. From the time they returned to the Canterbury Road, till the town of North Fleet was behind them, they neither saw nor heard a solitary soul. Not even an animal had stirred as they past, but now they were nearing Gravesend; notorious bastion of Free Traders. Darcy peered through the quarter lights and mused, *"The moon is not full; still there is light enough for these rogues to be afoot."* He knew the safe transport of contraband would leave these men little time or inclination to interfere with a mere coach upon the road, but should they chuse to take his presence as a hindrance to their passage, things could turn ugly, very quickly so he tapped on the roof and called out, "Tom, let us pick up the pace; the less time spent in these parts, the better."

"Aye, sir. Quite so. I had thought the same."

Darcy listened for the change in cadence of the horses gait and felt some reassurance when they broke into a gallop. Once or twice, he thought he might have seen something move in the surrounding brush; *"Probably a stag,"* he thought. Thankfully they past without incident and soon came upon a sign post for Rochester. The mouth of the Thames and the infamous marshes where smuggled goods were brought ashore were now far enough from the road as to be of little concern, so Darcy directed Tom to slow their pace in defense of the horses. It was essential that their strength be preserved for he intended to push on for Sittingbourne, which meant the horses would be driven about five miles farther than the generally accepted limit of twenty.

Darcy's watch told him it was quarter past three and he wondered once again, as he had so many times this night, how his sister faired. *"Dear Georgiana, you are so incredibly intelligent; I only hope your judgment has not been too far clouded."* Staring out into the darkness he thought, *"Poor, dear girl. Once you understand the true nature of the situation you have been thrust into, you will be mortified."*

Fatigue was beginning to set in, but he was far too restive to sleep. Even had he been able, he would have refused to give in to slumber. He needed to have his wits about him on the road just as much as when he arrived in Ramsgate.

Somewhere between Rochester and Newington, Darcy's thoughts were interrupted by the sudden slowing of the horses and Tom's utterance of profanity. It not being at all like Tom to swear in his master's presence, this was a portent of a most alarming nature. As Darcy leaned out to look ahead, Tom announced, "Trouble, sir. Seems as we 'ave comp'ny."

Making sure his pistol was ready to be fired, if need be, and his sword within easy reach, Darcy sat and waited. Three riders abreast, blocked the road and once the coach had stopt three more emerged from the brush next it. Of these last, two took up positions at the rear to block any possible retreat and the last advanced to the carriage. "They be some tired lookin' 'orses ye 'ave there. Hope as ye weren't thinkin' o' runnin' our blockade." he snorted to the coach-man, in a most unfortunate attempt at humour.

Tom was good at masking his emotions but Darcy knew him well enough to catch the anger in his voice when he answered, "The thought never crossed me mind." Darcy knew too, that the thought was *very much* in his mind, but so was common sense.

Moving closer to get a look inside the coach, the scoundrel espied Darcy, who gave him a polite nod. The man was genuinely surprised and with a nearly toothless grin, crowed, "Well now. What 'ave we 'ere?" Addressing his compatriots he announced, "He be a man o' the quality boys, and 'e 'as good manners, 'e does!" The sarcasm was maddening, but to take offense would have been to jeopardize the mission, so Darcy held his peace. Again turning his attention to the inside of the coach, the scoundrel queried, "Quite interestin'. Now what would the quality be doin' drivin' a yellow bounder in the dead o' night?"

"I am traveling light, for time is of the essence."

"Oh, time be of the essence now, be it?" mimicked the man. "And why might that be?" As he said this, the moonlight revealed that he employed a gold tooth pick which clearly must have been amongst the spoils of some previous thievery.

"Sir." Darcy replied in frustration, "I really have no time to spare. If it is my purse you require, here it is." and he handed out the pouch of coins he always carried on the road, at the ready for just such an occasion as this.

Snatching the purse, the man crowed, "Oh ye are a feisty one, ye are; but you'll not be rid o' me so fast. I do believe your story would be worth as much to me as your purse, being as how I don't get to Drury Lane much."

Darcy's patience was wearing thin; there were irritated mutterings from the footmen and Tom was beginning to visualize his hands round the impudent scamp's skinny, little neck. Darcy tried again, "Sir, I really must ask you to let us by. I have offered you all I have. My plan is to be away one night alone, so as you see, I carry naught but a small satchel of clothes."

Completely ignoring Darcy's request, the man continued where he had left off, "So why all the rush? Might ye be runnin' from the law?"

"Absolutely not!" Darcy parried, supreme indignation forcing a decided edge into his voice. "Now will you please ask your men to stand aside? We have nothing more to give you."

Heartily enjoying the situation, the man continued in total arrogance and disregard, "Be it a matter o' life or death?"

"It might very well come to that, for it is a matter of honour and the longer I tarry, the worse the situation becomes."

For the first time, there shewn some semblance of common decency in the man's face and he said, "Oh, well then ye should 'ave said so from the start! If it be a matter o' honour, that makes all the difference i' the world! If there be one thing Long Neck Jack will let a man by for, it be his honour, for nothin' be so important as honour!" Tipping his dirty cap to Darcy, he backed his horse away and called out to his men, "Clear the road for the gentleman boys." Turning back to Darcy he said, "Good luck to ye, sir." and holding up the purse he laughed an odd little laugh and added, "Let us say as you're all paid up for your return trip home. Highwaymen have our honour to uphold too ye know."

Darcy nodded politely and said, "Thank you and God speed."

"Same to you, sir. Same to you." He gave a quick, shrill whistle and as suddenly as they had appeared, Jack and his men were gone; vanished into the brush.

Continuing on their way, none of them could believe the farce that had just transpired. The whole encounter had lasted not ten minutes and one could almost convince oneself that it had not happened at all. As shocked as he was relieved by the peculiar resolution of the incident, Darcy could do naught but shake his head in wonder. *"How,"* he mused, *"can anyone ever question Providence? Could anything but God's grace have seen us through a confrontation such as that; unscathed as we were? I think not. Dare I hope this means I am intended to arrive in time to save your honour Georgiana?"*

They were about a mile shy of Sittingbourne when first light began to break and as they entered the town, the clock tower in the square was chiming five o'clock. People were beginning to stir; the baker's ovens scented the air, the grocer was beginning to put out his fruits and vegetables, a fish monger was trundling a cart up the road, as was a boy pushing a wagon of caged hens. Outside a still closed draper's shoppe, a small flower girl worked industriously to arrange her display to best advantage. Darcy had his pick of coaching inns for there were many large ones along the length of the High Street. It was a very cheery red brick Inn with large glazings that drew his business, for not only did it look inviting, but as they approached, the mingled scents of eggs, ham, bread, coffee and pastries wafting from its kitchens were most persuasive in convincing him it was time they take some nourishment. The inn was a busy place, even at that hour, for they had many travelers anxious to continue their journeys; still the appearance of a distinguished gentleman called forth immediate service. It was a pleasant enough place and had he been traveling under any other circumstance he might well have enjoyed himself. As it was, every second of this necessary delay was a torture to him. When he had told the serving wench what he should like to eat, he reached a gold sovereign from his pocket and said, "When you go to the kitchens, please see to my men, and be quick about serving them."

Her eyes grew suddenly round and bright when she saw the coin. She gave a deep curtsey and almost sang, "Why, thank ye sir. Thank ye very much. Your men are as good as in your own kitchens, they are." As she turned away, Darcy saw her bite the coin and heard her whisper to herself, "A *real* gold coin." before tucking it in her bosom and hurrying off on her errand. He stretched out his legs beneath the table and chuckled in spite of himself, before drifting back into thoughts of his sister.

It was a quarter past six when they took to the road again. Being fed, rested and knowing they could travel much faster and probably more safely by day, Darcy felt somewhat relieved. They still had roughly thirty-four miles to go, which meant they would have to stop yet again, but if all went well they should reach Ramsgate in under four hours time.

That final stop was made in Canterbury and whilst his

men saw to a quick change of horses, Darcy betook himself to the Cathedral. Passing through the great doors he took solace in the familiar smell of a Church. His strides took him quickly the length of the Nave, up the Crossing steps and through the arch. Once inside the Quire he knelt, crossed himself & said one of the most heartfelt prayers of his life.

"Dear God, I beg you to hear me this day. At this very hour, my sister, one of your purest and gentlest creatures, is very much in need of your protection. She is in the worst sort of danger and I fear she will be lost if I am not able to help her. You have seen me safely through the night, for which I heartily thank you. Now I humbly ask that you direct my actions at Ramsgate that I may, through your guidance, see Georgiana safely out of danger. Amen."

At last alighting before the inn at Ramsgate, Darcy stood, collecting his thoughts. As he watched his coach turn and pass from view beneath the arch and into the carriage yard, he took a deep breath and summoned all the courage he possessed. Facing Georgiana and dashing all her hopes would be as painful for him as for her. *"In many ways,"* he thought, *"she is so mature, yet in other ways she is still very much a child."* He as yet, knew not how he would approach her. He hoped the words would come when he needed them. The model of confidence in most everything, few had been Darcy's lessons in matters of sensibility, hence much had he still to learn, and he was most displeased that a circumstance involving his sister's happiness should arise whilst he was yet so ill-prepared.

On entering the establishment Darcy had not to seek the proprietor, for his appearance, brought the man scurrying to him. "Good day sir; so kind of you to grace my inn. How may I be of service to you?"

"Good day to you, sir. I am Fitzwilliam Darcy; I believe my sister is a guest here."

"*Darcy*. Why yes of course. Welcome Mr. Darcy, sir. Will you be needing a room as well, sir? Your brother did not say you were expected so we are unprepared; my sincere apologies, sir."

Darcy had stiffened at what he heard and he certainly hoped the situation was not so bad as to require a stay, but thinking it well to be prepared just in case, he replied, "Thank you, yes; just for the one night. My *brother*, you say?"

"Why yes sir; your brother, George. So attentive he is too; visits dutifully with his sister every day."

The fine hairs at the back of Darcy's neck stood on end and he said, "He does, does he? Do you know if he is about at present?"

"No sir, he is gone out just now."

"I should like to see my sister, if I might. Is *she* in?"

"Oh yes sir, she is just shortly back from a walk." the innkeeper advised and he called to a servant girl, "Shew the gentleman up to Miss Darcy's rooms."

Surprised, yet not at all so, by this latest ploy of Wickham's, Darcy followed the servant girl up the stairs. As he walked, he steeled himself for a meeting that would have to be as carefully orchestrated as a military campaign. The time it took to make their way to Georgiana's rooms seemed at once interminable and far too short, for Darcy was, if it were possible, even more incensed by what he had just heard; he was apprehensive, wondering of what further offences he might learn and still undecided about how he should proceed. Just then the girl rapped at Georgiana's door. Darcy's chest tightened when he heard his sister's sweet, innocent voice reply softly, "Do come in."

The girl opened the door wide enough so that Darcy now saw into the room, but he still had not seen his sister. With a pleasant smile and a curtsey the girl said, "There is a gentleman here to see you Miss."

The happy anticipation in Georgiana's voice was obvious as she replied, "Oh how lovely… but… I was not expecting a visitor just yet. My companion is not about. … Perhaps I should come downstairs to meet him."

Darcy was most relieved by the implication of his sister's words; perhaps he was not too late. Not wishing to prolong her misconception, he stepped into the room saying, "No matter, Georgiana. It is I, Fitzwilliam." His perceptive eye caught every nuance of her reaction, which moved swiftly, from initial confusion, to recognition and pleasure at the realization of just who was indeed come to see her. He knew the moment her comprehension was complete for her eyes lit up and she fairly leapt from her chair to greet him.

"Brother!" she exclaimed. "Oh how happy I am that you have come to share my joy." Pointing to the table where she had been seated she said, "I was just now writing another letter to you, even though you had not yet answered my last; but you have done better than answer. … You *have* received my letter, have you not? Do you know my news? Is that why you have come?"

As Darcy listened, he smiled, in spite of everything, at the half ladylike walk, half school girl skip that brought her to where he stood. *"So lovely; so innocent."* he thought. *"What kind of man can that Wickham be?"* He had quickly to banish his rage so he might answer civilly. "Yes Georgiana. That is why I have come."

"Is not it wonderful?" she asked and threw her arms round his neck. Tall as she now was, she still had to jump a little to reach; he held her tightly and saluted the golden top of her head and as he had all her life, he held her aloft for a few moments before letting her feet gently back to the floor.

The servant girl had gone and closed the door behind her. Darcy now turned its solid brass key saying, "Georgiana, I must speak with you on a matter of the utmost importance and I should not like for anyone to interrupt us."

Becoming concerned, Georgiana said, "Yes, of course Brother, but whatever could be so serious as to require such measures?"

Darcy took his sister's hand and after a quick scan of the room, led her to a settee. There he said, "Georgiana, I must beg your leave to speak freely, for what I have to say will hardly be easy for you to hear."

"Dear brother, I cannot make you out. It frightens me to think whatever should cause you to speak so."

Still holding her hand Darcy began, "Georgiana, before even I make a start, I must ask your forgiveness for I have no experience speaking on matters such as I must today and I fear that in my want of talent, I shall pain you greatly."

"Brother, I cannot imagine what you, of all people, could ever have to say to me that I should need to forgive."

Darcy saluted her hand, inhaled very deeply and taking up her other hand now as well, forged ahead. "Georgiana, your news, rather than giving me the same joy it has given you, has alarmed me much indeed."

The stricken look of disbelief on Georgiana's face already threatened to undo Darcy's resolve and loose him from his purpose. There was nothing for it but to take the jump and hope for clear ground beyond the hedge. "First, I need to know… Georgiana… has Wickham tried to… did he… have you ever been alone with him?"

"No Brother; we have always Mrs. Younge with us."

"Thank God." Darcy thought and his sigh was most audible.

"Brother, are you unwell?"

"No my sweet; it is rather a sigh of relief."

"I do not understand."

"Georgiana, in your letter, you say Wickham has told you he…" So disgusting did Darcy find the thought that he could not bring himself to utter the words. "The sentiments you have attributed to Wickham, I cannot believe of him."

Georgiana gasped and looked, for all the world, as if she had just been served an arrow through her heart. "Brother, how can you say such an awful thing?"

"I am truly sorry to be so direct, but I must. Please understand it is absolutely no reflection on you. It is that knowing Wickham as I do, I believe him incapable of such strong feelings for anyone but himself."

"You cannot mean that."

"Wickham has ever had the most happy manners. He is engaging, funny and he can effortlessly put people at ease, when it is to his purpose to do so, but I have known George far longer and far better than you have. Georgiana, this will pain you to hear, but nothing he does is without a view toward his own gain."

Georgiana replied in a hollow voice, "But he has been always so very kind to me; even when I was very little."

"Father was always very kind to George; far more so than ever he deserved and George is smart enough to have under-

stood it was in his best interest to do what would make him appear worthy in Father's eyes. True, he was always kind to you and friendly with me, but it was not because he liked us so well. Rather it was because it helped him earn Father's approbation."

Poor Georgiana was stunned. She knew not what to think. She just stared at her small, delicate hands still nestled in her brothers large, strong hands; his fingers wrapped protectively round hers and a tear escaped her eye. Darcy watched with grief as it coursed slowly down her cheek. When it fell to his wrist, it seared his heart and fueled the rage he felt for Wickham. Bringing her head to his chest he said, "I believe you know I want with all my heart for you to be happy so it pains me to have to tell you, as I must, that if you were to begin any serious association with George Wickham, it would only bring you sorrow and regret."

Georgiana began to cry. Her head was down and her sobs were almost inaudible, but Darcy heard them and he saw her shoulders begin to shudder. He despised Wickham for causing his sister such pain and for making him the instrument of it.

Shortly, Georgiana looked up with optimism in her tear filled eyes, "Brother, Mr. Wickham has been saying how very much he wants to marry me. Can it not be that he truly loves me, for why else should he so want to marry me?"

"If he has actually told you that is what he wants, it can only be that he believes he will profit from the union. Georgiana, when you do marry, it will be for the rest of your life, so I would want that you should find a man capable of making you truly happy. I am convinced George Wickham could not possibly be that man – even if he so desired."

"Please do not say so for everything seemed so perfect.

He has been so very attentive and he truly wants to marry me. Even as we speak, Mrs. Younge is gone to see to the arrangement for some clothes that are being made for me to take with us when we go. When you arrived, I thought it might be she returning."

"To take when you go where?"

"Why, when we go to get married. That is what I was just writing to tell you. Mr. Wickham says he loves me so well he wants nothing more than for me to be his wife and he should like for us both to have fine new clothes as we start our married life so that everyone can see what an excellent wife he has."

Darcy's lip curled, "Did he say where exactly he intended you to go?"

"To a place called Gretna Green; he says it is so very lovely there that it puts him in mind of me and once I have seen it, I shall think it the most perfect place in the world to be wed."

How Darcy would keep the anger from his voice, he knew not, but he must. "My dear, sweet, trusting girl, Gretna Green is a place just into Scotland where people go to marry when there is a reason why they must marry quickly or marry where they are not known; people do not go there simply because they so chuse. The marriage is often not even a true one in the eyes of the Lord."

These were shocking revelations to Georgiana; her eyes widened and her face paled, but Darcy knew he had to go on for he could clearly see she was not yet convinced against Wickham. "If you were to marry at Gretna Green, upon your return, if indeed you did return, you would be censured by all our connections. Surely Wickham knows this and if his intentions toward you were truly honourable, he would care more for protecting your reputation and maintaining for you, the approbation of your friends than for securing his own interests.

Georgiana, I have never known Wickham to shew one jot of concern for another living thing so I am much mistaken if his rush to marry under such clandestine circumstances is not largely due to the knowledge that at fifteen, you would require my approval to marry properly and that knowing Wickham as I do, I should never grant it."

Georgiana could hardly speak and Darcy had to strain to hear her ask, "How can this be? I understand all you have said, but I do not understand how it can be so."

"Have you any idea how you were to live? Has Wickham given you to know how he plans to make his living or how he might hope to support a wife?"

"That is not something we have discussed, but I am sure he has everything well planned."

Darcy thought crossly, *"Yes, I am sure he has."* Any illusions Georgiana still maintained must be quashed at once. "Georgiana, as you grow older and see more of the world you will learn that people are not always what they seem; Wickham is such a one as is rarely what he seems. I had not intended, ever, to share this with anyone, but I think now I must share it with you.

When father died, he left Wickham a substantial inheritance and believing Wickham intended to take orders, father asked me to see that the living at Kempton be given him when it became vacant. Wickham quickly squandered the legacy and assuring me he had no intention of ever becoming a clergyman, he demanded, and received, more money in lieu of the preferment.

This past spring, when Reverend Dibble passed on, the

news found its way to Wickham. Having gone through his second allotment as well, he returned to ask for the living, which by then I could not in good conscience give him. His circumstances must by that time have been bad indeed for he became most abusive on learning the preferment would not be his and now, four months later, I can only suppose he seeks to secure his future by making your inheritance his own." Georgiana's eyes were wide and she seemed to be stunned but Darcy needed to present every possible argument against Wickham. "I do not imagine he has said anything about what your marriage settlement would be."

"My what?" asked Georgiana.

"Great God," thought Darcy, *"my poor defenseless little lamb. You know not how much you lost when you lost your mama. I should think you would know of such things even now and perhaps you could have seen for yourself what he was about."* Quietly he said, "My sweet, when a lady marries, everything that is hers becomes the rightful property of her husband, thus when a man with honourable intentions decides to marry, he will generally settle on his wife an amount that is to be for her use alone; it is kept separate from whatever else he owns.

Wickham has for years, led a life of gaming, questionable associations and, let us say, unsavory amusements, so if he has talked at length of marriage but has not offered to settle anything on you, I am convinced it is because he has designs, of a reprehensible nature, on the entirety of the inheritance he expects you would bring to the marriage."

Pulling her hands away, Georgiana held them to her face and sobbed but she said nothing. She seemed to have taken in what her brother said but just in case she was not thoroughly convinced, he added, "I will *not* have you meet him

again, but if you wish, you may write to ask after a settlement. His answer will surely reveal the nature of his intentions."

Eventually she replied, "No Brother; that will not be necessary. What you say is awful, and of course I depend on
your judgment, but how is it possible that Mr. Wickham can
be so very bad?"

"How, I know not, but I assure you he is; has been for
many years, and I would have completely failed you, Georgiana, were I to stand by and allow him to ruin your life.

Tears were, by this time, streaming down Georgiana's
face. As Darcy wiped them with hands already salted by her
tears, she pleaded, "Oh dear brother, please do not be over
angry with him. This is as much my fault for having wanted
to believe him as it is his."

"His level…" Darcy proclaimed in a voice far more stern
than he had intended. He checked himself and began again,
"His level of responsibility… or I might say *culpability* far,
far outstrips your own. He is a master negotiator who I do
believe could sell sand to a Sultan."

Despite her distress, a faint smile crossed Georgiana's lips
and she thanked him.

"Georgiana how ever can you thank me when I have just
summarily dashed all your hopes and dreams?"

"No brother. You have saved me from myself. You have
also made me smile and feel protected, just as Papa used to.
The example you just gave sounded very much like something he would have said."

At that moment Darcy felt he could just possibly loose
his composure, so he forced his eyes from hers and cradled
her in his arms. They spoke of their father for a time then
Darcy said, "Georgiana, try to get some rest; if we can leave

by noon we shall cover much ground before having to stop for nightfall. We shall reach London early to-morrow and can start out for home tomorrow-next." He held her a while longer and though he still heard her sobs, they steadily grew fewer and fainter. Soon the stress of the interview exhausted her strength. Her breathing grew shallow and steady whilst her head grew heavy on his chest. Carefully rising from the settee, he situated her more comfortably on it and brought the counterpane from her bed to place about her.

There were still the matters of Wickham and Mrs. Younge to be dealt with and Darcy very much wished to be done with them ere Georgiana awoke. When Darcy rang for the servant girl to pack his sister's belongings, he was given to know that indeed Mrs. Younge had returned from her shopping trip but Mr. Wickham still was not in his rooms. Though Darcy was most anxious to deal with Wickham, it seemed their meeting would have to wait, so he went in search of Mrs. Younge. In answer to his knock at her door, the lady called out, "A moment please..." After some rummaging about and closing of drawers and trunk lids she continued, "Georgiana, is that you? Come in."

Darcy opened the door and stepped in saying curtly, "Georgiana sleeps." Immediately she heard who had spoken, Mrs. Younge gasped and swung round; her face ashen. Coming slowly toward her, in a manner menacing in its total calm, Darcy said, "Yes, well might you be alarmed, for your actions in my employ are such as should rightfully land you in goal."

"Mr. Darcy, sir. Whatever can you mean by that? I am always most attentive in my duties."

"I am in no humour to be toyed with Mrs. Younge. I am sure you know full well that I refer to your lack of vigilance regarding Mr. Wickham's attentions to my sister."

"Oh but Mr. Darcy, sir, you cannot blame me for the impetuous nature of two young ones."

"Mrs. Younge, I blame you for standing idly by, if not in collusion, whilst my young sister was deceived by someone even older than I; someone who is devoid of principle and who I now see must be far better acquainted with you than I had realized."

"But what was I to do, sir?"

"Your job, Madame. I expected of you nothing more than propriety and common sense demand, but you have failed me miserably. Mrs. Younge, you must realize that you leave me no choice but to dismiss you and you can expect no reference. I will not lie and were I to tell truth it would do you no service." Placing some bank notes briskly upon the table, Darcy said, "This should be more than enough to settle anything that is owed you. I shall expect you to be gone from this place within the hour."

Shewing a rage few would have dared, under the circumstances, she spat, "That is not fair, Mr. Darcy. What am I to do with no position and no prospect of finding one?"

"That, Madame, is something you ought to have considered long before now. It was a monumental error not to have recognized with whom you were dealing."

"You cannot do this." she screeched.

"I have done. Good day Madame." Darcy then left, closing the door behind him. As he walked down the hall to his sister's rooms he could hear slamming, stamping and some very unladylike utterances in his wake.

Again Darcy sent word below to inquire after Wickham; the news that he still had not been seen, incited Darcy's ire, for the man was costing him precious time in removing his sister to the comfort and safety of Pemberley. Darcy very much wanted the satisfaction of meeting Wickham, that the man might bare the full force of his displeasure, but he would not allow Wickham to cost them a day's travel. If he were not back in one hour, Darcy would just have to commit his sentiments to paper. Small consolation that, but it appeared he might be left no choice.

Feeling thoroughly agitated, Darcy yearned for a long hard ride on his horse, Albion. The last dozen hours or so had been amongst the worst of his life. *"Soon... soon we shall be home."* he thought. *"If all goes well, we shall be to Pemberley in three or four day's time. It will be better for Georgiana to be back at home, so I shan't tarry in London."*

Returning to Georgiana's rooms he was pleasantly surprised to find how quickly and quietly the girl was packing his sister's belongings; it appeared he would be able to take Georgiana away as soon as she awoke. That was welcome news for he dearly needed to remove his sister from this place and he did not fancy carrying her upon the road once darkness fell.

Suddenly realizing how emotionally spent he was, the thought of a pint of strong ale was somehow not unwelcome just then. He ordered one up and whilst he awaited it, he went to the desk to begin crafting his letter to Wickham. There, where she had left it, was the letter Georgiana had spoken of and it stung his heart to see it and imagine what joyful thoughts it must contain, thus he quickly turned it over and placed it beneath her writing box. Taking up some fresh sheets and choosing a sharp quill he began.

The Inn
Ramsgate
Friday, July 19ᵗʰ 1793

George Wickham,

This correspondence is something I should never have imagined necessary, and I very ill brook finding it so. To be sure, your presence in this place, at this particular time, can hardly have happened by chance. Having learnt of your recent association with my sister, I at once came hither, driven by serious doubts of the veracity of your affection for her. It is many years that I have been aware of your vicious propensities and your total want of principle; such being the case, it is highly unlikely that your motives here can be honourable or just. I have little doubt that you are driven by a desire to make my sister's fortune your own. If this be true, and it seems very likely so, it is a treachery that far outstrips anything I could ever have believed of you.

Knowing how much my excellent father valued your society and how completely devoted he was to your advancement, your betrayal of his trust is, in and of itself, a deceit beyond reproach, but to prey on the affections of his young daughter, someone so pure and gentle, who has the kindest heart and for whom suspicion is not in her nature, is a depravity of the worst kind. Had you succeeded in carrying forward your scheme, complete indeed would have been her tragedy for I do not doubt but that you would have abandoned her once you realized the fatal flaw in your plan.

The particulars I am about to make familiar to you are such as I do not willingly share. I do so purely in defense of my sister, for having taken this false step, I would expect you are fully capable of attempting further designs on Georgiana. My father's will sets aside an inheritance for my sister that becomes hers when she comes of age; however, the money will remain in trust and under my control, if before she comes of age, she marries without the full consent of both myself and our cousin, Colonel Fitzwilliam, who shares her guardianship. Surely you must realize that knowing you as we both do, you would never receive our consent.

Your actions have been wholly unconscionable and it is my heartfelt belief that for them you should be exposed to the world's censure and derision. Would that it were possible to serve you up to justice and still protect the character of my beloved sister! Since it is not possible to do both, in this transgression at least, you shall be spared your just desert. I do not doubt that in time, other offenses will be laid at your door for which you will be held accountable, but know this Wickham; if you ever again dare try to harm my sister or in any way insinuate yourself into the affairs of our family, you will pay dearly for your interference.

I had long since believed all connection between us to have been dissolved. Understand that you are, from this day forward, to consider your connection with the Darcy family completely and unequivocally at an end.

Fitzwilliam Darcy

When Georgiana awoke it was to the news that within an half hour of Darcy's interview with Mrs. Younge, a stable boy had seen Wickham and the lady ride off in a curricle, fully laden with baggage and parcels. Neither Mr. Wickham nor Mrs. Younge was seen there again and nothing of either was left behind; nothing except Darcy's letter, which lay crumpled in the dormant fireplace of Wickham's room. Neither is it surprising that Wickham's debts, including a number for gaming, were left unpaid and as he had assumed the name of Darcy, settlement of those debts became yet another insult that squarely met its mark.

On their way at last, brother and sister sat opposite one and other in the carriage. Georgiana was of course devastated; she would remain so for some time to come, but disappointment was already beginning to be replaced by compunction.

"To think," said she, "that I have been so very senseless and naïve as to have believed all Mr. Wickham said and to have thought Mrs. Younge my friend. You know not all the things she and I have spoken of."

"Georgiana, you are far from senseless and as you are but fifteen, it is expected that you should be naïve; it is proper. You have no idea how it pains me to have been obliged to bring you such sorrow. Would that there had been someone else, better suited to have this conversation with you; I am sure it need not have been so harshly done."

"Brother, you did what was necessary."

"Georgiana, I would have thought to be married myself before ever having to consider your marriage. That way you could have had a lady to speak with, rather than a stern brother who knows nothing of defending a lady's sensibilities."

Managing a slight smile, Georgiana said, "Brother you have been as kind and gentle as ever you could. I do not think any lady of my acquaintance could have done better."

"No," thought Darcy sadly, *"nor any lady of my acquaintance either, yet there must be someone, for how inadequate am I in this situation. Never till now have I seen any urgency in finding a wife, but who? Where?"*

His sister's voice roused him from his solemn contemplation. "Thank you Brother. Thank you so very much."

He offered a sad little smile in response. *"'Thank you.' she says. Imagine that she should chuse to thank me when I have brought her such pain."* He pondered his sister's words and watched her eyes as they slowly traced the lines of his face; he was humbled, but truly perplexed. He was also thoroughly exhausted.

Georgiana soon forsook the seat opposite to move beside him. Believing her to act from a need to feel more secure, he placed a protective arm gently round her. Within minutes, as she sat watching the country side pass to the rhythm of the moving coach, heavy grew her brother's head upon her shoulder and she smiled to herself. It was not till their first coaching stop slowed them at Eversham that he awoke. Realizing his lapse, he sat bolt upright and apologized profusely for having allowed himself to give way to fatigue. Georgiana simply giggled softly and said, "Brother, there is something amiable in allowing of one's limitations.

Strangely, it is somehow comforting to know you are not wholly without fault."

Darcy was not sure he knew just how he should perceive her words but he thought it best not to seek clarification. Still, her comment made him suddenly see his *little* sister very differently and he realized he would have to rethink his understanding of her. There was some conversation during the remainder of the journey, but for the most part they traveled in a companionable silence, both lost in their own thoughts; both tending their emotional wounds in their own ways.

Somehow the trip home seems always shorter than the trip out, but for Darcy, this trip home, calm and uneventful as it was, with his sister safely by his side transcended the passage of time.

Chapter XIV

THE MERYTON ASSEMBLY

1793

CRISP autumn breezes rushed through the open carriage window, bringing with them the heady scent of nearby hearth fires. Drawing in a slow, deep draft of the bracing night air, Darcy surveyed the passing countryside. The full moon brought neat fields and pleasant cottages of the Hertfordshire countryside into his view, but their bucolic splendor was lost on him for he was completely absorbed in his thoughts; he considered his current situation and wondered, with regret, how he had allowed such folly to come about. *"How indeed?"* he puzzled. He reviewed the course of events that had led him hither and mused at the extraordinary difference betwixt himself and the man seated opposite him, for a surreptitious glance shewed Bingley, to be all eager anticipation.

As they drew nearer their destination, he sensed Bingley's excitement increasing. Darcy on the other hand, grew steadily more wary. "Bingley," he queried, "how can you be so pleased at the prospect of an evening spent in the company of people whose society is so decidedly beneath your own?"

"Darcy," replied his friend, "there are interesting and agreeable people to be found everywhere. One has merely to seek them out."

"Humph," was all the response Bingley was to receive.

"I am most serious." Bingley offered, "Tonight for example, I am certain there will be many handsome young ladies at the assembly, all very pleasant and eager to dance with us."

"Eager to dance with our purses more like. Bingley, you must know that news of our position in society and more importantly, our wealth will be in circulation immediately we arrive."

"Darcy, do not be such a cynic. Not every lady is driven entirely by thoughts of riches."

"But most are. It seems all in *my* acquaintance have been."

Bingley laughed, "*You*, Darcy? I am inclined to believe that an exaggeration. You have many qualities, besides wealth, that excite a lady's esteem. Nevertheless, Darcy, I will *not* let your dour mien spoil my evening. I intend to dance all night and to have a most pleasant time of it and I should hope you might do the same."

Soon Bingley's carriage pulled to a gentle stop before the modest assembly hall in Meryton and Darcy thought, *"I have now to pass an entire evening at a country dance that is sure to be attended by no one of consequence; no one whom I could ever wish to know."*

As soon as the footman opened the door, Bingley sprang eagerly from the equipage and looked expectantly about, his face suffused with a warm smile. As for Darcy, the effect was not so pleasant. He was immediately accosted by the strains of a simple country jig, played with little mastery and even less style. *"Clearly,"* he thought, *"this is a portent of what is to come. I must now waste a whole night together trying not to see or hear any of the nonsense about me."* He sighed deeply and alighted from the carriage. As they awaited Caroline and the Hursts, who were just then emerging from Hurst's carriage, Darcy steeled himself for whatever was to come. "Miss Bingley," he said and proffered his arm.

"Mr. Darcy," she cooed and placed her hand possessively in the crook of his arm. "Let us hope the evening's *entertainment* is of short duration."

With only the slightest nod in reply, Darcy fell back into his own contemplation. Their party now complete, they moved slowly forward. Propriety bespoke an evening spent in this manner to be insupportable, yet here they were. As they progressed up the stairs, Darcy inwardly chastised himself, for verily duty, honour, and decorum ruled his life. Yea, it had always *been* thus, and it would always *be* thus. "*Remember who you are.*" he thought. Nearing the door of the Assembly Hall, Darcy was not so sure he was living up to his father's expectations just then, but he would do the best he could under the circumstances. He was a Darcy, and a Darcy had a responsibility to hold himself to the highest standards; to conduct himself with the utmost comportment. Yes, duty, honour and decorum would rule, this night and always, regardless of any obstacle Bingley, or anyone else, saw fit to throw in his path.

Their entrance caused a current of excitement that quickly radiated throughout the room. Fast upon the initial stir, Sir William Lucas appeared to welcome them. He thanked them profusely for having been so kind as to have accepted his invitation and told them he was gratified indeed that people of such decided fashion should grace Meryton's little assembly.

The evening moved forward precisely as Darcy had expected. The company; the entertainment; the refreshment; none of it was to his liking. When he had danced once with

Caroline and once with Louisa, there was nothing left to entertain him and he spent the remainder of his time in walking about the room, praying for an end of the evening.

Long into the evening, Bingley, who had been engaged for every set, left the dance to encourage Darcy to join it. Darcy replied that aside from Bingley's sisters, there was not a woman in the room with whom it would not be a punishment for him to stand up. On Bingley's suggestion that he consider the sister of the lady *he* was then dancing with, Darcy turned round to see whom he meant. On catching her eye, he quickly looked away; a most unsettling feeling having taken hold of him. Somehow he could still feel the pair of bright inquisitive eyes looking on him; dismissing his friend's entreaty, he quickly walked away.

The lady was not long without a partner and more than once as the evening progressed, Darcy happened to see her moving gracefully through a dance. She spoke and laughed amiably with whomever she happened to be dancing with at the time.

Once as she moved through the set, she happened, for a moment, to catch his eye and if he was not much mistaken there had been the hint of a smirk on her face. He quickly looked away and headed for another part of the room but as he did so, he became aware of a tightening in his chest and sought to redirect his thoughts. *"If I can just get through this night, in the 'morrow I shall give Bingley to understand that he is not ever again to accept an invitation on my behalf."*

Walking through the crowd, the tightness in his chest remained. He believed it to be born of exasperation; to be grounded in rational thought. His unschooled sensibilities would have argued to the last, against even the remotest possibility that it could have been the result of anything else; and yet into his sober thoughts now crept the vision of a most amiable expression of face and comeliness of person together with a decided liveliness of spirit. It would be days before that small notice would work its way into his consciousness and weeks or perhaps even months before it would be acknowledged.

As he suffered through the length of that interminable evening, nary a chance had he of guessing that even then, Providence was fast at work, setting him squarely on a path that would cause him to question the very principles upon which he determined his actions; a path that would monumentally test his mettle, plumb the depths of his understanding and challenge his character. It was a path that would forever alter the course of his life.

Made in the USA
San Bernardino, CA
13 December 2013